The Cassiopeia Chronicles

Maxwell Pearl

The Right Asteroid

Chapter 1.
New Bureau Chief

Sam, April 2105

"Approaching Strelix Station, Sam." The voice of Sam's AI spoke, bringing Sam to attention. It was time for a break. They'd been asteroid hunting for months without any luck, and it was time for them to get some rest before they lost all hope. Besides, they needed supplies.

They wondered whether Sky was on station right now; it would be good to see her. Even though Sam did well without any human contact for a long time, it would be nice to spend time with someone who knew them well. And Sky was always good company.

Sam pushed some icons on their comm panel. "Sam Julian, here, calling Strelix station, request docking permission."

"Permission granted. Docking bay 25B."

"Affirmative." To their AI they said, "Got that, Jane?"

"Yes, Sam. Adjusting attitude and direction now. Homing beacons activated. We'll be docked in six point five minutes."

When they first bought the AI, they decided to name it, although most people thought that was kind of creepy. AIs weren't supposed to have a personality, but sometimes they suspected this one did. Anyway, they liked using a name.

Sam just let Jane fly the ship as they were thinking about their short shore leave. They could only afford a week. They didn't have enough money left to pay for more than that and resupply.

Sam had become a solo asteroid hunter about five years ago, after spending ten long years employed by Strelix, Inc., crewing a number of ships. Strelix was the largest asteroid hunting corporation that existed. Sam had spent nothing, and saved everything, even shore leave allowances, so that they could lease a ship of their own someday, and go solo. They didn't want to build a company to compete with Strelix, they just wanted the freedom to explore on their own, and reap all of the rewards. They learned over time, that it also meant taking on all of the risk.

They'd found one small asteroid early on, and it was only moderately successful, the asteroid miners they'd sold it to refused to take a flat fee; they only wanted to give them a percentage. It turned out to be a C-type asteroid, mostly carbon, with only a little bit of magnesium, iron, and other trace minerals. It paid for itself, finally, at least.

They went for a year without a decent find. They remembered how lean that year was, and how close things got. They then had several mediocre finds, one complete dud, then, a good solid find. But that had been almost 2 years ago. If they didn't find a good asteroid soon, they wouldn't have enough Yuan left for payments on the ship. In a few months of that, their ship would be repo'd. They would do everything they could to avoid that fate.

They loved their ship. They looked around at it for a moment. They found the space cozy, even though many would find it cramped. It had small cockpit, with only one seat. There was a work area with a workstation and all of the equipment Sam needed to take samples and gather the data that would provide information for the mining ships who would buy asteroids from them. The ship had a small living area, with a tiny galley, and a dining space for one, with a bunk that folded up at night. They dreamed one day that maybe they'd upgrade to one of the faster explorer class ships—maybe one that spun for gravity. Not much more space, but more oomph to help find better asteroids.

The mild shudder of the ship that meant it was docked brought Sam out of their reverie. They could feel the increased gravity from the spin of the station.

"Jane, docking sequence, please."

"Yes, Sam."

Sam got up from the seat and walked back to get their stuff. They climbed up the ladder to the top docking door, engaged the airlock, and climbed up to the embarkation area for bay 25B. They closed and locked the door, hefted their bag, and walked to the hostel.

After they'd checked in, and unpacked their meager belongings, they checked their tablet to see whether Sky was on station. She was. They sent a message to Sky and got back a brief message in return. "I'm leaving the station in a few hours. Come over before I go."

Sam got up, left the hostel, and walked the corridors to Sky's place, on the other side of the station. Sam stopped in front of Sky's door and pushed the doorbell icon.

"God it's good to see you Sam!" Sky's arms were wide when the door opened, and Sam fell into Sky's embrace. They hugged for a while.

"Glad I came when I did. It would have been a bummer to have missed you this time."

Sam followed Sky into her quarters.

"Want a beer?"

"Sure." Sky threw Sam an aluminum bottle. Strelix beer was barely palatable, only really worth it for the alcoholic content.

"How the hell are you, Sam?"

"Alright, I guess. But things are lean. I haven't found an asteroid in far too long. It won't be long before my ship gets repossessed."

"Sam, let me loan you some money."

"Thanks, Sky, but I'll be OK."

"You'll wait until you are completely desperate, won't you?"

"Sky..."

"I know you, Sam. You don't ask for help from your friends enough."

"I try to be independent."

"You try too hard. Anyway, you know it's there when you need it."

"Thanks, Sky. So how are you? Where are you off to?"

"I'm shuttling the CEO of Strelix to Mars."

"Wow. Why?"

"They are trying to negotiate some new contracts, but things are getting sticky. Mars is itching for independence, and that's the last thing Strelix wants."

"Mars isn't going to get independence in either of our lifetimes, Sky. SolGov won't allow it."

"I'm not so sure of that, Sam. I've been hearing some interesting rumbles, and if Strelix is worried, something real is happening."

"Well, keep me posted. If I go completely broke, I might rather end up on Mars than on the Moon again."

"Sam, work with me. We'd hire you."

"Strelix would never hire me back, Sky, and I rejected the pilot's union's offer a while ago, so I'm screwed there, too."

"You'll be fine, my friend. I know you. You always end up doing alright."

Tina, April 2105

The low voice of her AI indicating that it was time to get up pulled Tina out of a dream. As she opened her eyes, she struggled to remember what it was about, but it all slipped away so quickly as the realities of what was ahead of her today came to the fore in her brain. And, as with every morning, all of the extra weight from being on Earth seemed to keep her glued to her bed—she always had to pry herself up, and stumble around at first.

Today, she was covering more hearings on the future of Mars. It was ridiculous, really. SolGov wanted to control all of the Solar system, but that was, for practical reasons, impossible. It took many days to get from Earth to Mars, and it wasn't even possible to have a synchronous conversation between the two planets. The Mars governor and the now 500,000-plus people who lived in the six colonies on Mars wanted much more autonomy. Now, Earth needed Mars far more than Mars needed Earth, but Earth-centered SolGov could not admit it. Mars had ample water, energy, and finally, Mars had become self-sustaining in food and manufacturing. Mars had the scientists it needed to start their terraforming project in earnest. Those scientists predicted that within 200 years, Mars could be habitable across the whole surface, without domes. After that, all bets were off.

She slowly got up out of bed and went to the shower. She thought more about her current work as the hot water flowed over her body, warming her to the core, and energizing her so she didn't feel so heavy. She was beginning to realithey she was somewhat obsessed with Mars. She had been given the Mars beat by her boss mostly because none of her other colleagues wanted it. As one of the newest members of the SolGov reporting team, she got the assignments no one else wanted. Everyone wanted to get to be part of Volkov's press corps. If not, then one of the high-end governors, like Xien of China, Harrison of the US, or Grendel of Germany. If not those, then they wanted to cover the Solar Senate, where the city-state of Monaco had the same number of representatives as Mars.

But no one else at the *Times* wanted to show up at hearing after hearing about Mars governance. Except her. She hadn't wanted to do it at first, but after a while, she had become fascinated by it. She was intrigued by the problems the Mars colonies faced, interested in the issues involved in immigration, and engaged by the relationship between Earth and Mars. At one point, she wished she could go to Mars to see it and see what it was like to live there. It was at that moment that she finally understood her long lost ex-, Sam.

She got out of the shower and started to dry off. As she went through the rest of her morning ablutions, she thought about Sam. Sam had been her first lover, and Tina thought of Sam as The One Who Got Away. Tina had been born on the Moon, her grandparents being early settlers in the first permanent colony on the moon that allowed families to settle in the early 60's. At the time she met Sam, she had been working as an administrator at the same mining company, before she started her journalism career. Their relationship lasted until Sam decided to leave the Moon and head for the asteroid belt. Tina had always wanted to move to Earth, but it was no use trying to convince Sam to join her. That Sam, who liked spending days out in a Moon rover scouting for good sites to get more of this or that mineral. The Sam who she knew was right now out finding the right asteroid. She shook her head as she got dressed. Her AI started to speak.

"You have an incoming synchronous message from the *Times* editorial desk. Shall I put it through?"

Tina wondered what it could be about. She hurriedly finished putting on her jacket.

"Yes, please."

She walked over to her wall screen and the image of her boss' boss appeared. Even though the original family that had owned the company that used to be a newspaper was long gone, somehow, this strait-laced, upper-crust Manhattan born-and-bred editor reminded her of someone who might belong to that family. She remembered how surprised she was that it turned out that he was the great-grandson of old rock and roll stars.

"Ms. Fiorici, I'd very much like to talk with you in person."

"Sir, the Mars hearings..."

"This takes precedence. Please come to my office. When can you arrive?"

Her AI flashed a tentative schedule in the lower right-hand corner of her wall screen. There was a shuttle to New York she could grab in about five hours, and she'd be there first thing the next morning.

"I can be there by 9 AM tomorrow."

"I'll see you then. Oh, and pack all of your things. You aren't going back to Beijing, at least not for a while."

She tried to hide her surprise. "Will do." His picture disappeared.

There were only two things that this could mean: a promotion, or she was fired. The latter was rather unlikely—she'd been headhunted for the job at the *Times* after having spent years on the government beats of smaller operations. The *Times* was a plum job—journalists had vied for positions there for hundreds of years. All of her performance reviews had been stellar. Besides, one's boss' boss didn't fire you in person. An email or call from your boss would do fine. So what could he possibly be promoting her to? She had been on the Mars beat for three years now. She didn't want to be an editor; she liked her job. She also knew there weren't any editor positions even open. Her colleagues kept track, and she'd have heard about it by now.

She put away her questions and packed her things. She hadn't brought much with her to Beijing this time—these Mars hearings were only supposed to go for another two weeks. She was happy that she'd get to sleep the next night in her own bed. She put her clothes haphazardly in her bags—she'd just put them in the laundry when she got home.

When she was done packing, she sat at the desk, logged into her work task list, and saw that it was completely empty. Last night, it had four requests in it. A request for a summary article about the major sticking points around the Mars proposals for autonomy in the realm of immigration, a research request for an opinion page editor about the terraforming project, and a couple of other requests she couldn't remember at the moment. They were all gone. So she whiled away her time reading the latest news, catching up on what was happening in the City, messaging some friends she'd neglected that she'd be home for a while. She even spent some time on WayBack checking up on some old acquaintances. Nothing from Sam in ages. She wasn't surprised. Sam was never one to spend much time doing that sort of thing. Tina thought the last status message she saw from Sam on WayBack was years ago about some asteroid.

She said to her AI, "Please send a check-out message to the front desk, prepare my home system, and remove yourself from this matrix."

"Commencing."

The standard welcome message for the hotel's matrix now replaced her own AIs custom screen. A bell chimed at her door, and Tina opened it, and saw a luggage cart making its way towards her. It stopped a few feet from her, and she lifted her luggage onto it. She was glad they had those things—she was generally unable to carry her own luggage. It proceeded ahead of her quickly, and she made her way to the elevator. When she got outside the lobby, she and her luggage were reunited for the taxi ride to the airport.

Getting from Beijing to New York was pretty easy these days—a nonstop hypersonic flight took only a few hours. She'd be gaining time on the way, and at least for a few hours of the day, she'd be completely functional. On the flight, she obsessively perused the news, especially from the MetaNews sites, looking for possible clues to why she was called in. She landed at JFK, sent her bags home by courier, and took a taxi to the office. When she got to the suite where her boss' boss' office was, she was ushered into his office immediately by his assistant.

She sat down, and he immediately told her what he had in mind.

Tina sat looking at him, and she was sure that even though her mouth actually wasn't open, he could see her jaw drop to the floor.

"Mars? You actually want me to do the Mars government beat... on *Mars*?"

"Actually, you won't be doing the Mars government beat. You'll be doing the Mars beat—all of it."

"I'm confused."

"We are promoting you to run the Mars bureau."

"But there isn't a Mars bureau."

He smiled. "There is now."

She was astonished. And honored. "What prompted this change? *The Times* has always been very Earth-focused."

"We have decided that is a mistake. There has been a lot happening on Mars lately, between the sounds that the Mars government is making about autonomy, to the insistence of Mars educational institutions to have their own accreditation system. There's so much going on, we want to make sure there is someone there on the ground."

"I don't know what to say besides thank you for this opportunity, and yes, I'll do it." She could hardly believe what was coming out of her mouth. "Do I get some assistance?"

"Yes, we're sending you one junior journalist, and one imager." Tina remembered that before this meeting, *she* was a junior journalist.

"Do I get to state my preferences?"

"You have some? We haven't made any offers as of yet."

"Yes. Joseph Dunnely has done an amazing imaging job—and he's unusual in that he does 2D and 3D, still and moving, all really well."

"Sounds reasonable. He's been working with you a lot, and he's done some work on Mars."

"Yes. And for the journalist, I'd suggest Ama Shabazz. She's smart, has been working on the Moon beat for a while, and I think this would be a good stretch for her. And we work well together."

He nodded his head. "OK, I'll add them to my list, and I'll let you know what happens. I want you on the next possible ship to Mars. You'll have an assignment list probably before you leave."

He rose and stuck out his hand. Clearly, she was being dismissed. She rose as well and shook his hand.

"Good luck, Ms. Fiorici."

"Thank you, sir."

She walked out of the room, and for a moment didn't quite know what to do. Ah, she thought. Go home, do laundry, pack, and figure out when the next Mars ship is leaving VirginGalactic One.

Chapter 2:
To Mars

Lodan, April 2105

Today was the day. Lodan woke up, feeling warm in her blankets, but she knew that it was bitter cold in her room. She relaxed in the warmth of body and blanket until she just couldn't anymore, and pulled the covers back, looking around. The glass of water on the end table had a layer of ice on the top, and there was frost in all of the windows. It was, so far, the warmest winter in the last 20 years, but the temperature hadn't gotten above twenty below zero in a week.

She hurriedly got up, put her slippers on, and threw on the coat she had next to the bed. She walked to the living room and turned on the geothermal heat. After a while, she could begin to feel a little heat from the floor. Soon the whole cabin would be warm.

As her brain started to thaw, she thought more about what was in store for her today. The application for the new Mars colony had been an arduous process, but she was happy that it had come close to the end.

A few years ago, she'd relocated from Phoenix, Arizona to Massachusetts, where they were trying some re-settlement. Living here had been much more difficult than she'd imagined—the mini-ice-age brought on by the shut-down of the Gulf Stream fifty years ago was just beginning to thaw, but the living was still difficult. The growing season was so short that only the hardiest vegetables, like potatoes and kale, could be grown outside. The rest of the crops had to be grown inside greenhouses. She was living with a few people in a compound, where they grew what they could and bred hardier and hardier varieties of crops to deal with the cold. They were working to rebuild so that people could begin to relocate out of the crowded southern part of the country.

She was nervous. She'd done great work over the past few years, but somehow, she didn't quite believe she'd be chosen. The new Mars colony was at Stage Three. There were greenhouses, lots of domes, and enough resources that a reasonably sized colony could begin the work of becoming self-sustaining. The earlier Mars colonies had been a success, and they'd even set up a university there. But this new one, in a totally new area of Mars was designed to try new techniques and begin the true terraforming process.

She realized she was running out of time—she needed to catch the next bullet train to Washington, DC. As she gathered her things, said her goodbyes, and walked out of the entrance to the group of dwellings, she knew that she was unlikely to return here. Either she'd make it into the program, or she'd return to Phoenix, and take the standing job offer at FoodTechSystems that had been waiting for her for the last few years. There weren't any other jobs in space for agronomists—the ones on the current colonies or the Moon colonies were all taken.

After the train ride, she walked into the Mars Settlement office. She looked around at the people who were in the waiting room. One man sitting in the corner looked like he'd just come off of a construction site—he wore dusty carpenter pants and a heavy jacket. Another man was wearing a suit that didn't quite fit; it looked like it might be borrowed. She knew that many people in desperate straits were vying for the new colony. The avenues to get into the established colonies from Earth were few and far between if you didn't have connections or a lot of education or expertise.

She walked up to the desk where a young woman with dark hair and bright yellow shining contact lenses looked up at her.

"Hello. Do you have an appointment?"

"Yes. My name is Lodan Greenfellow."

"Just one moment please...."

About 30 seconds later, a tall, uniformed man approached the desk from behind, and signaled to follow him. Lodan walked around the desk, and into his office.

"Please, Lodan, have a seat. I'm Lieutenant Bob Jordan." He pointed to the chair in front of his desk. She sat down. He fiddled with his tablet, and then looked at Lodan.

"You've been approved for the new Mars Colony." That felt like a surprise to her.

"Wow, I'm glad to hear that. Thanks! I thought there would be a few more steps in the process."

"No more steps. We really need your expertise on Mars, now. And we're very sure of you."

She nodded, although she was sure her surprise showed. "OK … what's next?"

"You need to have a briefing with Mission Commander Kelley. He'll fill you in on the details of the new colony mission. Then, you'll get on the next ship heading out—it's leaving tomorrow from VG1. There is something you should know, though."

"What's that?"

He paused, as if weighing carefully what he was going to say.

"The colony is in a lot of trouble."

"What kind of trouble?"

"It's hard to explain... I'm not sure even I understand it. The crops are failing."

She gulped and nodded. This might be even harder than living in the new ice age.

He picked up a tablet sitting on his desk, and touched it a few times, and then began to speak.

"Commander Kelley, Lodan is here. She's ready to ship out with you to Mars. Are you ready?"

A slightly tinny voice come out of the tablet. "OK. I'm just finishing up my briefings with the brass. I'll be over in about 20 minutes to pick her up."

He looked up at her. "You heard that?"

Lodan nodded. He got up from his desk and showed her out of his office. He pointed to some seats toward the back of the outside office. "Please wait there. Do you need anything? Coffee? Water?"

"No, thanks, I'm fine."

"Alrighty then. It was nice to meet you. Good luck on Mars."

"Thank you, Lieutenant." He shook Lodan's hand and went back into his office. The woman with the contact lenses seemed to be looking at her with some sympathy.

Lodan sat down and decided that it would be a good idea if she could find information about the current status of the new Mars colony. She hadn't heard anything about trouble, and she wondered how much of this was still secret. She took out her tablet and gave her AI instructions for what to look for.

After the first few articles the AI indicated she should read, she could tell that the situation was still secret. The most recent article about the colony suggested that they had delayed emigration of non-expert families, which was telling, but there were no details about what prompted that delay. The absence of information about the new agricultural development processes was also telling. Taken together, this was pretty indicative to Lodan that there were some serious problems.

Lodan kept reading, and then got absorbed in reading a recent scientific article which investigated approaches used for growing warm-weather crops on Mars, when a voice surprised her.

"Lodan Greenfellow, I presume."

Lodan looked up to see a tall man, with a dark and wizened face, a grey mustache, and a broad smile looking at her.

"I'll bet you're reading the latest data from Mars, yes? You don't seem the type to pass the time on WayBack."

Lodan couldn't help but smile. She instantly liked Commander Kelley. She got up and extended her hand. "Commander Kelly, nice to meet you."

"Please, call me Josh. Everyone up in the new colony does. Let's get going, I'm finally ready to get off this rock. I've been missing Mars, and briefing the brass kept my interest only so long."

He turned, and she followed him out after hurriedly shoving her tablet into her bag. He stepped around a small vehicle, just large enough for two, and opened the trunk, indicating where to put her bags. They both got in.

He spoke to the AI in the vehicle's dashboard. "Dulles Space Port."

"Berth?"

"20."

"Acknowledged. Approximate arrival time, 15:20."

The car started to move and joined the traffic heading toward the expressway.

"I've been following your work in the Northern Resettlement Project for quite some time—even before you applied to join the new colony. I've been quite impressed by your applications of ancient agricultural techniques to solve modern problems. I've been especially interested in your anthropological approaches that include applying strategies of older civilizations to current agricultural problems."

"Thanks. I appreciate that—but to be honest, I'm not at all certain that ancient Earth agricultural techniques, or anthropology are going to help on the colony."

"Well, you'll get a chance to be the judge of that, once you'll go through some of our data… and findings. These are findings we have not released to the public."

"I noticed you delayed emigration."

"Yes, we did. We have about 100 families on Earth that were slated to come with us on this trip, as well as several hundred from other colonies on Mars. Of course, they are not at all happy. But there isn't anything we can do about it, for now."

"So, what's going wrong?"

"I'd like to wait until we get underway, so I can show everyone coming up with us all of the data we've got. I'm also pretty careful what we say here on Earth—this information can't become public."

Lodan nodded, but she couldn't for the life of her imagine what could be that big of a deal. Everyone knew that the efforts to terraform Mars were going to be risky, and not necessarily generate the results wanted. And the new techniques they were trying out were certainly theoretically sound, but if they failed, there were other well-established techniques already available on Mars.

The first colonies on Mars had been quite successful. The greenhouses had worked well, and the combination of water transported from the poles, mining for minerals and using solar power had made those colonies self-sustaining in a matter of a few years. They had begun to raise chickens and goats in some colonies.

But building out more colony space was extremely expensive, and VirginMars had expended a lot of capital to get the initial colonies going. No other corps wanted to take the risk of starting new colonies, so SolGov had to. Earth was too crowded, especially since the mini-ice age that had made all of Northern Europe, all of Canada, and a swath of the United States about 300 miles south of the Canadian border into barely habitable lands.

The good thing was that the mini-ice age, which came upon the world relatively quickly, had been enough to get everyone extremely serious about dealing with global climate change. The Gulf Stream was eventually re-started with a gargantuan global effort, and the predictions were that in another 15 years or so, those regions would be back to the climate they had been in the 18th century.

Lodan was jarred out of her reverie by the car slowing down, ready to enter the spaceport gate. Josh opened his window, and flashed his ID to the guard, who waved them through. The car made a right turn, and eventually pulled up in front of a squat metal building that almost looked temporary.

"OK, let's go."

Lodan knew the drill. The ship going to Mars was in orbit, and this would be a short shuttle trip to dock with VirginGalactic One, the space station that served as a space dock for most ships leaving the Earth orbit, on the way to the Moon, Mars, Ganymede and a dozen other colonies, as well as the numerous asteroid mining and transport craft coming and going. Lodan had once been to VirginGalactic One on her way to the Moon.

Several hours later, Lodan was stowing her gear in the small closet next to her bunk, inside the quarters she was sharing with four others on their way to Mars. There was a group orientation meeting before they were to undock from VG1. She walked down to the large conference room. The personnel from the Colony had commandeered a chunk of the transport going to Mars, including some of the nicest meeting space. They had, thankfully, started spinning the habitat ring, which had settled her stomach. During the shuttle ride up, and the transfer from VG1 to the ship, there had been several segments of time at zero-g. She hated zero-g.

Commander Kelly was speaking. "Welcome to the *Acheron*, everyone. Now I'm going to give you an idea of how we'll be spending our time during the 15 days we've got to get to Mars."

"We've sent everyone a full brief—it's hundreds of pages of data. I know it will take you a while to process. There are two important pieces of information to focus on. First, we have been unable to grow anything, except plants that are kept in sterile, hydroponic environments. There is something toxic in the processed regolith that we cannot identify, but it prevents seeds from sprouting, and seedlings die after several days. The regolith has been processed the way we've been doing it on Mars for years, to eliminate perchlorate, acidify it, and add nutrients. All analyses of this processed regolith suggests no presence of anything toxic to plants that we can find.

Second, and probably most important, is the discovery of artifacts in caves at this new site. There are photographs and details in your briefings, and I don't want to begin to discuss these until you've fully brought yourselves up to speed on what we've found. It is our current theory that these two things are connected somehow—we just don't know how yet."

There was a lot of murmuring, and Lodan decided to be one of the first to head out and find a comfortable place to sit and read all of this material. She found her way to one of the living rooms, with comfy chairs and a large view screen showing earth. It was nice to get to see Earth while they were slowly pulling out of orbit. They wouldn't start seriously accelerating for another few hours. She sat down on a chair, and started to take out her tablet, but she was interrupted by someone speaking in front of her.

"Hi there, my name is Michael."

Lodan looked up, to see a young-looking man with a small goatee smiling at her. She thought that his eyes belied the young look of his face—Lodan bet he was quite a bit older than he looked. She smiled and waved.

"Hello. I'm Lodan."

"Hi Lodan. Where are you from?"

"Originally, Utah and Arizona, but I spent the last 3 years in Massachusetts."

He smiled, even more broadly if that were possible. "I just got back from Minnesota."

She groaned. "I did my best to avoid Minnesota and North Dakota. Massachusetts was bad enough."

"I was low man on the totem pole, so I took what was offered."

"Well, not many people wanted to be part of the resettlement program—it takes a certain kind of person..."

"Yup, like the kind who will fly headlong into a new troubled Mars colony."

Michael seemed her sort of person. He came to sit down on a chair next to hers, facing Earth.

"So, what's your specialty, Michael?"

"I'm an anthropologist. My major role in the resettlement program, besides chopping wood and carrying water, was to do ethnographic studies of people's accommodation process to situations like that."

"Oh, you're Michael Gerald!"

"You know my work?"

"I do! I'm an agronomist by training, but I have a very serious interest in anthropology, and I have used anthropological research to apply ancient agricultural methods to modern situations. I came across your study of "The Holdouts." It was fascinating."

"I loved doing that research—well, except the months inside my RV. Good thing it had been specially built to withstand the cold! I was amazed how these folks had managed to eke out a living and stay in the areas that never saw spring. I could never have spent my life in perpetual winter."

Lodan nodded. "It was hard enough living up there after the warming started. I can't even imagine dealing with a winter way below zero all the time, and summers barely breaking the freezing point during the day."

"It's hard for me to leave Earth. I love it, even in its extremes. My contract is only for three years. After that, I decided I'd go back to Minnesota. I bought some land already."

"Cheap, I'm sure."

"It was when I bought it, 15 years ago. I had a small inheritance from my father, and the efforts to re-start the Gulf Stream again had just begun, and I was betting that it would be successful. So, I got 50 acres of land in suburban Minneapolis for a song. It's worth about 30 times what I paid for it now. I already have a few folks interested in helping me farm it in a few years when it becomes fully arable."

Lodan laughed. That was pretty smart. She hadn't thought that far ahead back then—but also, she didn't have an inheritance to spend. There was a moment of envy, but it passed. Her early life without her biological parents had been hard, but she'd managed fairly well in the end.

"I don't know how long I'll stay. I have an open-ended contract, and had expected that it would be possible, even likely, that I'd spend my life on Mars. But with the current troubles ... who knows what will happen. I may end up being a farmer on your land in Minnesota!"

He smiled. "You'd be a great addition to the team!"

The ship shuddered slightly, and Lodan could see Michael flinch.

"Spaceflight not your thing?"

"I've never been in space before. This is an exciting opportunity, and I couldn't pass it up, given my earlier work..."

"Earlier work?"

I actually made my name originally in archeology. I was one of the folks who discovered that ancient, semi-technological society in Eretria."

"Oh! I remember that find. It was so exciting and unexpected. I guess I didn't remember you being connected with it, but I learned about it before I went to grad school."

Michael smiled, "I guess that dates me. But I was a grad student myself."

Lodan smiled, "It must have been such an amazing adventure to have discovered that."

"Yes, it was. I guess that's mostly why I'm here. Speaking of, I guess I'd better get to reading. I haven't even cracked this open yet."

"Nor have I." They took out their respective tablets, and began to read, as the Earth slid slowly by on the screen.

The image of caked dirt inside of a boot floated inside Lodan's head as she drifted awake. As that image made its way into her conscious mind, she sat bolt upright, hit her head on her bunk, and swore.

The head with the long, blond hair of her roommate, Olga, showed itself above Lodan.

"You OK?"

"I'm fine, sorry. Hit my head."

She got up out of the bunk, got dressed quickly, and asked her AI for the location of Commander Kelley. He was in the mess. She hurriedly made her way there.

"Commander Kelley, I need to urgently speak with you."

He looked up, from his bowl of cereal. "Sit, please." He motioned her to a seat across from him. "Want breakfast?"

"Not until I ask you a question."

"Go ahead. This sounds important."

"It is. What is the decontamination procedure of people entering Earth atmosphere who have been on Mars?"

He looked puzzled. "Well frankly, there isn't one. You know there are no microorganisms on Mars. After 20 years of Mars colonies, and 30 years of our presence, there have never been signs of infection after exposure to the Martian environment. We decided a long time ago that a decontamination process would not be necessary."

She felt the blood draining from her face. He looked at Lodan, and she could see that he was concerned.

He said, "Why? What am I missing?"

"I don't know yet, but I am very worried. The data on the crop failures suggests that it isn't a lack of nutrients, nor an imbalance of chemicals, or too much perchlorate. It suggests something more dangerous—some sort of herbicidal like substance."

"What do you mean?"

"The data I've seen so far seems to suggest that what is causing the crops to fail is quite different than the ways in which crops respond to different factors such as lack of nitrogen, sun, water, or soil acidity or alkalinity. Further, the experiments on hydroponics using regolith-treated water suggest a water-soluble factor."

"Certainly, our biochemists and microbiologists would have found something—they have found nothing so far."

"I understand that—but the effects on the plants are pretty clear. My fear is that there might be some regolith from this region carried to Earth on your boots, for instance, or on clothes."

"Ah, well, water soluble did you say?"

"Yes."

"OK, good. You don't have to worry. We do wash everything—all clothing and footwear, as well as ourselves, before we board the ship to go back to Earth."

"Ah. OK. That makes me feel a lot better."

Lodan was relieved, but something still was nagging at her. She wasn't going to figure it out without breakfast, though.

Lodan, May 2105

They arrived at Mars station just as Lodan had gotten used to life aboard the ship, and just when she'd finished absorbing all of the data given to them. The information on the artifacts was interesting to her, but she had to focus all of her energy and time on the issues of crop failures.

"What we really need is some very high-resolution split-beam electron microscope images of the regolith. I wish we had one."

"I can't imagine why that would help—there's nothing in the soil to look at!" One of her team members, George, who was the team leader, was always convinced he knew more than anyone else. Besides having somehow managed to land a job at Harvard, Lodan couldn't imagine why he was the team leader. Although prolific, Lodan thought his research was pedestrian at best.

"I think there's something there we can't see with a regular microscope and can't see in the chemical analyses. Something on the scale of a few hundred atoms. Some mineral formations that get in the way of nutrient absorption, maybe?"

George shook his head, and Peter, who had yet to suggest anything, shook his head as well. Lodan was outvoted in her suggestion to get Regolith samples to a hi-res EM lab.

A loud voice spoke, drowning out Lodan's next comment. "Your attention, please! We are arriving at Mars station. We will be turning off spin in approximately 10 minutes. Make sure you are prepared. Please exit the *Acheron* in the docking bay, section 5."

It was time to take the shuttle down. Lodan went back to her quarters, where the return of zero-g happened just as she took out her bags. She pushed herself out of her quarters, and down what used to be a hallway, but now she was using handholds to propel herself to the docking bay, towing her bags behind her. Even though she felt like she wanted to vomit, at least her bags didn't weigh anything.

She got to the docking bay, and could see a lot of people, some were headed to the new colony, and there were varied passengers on their way to other colonies. She got in line to go through the docking doors and found herself on a little tram to the station's habitat ring. One moment she was strapped into the seat, and the next moment, as the tram curved to meet the habitat ring, the straps went slack, her stomach settled, and there was now a real "up" and "down." She felt much better.

After a little time on the station, Commander Kelley herded them to the shuttle which would take them down to Colony 6. It was a fairly painless process, and in just a few hours since they'd arrived in Mars orbit, Lodan was on the ground, on Mars, walking to her assigned quarters, and settling in.

Lodan heard the sound of her AI, which woke her. "Call from Commander Kelley". It was still dark in her quarters. She was glad for the cycle of lights in the colony, but she still hadn't gotten used to how dark it was at night. All of the quarters were underground, so there was no ambient light.

She looked at the clock on the table next to her bed. 4:00 am? What was going on? She got up, put on a shirt and pants, sat down at her desk, and answered the call. Josh's face looked like he hadn't slept in a while.

"Hi Josh. What's going on?"

She could see him take a breath. "I'm not sure exactly how to tell you this."

She didn't have any family, so it wasn't that someone died. What could it be?

"Just tell me."

"Well, its late spring now, in the US. As you well know, the northeast US is struggling to grow food again."

"Yes, and...?"

"A large swath of southeastern Pennsylvania and some of Maryland have had serious crop failures. Reminiscent of what's happened here. When I heard about it on a news program, I remembered your concerns."

"But how would regolith from the new colony make it to Pennsylvania?"

He took another breath.

"We delivered to a certain company 500 pounds of regolith from the region of the new colony. They were going to analyze it for new possible commercial uses."

She was speechless. She collected her thoughts. "Why?"

"Well, honestly, this company was willing to spend a hundred million Yuan on the sample, and a 5-year exclusive contract for regolith mining near the new colony. The program needed the money. And what I just found out is that the company is based in Harrisburg, PA."

"And they fucking washed the regolith down the drain, didn't they?"

"I don't know—but I expect its likely."

Crap. That meant that whatever they could do to solve the problem on Mars would be way more important than Lodan could have ever dreamed.

The next morning, Lodan was meeting with George and Peter, going over this new problem. She again suggested high resolution EM imaging.

George said, "I'm still not in favor of that, I'm sorry."

"George, I don't care. I'm going over your head on this one—there is too much at stake, now."

Lodan turned and left the meeting room to go to Josh's office. As she arrived, she saw Michael leaving.

She said, "Hey there—how is the artifact analysis going? I'm so sorry I haven't had time to check in with you."

"It's pretty fascinating—and impossible. I'm at my wits end, frankly."

"Well, you and me both. Maybe sometime we should have a chat. Maybe fresh perspectives might be useful."

"Sounds great—I look forward to it."

She watched him turn and walk away, noticing how she appreciated his body as he moved. She knocked lightly on Josh's door.

She heard, "Come in."

"Hi Josh. I need a favor."

"Sure thing."

"George won't agree to a hi-res SB EM look at the regolith. I think it's necessary. We're drawing complete blanks using every other method. I think George vetoed it because it's expensive, and he is always looking at the budget. Plus, I think he thinks I don't know what I'm doing."

"Look, anything we can do to solve this is important—were in trouble here. Apparently, the crop failures are spreading."

She said, "Let me know who to send my official request, and I'll spell out the specifications for specimen preparation."

"Alright, we'll make it happen."

It took more than a week to get the images back. There were some regolith samples from the new region tucked away at a couple of different national labs, but they had to be sent directly to USAMRID for imaging, because they needed the regolith to stay in the highest possible containment area.

Lodan had been right... sort of. The hi-res SB EM images showed clear evidence not of any crystalline formations that she'd expected, but of artificial nanoparticles.

She realized that her conversation with Michael was far overdue. She wondered if the key to understanding was in his bailiwick. She went in search of him, and found him in the colony lounge, reading. She took a moment to observe him. She'd come to really appreciate his points of view, and his sense of humor. She realized that she was attracted to him. She smiled, and went to where he was seated, sat next to him, and told him what they'd found.

Michael said, "I don't understand."

Lodan answered, "Nanoparticles are not naturally occurring, although of course George thinks I don't know what I'm talking about. I've gotten permission from Josh to talk with some nanotechnology experts I know on Earth and have them see if they can figure out what these particles are."

"I never really liked George. Anyway, these are definitely not natural?"

"Definitely. These shapes and sizes just don't occur in natural crystals. These are absolutely artificial in nature."

"Well, let me tell you about the artifacts, then. We can see if anything comes to us. They aren't very revealing. They are some geometric shapes, made out of something resembling plastic. Definitely carbon based, but with some unusual elements, too. Sort of like Poly Vinyl Chloride."

"Kid's toys?"

"It's funny, when I first saw them, that is actually what I thought of. They are about the right size, even. I had this image of a bunch of aliens hurriedly leaving Mars, and the kid having to leave behind their toys."

"So that's all?"

"There are 40 of the shapes. Some are different geometric shapes—a couple of tetrahedrons, some cubes, and a lot of dodecahedrons and icosahedrons. All platonic solids. There are some very enigmatic carvings and symbols on the walls of one of the caves, and about 30 small fragments of materials that seem part of some sorts of mechanisms, but we can't figure them out."

"Did you say Platonic Solids? What are those?"

"I heard that from Maria, the mathematician. They are regular, with congruent sides."

She took out her tablet and showed him pictures of the nanoparticles.

"That there looks like a dodecahedron with patterns on the sides."

"Yes, these nanoparticles seem to be all dodecahedrons."

It didn't make any sense to Lodan. Why would an alien species leave nanoparticles in the regolith, as well as geometric shapes behind?

"Is this the only place where these have been found?"

"Yup. They were found in one of the caves. Apparently, nothing else like this has been found in any other areas that have been explored on Mars."

Michael said, "So that means they are probably local, just like the artifacts."

That sounded right to Lodan. "Let me find out."

She had her AI send a quick request to Josh. There had been regolith samples taken from all over various parts of Mars. After a few days, the results came back—Michael had been right, the nanoparticles were local. Everyone was now in the process of determining a new site for Colony 6. In the meantime, she'd sent requests to some old colleagues of hers who were nanoscientists. She'd hoped they had a solution for their problem—not the one on Mars, but the one on Earth.

About two weeks later, she was sitting across from Josh in his office which was full of half-packed boxes.

"Well, Lodan, it looks like you'll finally get to grow some crops."

Lodan smiled broadly. "Yes, I'm quite looking forward to it. I'm glad we found a new suitable spot not too far away, with both caves, and space for greenhouses, and no sign of nanoparticles."

"The whole thing is still a mystery to me, but I'm sure glad that your nanotechnology friends knew how to dismantle those nanoparticles. Otherwise, we might have had a serious disaster on our hands on Earth. As it was, thousands of farms lost a growing season."

"Josh, it's still a mystery to everyone. The current theory is that the nanoparticles were just some refuse of the aliens, maybe just garbage. It didn't hurt them -it just happened to hurt Earth plants."

Lodan walked out of his office, went to the storage locker to don her pressure suit. She then joined the team disassembling the greenhouses.

Tina, June, 2105

It had only taken Tina two weeks to get on a transport to Mars. That gave her time to pack what she'd want for Mars, put the rest of her things in storage, arrange for a sublet for her apartment. Even as she did all of these things, she noticed that she only put things she felt she could part with in storage. Some part of her knew somehow she wasn't coming back.

It wasn't at all logical—Tina worked for the *Times* and hoped to work for them for as long as she could. The *Times*, unlike the rest of the news organizations, was very old school. People actually worked there for twenty or thirty years, once hired. She actually had hope that she could work at the *Times* until her body gave out, and she'd have to retire to the Moon. The good thing about spending a few years on Mars would be that her body clock would stop ticking quite so quickly, since the gravity was so much less than Earth's. But she knew that by the time she was fifty, or perhaps at most sixty, she'd have to return to the Moon to spend the rest of her life.

She was thinking about this as she was enjoying the zero-g gym at the center of the Mars transport. She'd be on this ship for about 45 days—Mars and Earth were pretty far apart at the moment. She did a few final exercises, then headed back to her quarters. Her stomach was grumbling, so she planned to head to the mess hall after she cleaned up.

When she arrived in the mess hall, there weren't many people there. She picked up her food, went to one of the small tables toward the outside of the hall, and ate while she looked over her AI's picks for the most important stories from Mars for the day.

Once she'd started to really read the news reported from Mars, she got a much fuller picture about what was going on Mars than she'd had when following the Mars government beat on Earth. There was an active Mars independence movement that was much more popular on Mars than anyone on Earth had reported. The results of one recent poll were that an independent Mars was favored by 75% of the populace. With those kinds of numbers, it made all sorts of sense that the representatives Mars sent to SolGov would be pushing for more autonomy. And the pushback, Tina realized, was bound to make things less stable, not more stable, for SolGov. Tina at first was shocked at how uninformed she had been, but she gave herself some slack—her job hadn't been deep investigative reporting on Mars—it had simply been reporting on Mars representatives on Earth. She was looking forward to doing some real investigative reporting.

The assignments that *The Times* had sent her were laughable, given what she was learning about the realities on the ground on Mars. It was then that she realized something of her true job—the job they hadn't told her she had. The *Times* had SolGov's back, and the *Times* wanted to have SolGov's back on Mars. She didn't know what to think of that. She'd do what they asked, but she suspected that after a while, it might be hard to maintain. She'd worry about that when the time came.

She did get Ama Shabazz as her junior journalist, and she would be on the next transport, several weeks hence. She hadn't gotten Joseph for imaging. Strangely, Joseph had just been transferred to the sports desk. Tina couldn't understand what was going on—Joseph was totally wasted imaging sports, and he'd spent a lot of time on Mars. She shook her head, choosing not to delve too much into speculations on machinations at *The Times*. She'd been assigned Holly Trimble—she knew that Holly was a decent imager and would do fine. Holly and Ama were heading to Mars on the same transport.

The first thing on her list to write an investigative story on was the movement of Colony 6. Just one month ago, for reasons that no one would talk about, the entire colony moved from one place to another. Interestingly, they were trying to pass it off as a problem with the local regolith, but Tina knew enough to know that didn't really make a lot of sense. The regolith on Mars did differ from region to region, but not enough so that the known ways to treat it so that plants could grow in it wouldn't work.

She had a list of a few folks she would request interviews of. She saw an anthropologist on staff for the colony, which made no sense to Tina—he would be the first she'd request an interview of, as well as the Colony Commander. She set a number of reminders for her AI, including background research on the anthropologist, and then kept reading.

Tina, July 2105

The alarm next to Tina's bed rang, and she woke up, feeling more refreshed and ready to go than she'd felt in years. Although Mars had twice the gravity of the Moon, where she was born and raised, it was just over one third of Earth's gravity. So being on Mars, even for a few days, had been a surprising relief, even from the .6 gravity in the Mars Transport generated by the spinning habitat rings.

Today, she was taking a day trip to Colony 6 to talk to a few people about the move. She had contacted Michael Gerald and Lodan Greenfellow, both of whom were willing to talk to her, but warned her there was much they could not talk about. The colony Commander had declined her request for an interview. She understood, and she knew she'd be getting less than half the story, but it was worth reporting anyway.

On the shuttle to Colony 6, she did a re-read of all of the information she had. They had tried to grow plants using the same techniques of modifying the regolith as usual, and it hadn't worked, so they moved. It seemed very straightforward, and also quite strange. It didn't look like any scientific studies about the regolith had been published, or were even in process, from what she could see. No funding had been released by SolGov to research the problem, no theories about the problem had even been blogged. It was as if they said "Can't grow anything here, don't know why, doesn't matter, we're moving." On its face, for most of the public, that might seem reasonable, but Tina knew enough about Mars and about science to know that it wasn't, not at all.

When the shuttle arrived, she made her way to the central dome, which looked to be in complete chaos. Containers were scattered about; people were dashing to and fro. She could hear the loud sounds of machines digging into the caves to create caverns. At times the sounds became almost deafening. As she was looking around, trying to figure out how to find the people she was supposed to interview, a tall man with a goatee came up to her.

"Tina Fiorici, I presume?"

She smiled. "Michael Gerald?"

"One and the same."

She stuck out her hand, and they shook hands.

"Come this way—we found a quiet place where we can do the interview."

She followed him through the chaotic dome, through a corridor which led underground. They went down a hallway, and into a room which looked like it was being prepared to be offices. A woman with dark curly hair stood up to greet them. Tina recognized Lodan from her background research.

"Ah, Michael, you found our journalist!"

"Yes, indeed."

"Please, Ms. Fiorici, have a seat."

"Feel free to call me Tina."

"So, Tina, how can we help you? I'm hoping that you don't think this visit ended up being a waste of time."

"I know, you warned me that there wasn't much to tell me. But anyhow..." Tina took out her small pocket recorder, and placed it on the table between them, which was strewn with assorted papers.

"So, I'd like first to learn a little about both of you, and how you became attached to the colony."

Lodan started, and, from Tina's perspective, her involvement in the colony didn't have much to do with the move. Tina had already learned that she was a very well-regarded agronomist, with particular expertise of the sort that would be extremely useful on any Mars Colony.

Lodan finished up by saying, "... and the problems that the colony had faced weren't really ones I'd been familiar with but were certainly in the realm of things I could deal with."

"Thank you, Lodan. That's very informative." It wasn't really, but Tina was trying to be friendly. "Michael..."

"I was recruited primarily because of my work researching how people deal with living in harsh conditions. The earlier colonies hadn't had any folks on staff to help with that kind of research. My work on 'The Holdouts' in the northern US during the mini-ice-age was the primary reason I was added to the Colony. And if you've done your homework, which I imagine you have, you've seen that I've already published one ethnography about the first members of this colony."

Somehow, Tina didn't believe a word of what he was saying, other than the fact that he'd published an ethnography. She'd already read it. On its face, the reasons he stated that he was sent here made a tiny bit of sense, but in her years of covering SolGov, she knew how little they regarded research that didn't have clear, material ends. VirginMars would be more likely to hire an anthropologist than SolGov. Further, although Michael's more recent work was ethnographic, Tina found that he had done a lot of significant archeological research, and he was better known for that than his ethnographic work. This just wasn't passing the sniff test.

"OK, thank you both. Could you now recall for me the events that led up to the need to move Colony 6."

Lodan replied, "Of course. We had heard on the trip out that the crops were failing—there had been no successes in treating the regolith in ways that had been used all over Mars before to allow any crops to grow. There seemed to be some sort of toxic compound in the soil that prevented that from happening. We did a lot of testing and investigation and realized that this colony site was just not going to be viable, so we found another site where we could grow crops, and we moved here."

"Did you find the reason that the regolith was toxic?"

Tina noticed a slight hesitation in Lodan's voice, and she detected the most subtle flick of Lodan's eyes toward Michael.

"No, we don't really know why the toxicity found in the regolith prevented seeds from sprouting or prevented plants from growing."

Tina knew this was the truth, but she also knew that it was hiding quite a lot.

"What kinds of tests have you done?"

"All sorts. EM, spectroscopy, using different kinds of treatments for the regolith, you name it."

"Can I see that data?"

She shook her head. "No, I'm sorry. SolGov has classified that data."

"Classified? Why?"

"You'll have to ask them that."

"Michael, do you have anything to add?"

For a quick moment, he looked a bit like a deer in headlights—then that expression passed.

"No, I wasn't involved in the testing of the regolith at all—not my department, as they say."

Tina internally shook her head. There was something very big lying under this blanket they had hastily thrown, and she could see it was big, but couldn't see the shape of it. And she could tell that she wasn't going to get anything of substance from them. But it had been worth coming out here in person, to see their reactions to her questions.

"So, now that you've moved, how is it going?"

They chatted amiably about the new colony site, the progress that was being made, and the date that they thought the first set of non-expert families would arrive—sometime in the spring of next year. She left, and as she was sitting in the shuttle to Colony 1, she started to write the article. She did a basic report, and then added the questions that she still had for SolGov. She'd try to get answers to those questions when she got back.

In retrospect, as she looked at her message in-box with messages from varied SolGov officials with "no comment" said in twelve different ways, she should have known she'd hit a brick wall. She sighed and started to write her article. She started out with the article relaying, basically at face value, what she had been told by Mr. Gerald and Ms. Greenfellow. She then added a few paragraphs with her own analysis, explaining why it didn't make sense that regolith would be toxic enough to force a colony move, that it seemed out of character for SolGov to hire Michael Gerald, and that classifying this information suggested that there was something going on that SolGov didn't want the public to know. At that last, she got a twinge of worry—how would her editors look at this? She didn't know, and she decided worrying about it now wasn't going to make any difference. She'd asked incisive questions before in her articles—this wasn't much different.

The next day, as she prepared her research for an article that wasn't on her assignment list, but she felt was an issue on Mars that was important to cover, her AI signaled her.

"Video message from *The Times* editor has come in." *Video*. Uh oh.

"Play on the view screen, please."

She turned to look at the large view screen that was hung next to her desk. The formally dressed visage of her boss appeared.

"Ms. Fiorici, I want to thank you for your investigative reporting of the move of Colony 6. However, you have gone too far in indicting SolGov for blocking the news of the reasons for this move. This is very straightforward, and I am concerned that you are being fed some sort of disinformation that is leading you to draw erroneous conclusions about the motives of SolGov, which, as you know, are always above board."

She was glad this couldn't be synchronous—he would have not been happy at the snort she let out at the last statement.

"Please review the article as we have published it. And please understand that we have invested a lot in your presence there on Mars, and we expect better of you."

His image was replaced by a blank screen. Numbly, she brought up today's *Times*, and found her article, which she noticed was well buried. The entire last part of the article had been replaced by pablum about SolGov's commitment and investment in Mars Colonies!

She sighed. That unspoken job she realized she had? It became clear to her that it really was her job. She had to find a way to report on Mars truthfully, without making SolGov look bad. And she wasn't at all sure that was possible. But she knew that making SolGov look bad would get her fired. So, she was going to have to tread very carefully.

Chapter 3:
The Right Asteroid

Sam, October 2105

Sam looked up from their console at the asteroid as their ship moved toward it. They'd been folded into their seat for way too long, and their back had started to ache. They took off the straps and moved around a bit to loosen things up. Their console had a view screen that curved around the seat. Sam peered into it—they couldn't really see the asteroid—it was more like a tiny black blot on the canvas of stars, about 1,000 kilometers away. This was the asteroid they'd been tracking for the last hundred thousand kilometers or so, and it looked to be a gem.

It was time for their to have the ship decelerate. "Jane, calculate forward thrust to place us in line with the asteroid."

The dulcet voice spoke from her console. "Calculated."

"Engage."

"Engaged."

They felt the slight shudder of the ship as the forward thrusters were engaged, slowing their approach to the asteroid. About 100,000 kilometers ago, they'd gotten some positive preliminary spectrographic data from this asteroid. They'd spent the last of their financial reserves, as well as borrowing money from Sky, to claim it. If it was a dud, they were done—they'd have to return to the Moon, completely broke. Likely they'd end up working as a grunt in a mine. They'd rather avoid that fate.

They took off the belts, and floated out of their chair. They had a lot of work to do, once their ship made contact with the asteroid. They propelled themself back into the work area and got to work. There would be core samples to take, and spectral analyses to run. It was a large asteroid, and they'd been amazed to find early on that it hadn't ever been claimed, given the early spectrographic data from it.

They sat down at their workstation, strapped in, and started their report on it. They'd learned, over time, that although the asteroid miners pored over the data, the presentation would influence the price they was able to fetch for the rock. They were determined to put together the most convincing and well-presented report they'd ever done.

"Telemetry data, please."

"Telemetry data complete." Information about the direction, velocity, acceleration and spin of the asteroid appeared on her screen. Wow, this was strange, they thought. The direction and velocity suggested that the asteroid was moving *across* the plane of the asteroid belt! And really fast—it was accelerating! No wonder it hadn't been claimed already. It hadn't been around. They began to ponder what this might mean about its composition.

"Rerun remote spectroscopy please."

"Complete."

They reviewed what showed up on their screen. The data was clearer now that they was closer. The majority of the asteroid looked to be carbon. Not too surprising, it was common for asteroids. But what was good was that there was also plenty of iron, good amounts of nickel, tin, and aluminum, and what looked like a band suggesting some amount of platinum or gold! Yes, this *was* a gem. If the core samples confirmed this data, they could retire in style back on Earth once they'd sold this rock. More likely, they'd buy themself a brand-new ship, and keep exploring.

"Contact with asteroid in 5 minutes." Their AI's smooth voice came from the speaker next to them.

"Start initial contact procedures. Extend grappling hooks."

"Hooks extended."

"Deploy external sampler."

"Sampler deployed."

This was the first step. Grab a bit of the rock and put it inside the small isolation unit they had aboard ship. Take a visual look at it, grind up a bit and analyze the real composition, and make sure that there isn't anything potentially dangerous about it. After that, take a big core sample from below the ship, and store it. Sam would go outside and take three more core samples from different areas of the rock. Do a final analysis, and then send it all for bid in the asteroid auction market.

This part was short. They should be done with all of the analyses within 12 hours or so. The long part was waiting for a bid they'd take, and then waiting for a ship to show up to take their own samples and make the final transaction. But if it all went well, they could be taking shore leave on Mars sometime next month.

"Contact with asteroid made." They was jolted from her reverie by Jane.

"Connect to asteroid with grappling hooks."

"Hooks engaged." They felt a small movement in the ship, then it was still.

"Ship attached to asteroid. Commencing first sampling." They could hear the slight whine, pause, and whine of the sampling arm extending, grabbing a sample, and retracting.

A beep started to sound on her console, and they went back to look at what it was. On her console, a small green LED was flashing, which indicated the presence of radio transmissions coming from the asteroid. They couldn't believe it.

"Jane, what's the transmission?"

"A very high frequency transmission coming directly from the asteroid."

"When did it start?"

"Calculating ... It started when the sampler made contact with the asteroid."

They thought a moment. This was certainly going to mess with their plans. But then again, what were the possibilities? It was either someone else's asteroid already, in which case they was in deep trouble, or it was something else entirely. Something very interesting.

"Can you make any sense of the transmission? Anything identifiable? Is it a standard claiming beacon?"

"It is well above the frequencies used by the industry for claiming beacons. It does have a pattern. Displaying pattern now."

A graph appeared on her console. It didn't look like anything they'd seen before.

"Can you analyze this?"

"Negative. The pattern is not recognizable."

"Are there any reported signals of human origin with that signature that might apply here?"

"Negative."

Sam didn't know exactly what to do. This was clearly alien. In general, there wasn't much interest from anyone about anything related to alien life. The deep problems of Earth had overshadowed this interest many years ago, with all available resources going to help reverse the catastrophic climactic changes. The moon and Mars had become insular, with only attention being paid to making habitable spaces and profitable enterprise.

They kept up with astronomy and planetology, and had even written some articles, and they knew that most scientists who studied them were now on Mars at Terra University, on Arabia Terra. They knew they were stuck. Give this asteroid over to the scientists, they'd get nothing, and would end up in the lunar mines. Ignore the signal, and send a report to the asteroid miners, and when they came to claim it, they'd find the signal, and probably nix the deal. And they'd end up in the lunar mines.

They decided that if they were going to end up in the lunar mines anyway, they might as well do the right thing. And maybe the scientists would take pity on them and give them a job on Mars washing test tubes. That would be a better fate. It wasn't the shore leave they had hoped for, but it was better than being underground for the rest of their life.

But they needed more data before they sent the report to Terra University.

"How's the sample analysis going?"

"Sample analysis complete."

They must have been absorbed in the dilemma for longer than they thought.

"Display at my workstation, please."

They propelled themself back to their workstation, and looked at the screen. At first, they thought it was mighty strange. But then, the composition of the sample made perfect sense, if it was indeed some sort of alien ship or capsule.

The sample was 100% carbon. Completely 100% carbon. The microscopic images clearly showed it was full of carbon nanotubes. In order for her to have found metals in the remote spectrographic data, there must be some exposed areas not covered by the carbon.

They sighed. Time to write up the report and find out who to send it to. They started to do research on faculty at Terra University and found a professor who not only looked to be still interested in SETI, after all these years, but also seemed like a good bet for someone who would be sympathetic to their plight. Sam wrote up the full report and sent it to Professor Kylee Mason.

They looked at her clock—time to catch some sleep. They had no idea how long it would take Dr. Mason to read the report and reply. Might as well get some rest. they pulled the bunk down, pulled themself in, strapped in, and fell promptly asleep.

A gentle chime woke Sam up. They'd asked Jane to wake her if there was a response to their message.

"Jane, response from Professor Mason?"

"Affirmative. On screen."

They looked up at their small console over their head in their bunk. A round young face appeared with warm terra-cotta skin, deep brown eyes, and short, curly hair. She was smiling broadly. Sam felt a jump in their chest—Kylee looked a lot like Tina. Sam was surprised at how strongly they felt the sadness. They still missed Tina, after all these years. Sam wondered often how Tina was. They imagined her a famous journalist on Earth by now. Well, that was then, and this is now. They forcibly moved their mind back to the problem at hand as the message played.

"Hello, Sam Julian. You have sent us amazing data, and we are astounded at what looks to be clearly some sort of alien artifact. We have a problem, however. You might be surprised to learn that Terra University has very little presence or influence in space. In fact, we don't own any ships other than ground-to-orbit, and we have been unable to contract with companies with ships given the current shortage. Thus, we will be unable to send anyone to you to take over the asteroid or help you in any way analyze the find."

There was a pause, and Sam's hope of getting out of their problem were dimming by the moment.

"However, given your expertise, we were hoping that you would be willing to contract with us to continue to explore the asteroid, with our remote help. Is that possible? Please let us know. I imagine that we could settle on a reasonable fee, and we possibly could arrange some percentage of payment up front."

Sam almost hit their head on the ceiling in surprise and happiness. This professor was clearly sympathetic. Or, perhaps, just realistic. They got down from the bunk, and sat down at their workstation, and began to figure out how much money they needed to make the lease payments, and get their supplies and food for the next run out. They also included reimbursement for the claim reservation. They sent it off and hoped that would be acceptable.

"Asteroid velocity has changed."

"What?" Sam got up from her workstation and ran to the cockpit.

"Velocity has slowed by 20,000 miles per hour and is continuing to slow. Direction has changed as well."

"Direction? Jane, plot new direction, please."

An image of the solar system appeared, with bright blue line, indicating the path of the asteroid. It led right to Mars. But there was something else. The path indicated that it was going to go right through the center of Strelix, Inc. space. Strelix. The company from whom they leased her ship. They was screwed. Once they got into Strelix space with this asteroid, they would claim their ship, and probably the asteroid to boot, just because they could, even though they'd put a claim on it. They knew that they didn't have the resources to fight it.

Sam sat for a while, thinking this through. They had no idea what to do, except send a message to the professor to let her know what's happening, and hope, by some miracle, that no one from Strelix would notice an asteroid that was a half kilometer in diameter streaking through their space. Yeah, right.

There wasn't much else they could do, once they'd sent the message off. They guessed they could try and unhook from the asteroid, but that wouldn't help things. Their time was up. They had no more money to claim another asteroid anyway. So, they might as well ride this out.

They decided to spend the time looking more deeply at the samples they'd gotten. They'd need true electron microscopy to get more detailed data—equipment they'd never been able to afford to add to the lab setup. They did find out that it was unlike any kind of carbon nanotubes that humans had managed to make, but that wasn't much of a surprise.

"Sam, incoming message from Strelix."

Sam sighed. This was it.

"Put it through, Jane."

They looked at her console, and a familiar face was grinning at them. Georgio Morone. He was the one who'd leased the ship to them. Damn.

"Sam! How nice to see you. Bringing us a sweet present, are you?"

"Hi Georgio. No, it's not a present for you."

"Ah, I think it is, my friend. How did you get it to swing by this way?"

Sam didn't want to let Georgio know anything about the asteroid.

"It wasn't quite in my plan to come in this direction."

"I can imagine it wasn't. Well, anyway, a ship is on its way to rendezvous with you in about 45 hours. Be prepared to be boarded. No funny business!"

Sam turned off the console. They didn't really have a choice. The ship, and the asteroid, were going to end up in Strelix's hands, no matter what they did. Then they smiled—funny business indeed! Yes, that might work... They spent the next several hours preparing for the handover of their ship to Strelix. When they were done, they decided they had some time to sleep.

A quiet chime woke her.

"Message from Mars."

"Display."

Kylee Mason's face looked concerned this time.

"Sam, I got your message. I don't know what to suggest. We don't hold any sway with the big corporations–we are almost always working on opposite ends of things these days. I can't help. It's horrible to think that the asteroid will fall into their hands, but there isn't anything I can do about it. I'm sorry.

"I hope there is some way you can make it to Mars with the samples you've taken so far. And we can find some work here for you, if you can."

Washing test tubes, Sam thought.

It was time to complete the preparations. They'd spent hundreds and hundreds of hours customizing the nav and communications systems, and they were damned if Strelix was going to get that code, or the analyses of the asteroid. And they owned their AI outright. They took out the holographic storage cube they kept for emergencies just like this. They were going to dump the source code for everything: customizations, AI, analysis algorithms, asteroid data, all of it.

"Jane, please copy all source, and verify."

"Copying." Several minutes went by. "Verified." Sam removed the cube from the console and buried it in a hidden pocket in their clothes bag, right next to their dirty boxer shorts.

"Jane, when I say the words 'well, hello Strelix', I want you to activate the new self-wipe sequence 4b."

"Understood."

They then found her sample container. They screwed it into the sterile sample holder.

"Jane, transfer asteroid samples to container and seal."

Sam heard the sucking noise of the samples being transferred and the container sealed. They removed the sealed container, and wrapped a t-shirt around it, and packed that along with her clothes. None of these would pass careful inspection, but they hoped they weren't in that kind of mood.

"Jane, take the old asteroid sample from A453, and place it in the sample holder."

They heard some more sucking sounds.

"Complete."

Once the system wipe was complete, the only data left would be that of her most dud asteroid. And the only samples left would be those of the same asteroid. They hoped that they would take a quick look at the data, and let the asteroid go on to Mars.

"Proximity alert!"

That would be Strelix calling.

They heard the clanking of the docking rings engaging.

"Incoming message."

"Go ahead, Jane."

"Sam Julian, this is Josh Winter, for Strelix. Please unlock your hatch."

Josh Winter, one of their least favorite people, and perfect for their plans. He'd been the communications officer of a Strelix ship they were on early in their career. He cared about no one except himself. Stepped on the backs of many people to get as high as he could in Strelix. They wondered who he had pissed off to get repo duty. The good thing was that he wasn't very smart, but he didn't know it.

"Affirmative." This was the end. They looked around their ship, one last time. Their bag was over their shoulder, and they were ready to go.

"Jane, unlock the hatch."

"Hatch unlocked."

"Well, hello Strelix."

"Wipe commencing. Goodbye, Sam." Sometimes, Sam did think Jane had a personality.

"Wipe complete." A tinny, flat voice had replaced Jane's deep, complex tones.

The door to the hatch slid open, and they could see a man standing stooped down in the dock so that his head didn't hit the ceiling.

"Sam, excuse me, please."

He shoved past them into the analysis area. His fingers moved quickly over the workstation.

"Don't do much customization, do you? I never thought you were that smart, anyway. Gee, this one was sure a dud. Why is it not in a standard orbit?"

They shrugged. "Got me."

"Damn. OK, I'm letting it go; I don't have time to deal with a dud asteroid."

His fingers moved across the workstation again, and the grappling hooks came undone. They could feel the slight change in acceleration from no longer being connected to the asteroid.

They sighed with relief. John looked at them sharply.

"I'm just sorry to leave this ship. I love it." Sam was, of course, telling the complete truth.

"You were such a sap. OK, time to get this back to Strelix Station. And unfortunately, I'm not allowed to space you. Come on, get inside my ship."

They hoped They could hitch a ride to Mars from the station. Their asteroid would probably make it there first. They crammed Sam in a tiny space, with a narrow, thin mattress that took up all of the floor, and threw in a bunch of "Meals Ready to Eat" in with them. They couldn't actually stand or lie straight in the compartment. No windows or view screens were in evidence.

"The bathroom is over there. Besides going there, don't leave this room until we get to the station, OK? I don't want you wandering around this ship."

"Fine with me."

Sam didn't think that the MREs were going to be enough—the main Strelix station was, in their estimation, at least 5 days away at maximum thrust. They guessed they would go a bit hungry at times, but they'd been hungry before. They spent their time mostly thinking about their next steps. They'd lost their ship, and probably lost their chance to go back to asteroid hunting forever. They couldn't imagine a situation that would allow them to save up enough money again to lease another ship. Once one left a company like Strelix to become a freelance asteroid hunter, it wasn't ever possible to go back—they never trusted you again. They couldn't be a pilot—they'd lost the chance to join the pilot's union years ago, and pilots, who worked for either VirginGalactic, SolGov, or another big corp, and independents like Sam were like oil and water—and none of the employers would hire them.

Any other jobs they could do with their experience were mostly on the Moon, and mostly menial—they might be able to scrimp and save a little, but never enough to get another down payment on a ship. They didn't know what was in store for them on Mars. Professor Mason had offered Sam some sort of work, but they couldn't imagine what it might be, and they doubted it would pay well enough for them to save again.

They realized that spending their time being despondent about losing their ship wasn't very useful. They were still young and had a long future ahead of them—they just had to figure out what it was. Sam wondered if they could get reduced or free tuition at Terra University on Mars. They didn't know if they gave credit for informal work completed. Maybe they could finally get their degree in planetology. That was it, really. It wasn't that they loved asteroids, although they did enjoy studying them. It was really that they loved being in space. Well, that is, when they could see around them. Sitting crammed in a tiny compartment with no way to see out was maddening.

After they ran out of MREs, when they were beginning to wonder whether or not they'd starve to death, they felt a slight shift in the ship's movement and the sounds of the ship. They realized they probably had arrived at Strelix Station. Eventually, they heard a knock on the door, and a voice.

"Time to get out. We've arrived. Georgio wants to talk with you."

Sam gathered their things and followed a crewmember whose name they never learned, through the ship and out to the dock. They floated together out of the airlock and into the docking area of the Strelix Station. The crewmember bid her goodbye, and Sam made her way to the tubes to the outer ring of the station. They knew exactly where Georgio's office was, and walked down the ring's main hallway to get there.

As Sam was walking, they felt a sense of anti-nostalgia. They had never liked this station and had been glad to leave. They were happy they would not be here very long if they had anything to do with it.

The door was open, and they peeked in, to see him sitting at his large, ostentatious oak desk that must have cost a fortune to ship out here.

"Hello, Georgio."

"Ah, Sam, please sit down. How are you today?"

"I've been much better, frankly. Besides losing my ship, I spent the last 6 days without enough to eat in a closet."

"I'm sorry about the closet—I'll have a chat with Mr. Winter about that. And, well, sometimes, it's just tough luck out there in the asteroid hunting biz. Sorry to have to take your ship, but it's just business, you know."

Sam was not really interested in talking with Georgio about their current problems.

"Is there anything you need, Georgio? Why did you want to see me?"

"I have some questions about the asteroid my idiot employee Mr. Winter released." Sam could hear the anger in his voice. Sam could tell Winter was on his way down to something worse than repo duty. Sam knew they had to be very careful, here.

"What kind of questions?"

"Sam, Josh Winter might think you are stupid, but I watched you during your years in this company. I happen to know that you are the smartest asteroid hunter I've ever seen. And I saw the telemetry data on your ship."

"On my ship? You were tracking me?"

"That's for damn sure. You were flying a million Yuan ship of mine that I wanted back."

"OK, so what are you getting at?"

"You approached a spot within the asteroid belt, I'm assuming that's where you met the asteroid. Your direction and speed, which one would think would match the asteroid, did some very strange things. First, you seemed to follow a track across the plane of the belt. Then, you seemed to make an adjustment, slow down and begin a big sweep toward Mars. Now, the weird thing is that it was clear you were going to fly through our space. So why did you make that shift when you knew we would get your ship in the process? It doesn't make any sense to me."

Sam didn't know what to say. They couldn't imagine how to lie convincingly—there were too many holes in anything Sam would say. On the other hand, they weren't going to tell Georgio anything about the alien craft. So they decided in the end to not say anything.

"Is that all, Georgio? I don't have anything to tell you, and I would like to go now."

He looked at Sam for what seemed like hours, but was probably only about 30 seconds.

"Alright, have it your way. It's true, you are under no obligation to tell me anything, and we have no claim on the asteroid, legally, since you bought the claim. By the way, I've sent you the final accounting. Surprisingly, we owe you a little money."

"You owe me?"

"Yes. You gave quite a hefty down payment, and the contract states that in case of default, we'd measure depreciation and damage, if any, on the craft, as well as interest on the value of the ship, and subtract that from the total of the down payment and the lease payments you made. We try to be fair, and you kept very good care of that ship. It's not much, but it might get you some meals and quarters on Mars for a few days."

Sam decided it was best not to say anything. They got up, said goodbye, and walked toward the operations desk, so they could find a ride to Mars. Luckily, there was a transport heading to Mars station in a few hours, and there was a berth left. It would take a few days to get there.

They sent a message ahead to Professor Kylee Mason, letting her know when they'd be arriving, and also giving her the latest data on the asteroids location, speed and direction. Kylee answered with enthusiasm and also to tell them that they had begun to track the asteroid.

Sam had been surprised that Georgio had told them that he knew they had a legal claim on the asteroid. It made them wonder whether or not getting Winter to release the asteroid had been the best decision. But in the end, here they were, with a little bit of money in their pocket and an asteroid that was legally theirs on its way to Mars, where it could be properly studied. And, perhaps, in the end, it could be worth a little something.

John, November 2105

John walked at a brisk pace down the hall toward Admiral Matira's office. He had just gotten off of the shuttle from the Moon, where he was regularly stationed. He had been puzzled by being recalled—he was told that he was no longer to be stationed on the Moon, but he hadn't yet received his orders, save to report to Admiral Matira, at headquarters in Beijing. That was highly unusual.

He arrived at Admiral Matira's office, and the Admiral's assistant opened the door. As John walked in, saluted, and stood at attention, he noticed his old teacher and mentor, Captain Benjamin McAdams, in the room. Several other officers were present that John didn't know.

"Admiral Matira, Lieutenant Commander Herman reporting for duty."

"At ease, Lieutenant Commander. Everyone, have a seat, please. Lieutenant Mitchell, please make sure we are not disturbed."

"Yes, sir." The assistant left the room, closing the door.

"What I am about to tell you all is classified at level nine. Last week, we received word that an asteroid hunter had discovered an alien probe of some sort. That probe is headed on its own propulsion toward Mars. It might have already arrived there by now. We have classified the existence of the probe, and the data about it. We have been in contact with a scientist, named Dr. Kylee Mason. Dr. Mason was, for some reason, contacted by this asteroid hunter when they discovered that it wasn't an asteroid they had found. Dr. Mason already has level six security clearance because of a previous SolGov contract with her lab, and we have increased her clearance to level seven. She will be handling the analysis of the alien probe.

"We suspect that the probe's origin is the same species that the Chinese Government encountered on the Moon in 2025."

Captain McAdams interrupted, which surprised John. Perhaps McAdams and the Admiral had a more cozy relationship than John knew.

"Admiral, what makes you think that?"

"Some of the spectrographic data matches alloy samples we've got from the Moon. In addition, the carbon nanotubes the asteroid hunter described sound a lot like the ones we've also seen. In addition, the probe is on its way to Mars—where the abandoned alien colony was found."

McAdams nodded at the Admiral, and she continued, as if the interruption were of no consequence.

"We had already begun plans for a new class of interplanetary ship, and because we are concerned that the existence of this probe suggests the continued presence of this species in our system, we have accelerated the pace of construction. The President feels that this species is a clear and present danger to SolGov, and this ship will be our primary defense. It will have some very new fusion weaponry we've been working on.

"Captain McAdams will lead the construction effort and be ship's captain when the time comes. All of you will be officers in various capacities on this new ship. Lieutenant Commander We Ying, you will lead navigation and communications, Commander Marianne Julta, you will lead security. Commander Gustav Androv will be in charge of ship's systems, and Lieutenant Commander John Herman, you will lead alien contact logistics."

He was taken aback by that assignment. He had plenty of space and air combat duty under his belt—the Delta Colony uprising on the Moon that finally ended in 2103 and the Senegalese war in 2096. But he wasn't a scientist. It troubled him momentarily, but then he realized that they must know something he didn't and have a good reason to put a combat veteran in charge of this mission.

"You'll all be headed up to SolGov Military Shipyard in a few hours—we've got a shuttle waiting for you. Get your things together and meet there at 1500 hours. You are dismissed, except for Lieutenant Commander Herman."

Everyone left the room, except for the Admiral, McAdams, and himself.

The Admiral said, "Lieutenant Commander Herman, it is my understanding that you are due a promotion."

John was surprised, again. "Thank you, Admiral Matira." He stood up.

The Admiral handed McAdams a box, which John knew had his new Commander's insignia. McAdams opened the box and pinned the stripe onto John's jacket.

"Congratulations, Commander Herman."

He smiled. He was a proud man. Proud of the life he had made for himself out of nothing, and proud to be part of the SolGov military.

"Captain, I know that you'd like to spend some time catching up with your officer, here, and I've got a lot to deal with. Dismissed."

John and Captain McAdams left the office.

McAdams said, "John, let's head to the American restaurant for lunch, shall we? I know that you are already packed."

John nodded. "Lead the way—I've only been here a few times."

They walked down a number of corridors and emerged in an open plaza. There were military and civilians of all sorts walking around, sitting on benches, or on grassy areas, and eating at tables that spilled outside of varied restaurants around the plaza. McAdams led them to a large restaurant that wasn't too crowded, and they sat at an outside table. A waiter came right away and took their order.

"This is my treat, *Commander*. It's been a long time since I've seen you, even though I've followed your career closely." McAdams said the word Commander with a smile, and John thought a hint of personal pride.

"Captain, I'm looking forward to serving under you again." The last time John had served under McAdams was during the Delta Colony uprising. McAdams, then a Commander, led his attack platoon.

They talked amiably about the Moon, and John asked whether McAdams missed it at all.

He said, "No, I don't. It was too insular—both in the military and the civilians. I like being here on Earth. My wife certainly appreciates being back home."

"How are your wife and kids?"

McAdams smiled, "She's fine. Jason is in his third year at West Point, and Maria wants to be a scientist and is hoping to get into Harvard, Nanjing, or Oxford. She doesn't want to go to the University of Beijing—too close to home."

They continued to talk amiably, although as always, the topics they talked about skirted the fact that John had no romantic life, and no family. As John was just finishing up the last of his French fries, McAdams became serious.

"John, I need to make sure you have my back."

"Ben, of course you do." John didn't often call McAdams by his first name, but he'd had permission to do so for years, and used it sparingly. This was one of those times it seemed appropriate.

McAdams nodded. "This is going to be a tough, and politically charged mission. It's bad enough that there seems to be an alien threat—but now, with all of the noises Mars is making about independence..."

"Ben, why is everyone so sure they are a threat? The data I've seen about the colony that NATO destroyed on the moon..."

"The colony was destroyed, John. If the aliens find out..."

John got it. If humans had ever found out that aliens had destroyed a colony of theirs...

"I see. Well, in any event, Ben, you know you have my loyalty. If it wasn't for you, I'd have washed out of basic training and probably dead now."

"I think you sell yourself a little short, my friend. But I'm glad you're with me. It's going to be an interesting time. We should get to the shuttle."

They made their way to the side of the complex that had a terminal and a large tarmac for planes and shuttles to land and take off. They could see the short-range shuttle sitting attached to the terminal. John had stowed his belongings in the terminal luggage area, and he went to claim them. He dropped off his luggage as directed in one of the carts on the way to the shuttle. They ran their ident cards over a reading station, had their retinas and fingerprints verified, and walked down the entryway to the shuttle.

The officers John had met were already on the shuttle, as were a few other people who he imagined were headed up to the Shipyard for duty. John had never seen the Shipyard, although he had certainly heard a lot about it, and was happy that he would get to spend some time there. It was the largest station that had been built in space, by human beings, at least. It had three parts—a large, rotating station for people to live and work in, a very large construction bay, and a ship repair and storage bay, which was enormous, and held many ships in varied states of disrepair. It had been built after VG1, which had been, up to that time, the largest station in human space.

He had known about the existence of the destroyed alien colony for years, so unlike most humans, he knew that they weren't alone in the universe. He sobered, imagining that they might actually *meet* these aliens.

Sam, November 2105

Overall, the transport to Mars was uneventful, except for the gorgeous view of Mars on approach to the Mars station. Sam had only been to Mars once in their life, and only to Mars station—never to the surface. They did have several very interesting conversations with people who were now living on Mars. They had no idea that there was an independence movement, and that so many 'Marsies' as they called themselves wanted SolGov to go away. It appeared that SolGov was only taking—sending emigrants, taking resources made on Mars, and not giving anything back. Mars was self-sufficient and didn't really need much from Earth anymore. It was an education for them— they'd been so used to life on the Moon and on Strelix station—both were dependent on shipments of food and manufactured goods from elsewhere—including Mars.

As they walked out of the airlock of the shuttle into the bustling Mars colony spaceport, they felt a bit overwhelmed with the size of the space. They noticed the light gravity—lighter than the gravity of the spinning Strelix station, but heavier than the gravity of the moon, where they'd spent several years. They looked around for indications of how to find her way to the university. They walked over to what looked like an information kiosk and began to ask the AI about how to get to Terra University.

"Sam!"

They turned around to see Kylee's smiling face.

"Professor Mason! I had no idea you'd meet me here."

"Please, call me Kylee." She put out her hand, and Sam shook it.

"Thanks for picking me up, Kylee. I wasn't sure how I was going to find my way around here. It's a bit confusing... and honestly, I haven't been on a planet in a long time—I'm used to much smaller spaces."

"No worries, Sam. Come with me."

They walked toward the outside of the large central domed space. Sam could see what looked like a transit car slowing down to stop.

"We need the next one—that one is going to dome complex 4. We're going to the dome complex 3, which houses Terra U. I took the liberty of getting you a staff apartment. I hope that's OK."

"A staff apartment?"

"Yes. They are pretty small—smaller than the apartments that most people who work on Mars get. But they are adequate for everything you need. And they are very close to my lab, where we'll be working."

"Thanks, I'm sure they'll be fine. I just spent 6 days inside a closet."

"Oh, my, I'm so sorry about that."

"It's no big deal. I survived." Sam smiled. They were quite happy to be off of that ship, out of Strelix space, and on a new adventure.

They got on the next transport that went quickly underground.

"Most of this colony is inside caves to protect us from solar radiation. The domes are specially coated, but it's much more expensive to build and maintain large domes than it is caves. The second Mars colony decided to try doing primarily domes, but much smaller, interconnected domes, which seems to work pretty well, although it's very easy to get lost there."

Sam hoped they'd get to visit all of the colonies at some point.

"How many are there now? I remember hearing about problems with one of them—they had to move or something?"

"Well, the details on that are still classified, I don't know what happened, but I do know they had to relocate to a different site. They are using a combination of domes and caves, much like this colony. But anyway, there are 6 total colonies on Mars right now."

The transport slowed to a stop; they walked out and down a long series of corridors with fewer and fewer people. Sam quickly lost their sense of direction.

"Is there a map, or something? I already feel lost."

"Sure, you can bring up maps on your tablet. Also, notice that at each tunnel intersection is a small display, which will tell you where you are."

"Ah, good, that's useful."

"It is a warren, but it gets easy to find your way around once you get used to it. OK, staff housing is over this way."

They took a right-hand turn and entered into a hallway with a number of halls off of it.

"Your apartment is section 9, apartment 2." They turned at the hallway marked "Section 9," and stopped in front of a door, with a large 2 stenciled on the side of it.

"Your ident card should get you inside. Try it out."

Sam waved their ident card in front of a small, raised square on the inside of the door jamb, and they heard a click, a gentle rush of air, and the door stood a bit ajar.

"You should read the safety procedures. I know that you are used to this, living on the Moon, and in space, but it's good to know where the breathing masks are kept, and suchlike. Things are a little different on Mars."

Sam and Kylee walked into a spacious room, with 3 large view screens showing the Mars landscape, and furnished with what looked like comfortable furniture.

"OK, you're home."

"Home? Where's the apartment you talked about—is it that small room over there?"

Kylee laughed. "I guess you aren't used to living on a planet. *This* is the apartment. That's just the bedroom. Over here is the bathroom, and the kitchen/dining room is through this door."

Sam was taken aback. "You said this was pretty small? This is probably 4 times the size of any space I've ever lived in in my entire life. It's enormous!" I might get lost in it!"

Kylee smiled. "Well, get used to it. I spent some time looking you up after you first contacted me. You might only officially have a high school education, but you seem to have managed to squeeze in graduate-level geology and planetary science based on your three peer-reviewed studies on asteroids. Based on those studies, I have made you an official staff scientist for the new alien asteroid project."

"Well, I mean ..."

"What, Sam, are you going to tell me those aren't yours? You aren't Samantha Julian?"

"No, no, they are mine, that's my real name. I did the studies and wrote the articles, but... I mean no one pays attention to that stuff, do they?"

"Sam, you spent a lot of time pretending you are far dumber than you are, haven't you?"

Sam shrugged. "Being smart never got anyone anywhere either on the moon or in the asteroid belt."

"Well, Sam, Mars is a very different story. You'll be welcome to stay here as long as you'd like. Besides, this alien asteroid of yours is going to take years to decipher."

"Speaking of that—how are we going to study it?"

"The planetary science department of Terra U has three ground-to-orbit shuttles, thankfully. Two of them are pretty old, and not in good repair, and we have to share them all with four of my colleagues... but this study will take precedence."

"Really?"

"Yes, really. There is much more to tell you, but Sam, you look exhausted. We've got plenty of time. The asteroid won't arrive for another couple of days, and we won't learn anything more about it for another 30 hours or so, when it begins its approach to Mars. Give yourself some time off. Sleep, rest, read about the colony and the University, and meet me in the lab at 0900 hours on Wednesday."

Sam was indeed tired. They realized They hadn't slept well in the 10 days or so since they first ran into that asteroid.

"Thanks, Kylee, I do need a rest."

Kylee smiled. "OK, Sam, see you Wednesday morning."

Kylee turned and walked out of the door and closed it behind her. Sam picked up their bag and walked into the bedroom. It was small, but had a double bed, with a little room to walk around it, and a small side table and a small alcove with a dresser and mirror. Sam put their bag on the bed and noticed some drawers below the bed. Opened, they saw a set of sheets, blankets and some towels. They took those out, and made the bed, and walked to the bathroom with the towels. They was surprised by the bathroom. A stand-alone toilet, a sink on its own, and what looked like a luxurious mist shower. They couldn't quite remember the last time they had taken a shower, and they'd never lived with a shower.

After spending time unpacking their stuff, their tiredness overwhelmed them. They turned off the view screen in the bedroom, and had a long slumber.

At 0845 Wednesday morning, Sam walked into Kylee's lab, with their sample jar in one hand, and their data cube holding all of the asteroid data, as well as all of the code customizations for their ship, and their AI, in their pocket. One of the first things Sam was going to do was find a matrix to install their AI in, so they could work with Jane again.

"Good morning, Sam!" Kylee looked happy to see them.

"Good morning." Sam raised the arm with the sample container.

"I've got the samples, and I need to set up a matrix to install my AI—she's got access to all of the data and can help us do the analysis. I've taught her everything she knows about asteroids."

"She?" Kylee raised an eyebrow.

Sam grinned. "Yeah, I know it's weird to name an AI, but mine is named Jane, and I can't help but think she has a personality."

"Sam, I want you to meet Curtis Wallace."

A middle-aged man, with long blond hair and a greying beard, got up and stepped out from behind a desk that had tablets strewn all over it, and three view screens facing it.

"Hi Sam. I can set up any matrix you need. Specs?"

Sam figured they'd use this as a good test for their resources—they aimed about as high as they could imagine they could set up.

"I need a matrix with... oh, CPUs at 10 THz, with 2K cores, 4 PB Memory and 10 EB holographic storage. If you can easily grab a copy of Spacenix 12.2, that would be great. Otherwise, I can get a copy."

"Easy as pie. Are you sure that's all you need? I can get one with 15.5 THz and 4K cores if you want. And no worries, on the 'nix—I've been beta testing Spacenix 12.4 for a while now."

Sam was speechless. The best matrix they'd ever laid their hands on was 1/10 the power of the one they were offering their as if it were nothing. Clearly, they had some things to learn about resources on Mars.

"Sure, whatever you've got. I'm happy with that. Jane will be happy with that."

"Sam, while Curtis is setting up your matrix, can we have a talk in my office?"

"Sure thing."

They walked back into Kylee's office, and they sat down on opposite sides of Kylee's desk.

"There are a couple of things to talk with you about. First, is your claim on the asteroid."

"My claim?"

"There are some things you should know. First, this is now a classified project, level seven. When you first contacted me, I'd sent the data you had to a colleague, and somehow, SolGov got involved, and put a lid on the whole thing. It was a bit strange, the way it was handled. Anyway, I got a message that SolGov wants to buy the claim from you. I believe you spent 5K Yuan on that claim?"

"Yes, the last 5K I had—well, actually, I had to borrow 2K from a friend."

"SolGov is willing to pay you 12K Mars credits for that claim—at today's exchange rate, that's..." Kylee looked down at her tablet.

"That's about 60K Yuan, if you wanted to exchange it back to Yuan."

"Why do they want to do that?"

"I think it's because they want ownership and control. What do you think?"

"Why didn't they just say they'd pay me back, or something? Giving me that much more..."

"Sam, that's hardly any money! I'd expect you to negotiate for more! I think that asteroid should be worth at least 100K Mars credits!"

"100K Mars credits? 500K Yuan? No way! I would have gotten maybe 2/3 of that if I sold a really prime asteroid to an asteroid mining company if I was lucky! They can't expect me to ask for that much!"

Kylee looked puzzled. "OK, you know this business better than I do."

Sam shrugged their shoulders. "60K Yuan seems way more than fair to me—it's downright generous. It means I can pay my friend back, with interest. Let me know how to make the claim transfer, and I'm happy to."

"I'll forward the form to you."

"Thanks."

"Second item is your salary. Your title is Senior Scientist."

Sam raised her eyebrows. "Seriously?"

"Yes, yes. You have the training for it, even if you got it informally."

"OK."

"Terra University has a range for salaries, depending on experience, and the whim of the lead scientist."

Sam could see the grin Kylee was showing. Kylee must enjoy playing with other people's money. And it seemed Kylee liked Sam.

"And SolGov just dumped a crapload of money on this project. We're getting some personnel from Mars colony 6, too!"

"Why personnel?"

"I'm not sure, but I've been told that we'll be completely briefed when they arrive. We're gaining one Lodan Greenfellow, an agronomist of all things, and a Michael Gerald, an anthropologist. Neither makes any sense to me. The one that does make sense is Tai Xien, who is a planetary geologist. He's read your work, by the way.

"That was a tangent, sorry. The standard range for a Senior Scientist here is from ten to twenty K Mars credits per month. I'm thinking with three published studies, and several years of primary research under your belt, you deserve at least 14K per month."

"Kylee, I am very happy to accept that. I just want you to know ..."

"I know, it's more than you could ever have thought you'd ever make in your life. Your life is different, now—get used to it. This is an important find."

Sam did some quick math in their head. In way less than a year, they could save up enough to lease a ship just like the old one. In 3 years, they probably could save up enough to buy a used one outright. If they owned a ship outright... they'd finally be truly free.

"Thanks, Kylee, I don't know what to say."

"Sam, I should be thanking you! Because you called me, I got a huge promotion, new staff for my lab, and a huge new budget to play with. And, if all goes well, I'll be famous. You'll likely be famous, too. And, most importantly, I get to be in on what is probably the biggest discovery in human history."

Sam couldn't help but smile, and nod. Kylee was right. Sam had done her a huge favor, professionally. But the truth was, the asteroid had done all the work, all Sam had done was to be lucky enough to find it.

Kylee said, "So, I think that's all for now. How was the apartment?"

"It was great, thanks. Very spacious, and the bed was very comfortable. Thanks for stocking the kitchen. I did manage to find the local market, but I got lost on the way back!"

"It does take a while to get used to the colony, Sam, don't worry. I got lost every other minute when I first got here."

They left her office, and Kylee showed Sam to a desk, which was a lot like the desk Curtis had. It was L shaped, with a series of three view screens curving around the L. They could see the text messages of the matrix build that Curtis was just completing.

"Sam, the matrix is doing its final configuration. After a reboot, it will be ready for your AI. There's a holographic memory reader right here." Curtis pointed to a small indentation in the top of the desk, where they could see a terminal ending.

"Thanks, Curtis."

"My pleasure."

While the matrix finished building, Sam brought up the current telemetry on the asteroid. It had slowed down, swung by Phobos, and looked to be approaching Mars orbit. They went back to their tablet and looked at the notes they had taken while in the closet prison on the way to Strelix station. There were a few primary questions they thought they needed to answer as soon as possible. First, could they extrapolate where the asteroid had come from based on its direction and speed when Sam encountered it? Second, what was its propulsion method? Third, what was underneath the complex carbon nanotube surface? They decided that the first question to start on was where it came from.

They looked up at the view screen and saw that the matrix had rebooted. They pulled the holographic data cube out of their pocket and plugged it into the reader. They typed in a few commands to get the matrix to copy the data from the memory cube, connect up the audio input and output, and start up the AI.

They saw the telltale symbols of the AI starting flash across the screen. After a minute or two, Jane's dulcet voice sounded out of the speakers on her desk.

"Hello, Sam. This matrix is adequate to my needs."

Sam loved Jane's sense of humor.

"Glad you like it, Jane."

"Adjusting my parameters for this matrix. You should notice a modest improvement in capacity and processing speed. Also adjusting for a stable, planetary existence...

"Done. Sam, care to update my records with events that occurred since I was copied?"

"Jane, find dated journal files on my tablet. Access code is the same."

"Accessing journal files. Thank you, Sam."

Sam noticed Curtis standing a bit behind her, and they turned toward him. "Want to be introduced to Jane?"

Curtis smiled. "Sure."

"Jane."

"Yes, Sam."

"I want to introduce you to Curtis. He'll be working with me. Give him access to all data and computation except those marked private."

"Hi, Curtis. Please speak so I can get a voiceprint."

"Hi Jane, my name is Curtis Wallace, Senior Scientist in the planetary geology department of Terra University on Mars."

"Thank you, Curtis. Voiceprint accepted."

Sam turned back to face the screen. "Jane, put the asteroid telemetry on visual."

"Acknowledged."

One of the screens had a small, white dot labeled with the ID number that had been given to them during the claims process, and a path behind it was displayed. Also next to the dot was speed and direction. As they watched it, they could see the speed slow.

"Jane, at current speed, when will it arrive here?"

"In less than 1 hour."

"Jane set a reminder to warn us when the asteroid changes direction."

"Acknowledged."

"Jane, can you calculate, based on the direction and speed of the asteroid, where it entered the solar system?"

There was a pause. "No, Sam. The asteroid was entering the belt directly from Jupiter, so it either originated there, or used Jupiter as a gravitational well. There is no way to tell from which direction it arrived at Jupiter."

Sam sighed. So much for that idea. The asteroid could be from anywhere. It could have been in this system for a long time or could have recently entered.

They heard some voices coming from the front of the lab and wondered whether or not the visitors from Mars colony 6 had arrived. The voices got louder.

"And back here is Sam Julian, who found the asteroid in the first place. Sam, please meet Lodan, Tai, and Michael."

Sam got up from behind the desk and walked forward to meet the visitors. In front of Kylee was a tall woman with olive skin and short, curly hair. There was also a squat Asian man with very close cropped, dark hair, and a medium-height, light-skinned man with short brown hair and a goatee.

"Hello, it's nice to meet you all."

"OK, Curtis, Sam, let's all meet in conference room 2."

They filed out of the lab and down the hall to a large conference room with actual windows looking out onto the landscape. Sam hadn't gotten the hang of the layout of the station yet—it surprised them to see it.

As they settled into chairs, Lodan, who seemed to be the leader of the group, sat at the head, and Curtis helped her get her tablet to send data to the room's view screen.

Lodan said, "Well, I guess we should start at the beginning. Before I start this briefing, I want to make it clear that everything I am sharing with you today, and until further notice, is classified. No one without at least level 7 SolGov security clearance can know about this. Eventually, all of this will be made public, but not until we get a better handle on it."

Sam's tablet started to flash, and Sam could see that Jane was notifying them of a change in the asteroid. The asteroid had entered Mars orbit, and, strangely, was taking geostationary orbit.

"Sorry to interrupt, I thought you should know something. Jane tells me..."

Lodan looked puzzled. "Jane?"

"Sorry, Jane is the name of my AI. Jane tells me that the asteroid is now in Mars orbit. It has taken up geostationary orbit."

Lodan smiled. "Ah, I get it. So... geostationary? Above what?"

"I don't know. It's not any of the current colonies. Here are the coordinates: 40.33321 Latitude and 12.3351 Longitude."

Sam looked up at Lodan, who had lost several shades of her color. Tai and Michael were busy on their tablets.

Lodan cleared her throat. "Well, that answers one very important question for us. It isn't an interruption of the briefing at all—it's a great place to start it. Those coordinates are the coordinates of the original placement of the 6th colony. Now I get to explain why it moved."

Sam sat and listened to the story of the original placement of the sixth colony. Now, it made perfect sense why Lodan and Michael had been sent. Lodan had been the one to isolate the problem with the crop failures. Michael had been the primary researcher of the artifacts found at the original site of the sixth colony.

Something was bothering Sam. The images that Michael showed them were oddly familiar to her. It was almost as if they'd seen them before, but they knew that was impossible. They wracked their brain—they couldn't think about what they reminded them of or where they could have seen them before. They hoped they'd figure it out at some point—things like that always bothered them.

Lodan said, "So, now you are fully briefed. When SolGov got wind of this asteroid, it seemed likely there was a connection between these two. Clearly, there is."

Kylee spoke next. "Well, we have our work cut out for us. We don't know how long this asteroid is going to be in orbit. The sooner we get up to it, and do whatever close analysis we can, the better."

Lodan nodded. "You have access to an orbital vehicle?"

"We do. I'm reserving it now. We should be able to launch within a day or two."

Kylee turned to Sam, and asked, "Sam, you're the only pilot we've got, now. The others don't have the security clearance. Do you mind?"

Sam smiled. They felt joy welling up inside her. "Mind? I'd be ecstatic!" Sam wondered what kind of craft it was.

"Can you send me the details of the craft model, so Jane can get up to speed on capabilities and control?"

"Sure thing—I'll have that sent to you as soon as I can."

Lodan turned to Sam. "Sam, if you don't mind—our team still needs to catch up on the details of the asteroid."

"Of course." Sam stood, and went to the front of the room, with the view screen.

"As you know, I'm an asteroid hunter. Basically, I look for asteroids that have high levels of heavy metals—the more metals, especially the really heavy ones, the more I get paid. Initial spectroscopy for this asteroid looked like this:" Sam pointed to the screen, remembering vividly when these graphs had appeared on the view screen of her ship. They missed the ship, suddenly.

"As you can see, there was evidence that this was a gem of an asteroid. Enough to keep me fed and watered for many years. But initial sampling of the asteroid gave us this:"

Sam showed the microscopic pictures of the carbon nanotubes in the sample.

"The spectroscopy of the asteroid was characteristic of a M-type asteroid with lots of carbon. They aren't that unusual. What was unusual was that the initial sample had nothing but carbon in it. And on further investigation, the carbon wasn't the normal type found in asteroids, it was full of carbon nanotubes.

"Clearly, the asteroid must have had some exposed areas for it to have spectroscopy like that. I'd say the nanotubes were a protective outer covering of some sort, perhaps, that had degraded over time."

Michael raised his hand. "Sam, what shape was the asteroid?"

"Funny, I never asked Jane that. Jane, any data on asteroid shape?"

"The asteroid is an icosahedron."

Michael said, "Just a reminder. An icosahedron is a platonic solid. Just like the artifacts we found, and just like the nanoparticles that caused the crop failures."

The briefing went on for another couple of hours, and then they decided to break until late in the afternoon. Sam was surprisingly tired—it probably had something to do with getting used to Mars time. They went back to the apartment to get some rest. They went to lie down on the couch and take a short afternoon nap. There had been so much information shared that their brain was about to explode. And there was more to come. Days of it.

As they were drifting to sleep, they found themselves thinking about the moon, and they had a vivid dream of a cave on the moon. When they woke up, they realized with a start why they had thought those symbols were similar—they *had* seen them before—on the moon!

They flew off the couch and found their tablet.

"Jane, please look up an incident on the Moon, at the Grethel-Xue mines, under Mare Insularum. Look for the name 'Mark Stewart'. You might find an article by Tina Fiorici."

They remembered the brouhaha. Mark had found this weird cave that turned out to contain a lot of Yttrium, which, if Sam recalled correctly, was in very high demand at the time. He was adamant that something was very strange, but the company couldn't afford to report this to the authorities—that mining area would have been immediately closed off to investigate. Mark reported it, and then got fired, and eventually arrested. The company accused him of vandalism and fabricating the whole story. He went to jail for years. The company destroyed the cave by mining it.

Tina had just left the company when this happened, to go work for the local Moon newsblog. Sam had convinced her it was a real story, and Mark was getting framed. Tina believed them, but the company squashed any further articles after the first.

"Sam, I found one reference."

"With photos?"

"Yes."

Sam looked at the tablet. There they were, plain as day. These looked a hell of a lot like the ones on Mars!

"Jane, compose the following message, send to Michael, Kylee and Lodan: 'Suggest we add this to the agenda for this evening's meeting. See attached story.' And attach a link to that story."

"Done."

Sam started thinking about Tina. Sam found that they missed Tina sometimes. It just hadn't been their destiny to be together, Sam thought, because Sam loved space, and Tina loved planets, especially Earth. Sam could never understand why Tina wanted to be on Earth, given how much work it would be for her body that had grown up on the moon. The moon had centrifuges that everyone was supposed to use every day, and most people did—otherwise, someone born on the Moon couldn't travel anywhere else, ever. Sam, who grew up on Earth, always thought that the Moon made life a little too easy—so they imagined the reverse would be brutal. Mars seemed a nice medium.

Out of curiosity, they did a search for Tina. What a coincidence! Tina was now Mars bureau chief—for *The Times* of all things! She had really come up far in the world. Without thinking, Sam sent Tina a message, and suggested they meet up sometime soon. Sam smiled. What a pleasant surprise! Sam couldn't help but wonder if she were attached. They were sure that Tina would find it surprising that Sam was planet-bound, at least for the time being.

"Sam, the meeting is starting in twenty minutes."

"Thanks, Jane."

Sam got off the couch, grabbed a snack from the kitchen, left the apartment, and started to walk to the conference room. As they approached it, Sam heard a shout behind them.

"Sam!"

Sam turned around to see Michael running towards them. They stopped just outside of the room, and Michael ran up to stand next to them.

"Sam, that story from the moon is... it's disturbing."

"Well, is it the same..."

"Yes, and more. There are definitely common symbols, and some different ones. But I did some more research, and there is something you should know."

"What?"

"Just a few miles from that spot is a crater that has been off-limits to satellite photography, visitors and exploration since the mid 30's."

"The mid 30's? That doesn't make sense. That's when the first Lunar expeditions to make a colony were launched."

"Yup. Even with my level seven security, I ran into brick walls in getting more information about that crater."

"Are you suggesting...?"

Kylee stuck her head out of the conference room.

"Sam, Michael, please join us."

They walked into the conference room, which was abuzz with activity. Clearly, Sam had dropped something of a bombshell.

"OK, quiet everyone, please!" Kylee's voice rang out with authority across the room. The room became silent.

She then said, "Sam, will you please review what you know about the Moon incident?"

"Sure. When I lived on the Moon, about fifteen years ago, I worked in a mine owned by the Grethel-Xue company. It was a pretty brutal place to work. Anyway, a friend of mine, named Mark, found a cave, and in this cave were those symbols carved into the walls of the cave. They had dug into the cave because that part of the moon had large quantities of Yttrium, which was fetching a very high price. He first reported it to the company, so that they would stop digging, and get some scientists in to look at the cave. They refused, so he reported it to the authorities, but then the company accused him of sabotaging the mine, and he was arrested. Of course, Grethel-Xue had all of the judges in their pocket, so he went to prison for years. The company mined the area and destroyed the cave. There was one news story on the cave, then none after the company squashed the story."

Kylee said, "Thanks, Sam. Michael, you have information?"

"Yes. I compared those symbols in the pictures Sam sent us to the images we have from the cave on Mars. There are 75 symbols over all, 35 symbols in common. Five are found on Mars and not the moon, and 35 found on the Moon and not Mars. They might help us to better understand these symbols, but I'm not sure yet—I haven't had time to really investigate."

"And there is more..." Kylee prompted.

"Yes. In investigating this, I ran into the fact that there is a crater somewhat near this cave that has been off-limits to any surface visitors, explorers, or even in-orbit satellite photography since the 2030's. I did look for some Earth-based telescopic photographs of the area, and I found a few from hobbyists, and there is some strange chatter about unusual formations in that crater. But even level seven SolGov security clearance doesn't get me any information about the crater."

"So, the suggestion is that there is something related to the aliens that SolGov already knows, but is hiding?"

"That's the suggestion, yes. It seems strange that there is that kind of security that has been maintained since the 30's. SolGov is only fifty years old. It must have been the old Chinese Government that kept the secrets on that crater, since they were the first to send missions to the Moon for purposes of colonization."

Kylee looked pensive. "Given that you weren't able to find any information with level seven security, I don't think we should include our knowledge of this incident, and any analysis of the symbols in the official report—I'm afraid of what might happen."

Tai spoke for the first time in a while. "I agree. A secret kept this long, and at that high a level is one that people at the top don't want exposed—if they know we know..."

Sam nodded. "We could be in some trouble."

Kylee stood. "OK, folks, I think we have a lot to chew on. I'm cutting this meeting short, so we have some time to rest. We'll have a big planning day ahead of us tomorrow, and the day after, we'll be in orbit."

The meeting broke up, and Sam could hardly keep their eyes open anymore, so they went back to the apartment, took off their clothes, and went immediately to sleep.

Two days later, the night before they were to launch, Sam was still awake long after they should have fallen asleep. They had spent the last 5 hours getting up to speed on the ship, launching policies and procedures, and the position of the asteroid. They would be leaving in just 8 hours, and they were tossing and turning, trying to get a little sleep. They decided it was hopeless, and got up, turned on the light and the view screen, and went back to looking over the mission briefing.

It should be fairly straightforward. Terra University's orbital craft were berthed at the spaceport. They'd gotten permission from the Terra U authorities, as well as clearance from Mars Central Command for the flight. They would approach the alien asteroid, take as many pictures of the exterior as possible, try and find some exposed regions.

It was a large object. Not huge by asteroid standards—something that size would probably be crushed by one of the very large asteroid crushers, rather than actually mined, like much larger asteroids. There wasn't going to be any way to get it to the surface or get it anywhere that they could study it better, given their lack of space resources.

Sam wondered what was inside. Was it machinery? They couldn't imagine life forms, but they guessed it was possible. After reading for a while, they finally felt sleepy, so they went back to their bed, turned off the lights, and slept a dreamless sleep.

"We've got launch clearance. We can go when we're ready."

"Everyone ready?" Sam heard assents all around.

"Jane, please take off."

"10 seconds to take-off, Sam. Nine, eight..." Sam braced herself. This was a small ship. It could be a rough ride, but Mars take-offs were always milder than Earth ones.

Sam never liked take-offs, even though they loved being in space. Most of their time in space was in small ships that stayed in space and got a bit of gravity feel from the acceleration toward whatever object they were pursuing at the time. This would be a very different type of trip. A take-off, weightlessness for a few days while they studied the alien ship, then the flight home.

"Alien asteroid in view."

"Thanks, Jane, keep a steady approach, then establish a tight orbit around the object."

"Acknowledged."

They approached the asteroid or ship, or whatever it was, and Sam could see it was still—not spinning at all. They started a slow orbit, staying about 500 meters away from the object. They intended to circle it for at least a day, in a sort of lazy spiral, so they could capture images of every inch of its surface.

"Orbit established."

"Thank you, Jane. OK, folks, orbit is established. Time to go to work. I'll be monitoring our systems and position, and alert you if anything strange happens."

There was the strange busy ballet of five of them going about their business weightless in a small, confined space. After a few hours, it was time to take a break, get some food, and debrief.

Kylee asked, "Curtis, how is the imaging going?"

"We're almost done. I'd say in about two more hours, we'll have very detailed high-resolution pictures of every inch of that thing. In addition, the spectroscopic analysis is going well."

"Great to hear. Lodan, you've been doing some sampling?"

"Yes, the robotic probes have been happily munching on nanotubes, as well as finding some stray metallic pieces. We've got a good bit of stuff to work with."

"Michael?"

"I've been looking at the images Curtis has been generating, and isolating regions we should look more closely at, if possible. There look to be some symbols written on a few sides, symbols that look a lot like the ones we saw on Mars and the Moon."

"And Sam, how goes it?"

"Everything is fine. Ship is in stable orbit around Mars, and in stable orbit around the asteroid. Jane has been monitoring transmissions from the asteroid. Also, we have successfully attached the beacon to the asteroid, so we'll be able to track it wherever it goes."

Kylee said, "OK, great work, everyone. We'll have a treasure trove of data."

They kept working for another few hours, then stopped for dinner. They were sitting around the cramped cabin eating their meals from tubes.

Kylee said, "My dad would tell me stories about eating at zero-g. He would spend many days at zero-g, going from one Saturn moon to another."

Lodan said under her breath, "I hate zero-g."

Michael said, "Lodan, why? I'm kind of coming to like it."

Sam saw Lodan give Michael a dirty look. He just smiled at her in response. Sam wondered whether the two of them had something going on.

Michael said, "My dad was also a spacer. He was one of the first employees of Kuiper Exploratory."

Kylee said, "Really? I bet our fathers know each other! My dad didn't work for Kuiper, but he did come in contact with Kuiper staff a lot, since they owned claims to most of the Saturn moons."

"It's possible my dad knew yours. My dad died a while ago. I still miss him sometimes."

"My dad is retired. He lives in Hawaii, now, but he left space a long time ago."

After dinner, they wandered not very far from each other into their respective bunks to sleep. Sam had given Jane permission to wake them if the status of their shuttle or the asteroid changed. They settled into their bunk, not quite sure that they'd get any sleep. They must have fallen asleep, because Jane's voice woke their up.

"Sam, please wake up." Sam came alert instantly and heard the sounds of others stirring.

"Status, Jane?"

"Sam, transmissions from the asteroid to the surface have ceased. In addition, the attitude of the asteroid has changed."

"Changed how?"

"It has rotated 180 degrees on one axis, and 90 degrees on another axis."

"Analysis?"

"I predict it is about to leave orbit."

Sam pulled themselves out of the restrictive hammock, trying their best to avoid pushing or hitting anyone else on their way out. They swam to the pilot's seat, strapped in, and looked at the telemetry data. The asteroid hadn't left quite yet.

"What's going on?" Kylee was behind her, looking over her shoulder.

"Jane thinks that the asteroid is leaving. It stopped transmitting and changed attitude."

"Asteroid velocity and position have changed."

"Any evidence of a propulsion system?"

"Yes, showing exhaust profile now."

The object showed up on the screen with a plume emerging from one direction. Jane was doing spectral analysis on the plume.

"Adjusting our position to avoid collision."

"Everyone sit down or stay in your hammock! We're going to be moving."

Sam heard the thrusters fire and felt the sharp sideways acceleration that lasted for a few moments. They watched as the asteroid got further and further away from them and then was lost from sight.

Sam, December 2105

Sam stood at the bar, fidgeting nervously with their beer. It had been so long since they'd seen Tina—they were almost worried that they wouldn't recognize them. They'd been early, as per usual, and had been waiting a while. At this moment, Tina was less than five minutes late—basically still on time.

They decided to stop obsessively looking at everyone, and turned toward the bar, and took a few sips of their beer. They felt a gentle touch on their arm, and they turned to see Tina's face, with a broad smile across it. She'd grown out her hair: it was currently in cornrows. Her eyes were as deep as Sam remembered them to be. Tina was dressed in her conservative usual—business suit with skirt, formal shoes, and neatly tailored shirt. Sam, in their spacer's standard shore-leave clothing of comfortable pants and pullover sweater over a t-shirt felt a bit shabby next to her.

"Never thought I'd see you here, sailor."

Ever since Sam left to work for Strelix in the asteroid belt, Tina liked to call Sam 'sailor'. These days, if one was not on Earth, it was the term given to people like Sam who spent most of their time in space, going from one place to another.

"Hi Tina." Sam, for some reason, immediately felt shy.

Tina said, "Sam, give me a hug—I've missed you."

Sam found themself enfolded in Tina's warm embrace, and they lingered in it for a while. After a bit, they separated, and Tina held Sam at arm's length, and looked them over.

"You look good—the last few years seem to have been kind to you."

"Well, I'm not sure I'd say that Tina. But I'm doing pretty well now. What are you drinking?"

Tina smiled crookedly. "The usual."

Sam motioned to the bartender. "Martini, sweet, for the lady here. Straight up."

"You remembered."

"Was that a test?"

"I guess a little bit. You passed with flying colors. And, truth be told, my current drink is whiskey, but I still do like a Martini now and again. So, Sam, why are you here, and not out looking for the right asteroid?"

Sam told Tina the parts of the story they could tell her. They warned her about the security clearance, and that there were things they couldn't say. But Sam knew that Tina was smart and would begin to put things together. They just wanted to make sure that Tina didn't quote her as a source.

Tina said, "Well, well. That is quite the story—or at least the parts you can tell me. I'm betting the whole story is even bigger."

Sam nodded. "It will be the biggest story of our time, Tina. I'm glad that I get to be a little part of it."

Tina looked sideways at Sam. "I think you'll be more than just a little part of it, my dear."

Sam said, "So what have you been up to on Mars?"

"Well, it's been interesting. I've been here now for about 6 months, and the distance between what *The Times* thinks I should cover and what I think I should cover gets further and further apart, the longer I'm here. Sam, Mars is on the cusp of something really big, and I want to cover it, but I know that *The Times* will want me to downplay what's happening. I covered the Colony 6 move and got slammed for questioning SolGov."

"Slammed? Tina, they should be questioned! They are hiding a lot." As Tina raised an eyebrow and smiled, Sam realized they'd better shut up.

Sam said, "Well, anyway, I'm sorry it's like that, and I'd better keep my mouth closed, or I'll get arrested for leaking secrets. But it's true—based on what I've heard, the independence movement is mainstream, and it wouldn't take much to move Mars out of SolGov. Not that SolGov would allow it."

Tina said, "What could they do? Invade? Not really practical."

"True. Earth and SolGov would have to just suck it up, I guess."

Tina reached forward and took Sam's hand in hers. "OK, so how about another topic entirely. I'm betting that you're still single?"

Sam smiled and laughed. "Yes, I've been single... for a while now. You?"

Tina let out a breath. "Single. My career has gotten in the way. Too much travel, and too much work to simply move around on Earth—I haven't had time or energy for a love life."

"Well, you know me—I'm always in space."

Tina whispered in Sam's ear, "But you and I are here, now. Shall we go to your place or mine?" Sam smiled and thought it would be nice to see what quarters the *Times* Mars Bureau chief had—must be even bigger than theirs.

Chapter 4:
A New Life

Gareth and Sharron. May 2106

Gareth Holbright walked in a strange, light gait, but bent down somewhat, since he was too tall for the tube leading to the colony entrance. He was feeling a combination of dread and excitement. Even though he knew he'd heard God's call to come here, he worried that he'd made the decision to move to this new Mars colony on a whim. But it would have been a whim born of deep grief. He looked back and saw his wife following several feet behind him. Her head was bowed down, as if she was studying the floor of the tube. But he knew she was feeling the same feelings as he was.

They finally entered the colony through a circular door which led to one of the large domes. Later, he would note how large and airy the space seemed, but right now, he felt claustrophobic. He thought that perhaps this wasn't such a good idea after all.

His wife asked, "Gareth, where are we supposed to go?"

"We need to follow that fellow up ahead, apparently."

He watched his wife look up and around at the dome and wondered what she was thinking. Perhaps she was doubting the wisdom of his decision to come here. She always was a good wife, following in his footsteps, allowing him to lead. He realized he was far from the perfect husband.

They followed the leader and were in the front part of the small crowd of new settlers that had traveled with them from Earth. It was the second wave of colonists for this colony, the last wave in a while, probably. There were quite a variety of people, including clergy, like Gareth, here to minister to the people of the colony.

This colony had a rough start, he'd heard. A year ago, it had to be moved, although no one was saying anything about why that was. He wondered whether folks here had any knowledge of that had they weren't sharing with folks on Earth.

A tall dark-skinned man with gray hair and a beard appeared from one of the far entrances to this dome. A woman with long, blond hair accompanied him.

"Hello everyone. I'm Commander Kelly, leader of this colony. I want to welcome to Mars Colony 6! I'd like to introduce you to my logistics officer, Olga. She'll be helping you with everything you need. There is a lot to get used to, but you'll have plenty of time for that. For now, I want to get you all settled in your somewhat temporary housing areas right now, then we'll reconvene for a meal, and then we'll get you connected to the proper teams."

Gareth knew that the colony was still undergoing a lot of growth and change, but he didn't like the sound of "somewhat temporary."

The group followed the two of them down some corridors that lead to the cave system. If Gareth had felt closed in during his time in the dome, he felt even more so now. The caves were well-lit, which helped, but as a tall man, he felt a need to watch his head.

Olga stopped them in the hallway. "OK, those with last names starting with A through F, go down this hall, and you'll find rooms with bunks. Couples and families get their own rooms, singles need to share. If you need extra mattresses, let me know." A group of people went into that hallway. He knew his group was next.

They found their room. A small affair, with two single beds, a large desk, and some assorted other furniture. No closet, and no bathroom. He saw his wife leave the room—he imagined she was in search for the bathroom. She came back fairly quickly.

"The bathroom is two doors down on the other side of the hall. It's pretty big, but it's not ..."

"What?"

"It's not private, Gareth. And it must be co-ed.

"Isn't there a door?"

"Yes, there is a door. I guess that will have to do."

They had dropped off their things, washed up a little bit, and spent some time in prayer. Now they were sitting in the dining hall, in one corner, among other new arrivals. Gareth had made his acquaintance with most of the people in this group and was sitting among some he had gathered to pray and read the Bible on the ship. The rest of the hall was busy and chaotic, with all sorts of people coming and going. It was toward the end of the lunchtime eating session, and it had slowly begun to quiet down.

He heard a series of thumps to his right and saw Olga banging one of the plastic mugs against a table. Next to her were several people he'd never seen before.

"May I please have your attention! Thank you. You've had your safety and emergency procedures orientation on the ship. Please make sure to review that information, now that you're here. It's time to introduce you to your team leaders and get you into place. First, the agronomy team."

A tall young woman with short curly hair and olive skin raised her arm. "Hi, I'm Lodan Greenfellow, leader of the agronomy team, and this is my associate, Peter. Those of you in the agronomy team, please come with us. We'll be getting you assignments and will put you to work immediately. We have a lot to do."

A large group of people, some of whom were at his table, got up, and went with the pair. After that, other teams, from engineering, logistics, and construction went on their way with their respective team leaders. Gareth looked at the remaining people sitting with them; he knew them all. The imam from Turkey and his wife and two children, the rabbi and his husband, the priest from the Vatican, the Unitarian minister and her wife and their son, the Buddhist monk from Thailand in his robes, the Mormon elder and his three wives and numerous children, and Gareth and Sharron. They were the clergy and families.

"Well, we don't have any permanent space for religious services yet, or for you to see your parishioners. We don't expect to have that sort of space for another six months at the earliest. But we have set aside two spaces for you to all share, and I will leave it up to you to figure out how to do that. I'm sure you can come to an amicable arrangement." She grinned. Gareth thought she grinned the ironic grin of an atheist who thought that they would be spending their time squabbling or maybe even killing each other over the space.

"Come this way."

They got up and followed her back into the cave system, and eventually came to a door. She opened it, and inside was one large room, and off of that room was a much smaller room. There was no furniture of any sort inside.

"Let me know whatever you need in the way of furniture—chairs, tables, desks, couches, etc. We can find them for you. I wish you all good luck."

With that, she turned around, and left.

Gareth took the initiative to talk to his fellow clergy.

"Hello, everyone. I know that we're just getting used to what it means to be of service here. Why don't we just take a brief look around, then send each other our proposals for how to split up the time. I'm sure that Sundays and Fridays will need a bit of negotiation among us, but I'm sure we can figure it out."

There was general agreement, and after a few minutes, they all filed out of the room and back to their respective quarters. When he and Sharron arrived, Gareth started to think about how to arrange times for worship for his congregation. Before he knew it, he was ready to fall asleep, and they found that their two single beds conveniently fit together quite well. They spent a little bit of time rearranging their quarters, and talking quietly, and the minute Gareth's head hit the pillow, he was asleep.

He saw his son, reaching out to him. "Help me dada, help me!" He couldn't reach him. Couldn't help him. He woke up sobbing. It had been like this almost every day, for months. The trip to Mars hadn't made a difference. He thought that maybe coming here and starting a new life away from Harrisburg would make a difference. Make his life better. Make him feel less sad, less full of grief.

He looked over at his wife, who was still asleep. It had been a horrible year. In April, completely inexplicably, their 5-year-old son had gotten ill, and died. None of the doctors could figure out what it was, although Gareth knew that there were a large number of other children who had died that month.

He had spent a fun day with his son, in a boat on the Susquehanna River. The river was fairly clean these days, given that most of the industry upstream of where they were had been shuttered since the global economic crisis of the twenty-teens. It was an exceptionally warm day in April, and the carp fishing season had just started.

He and his son were in the boat, fishing lines in place, just waiting for a bite, when he saw his son put his hand in the water and bring it up into his mouth. At the time, he hadn't thought much of it. He didn't think there was anything dangerous in the water. But he found out there must have been, although no one knew what it was, or was talking about it.

The next morning, his son was writhing in bed, and screaming in pain. They rushed him to the hospital, but the doctors had no idea what was wrong. His son's organs shut down, one by one, and by mid-afternoon, he was dead.

Joshua was their joy, and now he was gone. It had been a very difficult pregnancy for his wife. She had had 3 miscarriages before, and it wasn't even clear that she would make it through this pregnancy. They had been trying to have children for over 10 years. In the end, his wife had to have a hysterectomy just after Joshua was born. There would be no more children.

Even though Gareth knew that it wasn't his fault, he felt responsible. Felt responsible as the man of the house and the head of the family. Sometimes he even felt judged by God, but he tried to put those thoughts aside. It was just one of a string of failures that Gareth had experienced in his life. Instead of following in his father's footsteps in leading the mega-church his grandfather started in Pittsburg, he ended up pastoring a small church in Harrisburg. He was the eldest, and like his father, he expected to lead the Calvary Chapel. But instead, his brother was.

His father used to call them "Cain and Abel," and Gareth always ended up being Abel, sacrificed for his brother's ambitions. He knew his brother had been scheming for years, but he had no idea he'd managed to garner enough friends on the board to make sure that when the time came, Gareth would not be chosen to lead the congregation. Gareth had spent so many years preparing for it, and it had been heartbreaking.

The church he started in Harrisburg never really got off the ground. When he left for Mars, there were only 20 people in the congregation.

He was sorry to leave them, but he knew they God would lead them to a new church.

He could see the lights in the room begin their slow ascent to the simulacrum of daylight. He got up, grabbed his toiletries, and went to take a shower. He got dressed quietly, not wanting to disturb his wife's sleep. He sat for a few minutes in prayer, and then went out to find breakfast.

Gareth walked into the dining hall, which was already beginning to get crowded with people eating breakfast. He stood in line, and then took his tray, which today had oatmeal, raisins and some coffee, with some dried apples and peaches on the side, and looked around for a place to sit. He liked to meet new people, and talk with them, and get to know whether they would be open to hearing the Gospel. As he looked around, he saw the woman Lodan, the head of the agronomy team, sitting alone, and thought it was time to make her acquaintance.

"Mind if I join you?"

She pointed to the chair across from her. "No, not at all, please do."

"We haven't met. I'm Gareth Holbright."

"Ah, I've heard about you. The Southern Baptist preacher."

He wondered what she'd heard.

"Indeed. Does that make you uncomfortable?"

Lodan looked right at him, with a gentle smile on her face. "No, not at all. As long as you're willing to respect that I'm agnostic, I'm happy to respect who you are."

Gareth could tell that Lodan was someone he could get along with. Unlike many of his Southern Baptist colleagues, he actively enjoyed talking with people who thought differently than he did.

Gareth nodded. "I rather like respect, myself." He smiled.

"So, what brings you to Mars, Gareth? I've heard a bit about what has brought some of the other clergy here—a desire for new experiences, a change of pace. What about you?"

Gareth could feel the heavy curtain of his sadness fall over him. "Well..." He looked up, and he could see a sympathetic look on Lodan's face.

"Well, our son died last year, and it's been extremely hard for both of us. I felt God was showing us an opportunity for a change, a new lease on life."

"I can understand that, for sure. Do you mind if I ask how your son died?"

"No, I don't mind. It was a complete mystery. One day we were fishing in the river, the next day he was dead."

He looked up at Lodan and saw the most interesting look on her face. It was unreadable, but he bet that was because he didn't know her yet.

She said quietly, "Where are you from?"

"Harrisburg, PA. My son and I were fishing in the Susquehanna River."

Even though he didn't know Lodan, the look on her face became completely transparent. She knew exactly why his son died, and she knew she couldn't tell him, and it was ripping her apart.

Why would she know why his son died? It didn't make any sense!

Gareth said, "Can we change the subject?" The relief in her face was evident, and he could see her let her breath out.

"Sure, Gareth."

"How long have you been up here, and why did you come?" He thought maybe learning about her would help him unravel this mystery.

"Well, I've been up here for just over a year now. I've always wanted to come to Mars. Part of it is getting to try new things and the like. I spent 3 years in Massachusetts, starting to experiment with new kinds of hardy crops, and it made sense that I could use some of that expertise here on Mars."

"How does your family feel about having you so far away?"

Gareth could see sadness move across Lodan's face. "I don't have any family. My parents gave me up when I was an infant. I spent my childhood in the CPS camps."

"That's amazing you ended up here. You must have accomplished a lot in your life to make it up here."

Lodan nodded. "I did, but I am still surprised in being chosen for this program. I sometimes have imposter syndrome."

They laughed.

"Well, Gareth, it was nice talking with you, but I need to get back to work."

"I hope to get to talk with you again sometime."

Lodan nodded, but only a little. Gareth suspected she would be avoiding him in the future.

After finishing his breakfast, he went back to his quarters to talk with his wife. She had just come back from the shower and was getting dressed. He told her about the conversation with Lodan.

She said, "Gareth, it doesn't make sense that she would know about our son."

"I know, Sharron, it doesn't make any sense at all. But I'm totally sure of it. She knows!"

"Gareth, I know you are good at reading people's faces and emotions, but it doesn't make any sense. Why would she know anything about the death of our son in Harrisburg, when she was here on Mars?"

"I'm just sure of it. Let's review what we know."

"OK, Gareth, I'll humor you. First, we do know that more than 30 children in Harrisburg died that week."

"Yes, we know that."

"And we know that possibly hundreds of children died in the Susquehanna and Chesapeake watershed areas. And we also know that spring, there were massive crop failures in the area. We always thought they were connected, but no one would talk with us."

"Right. Every time we talked with people we were stonewalled, and every journalist or scientist we got interested in the story dropped it."

"So, something big must have been happening. Something secret. Maybe it had to do with the space program?"

"But what?"

"I don't know, Gareth. What was happening here a year ago?"

"They were moving the colony."

"That's right—the colony had to move. How could those two things be connected?"

"I don't know—but Sharron, that's the key. If we find out why the colony had to move, we'll know why our son died. I'm sure of it."

They talked for a bit more, and then she went to her agronomy class—she was learning how to grow food on Mars. He sat at his desk and drafted his proposal for worship. Patricia suggested that Gareth and she work together on compiling the schedule, and he agreed to meet her later in the afternoon. He spent the next few hours answering messages from home, and working on his first sermon for Sunday, a few days hence.

Later, Gareth and Patricia were meeting in the worship space, which now had about thirty folding chairs and a couple of tables. It was a start.

Gareth said, "I'm happy to have my service at 1:00pm on Sunday, so that Father De Luca can have mass at 11:00. The Elder is willing to have services at 7:00am, amazingly. Patricia, are you OK with having your service at 9:00?"

"Yes, Gareth, that's fine."

"I'm going to have worship also on Wednesday evening, and a prayer service Sunday night. Rabbi Weiss and Imam Sahin are all settled for Friday. Sahin will have prayers at 2:00pm, and Rabbi Cohen will have Shabbat services at whatever passes for just after sunset."

Patricia said, "He's also reserved every other Saturday for services as well. And Ajan Karuna has reserved the room on the other Saturdays, and Thursday evenings for meditation practice. I got a request from several people for space for varied Anonymous meetings, and it looks like Mondays and Tuesday evenings are free for those, as well as during most weekdays. I think Father De Luca was thinking of having mid-day Mass a few days a week."

"Looks like we're all set. I think our schedule for dividing up the usage of the small room for pastoral care visits is set as well. I'm sure Olga is surprised at how well we're all getting along."

They both laughed.

"Patricia, do you mind if I ask you an unrelated question?"

"Sure Gareth, go ahead."

"Have you heard anything about why the colony had to move to this location?"

"Only rumors, nothing from anyone who was actually here. They said there was something toxic in the soil."

"Toxic soil? Why would that be secret?"

"It wasn't quite secret. There was a news story about it. But it the underlying cause was never really determined. You know how governments are—anything that might be even a little bit damaging…"

Gareth knew there was a different answer. He knew it was way more than that. But he had one more clue than he'd had before. Toxic soil.

After they finished meeting, Gareth went home, and looked up on his tablet all of the news stories about the move of the colony that he could find. One of them was of particular interest. It had been published by *The New York Times*, but the author seemed to be on Mars, one Tina Fiorici. Gareth thought that she had asked some insightful questions, and he felt that perhaps she might have some more information than was printed in the article. He sent her an email and suggested that perhaps they could get together. Gareth could take a shuttle to Colony One and talk with her.

John, June 2106

John was weightless, in one of the tiny one-person repair ships that were common here. He was doing a run around the skeleton of their new ship, the *Corinth*. Calling it a skeleton hardly did it justice—a lot of the initial systems were in place. The huge new ion engine looked quite impressive. It was a monster of a ship—largest he'd seen, and largest interplanetary ship yet built by SolGov. He didn't even want to think about how many billions and billions of Yuan were being spent on building this ship at such an accelerated pace.

They'd tracked the alien probe, and it was traveling at high speed out of the system. There were military analysts determining all sorts of possible scenarios. The fact that the probe had not gone to the Moon suggested to them that the aliens likely did not know that there had been a colony there. But they all knew there was no way to know that for sure. Some of the scenarios suggested that they could have first contact with the aliens within the next year.

They supposedly would be ready to launch by the end of the year, but John thought that was a bit unrealistic. Captain McAdams had wanted them to make the ship space worthy by October. John thought that was insane, but he kept that to himself. Most of the systems in his bailiwick, including the fighter wings and most on-board defenses were in great shape. The one thing that worried him was the new fusion weapon designed by Dr. Lucia Wynn, a Nobel Laureate in

Physics. Although the mechanics of it were fairly straightforward, it would go into the *Corinth* largely untested, which unsettled John. They had a testing protocol in place that they would be doing after the ship launched, but it mostly consisted of modeling, rather than actual test firing of the weapon. His hope was that they wouldn't need it—all of the other contingencies would be enough.

He headed back to the habitat part of the Shipyard. He had three days of leave coming to him, and he planned to head back to the Moon tomorrow for some R&R. He'd spent a lot of years on the Moon, and had some good friends there, one of whom was getting married, for the second time. It was his old friend Vito, who he'd known since the beginning of his tour on the Moon, more that fifteen years ago.

Vito was the kind of guy that reminded him somewhat of the nicer gang leaders back home, when he was a teenager. Except Vito wasn't violent. But if you ever wanted to get anything really done on the Moon, you needed to talk with Vito. SolGov had managed to put the most closed-minded bureaucrats in power on the moon, so any projects required reams of forms and lots of fees, and many months to get through. Vito, though, knew how to cut to the chase.

He'd met Vito because one of his superior officers had wanted to hire a group of expert lunar geologists to help with a construction project. Since the lunar geologists belonged to some sort of association, they couldn't be hired without going through the Moon bureaucracy, which would have delayed the project by months, or more, and cost a fortune. After beating his head against a number of walls, someone told him about Vito. He went to meet with him and got the lunar geologists to work for them in a week. He returned the favor to Vito by expediting a contract for a Moon company with the military, and thereafter they were fast friends.

Vito was part of an old Moon family—the grandson of Marcus Fiorici, the patriarch of one of the first, and now grandest Moon families. John remembered going to Christmas dinner once with the family. There were siblings, cousins, all sorts of people there. It was a huge party, and for once, John hadn't felt out of sorts, or lonely. It was as if they accepted him into their family. John even had fantasies about Vito's youngest sister, Tina. They got along well, at first, and so John thought that it might be fun to ask her on a date. He came to find out that she was already involved. So much for that idea.

John could see the landing bay for the one-person ships looming ahead of him. He paid attention for a while navigating the ship into its berth. It was time for shore leave.

Tina, July 2106

Tina cooled her heels in the outer office of the Mars Governor. It had taken a gargantuan effort to get this appointment. In general, she'd had a tough time getting any face time with Mars government officials, simply because she was from the Earth-centric *Times* organization. She'd been trying hard to make friends in the Mars independence movement, but the ways her editors kept changing her articles didn't help her one bit.

She'd had a very fruitful meeting with the head of the Mars Independence Party, who would talk with anyone. Apparently, she had made a good impression on him, despite the hatchet job that the *Times* had done on her story. Somehow, he could see through that, and his positive opinion of her was opening doors. And this was the biggest yet.

"Ms. Fiorici, Governor Diallo will see you now."

She nodded her head to the assistant, who was waving her in. "Thank you."

She went into his office and was a little surprised by what she saw. It was spartan and utilitarian, with few personal items on the walls or on the desk. There were maps of each of the colonies on one long wall of the office, and some view screens and a keyboard. She took a mental note that he used a keyboard. He wasn't old, and although some, like scientists and programmers still used keyboards, most administrative types used their AIs as their primary interface.

The Governor himself looked younger than middle-aged, but somehow well-worn. He looked more like a technocrat than a politician—wearing the informal clothing of someone who spent more time working than trying to impress people. She knew from doing research on him that he was born here, in the first colony—one of the first people born on Mars. His parents were immigrants from Senegal.

"Welcome Ms. Fiorici. Please have a seat."

"Thank you, Governor Diallo. And please call me Tina. I really appreciate your willingness to meet with me."

"Kevin seems to think that even though you work for the *Times*, you are fairly sympathetic to the issues we face on Mars."

"Yes, Governor Diallo. Living here for even this last month has taught me a lot about Mars."

"Please, call me Marshall. So, what questions can I answer for you?"

"Thank you, Marshall. First, I know that you are unofficially connected to the Mars Independence Party…"

"Well, I wouldn't quite say that…"

Tina stopped and waited for a moment. She thought he would keep going, and he did.

"Look Tina, let me be frank, with you, off the record?"

"Of course, Marshall."

"If any of the top tier of the Mars Government were in any way, either officially, or, well 'unofficially' known to be connected to the MIP, we would be forced out of office. It's happened before, and we've learned our lessons."

"Happened before?" Tina was puzzled. Members of the Mars government were elected by the Mars populace.

"Check up on what happened to Governor Lewis." She filed that away and decided to change tacks.

"OK, Marshall, back on the record. What would you say is the biggest challenge for you in governing Mars?"

He laughed, hard. She didn't know what the joke was, and he could tell.

"I'm sorry, that question just struck me funny at the moment. Our biggest challenge, frankly, is managing expectations. Expectations from Earth, and expectations of those new to Mars."

"Marshall, I have been nothing but impressed by what you all have accomplished here."

"Thank you. I'm sure that won't make it into print."

She laughed. "Yeah, you're probably right. But it's true, nonetheless. What kinds of expectations do you need to manage from Earth?"

"They seem to think that even though some Marsies have been here for all of their lives, that they still have allegiance to Earth. The truth of the matter is that most people really don't. A recent poll, you might have seen it, said that more than 89% of people here had no intention of going back to Earth."

Tina nodded. "I'd heard about that poll, and the consternation of those on Earth. The funny thing is that Earth couldn't handle those people anyway—they are trying to get as many people off of Earth as possible, and Mars is the most likely place for them."

"Exactly. You see the challenge? They want us to take all of these people, and yet have them still somehow remain loyal to Earth and SolGov. Basically, Earth is our biggest challenge. We've done well here. All of the colonies except the newest one are self-sustaining in terms of energy, food, water and air. Mars has or makes everything our colonies need to survive and thrive. We have the most advanced technology for solar energy, and air and water recycling—we've even been exporting to the Moon! We are economically sustainable, since we have not fallen into Earth's mistakes of expectations of unlimited growth. We have as close as you can get to 100% employment, and we are beginning the terraforming projects in earnest."

"So, you don't see any challenges on Mars for the foreseeable future?"

"I wouldn't say that. We need to build at least five new colonies in the next ten years to prevent overcrowding of our current colonies. SolGov has told us point blank that Colony 6 is the last one they are paying for, so we've been having conversations with varied corps to figure out who is going to help us build these colonies. We have the manufacturing capabilities and machinery, but not the capital to be able to pay the folks with the expertise to build the colonies. And Earth wants to send more families without a lot of expertise—and it takes time, and money to train people to get them up to speed so that they can help build colonies."

"You'd think SolGov would pay, given that they want to bring so many more people here."

"You'd think... but they blame the problem with Colony 6 on us. 'Poor site choice', they say. It cost them almost twice as much as budgeted to build the colony because of the move."

The conversation continued for more than two hours, and Tina realized at the end that there wasn't much she was going to be able to write about. She decided to tell Marshall just that as she was getting ready to leave.

"Marshall, I want to thank you so much for this time. I've learned a lot, and, frankly, I can't write anything."

He smiled. "I'm beginning to see your predicament."

"Yes. Honestly, I'm in a pickle. The *Times* hired me to cover Mars, but they really don't want me to cover Mars. They want me to make SolGov look good. And that's getting hard to do."

He nodded, soberly, and said, "Well, I have heard the *Mars Monitor* is looking for good talent."

She laughed, then shook her head. "Thanks, but I'm pretty set on figuring out how to stay at the *Times*. Anyway, thank you."

"You are welcome, and I hope to see you sometime again." He seemed to be saying that genuinely.

She left his office, and went back to her apartment, thinking hard about what she could write. She decided to write a background piece on him—his family, how he got into the position he did. The article wouldn't say much at all about their conversation.

Gareth, August 2106

Gareth sat looking out of the window of the Mars shuttle to Colony 1. Colony 1 was on the other side of Mars from Colony 6, and they were further apart than any of the other colonies were to each other. For long stretches of time, he could just see the bare ruddy Martian landscape, but there were occasions where he would see some isolated domes. They flew over Colony 3 and Colony 2 in order to reach Colony 1, and it was interesting to notice how they were different. Colony 2 did not have caves at all—it was all domes. It looked to Gareth like this complex network—he couldn't imagine not getting lost in it. Colony 3, however, was largely underground, on the side of a large plateau. If the pilot hadn't gotten on the comm to let everyone know they were passing over, he probably would have missed it. They flew over the plateau, which had nothing on it to speak of, but as they passed it, they could see the large number of windows looking over the plain.

He was on his way to talk with Tina Fiorici. She gave him all sorts of warnings—she didn't know much, etc. But he told her his story, and he insisted, so she relented and agreed to meet. They were meeting at a cafe in the central part of Colony 1 in a few hours. He also had a long shopping list, mostly from Sharron, but there were a few things he wanted for himself. Even though he had lost the leadership of the church to his brother, he still did get his share of his father's inheritance, which was significant—he and Sharron had no money worries.

Gareth had begun to feel like he was fitting into the Mars colony. He had a steady congregation with some people who were emerging as friends. Gareth thought that God was showing His grace to him in many ways. He was glad he listened to God's call for him to come here. And he knew that many of his congregation had been glad to finally have a pastor.

The shuttle finally landed, and Gareth made his way among the crowd out of the terminal area. As he went through the large doorway into the main part of the colony, he was astonished at how large the central dome was. On one side was a transit station that he knew took people to different dome complexes. Toward the other side was the beginning of what he knew was the large commerce mall, full of stores. Tina had told him that the café was not hard to find, and he followed her directions through the entrance to the mall, into a part of the mall with many little avenues. It almost reminded him of a city on Earth. He found the café—it was small and intimate. He was early, so he found a seat toward the back, where he could see everyone come in, and he took out his tablet to read the news.

His AI reminded him that it was time for his meeting, and he looked up, and saw Tina walking into the café. He waved, and she saw him, and headed back to his table. When she arrived, he got up, and shook her hand.

"Thank you so much for agreeing to meet with me, Ms. Fiorici."

"Please, call me Tina."

"OK, Tina." They both sat down.

"So, as I said, Gareth, there really isn't anything I know beyond what I reported. I will say that the Times edited out my questions about SolGov's behavior."

"What questions?"

"Well, classifying any analysis done on the regolith in that area. Making that whole area now off-limits to visitors of any sort. Simply moving the colony as if the problems with the regolith weren't solvable."

"What if they weren't solvable?"

"Well, I guess that's possible—but why wouldn't they release that to the public?"

"Good question."

They talked for a while, and Tina seemed to Gareth to be completely forthcoming, but he felt as if she was holding something back—she knew something that she couldn't tell him. It wasn't quite the same as with Lodan, but he still got that sense. Perhaps asking her more about Lodan would break something open.

"Tina, you know Lodan Greenfellow?"

She looked a bit taken aback, and something about that surprised Gareth. "Yes, I do. I interviewed her for the piece you read—she's how I know what I know about the whole issue."

"She leaves Colony 1 quite often, did you know that?"

"Yes, I see her here on occasion, socially. She's a friend and colleague of my lover, Sam."

"What does he do?

"What does who do?"

"Sam."

Tina laughed. "Sam is a ze, Gareth."

Gareth nodded. On Earth, he lived a life around very few non-binary people—his church was still quite strict about the gender binary, and heterosexuality. So strict that his queer brother Percival left the family at 18.

"So, what does they do?"

"Ze's an asteroid hunter, and pilot."

"Why is they a colleague of Lodan's?"

Gareth saw Tina literally pull herself back.

"I'm sorry, Gareth, I can't say."

"I see." Another brick wall. He felt his deep sadness return and threaten to swallow him.

"Gareth, I can't tell you how I know—but I can say that you will know someday why your son died."

He looked up at her as if she was offering a sort of living water. "I will?"

"Yes, you will, Gareth."

"Thank you for telling me that."

"It's time for me to go. It was nice to meet you. I hope the rest of your trip to Colony 1 is pleasant."

He got up as she did, shook her hand again, and watched her walk out of the café. God was good. He would know why Joshua died. He would just have to be patient. God would provide the answers.

John, August 2016

He stood in front of his logistics team in the large conference room that had been reserved for their use. Over these last few months, they had fallen into a very friendly working group. Many of them would gather for drinks after work hours.

"Lieutenant Mumea, how is the design for the projectile and laser weapons systems going overall?"

"Very well, Commander. One problem is that I'm trying to figure out a way to get the best balance of weapon types and strengths. It would be a waste of our space if we brought, say 50 weapons of all conceivable types and strengths. We would be better off bringing more of only, say 5."

"That makes good sense to me."

"The problem is, we just don't know enough about how the aliens build things."

"Would more detailed spectroscopy analysis from the alien probe help?"

The Lieutenant nodded. "If we can get it—is that data available?"

"I'll find out. Send me specs for what you need, and I'll get it done."

Sam, August 2106

Sam let themself into Tina's apartment. They loved to hang out here. It was about three times as big as theirs and had real windows— something that was a luxury. They could imagine how much Tina was shelling out for it. True, Tina didn't have the best view—but Sam liked the view better than Tina did. They could watch the construction of a new section of Colony 1. They sat on the couch facing the windows, and watched for a little while.

They'd brought her work with them. It was Friday, which was always a good thing, but they had a ton of work to do. They were doing some analyses on the remote spectroscopy from the asteroid that they had gathered while they were orbiting it last year. Some big brass bossman in the SolGov military had requested a re-analysis of some portions of the data, and it fell to Sam as the expert in this area to do them. Some of it was grunt work that Jane was tackling, but some of it required some human discernment. That was their weekend's work.

They'd been planet-bound for more than nine months, and they were getting used to it. Sam got up into orbit about twice a month or so acting as a pilot for research flights. Since they were already on the Terra U. payroll, it was much cheaper to have them fly than to hire pilots, especially for the flights, which had been the standard before they joined. The pilot's union was far from happy, but they were satisfied with the arrangement.

They realized they liked being in big spaces, walking around, and getting to see people more than just on occasion. And spending more time with Tina than they ever spent on the Moon was a real treat. They kept reminding Tina that it was temporary, that they would be out in space again as soon as they could arrange it. But they had to admit that they weren't so sure. Maybe they were getting older, or something. They did find it hard to believe that they wouldn't get themself out in space again sometime soon.

They heard the door whoosh open, and Tina walked in, looking troubled.

"What's up, sweetheart?" They briefly kissed, and Tina flopped on the couch next to Sam.

"I just met with Gareth Holbright of Colony 1."

"Oh, right, I remember you telling me about that."

"It was hard to keep what I know from him—given how his son died."

"Lodan hates not telling him. But if he finds out..."

"I know—you are all in very big trouble."

"Yeah. He'll find out soon enough."

"I know. I told him he would. That seemed to make him feel a lot better."

"I'm glad to hear that. How was your other meeting?"

"Fascinating, and fruitless."

"Meaning?"

"Every Mars official I interview tells me things I can't write about for the *Times*. The Director of Immigration was no different. I keep ending up writing puff pieces about their backgrounds and such."

"Your bosses seem to like that."

"Yeah, but I don't."

Sam put their arm around Tina. They knew that Tina's patience for this was wearing thin. "Love, I think it will get better. Earth will soften its stance, and then you'll be able to report more freely."

"I certainly hope so. So, what's for dinner?"

"Was I supposed to cook?"

"Um, yes, you were, sailor."

"OK, how about I treat you to a dinner at Sir Wallace?"

"Sir Wallace? Wow, aren't you being extravagant! I thought that was against your nature."

Sam smiled. Sir Wallace was one of the best restaurants on Mars, and they spontaneously decided it was time to try it.

Sam got suddenly concerned, "Think we can get reservations tonight?"

They saw a broad smile form on their lover's face. "Being *The Times* bureau chief has to be worth something!"

Tina picked up her tablet and called in a reservation. Sam smiled. Table for two at 2030. Perfect.

Chapter 5:
The Arrival

Lodan, October 2106

Lodan took a big chug of her beer.

"This is pretty good beer. I'm surprised you can get such good beer on Mars."

Kylee laughed. "Lodan, you'd be surprised what you can get on Mars."

Sam said, "Well, from my perspective, you both are spoiled. The beer on the moon tastes like piss, and the beer on Strelix station... well I won't even go into it."

The three of them laughed. The team, led by Kylee, made up of Lodan, Sam, Curtis, Michael and Tai, had met again in October of 2106. After months and months of ongoing reports, they had finally finished the last report they would be sending to SolGov, excluding, of course, what they knew about the Moon. Lodan hoped that eventually, this whole thing—everything from the Mars colony move, the artifacts, the asteroid, the dumping of toxic Mars regolith in Pennsylvania, and the cave and structures on the Moon could finally be made public. It certainly would help Lodan's conscience.

She thought often of Gareth Holbright's son, and it wrenched at her that she couldn't tell him what she knew. Sometimes she fantasized about telling him, but she knew if SolGov found out that she was the breach in security, she'd lose everything she'd worked for her whole life.

Michael, Curtis, Tai and Kylee's husband Mark were off somewhere else in the colony finding fun, which left the three of them sitting in Kylee's apartment drinking beer. Lodan liked spending time with Kylee and Sam. Sam was brilliant, but so easy-going, and shared her history of living in CPS camps, even though they'd lived in different places. Lodan appreciated Kylee's ability to put things together. She and Michael were already working on a possible alien alphabet.

Lodan looked at the container of beer in her hand. It was called "Cassiopeia 2081." It was named after the famous supernova. She was just a kid when it happened, but it had been such a defining event in so many people's lives. Everyone who had been alive had a story of what they were doing when it happened. She held up the container.

"Hey remember this? I was in one of the camps, in Utah. It was unusually cold that night. Someone was shouting outside, saying come look, come look. And we all ran outside in our pajamas, looking at the sky. It was so bright. We figured at first that it was some kind of explosion in space. We couldn't imagine a supernova."

"Yeah, I was in a camp in Florida. It was incredible. I guess we're so used to seeing the cloud in the sky now that we forget how bright it was. It was that nova that made me interested in space. That's why I left to go to the moon, in hopes of getting to travel."

"I was living in New Mexico, my dad had just gotten back from a stint exploring the moons of Saturn, and he got a job at University of New Mexico. He took me outside and showed me the nova in a telescope. It was so amazing to look at. If it weren't for that nova, I'd probably be studying biology or something else, back on Earth."

They talked companionably for a while about their memories of that time, then Lodan and Sam left Kylee's apartment, and walked toward their own apartments.

As they were walking, Lodan said, "So, Sam, how's Tina?" Lodan could see Sam smile.

"She's fine. It's nice to spend time with her, after all these years. And it's hard not to tell her everything. I think she'll kill me when she finds out what I know."

"Naw, she'll understand."

"I certainly hope so. By the way, she got a visit from Gareth Holbright."

"Yeah, he's still looking for answers."

Sam nodded. "So... speaking of love interests, have you and Michael finally hooked up?"

Lodan laughed. "Well, yes, we have finally admitted to each other that we like each other a lot and find each other sexy. But we haven't actually done anything about it yet. We're taking it a little slowly."

"Slowly? You and Michael have had the hots for each other for how long? A year? More?"

"Sam! Give me a break."

"I'm just sayin'. I've seen something between the two of you pretty much since I met you. He seems like quite a catch, and, if I'm not being too forward, so are you."

Lodan smiled and knew it to be a nice compliment. "Thanks, Sam."

Lodan had reached her door, and Sam wished her goodnight. Lodan was tired and was looking forward to going back to Colony 6 tomorrow, to dig her hands in the dirt again.

Tina, November 2106

Tina had spent the last five months or more writing personal interest stories—the kind the *Times* would print without much editing. She had started this trend by writing a story about the Governor, and it had been so well received by her boss, that she kept going in the same vein. Heroic stories of hardship and stress in the new colonies, and stories of lives turned around. The fun part was that she had a hidden agenda to paint Mars leadership and significant characters in a positive light. Somehow, her boss hadn't caught on to this at all. She figured it was because SolGov was trying to encourage as many people as possible to emigrate to the Moon, although from what Tina could tell, there were still far more people who desired to come to Mars than Mars could currently take. She felt her stories were paving the way for people on Earth to appreciate people on Mars when it finally came time for them to ask for independence. Tina thought that was coming very soon.

The week before, Tina had been hanging out with Kevin, of the Mars Independence Party. They had become good friends, and he and Sam really hit it off. The three of them would socialithey often, and sometimes he would bring his wife Leila, who was the Manager of Colony 4. He said that the MIP was getting their "ducks in a row" and would be ready to call for independence in about seven months. They were looking at contingencies, in case Earth wanted to embargo Mars. They were also working out how an independent Mars government would work. It was exciting, and Tina was completely on the side of Mars independence by now. It was a good thing her bosses didn't know.

She was in the shuttle on her way to Colony 3. There had been a horrific triple homicide, the first of its kind on Mars, and the first homicides in a year. It was a clear-cut case. A man broke into a wedding and killed his ex-girlfriend and both of the people she was marrying at the altar. He was killed when the police arrived, and he opened fire at them. Apparently, he was a fundamentalist Christian, and left a long letter to his family about how abominable this new arrangement of hers was.

Plural marriage of all sorts were legalized on Earth over 80 years ago, and they had been legal on Mars since the beginning. There were still those that decried it—like they decried the sorts of relationships she got into. She laughed, grimly. This reminded her of that quip of Sam's when they had talked about a somewhat similar situation on the Moon, when a man had killed his ex-wife and her female lover, ostensibly because he thought they were an abomination. She'd said at the time, "What part of 'Thou Shalt Not Kill' doesn't he understand?"

In general, Mars had very little violent crime. For one thing, it was extremely difficult to obtain a projectile weapon of any sort, since it put everyone in danger if damage happened to one of the domes. Luckily, this wedding had happened inside the cave structures. It was still unclear how the assailant got a gun in the first place. Even the police didn't carry them—they carried laser weapons specially tuned to only affect human tissue, and not dome material.

In addition, somehow, whether it was, as most people suggested, a "sampling bias" because of the people who chose to emigrate to Mars, or some other factor, Marsies just didn't display much in the way of violent behavior. There were exceedingly few bar brawls, and that sort of thing. So, a crime like this really shook Mars.

When she arrived at Colony 3, she could feel the tension and fear in the air. There were a lot of other journalists, many of whom were from Mars news organizations that she had met recently. Others were journalists from Earth news organizations that had Mars bureaus—the *Times* was one of the last to have one. She greeted some that she knew, and she went in search of Ama and Holly. They had their work cut out for them.

John, November 2106

John was sitting in the small mess hall, eating a quiet dinner. Unlike most of his colleagues he liked this mess hall better than the main mess hall. Yes, it had a smaller menu, but it was very quiet, and it had a great view of one of the large construction bays. It wasn't the one with the *Corinth*, but it didn't matter. It was currently occupied by the *Valiant*, another ship of the same class as the *Corinth*, but several months behind.

John had heard that SolGov had plans for three ships in the *Corinth* class. The official story was that these were all in anticipation of the alien threat. John trusted his superiors, but he couldn't shake the idea that they weren't in the kind of danger that everyone thought they were.

Of course, if we found out that an alien species had eliminated one of our colonies, SolGov would be ready to go to war, and John would be ready to defend Earth and humankind. But John knew that didn't necessarily apply to other species. And he further knew that there was no guarantee that the aliens even knew about the destroyed colony. He continued on this train of thought and was surprised to see someone standing in front of him.

"Commander Herman?"

He saw one of the Ensigns assigned to the *Corinth*.

"Yes, Ensign Andreas?"

"You are needed immediately by Captain McAdams, sir."

"Immediately?"

"Yes, I was told to tell you to drop everything at once."

John sighed, took his tray with his half-eaten dinner to the refuse chute, and followed the Ensign back to Captain McAdam's office.

As they walked in, John saw the other department heads already present.

"Ah, Commander, welcome. You are dismissed, Ensign Andreas. Everyone, please sit."

The Ensign left and closed the door.

"We have received the following images from Kuiper exploratory." He pointed to an image on his large view screen. John couldn't quite figure out what it was. It looked like a row of five spheres connected to each other—except they weren't spheres—maybe some sort of dodecahedron.

"It is, without question, an alien craft, of enormous size. We tracked the alien probe as far as this sector of the Kuiper belt, so we're sure this is the ship that sent out this probe originally. Folks, we launch in 1 week. We need to stop at Mars to pick up the team that has been analyzing and monitoring the probe. Then we'll head out to intercept and will likely have contact in seven and a half months from now.

"So, I need your reports. How can we be ready to launch in a week?"

Commander Androv, in charge of ships systems, was the first to speak.

"Captain, may I speak freely?"

"Of course, Commander."

"There is no way we can launch in a week. The computer for the environment controls has just now been finally installed, and it hasn't been tested or really well configured yet. The bulkheads aren't built everywhere on the ship—that will take at least another month. The propulsion systems are in place, but we have not fully tested them yet. There are a half-dozen other ship systems that are still in process."

"Commander Androv, what if we were to get twice, or even three times the number of staff to help?"

"That might help, Captain, but of course it takes time to get new people up to speed..."

"I see. Anyone else want to tell me why we can't launch in a week?" John thought McAdams was getting angry. He spoke next.

"Captain, Logistics is actually in good shape. We can finish anything we need to do in transit."

"Thank you, Commander. Lieutenant Commander Ying?"

"Sir, most systems are in place, and we can handle most things in transit, sir."

"Alright. Everyone except Commander Androv is dismissed. You have your work cut out for you."

John got up and left and felt quite glad that he had not been asked to be in charge of ship's systems. Of course, Androv had the hardest job, with the most things to worry about. He also knew the Commander to be extremely careful and risk-averse. He was pretty sure that McAdams could get Androv to agree to launch in a week. And what a week it would be!

Lodan, November 2106

Lodan was dreaming. She was in Utah, again, at the CPS camp. She was looking at her tiny bunk, and small trunk at the foot of it, filled with everything she owned, which wasn't much. She heard shouting, and ran outside, to see the bright, bright cloud of Cassiopeia hanging in the northern sky, not far above the horizon.

She hears this insistent sound, and turns back toward the building, but it's gone. Everything is gone—there is just her, and the supernova. And the sound. She swims awake, and realizes her AI is signaling an urgent message.

Her room is completely dark. She looks for the dimly lit light switch on her bedside table and turns it on. She walks over to her desk and picks up her tablet.

"Display message."

Kylee appeared on her tablet, looking tired and worried.

"Lodan, it's Kylee. Sorry to bother you. I got a high-priority message from SolGov. Please call me as soon as possible, so I can talk with you live. And book the next shuttle to Colony 1 for you, Michael and Tai."

Lodan straightened and decided that it might be a good idea to get dressed before she talked with Kylee. Somehow, based on Kylee's demeanor, she doubted that she'd be getting any more sleep tonight. She took a shower, dressed, and sat down at her desk, and had her AI contact Kylee.

Lodan asked, "Kylee, what's going on?"

Kylee said, slowly, "Remember we followed the asteroid out as far as the Kuiper belt, when, for some reason the signal stopped?"

"Right, it was in the final report."

"There are several long-standing stations out there..." Lodan was trying to figure out what Kylee was getting at.

"Yes. Sam told me about them. They had thought about going out there to work at one point."

"Well, one of those stations caught sight of a ship. A large ship, heading in-system."

Lodan was confused. "Huh? What are you saying?"

"The aliens—the originators of the asteroid and the Mars artifacts. They are coming."

"Wait, what? How do you know this?"

"It has to be. Think about it, Lodan. The alien asteroid goes into one particular part of the Kuiper belt, and the tracking signal stops. Out of that same part of the Kuiper belt comes a huge, unidentified alien ship. What else could be going on? Anyway, SolGov certainly thinks it's a big deal— there is a ship on its way to Mars from Earth right now—with a large crew, and they are going to pick us up at Mars station in 20 days. We'll leave from there to rendezvous with this ship. In the meantime, we have our work cut out for us."

"Wow. I'm trying to let this all sink in. I'll go wake up Tai and Michael, and I'll see you at Colony 1 in a few hours."

She quickly made priority reservations for the first shuttle to Colony 1, and then walked out of her quarters, and followed the very dimly lit corridors to where Michael had his quarters. She had just spent the night with him in his quarters a few days ago for the first time. For some reason it seemed a little surreal now.

She knocked lightly on the door, and stepped in. He was stirring on his bed. She walked up to it and kneeled down.

"Michael."

He turned around to look at her. He smiled.

"Lodan. Mmmm, nice to see you. What's up?"

She figured he was now awake enough to see the look on her face, because he sat up and said next, "What's wrong?"

"Kylee called. Apparently, a station out at the Kuiper belt saw a big alien ship heading toward us."

"You're kidding."

"No, no joke. Pack your stuff. I gotta go wake up Tai, too. I already made reservations for us to get to Colony 1. Shuttle is leaving at 0800."

"I bet Tai is already awake."

"It's 0500!"

"He's an early riser."

Michael got up and went to his desk and asked his AI to connect with Tai. A freshly shaven face looked back at him.

"Tai, Lodan just came to wake me. Pack your stuff, dude, and give your second the keys to the kingdom. Kylee said the aliens are coming! We're headed back to Colony 1 at 0800."

Tai nodded and signed off.

"See, I bought us a bit of time."

Lodan smiled. "Time for..."

Michael was smiling so broadly that the dimple that only sometimes made its appearance showed up. She loved that dimple.

"Use your imagination, honey."

Later, Lodan, Tai and Michael were sitting at a table in the corner of the room, talking in very hushed tones.

Lodan said, "So you think you can talk with them? Really, Michael?"

"Well, no, not really, but perhaps make a beginning. We do have what we think may be an alphabet, based on the symbols on the walls of the cave and the markings on the asteroid. But we're running into some dead ends. I'm hoping that the time we have on the ship will allow us to crack it."

They were hurriedly eating their breakfast, on the way to a Colony 1 shuttle in 30 minutes. Lodan knew that it would be a long time before she got back to the colony, so she packed everything she had, and put her assistant Peter in charge of the Agronomy team. She wasn't all that happy about it, but she really wanted to be a part of this team—she wanted to see this whole thing through.

They had been privy to the knowledge that Earth humans weren't alone in the universe for more than a year, but it had been frustrating to them that SolGov refused to release information about either the Mars colony issues, or the alien asteroid. And there was absolutely nothing they could do about it.

She looked up to see Gareth looking at their table. She knew he observed their comings and goings, and knew that of anyone in this colony, the three of them were gone more than anyone. She knew he knew it was all related to the movement of the colony more than a year ago. Patricia, who had become a friend of hers, had confided in her that Gareth was doing some very deep investigations of her activities. Tina had told her that he had asked to meet with her. She let it go. If he discovered it on his own, that would make her feel a lot better.

"OK, ya'll we gotta get going."

They got up from the table, disposed of their dishes and trays, and walked out of the dining hall. She smiled at Gareth on the way out.

As they walked toward the central dome, Lodan asked, "Tai, how did Marlene take the leadership change?"

"She'll do fine without me. She didn't ask, surprisingly."

"That's good. Peter grilled me, then yelled at me for not giving him more information, and then got pissy because he hadn't been chosen to come. He's felt out of the loop since we moved the colony."

They were all glued to their tablets on the shuttle ride to Colony 1, reading everything Kylee had sent about what was known so far, and they hurriedly made their way through the transit system and then to the conference room at Terra University she was all too familiar with. Lodan almost felt like she lived in this conference room. She'd spent so much time in it with these people around the table that it felt like home. They each had their preferred seats, and some of them would even get testy if a guest happened to sit in their preferred seat. Luckily, they didn't often have guests.

Projected on the screen was the image taken from a telescope on one of the stations. It was hard to know how big the ship was. They estimated that the ship might be as large as five kilometers in length. It looked like nothing human beings would make. It was definitely a set of regular geometric shapes. Michael had said it was a series of five dodecahedrons. It was clearly metallic but was a very odd color—a ruddy red, not quite like rust, but close. It had symbols on it, which Michael said were similar to the symbols already seen on Mars, the Moon and on the asteroid. Lodan figured they needed to stop calling that thing an asteroid, and call it a probe, or a ship, or something.

Sam asked, "Any attempts to signal it?"

Kylee answered, "No. Believe it or not, there is a protocol. Some SolGov bureaucrat figured out a while ago what should happen in case of first contact, and they were sure that a commercial entity out in the Kuiper belt should not be in the position to make first contact. So, they are prohibited from attempting communication. Also, they are prohibited from telling anyone about it, but I can't believe that this is going to stay under wraps for too long."

"Where will we be when we rendezvous with it?"

Kylee said, "Not entirely clear. Probably outside of Saturn's orbit."

"Wow, cool. I've always wanted to go out there!"

"Sam, it's going to be a long trip!"

Sam smiled. "I don't mind."

Kylee turned to address everyone. "OK, so I talked with this guy, Captain McAdams. He is the captain of the *Corinth*, which is coming to pick us up. He is clear with me that he is serving as official SolGov representative, and he is in charge. However, we are leaders of the science team, and he is taking his lead from us. I've sent you the crew they are sending—quite a collection of prestigious people—but we're the ones who know the most, and we get to lead."

Lodan looked over the list, and she saw one person of interest: Lucia Wynn, from MIT, the youngest person ever to win a Nobel Prithey in Physics. That seemed quite odd to her, but she didn't feel like she had time to investigate it at the moment. The rest were scientists that she mostly didn't know. She'd heard of a few names, but she was the only agronomist on the mission. That wasn't too much of a surprise.

It had been a long 18 days of planning, communications, and, for Lodan, worrying. Lodan was at least enjoying her spacious accommodations on Colony 1. It was so nice when she was here—she got to stay in one of the staff apartments, which everyone here seemed to complain about, but was a lot larger than her room on Colony 6—and she had one of the biggest rooms available. She loved the large screens with Mars views—it almost felt like she had windows.

It was very late—she should be sleeping, but instead she was going over the latest plans for the Xenoscience team. She and Kylee would be co-leading it, and there were several biologists who were coming on the *Corinth* to join them. They had already had some email discussions on the plan. One of the scientists, Pedro Hernandez, was relatively well-known for his theories on different biological systems. He had some interesting ideas about the biology of these aliens based on the composition of the nanoparticles found on Mars, as well as some of the samples drawn from the alien "probe" they were now calling it.

Her AI beeped and spoke. "Priority call from Kylee."

"Take the call."

Kylee's face showed up on the screen. She was in her pajamas.

"Lodan, we have a big problem."

"And that is?"

"Someone from Kuiper Exploratory leaked the photos to the press. It's all over the news on Earth today."

"Oh boy. Now what?"

"Captain McAdams sent me a message—apparently there is a huge kerfuffle inside SolGov, but it's likely that they will come completely clean—he's heard from the President, and apparently the President is in favor of telling the whole story. He'll let us know when the press conference is."

Lodan took a deep breath. Finally.

"Does this change anything?"

"Yes and no. It doesn't change our basic mission, but it means we'll be watched by the whole Solar System during first contact. How does that feel?"

"Fucking scary. I mean it was already scary, now it's fucking scary."

Kylee laughed. "I feel you. Anyway, what are you doing up? Get some sleep—the ship arrives in two days!"

"Yes, ma'am."

Two days later, she had to chuckle at what she had gotten used to, even on Mars Colony 6, let alone Mars Colony 1. Her new dwelling was a bunk, in tiny quarters shared with 3 other people. One was Sam, which made her happy. The other two were not known to her—they were part of the engineering crew of the *Corinth*.

As their shuttle had approached the Mars Station where the *Corinth* was docked, Lodan had been impressed. It was an enormous ship—larger than she thought SolGov had. Sam had commented that it had some very unusual looking equipment on it. She suspected weaponry. That wouldn't surprise Lodan. The ship looked new, and once they got aboard, it smelled new. Lodan thought that they had possibly even launched it a bit sooner than it was fully ready.

She unpacked her belongings in the locker next to her bunk, and in the shelves inside the bunk. She had a top bunk, which she didn't mind at all. It was very comfortable.

"Attention all engineering and piloting crew. We are about to leave Mars orbit. If you are on duty, please report to your station. Otherwise, please find a seat or go to your bunk, and strap in. We'll be turning off spin and accelerating toward the Kuiper belt in 5 minutes."

Sam opened the door.

"Hey, Sam."

"Hi. They kicked me off of the bridge."

Lodan smiled. "Is this going to be hard for you—not getting to pilot?"

"Nah, it's such a different kind of ship—not my kind. It takes like five people to pilot it properly."

"Ah, I see." Lodan couldn't quite get Sam's obsession with spaceflight and piloting. But then, she figured Sam couldn't understand her obsession with food plants.

"We'd better strap in, huh?"

"Yup." Lodan got into her bunk, found the straps, and wrapped them over her knees, shoulders, and around her waist, and pushed the velcro in place. She wasn't going anywhere.

"Spin turning off."

She felt her weight slowly decrease, until she was weightless. She hated being weightless. She could feel her 1/2 eaten breakfast begin to rise in her stomach.

"Ugh. I hate this."

"Why, Lodan? It's fun. It's amazing what you can do weightless."

"I get sick."

"Oh, I'm sorry. I guess I've always had an iron stomach. Never had a problem. I once even made love weightless."

"Really? I can't even imagine that. I'd be too busy trying not to heave."

Sam laughed. "Well, it was a nice experience. You and Michael should try it."

Lodan felt her nausea and said seriously, "Not a chance! Besides, Michael hates space flight about as much as I do."

Then, she wondered about Tina. "Sam, how did Tina react to you leaving?"

"She was OK—she was excited for me, actually. I didn't get a chance to say goodbye to her yesterday, though. She was busy because of some brouhaha in Colony 3."

"Are you two going to get married?"

"No. I love space too much, and Tina knows that—she knows that what we have now is temporary. I was already getting tired of being on Mars, and I was beginning to make plans to get a ship again. I'm happy now that I'll make it all the way out to Saturn's orbit!"

"Well, you know me. Plants don't like space. They barely like Mars!"

Eventually, they turned spin back on. She undid her straps and got down from her bunk. A loud voice called from the comm system.

"Your attention please—all Xenoscientists and members of the logistics team meet in the fore conference room."

"That's us!"

She left the quarters with Sam. They walked down the corridor, toward the conference room where the first science meeting was to be held. She was glad that spin was back, and that there was gravity. It was .6—the standard for all interplanetary ships. More than she had gotten used to on Mars.

Lodan remembered approaching the ship from the shuttle. The *Corinth* was a monster of a ship. Large central core and a spinning habitat ring that extended about 1/2 of the ships size, centered in the middle. In the front part of the core was a large area that had the command stations and the bridge, in the rear were the engines and fuel.

Sam had said they'd spent some time researching the *Corinth*, and it was a brand-new design, with a new kind of Ion engine, and every bit of new technology available. Sam had said they wondered whether or not the ship had been built in light of the alien probe—preparing for the possibility of first contact.

"Hi Lodan. Ready for the meeting?"

Lodan turned to see the smiling face of Michael. She thought of kissing him, but thought the better of it, given where they were. Instead, she just touched him playfully on the shoulder.

"Hey there, you. I think so. Are you?"

Michael said, "Might as well get this part over with."

They walked into the conference room together. It was crowded, and there didn't look to be enough seats for everyone, but Kylee was up at the front of the table, and there were four empty chairs around her. She and Michael took two chairs. Sam and Tai were right behind them and sat down.

Captain McAdams was at the head of the table, and began to speak, even as some more people entered into the room, standing in the back.

"Sorry for the squeeze in this room. I think we won't have to meet as an entire group very often. The *Corinth* is designed more as a workhorse than anything, so there aren't a lot of spaces where many people can meet. Anyway, let's get started.

"Our scheduled rendezvous with the alien ship is in 6 months, as long as it maintains its current speed and direction toward Mars. It will intercept Mars in about 12 months, if we aren't able to stop it."

Michael spoke up. "Stop it?"

Captain McAdams put his hands up in the air. "Wait, wait, we're getting ahead of ourselves here. Now is not the time to talk in detail about scenarios. I just wanted to give everyone a timeframe for our work. We have a lot to assess between now and then. And you all sitting here right now are the ones who are going to do it.

"Also, SolGov will be holding a press conference in …" he looked at his watch, "Actually, about 5 minutes ago. The minute we get the feed from Earth, we'll pipe it in here. That should be momentarily."

Gareth, November 2016

Gareth walked into the dining hall. He wasn't especially hungry this morning, but he knew his day would go better if he had something to eat. He had dreamed about his son last night, again, but it was different than usual. It was more vivid, and there were other people in the dream this time, like Lodan. He didn't know what to make of it. Perhaps he was starting to heal.

He took some oatmeal and dried fruit and went to sit down in a corner. He wasn't interested in company this morning. As a pastor, he often had to be "on" all of the time. But he had noticed that if he sat away from people, they would leave him alone for a bit.

He was startled by hearing Olga's voice speak loudly over the com system. "May I have your attention, please! A very important press conference from Earth is about to start. Please come to the main auditorium immediately."

Murmurs started in the dining hall, and he heard the sounds of chairs moving, and people getting up to leave. He hastily dropped the remains of his breakfast into the recycling chute, and went to pick up Sharron from their quarters, which was pretty much on his way to the auditorium.

As he walked down their hall, he saw her coming towards him.

"Gareth, do you know what this is about?"

"No dear, I have no idea. Let's go find out, shall we?"

They walked down the hall and were joined by many others in the colony on the way. As he entered the large room, he could see that just about everyone was present. He wondered if this had any relationship to why Lodan and others had left earlier in the month. Gareth had heard rumors that it would be a long time before they returned, if ever.

On the large view screen in the front of the room SolGov seal was displayed, and the message below "Press Conference Starting in 2:03," and it was counting down.

"Gareth, when was the last time this happened? I can't remember."

"The last time there was an emergency press conference from SolGov? Maybe when Tsiou Chen was assassinated?"

"That was more than 15 years ago! Has it been that long?"

"Well, that's the last time I can remember. It's been mostly pretty quiet for SolGov for the last few years since the uprisings."

The screen changed from the seal to the President. His name was Andrei Volkov, and he had been a very unlikely candidate, as Gareth recalled. He began to speak.

"I know that this press conference is being broadcast all over Earth, the Moon, Mars, and all of our colonies and stations all over the solar system. We have come to a momentous time in our history as human beings. We have discovered that we are not alone in the universe. We now know of other intelligent life, and it has entered the solar system.

"We have known about this threat for over a year now. We first found evidence of other intelligences on Mars, where we found artifacts and toxic chemicals left by aliens in a proposed colony location last year. We then heard about a small alien craft which was found by an asteroid hunter and went to Mars. This small alien craft then went out to the Kuiper belt. Our furthest flung outpost made contact with a very large alien ship a little over a month ago, and I'm sure many of you have seen images of that ship. It is headed directly towards Mars. We have our most modern and powerful ship on its way to intercept it.

"We don't know what to expect. We don't know how dangerous they are, or what they want. We have our best military minds focused on the problem.

"I will take questions now."

Pandemonium ensued in the auditorium. Gareth could hardly hear what was being said.

Finally, a loud voice boomed across the room, "Quiet, everyone!!"

Gareth barely heard the rest of the press conference, until a woman of very small stature and graying hair asked the President a question that shook Gareth to his core.

"Mr. President, SolGov has released to the press a document which suggests that the crop failures last year were due to imported toxic regolith from the relocated colony on Mars. Was the origin of this toxicity alien?"

The President paused briefly before answering.

"Yes, we believe it was. We understand that 500 pounds of regolith from the original location of Mars colony 6 was imported to Earth by a company who was interested in commercial uses of the regolith. This company was based in Harrisburg, Pennsylvania. They illegally dumped a large portion of this regolith into the local river. We have now fined this company for negligence. These toxins were found to be alien nanoparticles."

"Mr. President, a follow up, please? Why wasn't this made public last year?"

"We realithey it was a mistake not to release this information sooner. We apologithey to all who were affected by this incident. Thank you, this press conference is now over."

Gareth turned to his wife, and said in a whisper, "I knew there was a connection—I just knew it."

She took his hand in hers and held it tightly. It made so much sense, now. Sam the asteroid hunter as a colleague of Lodan's, the anthropologist who was interviewed by Tina, and the general stonewalling he ran into over and over again. But there was more—

he could feel a kind of stirring in his heart. This was something very significant for him. He didn't know why, or how, yet. He knew God would show him. He knew.

Tina, November 2106

Tina wished she was on Earth for this press conference. She saw her *Times* colleague, Helen, ask the President the tough question about the regolith. She made notes—she would have a follow-up story to the story that she had broken months ago about Colony 6. The story ended up a lot less sensational than she'd written it—her editor had taken out most of the questions that she'd posed in the article about the actions of SolGov regarding the Colony. He'd made it clear that if she wrote another article questioning the actions of SolGov, she'd be looking for a job elsewhere. She was careful from then on.

She'd been writing puff pieces about Mars government officials, and human-interest stories about Mars immigrants to the different colonies. Every once in a while, a big story that was not about SolGov broke on Mars, like the triple homicide in Colony 3 earlier this month. It was a relief that she got to do good investigative reporting and tell the whole story without fear of it being edited into pablum by her boss. Although she thought about how that story had turned out—it was a little less complimentary to the work of the Mars police than she'd originally written.

Anyway, she now felt vindicated, but she still knew that she would have to tread carefully. She hadn't yet written the article about the Moon cave and formations suggesting a destroyed alien colony. She honestly didn't think SolGov was going to come clean about it—it was a secret kept far too long. Now wasn't the right time would be to break it, but she'd know when the time was right.

She wished Lodan and Michael were still on Mars, so she could do a new interview of them. It didn't really matter at this point, she realized. It was time to go get some Marsie-on-the-street interviews about the aliens.

She already missed Sam, who had been gone for almost three weeks now. She hadn't been able to say a real goodbye because of the Colony 3 story. She knew that Sam would be away for a year, and then back here for a while, just a while, before they headed out again to who knew where. Tina shook her head. She was hopelessly in love with Sam, and she knew that the only thing that kept Sam from being hopelessly in love with her was that Sam was hopelessly in love with space.

Gareth, November 2106

Gareth was standing in front of his small congregation, ready to give his sermon. Well, he wasn't really ready. This was the first Sunday since the announcement a few days ago, and everyone had been completely taken aback by the new realities of life. Gareth's thoughts were still in a jumble around the death of his son, and how this whole thing with the aliens was connected. He also had finally understood why Lodan hadn't been able to tell him anything. He didn't hold it against her.

"Please pray with me." He bowed his head. "Father, we come to you at this time with heavy hearts. We don't know what to make of the fact that we are not alone in this universe. Some say these aliens must be of Satan. Others say that they must be Your children. We are lost, Father. Give us wisdom to know what to do and help us keep our faith in You during this time."

He felt this lost-ness deep in his heart. God somehow felt to him even further away than ever, even though he realized that it must be God's will that he'd ended up here on Mars during this momentous time. He raised his head and began his sermon.

"Brothers and Sisters in Christ, we face a difficult road. Our faith has been sorely tested over these past one hundred years or so. We haven't been really sure who we are anymore, as Christians, or who we should be. And now, the most momentous occasion of our lives, and possibly the lives of modern humans, is that we learn that we are not alone in the universe.

"Scientists have been telling us this for many years: that it is likely that there are other planets that can sustain life. But we never believed it. We, as Christians, thought of the Earth as God's planet—the world He created, and we were the people He created. But it appears we really aren't alone."

He went on to tell the story of his son, and how and why he was here on Mars. He explained his own crisis of faith, and he also expressed his hope and expectation that God would make things clear. He left them with the advice to take it one day at a time and find the blessings that God has given in each day. He thought that was always good advice.

They had a prayer time, where his congregants prayed fervently for family and friends on Earth and in other places. They had already heard about rioting in London, Los Angeles, Bangkok and Shanghai. There had been huge protests in Pennsylvania and surrounding areas that had been affected by the incident with the toxic regolith.

He dismissed his congregants, and they drifted out of the room, leaving his wife, and his friend Frank, who was an engineer. He'd gotten to know Frank on the flight out to Mars. He was a quiet, soft-spoken man of deep faith. Gareth smiled at Frank.

"Frank, how are you doing?"

"Gareth, I'm troubled. My pastor from home sent out a message yesterday, and he insisted that the aliens must be from Satan, and a temptation for us to move away from Christ, and from the Bible. He is suggesting that SolGov is in cahoots with the aliens…"

"Frank…"

"I know, Gareth, it doesn't make sense. I don't believe what he is saying. But I don't know what to believe."

"It will come clear, Frank, God will make it clear."

Frank nodded, and he and Gareth shared a hug. The three of them walked out of the shared worship space, and Gareth and his wife walked to their quarters. Frank went off in the direction of the engineering area, and Gareth assumed he had duties to perform.

"Gareth, what do you think is going to happen?"

"I have no idea, dear. Time, and God, will tell."

"Gareth, I'm worried—worried for our safety. That ship is headed here."

He gathered his wife in an embrace.

"We will be fine. I'm sure of it." But truthfully, he was far from sure of it.

The next day, he was sitting in the library, watching the large view screen. It was showing the view that the Neptune station had of the alien craft. It was a live shot, and the craft was pretty far from the station—but the station had some powerful telescopes, and it found the ship. Everyone had a hard time understanding the sheer scope of the ship. It had been estimated that it was at least five kilometers in length, and about another kilometer in width. It was a set of five regular shapes—the coverage said that each shape was a dodecahedron.

He turned to the small screen with the results of his research. He didn't understand half of what it said, but it did explain the crop failures, and the death of his son. There had been nanoparticles, and he had finished a short summary article written by the anthropologist, Michael, that he'd met in the colony, that explained that these kinds of shapes must have significance to the aliens—the artifacts had those shapes, the nanoparticles that killed his son had those shapes, and the ship had those shapes. He said that theories as to their significance would have to wait until there was more information about who these beings were.

He decided to log into GalaxyMail to see what messages might be waiting for him. There was one video message from his brother. He touched the play icon.

"Hello Gareth. I hope that you are safe and sound on Mars. I know that the alien ship is headed your way, and I want you to know that if anything happens, and you need a place to come home to, you are welcome here."

Gareth shook his head. He found it hard to take that offer especially seriously, given all that had happened between him and his brother.

"Of course, I'm sure you'll be fine on Mars. In fact, I have a proposal for you. We are starting a new Institute—our church is working together with The Fellowship and Christians United for the Return of America. I'll be the director of this new Institute. Its goal is to fight any attempt to communicate with the aliens, and lobby for the immediate destruction of their ship.

"Knowing that you lost your son because of these aliens, I assume that I have your support, and a satellite office on Mars would be a very welcome addition to the institute. We have some big backers—we will pay you a salary to do this work and buy office space and better quarters for you. I know that being a clergy person on a Mars colony is far from the kind of riches God intends to shower on you, Gareth.

"I'll be sending by text information about the Institute, as well as a contract for you to sign. Take care, and we'll be in touch."

The window with the video closed, and Gareth looked at his list of text messages, and found the information his brother had left. He had to admit that he had an automatic distaste for it, just because his brother was behind it. But he promised himself he would read the materials and pray over this opportunity.

Somehow, he could feel deeply in his heart a tug in the opposite direction, the direction of curiosity. Who were these aliens? Why did they come here, of all places? Why Mars? He didn't actually think that the aliens purposely poisoned the regolith—he blamed the company that dumped the regolith in the river more than anyone. He opened the first message from his brother, which included the mission and vision statements for the new institute. He could barely get through the first few paragraphs before he stopped. He wouldn't have to pray over this, he could tell. A cool bell of clarity was ringing in his head, and in his heart. This Institute was nothing he wanted to be a part of. He filed away the messages and decided to wait for a few days before responding to his brother.

He wrote a brief message to Lodan. He didn't know where she was, and he didn't expect she would get it anytime soon. But he wanted to let her know that he didn't hold it against her for not telling him the truth. And he added that whenever she returned, he would love to buy her some coffee, or something.

He then started writing, and it felt a little bit like a compulsion, but he kept going. First, he started with his most burning questions: why? How? Why now? Who were they? Then he started writing the theological questions that came to his mind. What if these were also God's children? What was He saying by sending them here? He reviewed what he remembered of the theologies of Thomas Aquinas and John Calvin. There weren't any really obvious answers to be found, but he knew that he could eventually find the answer, with God's help.

Then, he realized that other religions must be having their own sets of reactions and theological questions too—maybe there was something to learn from them. As he thought that, a voice in the back of his mind was expressing its dismay at his willingness to listen to what anyone of another faith had to say. But he was always the unusual one among his peers—he was always willing to learn what other people had to say. He pushed that voice aside and typed a message to all the other clergy suggesting a meeting.

Sam, November 2106

Sam sat with everyone else, and all eyes were on the view screen, which at present had the seal of SolGov. There was a low murmur in the room as people whispered at each other in anticipation. Finally, the seal went away, and the face of the current president, Andrei Volkov, looked at them, and began to speak.

"I know that this press conference is being broadcast all over Earth, the Moon, Mars, and all of our colonies and stations all over the solar system. We have come to a momentous moment in our history as human beings. We have discovered that we are not alone in the universe. We now know of other intelligent life, and it has entered our system."

Sam was more interested in the reactions of those around her than they was at what the President was saying. Of course, they, and everyone in the room, already knew the whole story, and pretty much what the President would say. Everyone seemed quiet and attentive to what he was saying. Every once in a while, when the President would answer a question in a way that didn't seem completely truthful, a few people would snicker and talk to one another.

Sam noticed what some people in this room did not—the President said nothing about the Moon. Sam imagined that saying something like, "Oh, and one more thing—we've known about these aliens for more than 80 years," might be too much for the public. But they was disappointed nonetheless.

Finally, it was over. It was time to get back to work. The reactions to this announcement on Earth, Mars and other places were academic to them. They were on their way to meet this ship and try and figure out what to do—and how to keep it from going further inward.

Captain McAdams got up again, and the room quieted down.

"OK, I'm sure that the folks on Earth and Mars have things well in hand. We've got our work cut out for us. We have six months to figure out three things: What kind of beings they are, why they are here now, and what actions we need to take to deal with them. We're going to be divided into two teams. Your group assignments should be coming to your tablets momentarily. Most of them will be obvious. There will be two teams: Xenoscience and Logistics. These teams will meet first thing tomorrow to determine how their work will be organized. Kylee Mason is head of Xenoscience, and Commander John Herman is head of Logistics."

Sam definitely didn't like the sound of that last assignment—a military man overseeing Logistics. They shook their head and looked down at their tablet to see a new message icon and clicked it to see that they were assigned to "Logistics." Ugh. They wished that they'd been assigned to Xenoscience, but they bet that it was their piloting capabilities that landed them in Logistics. Perhaps, since they were the person who found the alien probe in the first place, they'd have some cred when they tried their best to talk them down from shooting first and asking questions later.

Sam saw a tall man, with extremely short blond hair come to the front of the room. He stood tall, and stiff, and overly formal. He seemed the epitome of a military man.

"I am Commander Herman. For those of you who are assigned to Logistics, we will meet in the aft conference room at 0730 hours tomorrow. Please make sure to read all of the materials sent to your tablet before then."

Sam looked at her list of messages and audibly groaned. It looked like she'd be up all night reading! And 0730 seemed rather early to meet. Sam looked up at Commander Herman, who was pointedly looking back at Sam.

Sam was disappointed at being assigned to Logistics because they felt, at some level, they "owned" the asteroid—or probe, rather, and they'd like to follow through with it. But they would go where they were told. One day, Sam thought. They had already almost finished testing their way to their Bachelor's degree in Geology and would be officially enrolling in Terra U to get their Doctorate in Planetology. That is, once this whole thing was over with.

Kylee Mason then got up.

"Hey, all of you in Xenoscience—meet right here at 0900 tomorrow. There is a packet of information on your tablets. We have a lot to cover."

Sam realized then that her primary disappointment was not getting to work with Kylee anymore. And 0900 seemed much more humane time to start.

Captain McAdams said, "OK people, it's almost time for dinner, and you all have your work cut out for you. Dismissed!"

Sam got up and followed the crowd out the door. They saw Lodan and Kylee up ahead talking to one another, and they sped up to drop in right behind them. Lodan turned toward them.

"I heard you got assigned to Logistics. I was bummed."

"Yeah, me too. I bet it's my piloting experience—you've got the big-league planetologists, I'm just small fry in that department. But I can sure fly." Sam smiled.

Kylee said, "We'll miss you, Sam."

They walked toward the mess hall, conversing about the different teams, and what was in store for them. They did have almost six months to get it right, but Sam thought that it didn't matter—they could meet the ship tomorrow, or in five years, and there were still so many unknowns. There were so many ways they could screw it up.

Gareth, November 2106

Gareth sat in the shared worship space in a circle of chairs with all of the clergy. Patricia sat at one side of him, and Alberto De Luca, from the Vatican, on the other side. Around the circle were Abib Sahin, the imam, Ajan Karuna, the Buddhist monk from Thailand, John Martin, the Mormon Elder, and Rabbi Abraham Weiss.

Gareth said, "Thank you, all, for agreeing to meet with me. I realized that although we don't share the same faith, we do share the same task of helping our congregations understand what this whole thing means. I don't even know where to begin, but perhaps we can just talk about what we are dealing with."

John, who was a quiet man that Gareth had come to respect, spoke first.

"Our Prophet has spoken. He has the testimony that these aliens are friendly, and we now have the new mission to bring them into our faith."

Gareth felt, rather than heard or saw Patricia bristle. He saw the Rabbi roll his eyes. He wasn't sure how he felt about that.

Patricia spoke next. "Well, as you might imagine, in our movement there are a lot of opinions." Gareth heard a snicker, and looked sharply at the priest, whose face became serious again. "But on the whole, people think that based on what we know so far, these aliens are probably friendly, or at least harmless, and we should try and contact them, and find out what they want or need."

Gareth nodded.

The priest said, "Well, the Vatican is far from willing to just assume that these aliens are benign, or subject to being converted. His holiness the Pope has yet to deliver his encyclical, but I have heard from the Cardinals that he considers these aliens to be hostile, and likely a test by God."

Gareth said, "I agree with you—it is a test by God. But what is it that you think God is testing us on?"

"Purity of faith, of course. God created Earth, and only Earth. Anything that suggests differently is either a test, or a plot by Satanic forces."

Gareth knew that all of the last several Popes had been more and more conservative and theologically orthodox. He didn't realithey it had gone quite that far.

He shook his head. "What if God is testing us on how well we welcome the stranger?"

Ajan Karuna said, "It is perhaps a test of how we can greet these beings with lovingkindness."

Father De Luca said, "Lovingkindess? That is reserved for other human beings."

The meeting didn't really get anywhere. But Gareth knew who he could talk with. That at least was progress. They broke the meeting up, and Father De Luca came up to him.

"Gareth, I have to admit I am disappointed by what I see as your emerging position. You are going against the words of your church."

Indeed, Gareth was. Every notable Southern Baptist, and most notable evangelicals of other stripes, had come out strongly against communication with the aliens. His brother was one of them.

"Father De Luca, you are correct, I am going against the words of my church, but my church is not like yours. I did not take a vow to obey my church hierarchy. It doesn't work that way for us."

"But Gareth..."

"Father De Luca, I need to follow my conscience, and what I feel to be God's leading. Those both tell me that we need to at least listen to what these aliens have to say before we try to destroy them."

Chapter 6:
Approach

Sam, January 2107

Sam had been quiet for most of this meeting. It was the umpteenth meeting where they talked about first contact scenarios. Most of the members of the Logistics team were career military, and it was impossible to suggest to them that they consider the alien ship friendly before they considered it a threat.

Sam had said at the first meeting about first contact that the alien probe had been completely non-threatening. If the aliens meant to threaten them, they could have done it by now. But these folks didn't want to listen. Commander Herman talked as if these aliens were the most dangerous threat mankind had ever seen. Sam felt like there was absolutely no evidence of a threat, but they wouldn't listen to Sam. They still hadn't told Commander Herman that they knew about the Moon, but they thought his suspicions about the aliens came from what he knew about the alien presence on the Moon.

They stayed quiet and did what they were told, mostly. They kept track of what the Xenoscience team was coming up with, in particular Michael's work on putting together some sort of alphabet or way of communication. They had asked that team to send Sam detailed data on the radio signal they had first heard when coming in contact with the probe. They thought they could figure out how to send the ship some information that would allow them to figure out how to communicate with it. So far, they had not had any luck deciphering the signal—nor had they had any luck deciphering any of the symbols in the caves on Mars, or on the ship. But Michael apparently had some ideas that they would try when they got closer to the ship. Their rendezvous was about two months from now.

"So we've decided that we will wait approximately three days for any kind of indication that they know we are present and want them to stop. If no indication comes, we will send out several small fighter ships in front of the ship to clarify that we wish them to stop."

Then what? That was Sam's question. What if they didn't stop? What were these military bozos going to do, shoot it? They expected something of the sort. They raised a hand.

"Yes, Mx. Julian?" They hated being called that. They wanted everyone to just call their "Sam," but military protocol forbade it.

"Sir, what happens if they don't stop? We might not be communicating the right thing to them. They might see us putting these ships in front of them as a welcome, not as a warning."

The Commander shook his head as if Sam was a child, needing to be educated.

"Mx. Julian, we are confident that we can communicate what is necessary to the aliens. If they do not stop, we are authorized to use necessary force to get them to stop."

"Even if they haven't used any force first?"

"Yes."

Sam didn't like this, not one bit, but they didn't hold any sway here, and no one else in the group seemed to agree with them. Even Dr. "Nobel Laureate" Wynn, agreed with this approach. She had been mostly silent throughout the whole exchange, although she indicated her enthusiasm for the destruction of the aliens by smiling when Lieutenant Mumea talked about the varied weapons plans.

Commander Herman and the rest of the career military went through the current analysis of the hull composition based on spectrographic data taken from a private ship that was in the region that the alien ship was traveling through. Apparently, SolGov had sent out a request and a bounty for any ship that could give them the data they needed, and there happened to be a transport headed for the Neptune station. The spectrographic data suggested a hull primarily of a kind of steel alloy with high carbon content, as well as large amounts of titanium and palladium. It appeared structurally different from the probe, but that made sense, given their different functions. Sam theorized that the ship was built in orbit—they thought a ship made of those materials would be too heavy to get into orbit from a planet. Of course, humans built pretty much all ships except small surface-to-orbit shuttles in space.

"Lieutenant Mumea, have you finalized the weaponry arrangements to have maximum impact on this hull type?"

"Yes, Commander. Models show us that this particular alloy is likely not very ductile, and is likely to be impacted most by missiles, rather than laser weapons. We are currently preparing a large number of missiles to be placed in the fighter ships."

"Thank you, Lieutenant. You all have your assignments for the next few days. We'll convene back here on Monday, at 0730."

Sam had taken a peek at the assignment. It was to work with Lieutenant Pogue to determine the best flight pattern options for the fighter ships in front of the alien craft. The whole thing still felt bad to Sam, and they decided to go find Lodan or Kylee and talk with them about the Logistics team, and what they were planning. It wasn't quite a time for a meal, so Sam started to walk in the direction of the Xenoscience workspace. They heard a clearing of the throat behind her, and they turned to see Commander Herman catching up to them.

"Mx. Julian..."

"Yes, Commander?"

"I want to re-emphasize to you that the content of the Logistics meeting is classified to level nine."

"I thought everyone on this ship has the same security clearance."

"No, actually, they don't. The Logistics team has a level nine clearance. The Xenoscience team has a level seven clearance."

Sam was frustrated. "So, you are saying that you don't want the Xenoscience team to know that you are planning to fire on the alien ship even if they don't fire first?"

"Mx. Julian, what I am saying is the content of the Logistics planning process is at level nine, and the Xenoscience team does not have that clearance. If you cannot abide by the classification, you can spend the rest of the trip in the brig."

They stopped in her tracks and weighed her options. The only viable one was keeping their mouth shut, which didn't feel like an especially good option. They nodded and turned around to go back to their quarters. As they walked, they realized that they couldn't even indicate to Lodan or Kylee that there was anything wrong—they would figure out something was up, and would go to their superiors, who would tell Commander Herman... Damn, and damn again. Instead of going to their quarters, they decided to head to the gym—they'd work off her frustration there.

Lodan, March 2107

Lodan looked at Michael, who was hunched over several tablets. She knew he was working hard on language but hadn't had much luck.

"Damn, Lodan, I wish I could figure out whether the symbols were part of an alphabet, like we use, or logograms, like the Chinese and Japanese use. Even so, when I go down either path, I get nowhere. And there seemingly is no connection between the signals Sam recorded from the probe and the symbols we've seen. Frankly, I'm stuck."

"And you've looked into the idea that they are either more complex, like pictograms, or somewhere in between logograms and characters?"

"Well, I'm not a linguist, and for some *stupid* reason, they didn't choose to include a linguist on this mission. That was a big, big mistake, from my perspective. And Dr. Marcus, as famous as he is, has been utterly useless. He seems to be waiting for the moment of first contact to wade in.

"Anyway, there are other language types in between logograms and alphabets, including syllabaries, and I've gone down those paths as well, to no avail. I'm stuck, Lodan, and there isn't anyone on this ship who can help, and there isn't anyone back home with the proper security clearances. I've asked, believe me."

"Michael, to be honest, I'm worried if we can't figure out a way to communicate with them. Sam has been extraordinarily closed-lipped of late, and the only thing they would say to me was 'Logistics is classified at level nine, and you only have a level seven, and I'm screwed if I say anything.' It suggests to me that they are planning something that they doesn't like, but they can't say what it is. And if they doesn't like it, we won't like it either. Do you think they are purposely hampering our efforts, so that we'd almost have to be in the position to fire on them?"

"I hope not, Lodan, but I honestly can't figure out why they have hobbled this communication effort so much. But I do have another idea."

"That is?"

"Well, it seems that it is likely that they are more advanced than we are. The artifacts we found are probably on the order of a few hundred years old. They were doing interstellar travel when we were still using horse and buggy. So, my idea is to send them, starting soon, a whole packet of information with the language key in the form of pictograms and words. My AI and I have been working on that key for a month now, and it's just about done. That way they can interpret it and learn our languages. We'll also send them direct feeds from various channels from Earth. We're hoping that will help them learn English and Chinese and increase the likelihood of communication. I'm only waiting on Captain McAdam's approval to get that process started. The sooner we get started on it, the better."

"That sounds brilliant, Michael. I can't imagine why the captain would deny permission."

"He would only deny it if they didn't really want to talk to the aliens, but just destroy them. Let's hope that's not the secret desired outcome of this mission. Anyway, Lodan, how's the bioscience effort?"

"Well, there isn't much to go on, Michael. The nanoparticles that we found in the Martian regolith were mostly made of carbon, with a fair amount of arsenic and trace amounts of Cerium and Promethium. Just like our nanoscience wouldn't tell an alien much about our biology, it doesn't really tell us much of anything about their biology. However, I found an interesting article that just came out which investigated the regolith much more closely than we had, with more sophisticated instruments. They found what they think are cells—and they think that these cells are made largely of carbon, silicon, and arsenic. They suggest that perhaps the genetic material of these creatures contains arsenic instead of phosphorus. I don't know that there is enough evidence of that, but their theory is interesting. And as you know, what was left on Mars didn't tell us much."

"Any deductions from the size of the ship?"

"Well, some. If this is an exploratory ship, they either are enormous creatures, or they need a lot of space. But my bet is that this is a colony ship. The fact that it isn't rotating suggests either that they have artificial gravity, or that they don't need gravity. I suspect the former is more likely. The alternative is that the insides rotate—but I doubt that. Anyway, until they give us more information, we don't have much on them."

"And if it's a colony ship…"

"Why did they choose this system? They've got to have known it's occupied. I think that's why the military types are scared—there just isn't a way for any species with their capacities not to know someone is here. Between the probe, and just listening to the airwaves, it's pretty obvious. And they've seen the Kuiper Belt Station—they came pretty darned close to it and didn't stop."

"Kylee's team has a theory about its origin. From the direction that it entered the Kuiper belt, it looked to be heading directly from Cassiopeia, and at speeds that are about .8 of light, it would take approximately fifty years from our perspective for them to get here from there. They think it's a colony ship from Cassiopeia, perhaps with the last of their people on it that left just before the supernova."

"Oh, my! But still, why here?"

"You got me. This is why we need to talk with them, Michael."

Tina, March 2107

She looked at the article, as published in today's Mars edition of the *Times*. She was angry—angrier than she had been in months. She was looking at the edited version of an investigative article that she and Ama did on the proposal for Colony 7. The article she was reading bore little resemblance to the article she wrote. The Mars government wanted to halt all new colony establishment until a new agreement could be reached that included a number of things, including giving Mars more autonomy. SolGov was going ahead with Colony 7 plans anyway. Her article made it seem that the Mars government was simply being obstructive for no reason.

She realized she was at the end of her rope. Over the last months of her tenure as the Mars bureau chief, the *Times* had used up any good will she had toward it. This had been the first substantive piece about Mars and SolGov she had dared write in the last few months—and she could see the result. And not only did she feel no loyalty towards the *Times* anymore, she felt an increasing loyalty to Mars. She wanted the *Times* to do Mars justice, and she realized it never would. Luckily, her bosses wanted more human-interest stories, and fewer political ones. She would oblige. But she needed to vent. She sent a message to Kevin, and suggested they have a beer after work tonight. She got a reply back to meet him at Filby's, one of their favorite bars. She was looking forward to it. It was too bad Sam was away.

Her day passed in a blur—she was occupied setting up interviews, dealing with varied news tips that came in, most of which she would not be dealing with, and talking with Ama and Holly about their next assignments. Holly was in the process of doing a very detailed photo essay of the history of Colony 1—Tina was looking forward to seeing what she came up with.

She left the office, and walked to the central dome, and into the mall area, where Filby's was. As she walked in, she could see a basketball game on the large view screen at the back of the bar. She remembered dimly that it was "March Madness"—the time of Earth college basketball tournaments. She looked around and saw Kevin with a man she didn't know in a corner booth.

"Hey there." She sat down next to Kevin, across from the man she didn't know.

"Tina, I'd like you to meet Jurgen. Jurgen, meet Tina."

They shook hands across the table. A waitress came up to ask them what they wanted.

Tina said, "I'll have a Cassiopeia 2081 please."

Jurgen said, "Can I have a Sternberg Export, please?" Tina almost whistled aloud. Even as *Times* bureau chief, she didn't feel she could afford a beer shipped here from Earth, no matter how good. She wondered if he were trying to make a point.

Kevin said, "I'll have an Acheron Catena, on the rocks, please." Tina rather liked that brand of Mars-made Whiskey.

"So, Tina, Jurgen is the owner of the *Mars Monitor*. I've wanted you to meet him for a long time, but the tone of your message suggested to me that this was the right time."

The *Mars Monitor* was the biggest news organization on Mars. It was headquartered in Colony 1, but had bureaus in all six colonies, in Beijing, on the Moon, and in a few other places. It was considered the best news organization outside of Earth and based on the fact that Jurgen had just spent what would be for her a day's wage on a bottle of beer, it must be doing well.

"Tina, I have been following you ever since you started writing for the *Times* on the Mars government beat in Beijing. You always seemed to have a balanced approach. And although many of the articles you've written recently have infuriated me, I have heard from Kevin that they were heavily edited Earth-side."

Tina nodded. "I just finished an article on the Colony 7 issues, and the article that has my byline is *not* the article I wrote."

"Would you like to write articles and not have them edited like that?"

"Of course! What are you suggesting?"

"That you come work for us. We want to beat the *Times*. We already do so here and in the outer colonies, of course, but I want us to be the first, everywhere in this system. I think people want news that isn't sanitized for SolGov. And I know good talent when I see it."

"Jurgen, I have to admit that I am tempted. Very tempted. But I'm not quite done with the *Times* yet. I suspect, though, that it won't be long. Will you keep this offer open?"

"It's open for as long as you like, Tina."

Their drinks came, they toasted to Mars, and had a nice conversation about the future. Tina liked Jurgen and thought that she could do well in his organization. She was glad that she had an out, if things at the *Times* went south. She amended that statement in her head... *when* things at the *Times* went south.

Lodan, March 2107

Lodan looked up to see Michael walking into the work room, looking triumphant. She, Kylee, and Tai were sitting around the conference table working, tablets strewn about.

Michael said, "I got it! I got permission to start the information message to the alien ship. We've commenced the sending process."

"Alright! That's good news, for once."

"I'll tell you, it felt like pulling teeth. It seemed that Captain McAdams doesn't actually want to talk with them. I get the impression that his mission is to simply stop them from getting to Mars, and he's not thinking much beyond that. I had to explain that talking with them would help stop them."

Kylee said, "Tai has a new theory about that."

"A new theory?"

Tai said, "Yes, my theory is that the aliens have just enough fuel to make it to Mars. Tai has been analyzing the exhaust plume. They seem to be using something quite similar to our current ion engines. One of the hallmarks of ion engines is that the exhaust can tell you a lot about the amount of fuel left. My bet, based on the changing spectroscopy of the exhaust plume, is that they are getting low on fuel. If they are forced to use extra to increase their deceleration, they will be stranded. And they will bet that this ship is the biggest we have. This ship can't tow their ship. There isn't much we'll be able to do to help them, even if we wanted to."

Lodan said, "So it behooves them to keep going, almost no matter what?"

Tai nodded. "Exactly."

"Oh, no."

"Oh, yes. We have to tell the Commander this theory."

"He might not care."

"We have to tell him anyway."

Kylee said, "I'll tell him, right now."

Lodan added, "I'll come with you." They both got up and walked toward Commander McAdam's office.

Lodan said, "Kylee, what do you think he will say? Do you think it will make a difference?"

"I don't know, Lodan. We can only hope. I think we should also make sure that the logistics people know this as well—I don't necessarily trust the Commander to share it with them."

Lodan nodded. I'll send a message to Sam with the data."

"Thanks."

They arrived at the Commander's door, just as Commander Herman was leaving. He nodded his head toward the two women and walked down the corridor. Kylee knocked on the door.

"Come in." They entered.

"Captain McAdams, Tai has been analyzing the exhaust from the alien ship and has a theory I thought you should know about."

"And that theory is?"

"That they have just enough fuel to get to Mars. They will be stranded if they use more fuel to decelerate when we ask them to stop."

"And this matters because?"

Lodan could hardly believe her ears, and she opened her mouth to speak, but Kylee put her hand on Lodan's arm, so she didn't.

"Commander, this means that the aliens are not going to stop. Even if they are completely peaceful, it is not in their interest to stop."

"You scientists don't understand one important concept, Dr. Mason. The aliens are *by definition* hostile because they have entered our system. If they stop, and hopefully turn around and go back to where they came from, then they won't have caused any problems. If they don't stop, then we have the right to stop them."

"Commander, you have read all of the analysis that our team has done—we theorize that these folks are the last of their kind, and they don't have anywhere to go."

"I don't agree with those theories."

"But what if they are right, sir?"

"It is irrelevant. My job is to protect humankind."

"But what if they are no threat to humankind?"

"They have to prove that first."

Ah, Lodan thought. Shoot first, ask questions later. How wonderful. She idly wondered if it was too late to get transport back to Mars and avoid what would likely be a bloodbath, possibly of both alien and human origin.

Gareth, March 2107

Gareth and Sharron were lying in bed after making love. It made Gareth happy that they were returning to the rhythm that they had before Joshua died. When he died, it had seemed that their sex life had died with him. Gareth felt that their sex life made Gareth softer and Sharron bolder. It was an interesting gender role reversal for them, one that he never seemed to mind. Nor did she. So, it came as no surprise that she started to talk about how she felt about the aliens.

"Gareth, I don't like the way people are talking about the aliens. I have been talking with a lot of people back home—our friends and family. They are all dead set against them. I don't really understand why—I don't think they are the threat everyone seems to think they are."

"I have a theory, Sharron."

"Is it about Biblical infallibility, or Calvinist predestination?"

"Biblical infallibility. I can't think of any other reason besides sheer stupidity."

"But, Gareth, thinking of the aliens as a threat simply because of what the Bible says *is* sheer stupidity, besides not even respecting what the Bible actually says."

Gareth had to admit she was right. There wasn't a way he could see to defend the stance that his brother and others were taking. He had to do something about it. And Sharron could help.

"Sharron, let's start a blog."

"A blog?"

"Yes. Let's start a blog examining the aliens from a biblical and theological perspective. You're the one with the theology Ph.D."

"But Gareth..."

"What? Are you disavowing that education?"

She sighed and snuggled next to him.

"No, Gareth. I guess I've just gotten very used to simply being your wife. It's a role I've enjoyed these past ten years. I didn't mind giving up my career when we married."

"Well, my dear, I think it's time to dust off that Ph.D. from Calvin Seminary. You are still my wife, but you are my brilliant wife, and it's time more people than just me knew it."

Several days later, Gareth was sitting with Sharron, Patricia, and a few others in the lounge, getting ready to hear the latest press conference with the SolGov president. There had been one every few weeks of this situation, and he didn't expect much different than the last, but he always watched. He also had been checking in with what was released from the group on the way to intercept the ship. There wasn't much—he knew that a lot of their work would be classified. He was interested to find out that they had begun sending a complex set of messages that they hoped would allow the aliens to learn English and/or Chinese. That had been the only recent news.

The President was on the screen, and Gareth started to pay attention.

"Hello, fellow humans, on Earth, Mars, the Moon and colonies. I have a short statement to read, and then I will take questions. The ship *Corinth* is about a month away from visual contact with the alien ship. As most of you know, the *Corinth* has started to send communications to the alien ship, which we hope will allow the aliens a chance to learn our languages, since we have been unable to learn theirs from the information we have. The major goal of the *Corinth* is to communicate with the aliens, determine their intent, and stop them from entering further into our solar system."

Gareth didn't like the sound of that last sentence. He would bet what he had left in the bank, which wasn't a small amount, that the last phrase was the real goal, and the first parts were secondary. He knew that many of the allies of this current President were like his brother—they weren't at all curious and thought that the aliens were a threat—either something Satan cooked up, or just simply some evil threat that needed to be eliminated.

"So far, however, the alien ship has been completely silent. We expect that this is because they have hostile intent. We are doing everything we can to protect humankind from this threat."

Gareth was angry now. He hated the way that they made assumptions about who the aliens were, and what they wanted. They couldn't have even waited very long for a response to their communication. And they also made assumptions that everyone would agree with them.

"I will take a few questions now. Yes, Margaret."

"We have been told that the SolGov military has sent ships and troops, and is working with Mars Militia, the Moon Patrol, as well as the Belt Police to strengthen defenses on Mars, the Moon and the colonies. What efforts are being made to protect Earth?"

"That's a good question Margaret. We will be increasing the number of troops present in the orbital platforms, and we will repair and scramble every military ship we can from space dock and put many of them into Earth orbit. We will be ready for anything. Yes, you there in the back?"

"Mr. President, what if these aliens pose no threat? There is a theory floating around in some circles that this ship is from Cassiopeia and might be a colony ship with the last of whatever kinds of intelligent beings lived on its planet."

"I've heard that theory, and it has been discounted by the military. They think that it is a threat and should be treated as such."

Gareth shook his head and turned to Patricia.

"This is crazy. He doesn't know what he's talking about."

Patricia answered, "I know, Gareth. But what can we do?"

Patricia had been a frequent commenter on the blog and had told him and his wife how much she appreciated their points of view on the topic. Over the past couple of months of writing and thinking, Gareth had become increasingly clear that somehow, he had something important to contribute. Some way to make the death of his son mean something. And he knew that by taking the stance he was taking; he was going against most of his Christian brethren. The Pope had come out with an official statement agreeing with the President that the aliens were a threat, and everything needed to be done to protect humankind from them. He was glad that he had spent time with some of his compatriot clergy here, like Patricia and Rabbi Weiss. It had given him the necessary boost he needed to keep going.

Gareth said, "I know that I need to go home. The blog has already generated a lot of interest, and we need to build on it to keep fighting this perspective. I don't quite know how, but we have to. Isn't he up for re-election?"

"Yes, although the election isn't until next year—several months after the ship will have arrived here. I've been doing some research on one of his opponents whose name is Geraldo Montoya, from Mexico. He has come out strongly in favor of communication and friendship with the aliens. He is trailing Volkov by at least twenty points. He certainly is the leading contender behind Volkov, though."

"We could start a political movement behind Montoya—that should pressure Volkov to moderate his tone. I think that's our best bet."

His wife squeezed his hand. "I'm ready to go home, too, Gareth. Let's get this started."

Gareth started to make plans to leave Mars and go home. He didn't know how well Mars and Earth were lined up right now, but he figured that he could get home in about a month, just in time to arrive when they finally made contact with the alien ship. It was too long, but it would have to do. In the meantime, he would keep fighting from a distance, and get themselves connected to the Montoya campaign.

John, March 2107

John sat in his cabin, looking again at the report from the Xenoscience team. He had just come back from a disastrous meeting with Captain McAdams. He was beginning to have doubts about their mission, and he had the stupidity to tell his commanding officer. He wanted to hit himself on the head for that. Didn't twenty years of being in the military teach him anything?

He couldn't shake the feeling that they were about to do something really bad. The Xenoscience team knew it too, but he knew that Captain McAdams was forcefully loyal to President Volkov and Admiral Matira, and would never back down, or defy them, no matter what the cost.

And, he had strongly aligned himself with Captain McAdams. If anything went wrong with his part of the mission... his career was over. And he didn't know what he would do if his career ended. It was everything he knew. It had meant life to him when he was 18, and just leaving the CPS camps. He'd have been dead many years now if he hadn't made that choice. He had no family to go back to, no wife, no children. No life. The military had been his life, and all he could see was a gaping hole if he left it.

He shook himself and went back to the scenarios for the attack waves, and looked at the models done by Mx. Julian. He thought that they were sullen, snotty, and undisciplined. They questioned every order, and he knew they did not agree with their mission. As he looked over their models, he whistled. Fuck, were they brilliant. They had set up what he was sure was the most effective pattern for putting down missile fire from fighter ships on a big target that he'd ever seen. And they didn't even want to fire the missiles! John guessed he would have to take 'undisciplined' off his list of their sins.

Well, wasn't this a pickle? He had to use the firing patterns of someone who didn't agree with the mission to do a mission he really, in his heart, didn't agree with. What kind of life was he living? He realized that now was not the time to answer that question. It was 0100 hours, and he had an 0750 meeting with Captain McAdams.

Chapter 7:
Contact

Sam, April 2107

It had been a very long six months for Sam. It was not enjoyable sitting in the Logistics meetings week after week, hearing about the thirty-five different ways they were preparing to destroy the alien ship. And they couldn't even talk to anyone about it!

At least they knew that they would be in the first group of fighters to contact the alien ship. They hoped that perhaps they could do something that would be helpful. Anything, except fire on it.

Unfortunately, those were their orders. They were to line up about 1000 kilometers away from the ship, in a formation that the military people thought would make it clear that they wanted the ship to stop. If it didn't at least show any sign of increasing its deceleration by the time the ship came within a few kilometers of their fighters, their orders were to fire at will. They didn't quite know what they would do when that happened, but it was hard to imagine that they would comply. Of course, they hadn't told Commander Herman that.

They was sitting in one of the lounges when Lodan sat next to them.

"Wow, that is a long face."

"You don't know the half of it."

"I know, and you can't tell me."

"Nope."

"Well, I can tell you something."

"What?"

"We've learned some things. Their ship is definitely from Cassiopeia."

"How did you learn that?"

"Well, for years, scientists have assumed that Cassiopeia was a classic Type Ia supernova. One of the hallmarks of a Type Ia supernova is the radioactive decay of nickel-56. Now that the alien ship is close enough for remote spectroscopy, we've found traces of nickel-56 and iron-56 that could have no other origin than a supernova. Between that and the direction they entered the solar system from, the only reasonable assumption is that they originated there."

Sam laughed. "I'll bet you a thousand Yuan that Commanders Herman or Captain McAdams will tell you that the aliens are trying to trick us."

Lodan said, "My dear, you have already won that bet! Upon reading our report about it earlier today, Captain McAdams said, quote, 'How do we know the aliens aren't trying to pull the wool over our eyes?' unquote."

"Geez. How stupid can you get? I guess he's never heard of Occam's razor."

"Naw, I bet he uses, I don't know, General Hortok's razor? Anything that you don't understand must be out to get you? Anyway, some other good news—there apparently is a growing movement on Earth and Mars to be friendly, and communicate, and only attack if attacked first."

Sam was silent. Sam realized that anything they said could be construed as a security breach.

"Well, then, you can't talk about that, eh?"

"Sorry."

"No, I'm sorry for you, Sam."

"Me too."

"Anyway..." Lodan was interrupted by a loud announcement.

"We have achieved visual contact with the alien ship. I repeat, we have achieved visual contact. All fighter pilots report for duty."

"That's me. Wish me luck."

They both got up, and Lodan hugged Sam. "Be well, my friend. Be strong."

Sam looked at Lodan and realized that Lodan knew them better than Sam thought.

"Thanks."

They picked up her tablet and walked quickly to the duty room. They arrived just as a number of the other pilots arrived. They saw Commander Herman at the front of the room.

"This is the moment we've been waiting, planning, and training for. You have your orders. Pilots, to your fighters."

Along with the other pilots, they left the tablet on one of the desks, and walked down to the closest hub tube, where they grabbed an elevator up to the hub. The section of the hub with the fighter ship bays was right by where this hub tube ended. As they reached the hub, they were all floating, and as the door opened, they moved hand over hand to the fighter bays. Sam found their fighter, and climbed in.

Sam did have to admit they liked this little fighter ship. It was smaller than their old asteroid hunter, but based on the test flights they'd taken during their trip out, it was a lot zippier and more maneuverable. Sam went through the standard pre-flight check. Everything was ready.

"Three minutes to launch. Please confirm readiness to launch." Sam recognized the voice of one of the Lieutenants in the control room.

They punched the comm, and spoke, "Julian here, ready for launch."

"Two minutes to launch."

They didn't usually get nervous at times like these, but they were today. This was something completely new—they would be encountering something no human had encountered before. And they were scared about how this would all turn out.

"Five... Four... Three... Two... One... Launch!"

Sam's body pushed back in the seat as the acceleration punched the ship out into space. They maneuvered into formation with the other fighters. Major Nguyen was in the lead position.

They were taking up a triple-diamond formation. Sam was part of the innermost diamond. Their orders were to stay in formation until the alien ship was within ten kilometers of them. When it reached there, and there had been no indication of deceleration, the two inner diamonds were to go first around the propulsion system toward the front of the ship. The outer diamond would stay where they were. All of them were supposed to fire their specially designed missiles when ordered to.

Sam still didn't have any idea what they was going to do, except not fire. Sam knew they didn't have it in them. They wished they'd had the bravery to tell Commander Herman before the mission, but then they'd probably be stuck in the brig for the rest of the trip, which didn't sound appealing to them. And somehow, deep inside, they thought there might be a way they could help.

They took up their positions and waited. Sam could see the small, bright dot that was the alien ship's propulsion system pointed toward Mars for deceleration.

Sam clicked on her communications system.

"Julian here, ready."

"Acknowledged, Mx. Julian."

Sam *still* hated being called "Mx. Julian."

So now, it was time to wait. It would take the ship about ten minutes to reach them. They could already see the bright light growing in size.

"This is Commander Herman to fighter group. On my mark, the outer diamond should accelerate forward at 100 kph. Inner diamonds use your flight patterns to reach the sides of the alien ship."

Sam was stunned. Commander Herman wasn't going to wait!

"Inner diamond, on my mark, engage engines and follow flight patterns."

There was a flurry of "Acknowledge" on the com system. They didn't bother to add her own. There wasn't anything they could do now. They put in the flight pattern and waited for the engage signal.

"Engage."

They pushed the icon, and felt the acceleration of her craft, toward the alien ship and outward. As they watched, the propulsion system grew larger, and then the rest of the ship came into view. As they approached it, they got a feeling for how enormous it was. They could see each dodecahedron in the series, attached to one another. There were what looked like windows and other varied things in the hull.

"Alpha wing, take up positions 1/2 kilometer from the alien ship. Keep pace with it."

They were part of the alpha wing, what had been the right-hand side of the inner diamonds. They kept the ship in formation and told the system to keep pace with the speed of the alien ship, which continued its regular deceleration towards Mars, but definitely did not increase its deceleration.

Relatively near to where they were, they noticed what looked like a door opening. They impulsively decided that they wanted to investigate, and they quickly put their system on manual and steered toward the door, pushing their thrusters.

They heard a shout from the communicator. "Back off! Back off!"

They didn't know who that was, but they ignored it. If the aliens were friendly, they'd hopefully prevent something unfortunate. If they weren't... well, they were betting they were. As they approached the door, which looked like it led into a landing bay, a shrill alarm went off. They looked at the indicator on their console, puzzled. Who would shoot a missile at them?

Then Sam realized what had happened. Someone had fired a missile into the door before they were ordered to, and they had ended up between the door and the person who fired the missile. Fuck. They were toast. The only thing Sam could think to do was push their thrusters harder and see if they could get inside the door. Maybe the missile would miss them and the door. The alarm got shriller, if that were possible. They flipped on their rear display and saw the missile coming right at them. Double fuck.

They felt more than heard the missile explode behind them. They had a moment to wonder why it exploded before it hit them, and they saw the door loom ahead of them, then knew no more.

John, April 2107

John sat in the control room in front of a large view screen showing the position of the alien ship and the fighters approaching it. Several Lieutenants were also sitting in the control room, overseeing their parts of the operation. The fighters were all in place, and the alien ship was approaching. There had been, so far, no change in the speed of the alien ship, and no communications from it, but it had only been a few minutes.

He sat back, ready to wait the ten minutes or so that it would take for the ship to arrive at the point that they had designated. He hoped that the ship would do something—he didn't want to have to start firing on it, but he would, since those were his orders.

"Commander Herman." That was Captain McAdams on the comm.

"Yes Captain?"

"Commence attack pattern now."

"But Captain, they have not arrived..."

"Are you questioning a direct order, Commander?"

John swallowed. "No sir. Attack pattern will commence."

He pushed the comm icon to reach all of the fighters at once.

"This is Commander Herman to fighter group. On my mark, the outer diamond should accelerate forward at 100 kph. Inner diamonds use your flight patterns to reach the sides of the alien ship. Inner diamond, on my mark, engage engines and follow flight patterns."

John heard and saw the acknowledgements of the fighters. He noticed that Mx. Julian had not sent in an acknowledgement. He filed that away for later.

"Engage."

He watched the view screen, seeing the inner diamonds accelerating, and moving forward toward the ship. It was time for Alpha wing to get into place.

"Alpha wing, take up positions 1/2 kilometer from the alien ship. Keep pace with it."

He watched the wing take up position. He hesitated. He didn't quite feel ready to start the attack. Perhaps if he gave the alien ship just a little more time...

Captain McAdams again on the comm, "Commander Herman, are fighters in place."

"Yes, sir."

"Commence..."

"Wait, sir." At that moment, he saw a small opening or door in the ship. He noticed one of the fighters accelerate quickly toward the opening. He then realized that another member of Alpha wing had just fired a missile toward the door.

He felt like time slowed down to a crawl. He saw the missile move toward the door, and the fighter was absolutely in the way, and it was likely to be destroyed by the missile. There was only one thing he could think of, quickly. He opened a comm channel to the fighter that had fired the missile.

"Alpha four, detonate the missile *now*."

"Sir...?"

"I said, detonate the missile *now*." Whoever was in that other fighter was running out of time.

He saw the missile detonate, and saw the fighter being pushed by the blast into the door. He couldn't tell whether or not the fighter was destroyed, but it looked quite possible.

He looked at who had been flying that fighter. It was none other than Sam Julian. Why was he not surprised?

Captain McAdams was back on the comm. "Commander, what just happened?"

"Sir, one of the fighter pilots apparently tried to enter the ship through that door that had opened. Another fighter fired a missile toward the door, not realizing that the first fighter was headed toward it. We don't know what happened to the first fighter. I had the missile detonated prematurely, to give the first fighter a chance at survival."

"That decreased the possibility of doing severe damage to their craft, Commander!"

John took a deep breath.

"Sir..."

"Commence bombardment of alien vessel."

"Yes, sir."

"Who was the fighter pilot that broke formation, Commander?"

"Mx. Samantha Julian, sir."

"Thank you, Commander."

He could tell that the Captain was angry and frustrated. He expected an item in his file about this incident.

"Attention fighter wing, commence attack on alien vessel. Fire at will. I repeat, fire at will."

Lodan April 2107

The entire Xenoscience team, less the career military, were sitting in the conference room, watching the proceedings. From what Lodan could tell, everyone was on edge. No one thought this would end well. Their final report had been completely disregarded, and the Captain was doing what he had been ordered to do by the President, stop the aliens from moving further into the system at all cost. Lodan was especially thinking about Sam. She half imagined Sam returning to the ship in handcuffs because she refused to follow orders.

They watched silently as the ships made the diamond formation. Then, much more quickly than she expected, the diamond formation broke, and the inner diamonds moved toward the alien ship. They couldn't control the image, nor zoom in on any one part.

Kylee was sitting next to Lodan, and turned toward her, and asked, "Do you know which ship is Sam's?"

"No idea. I don't know whether ze's on the outer, middle or inner diamond."

They kept watching, and Lodan saw something confusing. One of the ships that had been in the inner diamond seemed to go toward a newly opened door in the side of the alien ship. Then, she saw a large explosion right near the door. They couldn't tell where it came from, but Lodan assumed it was one of their own missiles.

"Oh, no, they are firing already? What about giving them a chance to decelerate?"

Then, they could see a lot of explosions, all over the alien ship. The good thing was that it appeared to be doing nothing. It stopped for a while, and it looked as if several of the fighters were converging on the door, which now seemed closed.

"I wonder what happened?"

"They captured a ship?"

"That seems unlikely."

They heard a voice over the ships intercom. "Kylee Mason and Lodan Greenfellow, please report *immediately* to Captain McAdams office."

Lodan looked toward Kylee as they rose.

"I wonder what this is about?"

"I don't know, Lodan, but I can almost guarantee you that we won't like whatever it is."

They walked out together, silently, and went to the captain's office. His door was open, and they walked in.

"Ah, Dr. Mason and Ms. Greenfellow, please have a seat. I understand that of anyone on this ship, you two know Sam Julian the best."

Kylee said, "Yes, Captain."

"Apparently, they blatantly disregarded orders and took it upon themself to enter the alien ship when given the opportunity."

Lodan wasn't shocked.

"We think that an unfortunate stray missile from another ship might have caused their death or grave injury, but we are unsure. In any event, their ship is within the alien vessel."

Lodan realized that was what the first explosion was.

Lodan said, "How can we help you, Captain?"

"I need to understand Mx. Julian's motivations. Were they looking for glory? Wanting to get inside and destroy the enemy from within?"

Kylee answered, "I think it's safe to say it's not those, Captain. I bet that it was pure curiosity."

"*Curiosity?*"

"Yes, sir."

He shook his head, and Lodan could tell he was reevaluating his decision to place them on the Logistics team.

"Thank you. You are dismissed."

They walked out together and went to the mess hall to grab lunch. They got their food and sat at one of the tables in a corner.

Kylee said, "Lodan, do you think Sam is dead?"

"I certainly hope not. I guess their life is in the alien's hands, yes?"

"I guess. Sam's death now can't be the end of their story."

"I know, they had so much potential."

"Don't use past tense, Lodan. I think they are still alive."

Gareth, April 2107

Gareth and Sharron walked out of the customs area, along with others they had shared the shuttle from VirginGalactic One to Washington Dulles Spaceport. It had been a long trip, and he was ready to settle into their new apartment in Washington.

Gareth and Sharron had become media darlings, and their opinions were highly sought after. Gareth thought that it was likely because they were two of the very few conservative Christians that were taking a pro-alien stance. It probably didn't hurt to have built-in drama: the two sons of the famous evangelical preacher, one of whom had a dead son, vocally taking opposite sides of the issue.

They had garnered so much attention, even from Mars, that the Montoya campaign had been happy to be connected to them and had given them both official employment with the campaign in the United States, as "religious liaisons," whatever that meant.

What Gareth assumed it meant was that he and Sharron would be traveling around the country talking about this issue, and Candidate Montoya's stance on it. Gareth appreciated Montoya's stance: assume the aliens are friendly, give them what they need or want within our capabilities, learn from them, and, if necessary, live in peace in the same system.

Before they would start to travel, they would settle into their new apartment near Woodley Park. He looked out at the group of waiting people, and saw the sign "Holbright," and pointed at it to Sharron. They both walked toward the sign.

"Mr. Holbright, welcome to D.C. Mr. Montoya sends his greetings."

"Thank you. Our main luggage is to arrive separately, delivered to our new apartment, so we can leave now."

"Very well, sir. Follow me."

The last time Gareth had been in D.C. was when he visited here to testify at a House committee hearing on the deaths in Pennsylvania. It seemed somehow appropriate that he was back, and this time to make some meaning of that original time—since they now know exactly what happened.

They got into a small vehicle, and rode quickly through the suburbs of Virginia, then crossed the Chesapeake River into Maryland, then south to Macomb street, where their new apartment was. The driver stopped the car.

"Here you are. I have the keys for you. Also, the refrigerator and pantry have been stocked, and there are linens and the like, so you should be all set for a while."

"Thank you so much."

They got out of the car and carried their few bags up the stairs. Their apartment was in a small building, with about five other units.

It was number one, on the ground floor. They walked back to the apartment door, unlocked it, and walked in.

"Gareth, I am dead tired. I don't even know what time it is."

"Well, I could tell you, but it wouldn't help. Let's just relax and settle in, shall we?"

It seemed like just a few minutes when Gareth's phone rang. He'd forgotten he'd turned it on when they arrived at Dulles. It had been over a year since he had used it last.

"Hello?"

"Gareth, this is Curtis Johnson from Montoya for the World calling."

"Hello Curtis. I know we have a meeting tomorrow."

"Yes, we do, but something urgent has come up."

"What is that?"

"We just received a wide-band message that had been sent from the alien ship. Apparently, one of the crew of the *Corinth* somehow ended up on the ship. The transmission is a conversation between the Captain of the *Corinth*, the aliens and that crew member. Get online, you can hear the whole thing."

"OK."

"We are having an emergency meeting at 6:00pm in the office, wired in with everyone in the campaign all over the world. A driver will pick you both up at 5:30." Gareth looked at the time on his phone. That was an hour from now. Just enough time for both of them to get a shower.

"Alright, we'll be ready."

Sam April 2107

Sam was dreaming about the CPS camp, when they heard some strange sounds. At first, their mind placed the sounds in their dream environment, but the sounds began to wake them up, and they opened their eyes. Sam couldn't see much—they were in a small room with dark red walls on five sides, and a sixth had what looked like perhaps a window, but they couldn't see out of it—it seemed misted over. They looked around the room and saw that they were sharing the space with some of the pieces of their ship, like the seat they'd been sitting on, a broken view screen, and some assorted parts of the cockpit. The sounds were coming from outside of the room. Very deep, irregular thrumming and booming sounds. They didn't like the sound of it.

They were cold, and they didn't feel especially well, and they looked down at their regulation gas meter and realized why. Way too much carbon dioxide! They knew they must be in the alien ship. And there wasn't much reason that the aliens would know precisely what gas mix humans needed. They would have to figure out how to talk with them, or they would likely get really sick and die soon.

They slowly got up from the floor and started to knock on the wall that looked like a window. Nothing happened for a while. Then they heard a voice. It was pitched low and a bit mechanical sounding.

It said, "Nin hau... Hello."

"Hello—I need your help."

"How can we help?"

Sam pointed to the gas meter on their belt. "The carbon dioxide level is too high. It needs to be 400 parts per million or lower. Does that make sense?"

There was a pause. It seemed a very long pause to Sam. They were worried they didn't understand. Then, slowly, they started to feel a lot better.

"Yes, thank you! I feel much better. Can you warm it up in here?"

"We are sorry. We had not carefully studied your planet's atmosphere, and the atmosphere in your ship was exhausted. And, of course, we don't know your... makeup. We will increase the temperature a few... degrees."

"Thank you! And thanks for saving my life."

"Of course, what else would we do?"

Sam didn't have a good answer, so they decided to change the topic.

"You have learned how to speak our language."

"Yes, we can speak both languages you sent us now. You are very... different than we are."

Sam was sure that was true.

"Why have you come here? Do you mind if I ask?"

"Mind... ah, no we don't mind. We need to explain ourselves."

"Yes, and I imagine we need to explain ourselves."

"We understand. We were once like you."

"Like us?"

"Wishing to destroy what was unfamiliar... alien."

"I am sorry that some of us are like that."

"Some of you?"

"Yes, not all of us agreed with this approach."

There was a pause. Sam imagined a hushed conversation, but they had no idea who they were talking to or what was going on.

"We understand now. Let us tell you why we are here."

"Wait... what are my people doing?"

"They are sending explosive projectiles at us."

"Idiots."

"I don't understand. They cannot damage the ship. It is stronger than you know—we had to build it to withstand interstellar space."

"Never mind. We should open communication with the ship—get them to stop."

"If you think that is right... We will open a narrow band channel to your ship like the one you used to send us your language data—you can speak with them, as can we."

"Wait... on top of the narrowband, also broadcast the entire conversation, both sides, on wideband. I want all of my people in the system to be able to hear this."

"As you wish."

There was another pause, and then the voice spoke again.

"Both channels are open."

"Captain McAdams, Sam Julian here."

There was a pause, and then they heard the captain's voice.

"Mx. Julian, are you a prisoner?"

"I am only a prisoner of circumstance, Captain. I am in a room with air I can breathe. I couldn't go anywhere else—I imagine I would die. They breathe completely different air."

"I see. Are you badly injured?"

"No, Captain, I am mostly fine."

"That is good to hear."

"Captain, they are on this line, can speak English, and are ready to tell us why they are here. I think you should listen. And while you are listening, can you stop firing the missiles? The only thing it is doing is giving me a headache. They say that you can't damage their ship with them."

There was a pause, and after a while, they noticed that the sounds of thrumming and booming stopped.

"Alright, we will listen to your purpose here."

The deep, mechanical, alien voice started to speak.

"Our planet is gone. Thirty-three cycles ago, our sun went... supernova. We had three cycles to prepare and could only build this one colony ship. It houses... about five hundred thousand of us, the last of our kind. We are in search of a place we can call home. We know that your third planet is poisonous to us—we could not live there, even if we wished.

"About four hundred and thirty cycles ago, an exploratory ship left our planet to come here to establish a colony on the fourth planet. We had expected this colony to thrive, but we have since learned that it perished long ago. We still don't understand why."

Sam said, "And why this system? There are others closer that might also have habitable planets."

"Yes, indeed, that is true. We know four systems with habitable planets within... ten light years."

The captain said, "You know of life in other systems?"

"Yes."

"So please answer Mx. Julian's question—why here?"

"Many, many cycles ago, more than twenty-five hundred, one came to us. This one told us that we needed to come here, to this star."

"Who was that? An alien?"

The captain seemed upset to Sam. They had to admit, this was a bit weird.

"No, it was one of us. We revere It. We follow what It told us to do, everything It told us to do."

Sam groaned inwardly. Oh, no, they thought, just what we needed: religious aliens!

"So, what do you need now?"

"We need a place to call home. If you would allow it, we would settle on the fourth planet—where the old... colony was supposed to be."

"We cannot allow that."

"Then we will die drifting in space."

"Captain, we can't let them..." Sam heard murmuring that they couldn't understand—definitely human voices coming from the *Corinth*. They seemed urgent. Then, the Commander spoke in a clipped, angry voice.

"This conversation is over!" There was dead air.

Sam felt the blood drain from her face. Sam was in big trouble. They discovered the wideband signal and decided that they would rather stop the conversation than have it broadcast.

"What happened? Did we displease them?"

"I displeased them. I guess they discovered the wideband signal and realized that the secret is now out."

"Secret?"

"It's a long story."

"We have some time. Is your name Mx. Julian?"

"Not really. The name I go by is 'Sam'."

"I can call you Sam?"

"Please do. What is your name?"

"My name is Droat. That is changed so you could say it. My mouth couldn't say 'Sam', and your mouth couldn't say my name. But that will do."

"OK, Droat. May I ask what you look like?"

The window side of her room started to clear, and they saw a very strange-looking creature sitting on the floor of a room about the same size as hers. Its mouth started to move.

"Here I am, Sam."

Droat was very large, certainly by human standards. It had what looked to Sam like overlapping scales on the outside, except they seemed to them that they were made of some sort of tightly woven fur rather than a hard substance. It had four long, strong-looking legs, which were folded under it, and two arms, each with seven fingers— two looked like thumb equivalents. They imagined that they would be capable of very fine manipulation. It had a long tail that whipped about on occasion. They realized that the closest thing they could think of that it looked like was a centaur.

Droat's head was rather large, with large, almost rabbit-looking ears, but wider, and eyes that were huge and oval in the horizontal direction. Sam guessed their horizontal visual field would be greater than 180 degrees. Their mouth was smallish, in comparison to the size of their head, and Sam could see a row of blunt looking teeth. They weren't an expert at this, but they would bet anything Droat's people were herbivores, with the eyes and ears to detect predators.

Sam was curious about one particular thing Droat had said.

"Droat, why did you call that one you followed 'It'?"

"Yes, Sam. We are born… without sex and choose a sex for our first mating. We then change sex several times during our lives."

"That is quite different than us. Most of us are born and live as one sex; some of us, like me, choose differently but can't change sex for mating. You must think us weird, perhaps."

"No, not weird. We have encountered beings like you before."

"Before?"

"Yes. It is a long story. It will have to wait for another time."

Sam didn't like the sound of that. It seemed that Droat felt bad for something, but they couldn't tell what it could be. There was a pause, then Droat began to speak again.

"Sam, what is next?"

"I don't know, Droat. We could try to recontact them just in narrowband. Or we could wait a while and see what they do. I know that eventually, they will want to recover me."

"You will need to return to your ship soon."

"Why?"

"We cannot feed you. There is water to drink on that side panel— we have purified it for you. But any food we produce for you would be poisonous."

"Then I guess you are right, Droat. I need to go back soon."

"Calling the aliens and Mx. Julian…"

Droat said, "Sam, they are communicating by narrowband."

"OK, answer them also just in narrowband."

After a brief moment, Sam said, "Yes, Captain, we are here."

"That little stunt of yours will cost you, Mx. Julian."

Sam was silent.

"You, alien..."

Sam could hardly believe her ears.

"Its name is 'Droat'."

"Well, then, Mr. Droat... We need to retrieve Mx. Julian."

"Yes, they must return. We cannot feed them."

"How can we accomplish this?"

"We are in the process of building a docking ring using a design we gleaned from observing your ship."

"We would like to send you detailed specifications..."

"That would be most welcome."

"The specifications are now on their way. How soon can you have this docking ring completed?"

"In... twelve of your hours."

Sam was only moderately surprised. They imagined that Droat's people were at least several hundred years ahead of humans in terms of technology, possibly more. They got prepared for a wait; They hoped they'd be able to ask Droat questions while they waited.

They realized they were thirsty and decided to try the water Droat said that was on the side of their room. They could see what looked sort of like a faucet, although it seemed that the water would be coming directly up at their face if they turned it on.

"Droat, can you give me a little instruction in the use of this water faucet?"

"Certainly, Sam. Push the green button there on the side, the longer you push, the more forceful the water will go out of the faucet."

Sam put their head above the opening in the faucet, and touched the green button briefly, they thought. Not briefly enough, obviously. A powerful stream of water hit them right in the face, getting in their eyes and nose, and drenching their head immediately. They sputtered and coughed, but they managed to touch the button again quickly.

"I'm sorry, Sam, clearly that isn't calibrated for you. Just a moment. Try it again."

This time, they cautiously kept their face away from the faucet as they touched it, and a gentle flow started, which they then were able to easily drink from. The water tasted fine and was refreshing. They touched the button again and sat back down facing Droat.

"Thank you, Droat."

"You are welcome, Sam."

"Droat, do you mind if I ask you some questions? We have time to wait."

"Indeed, I'm happy to."

"How old is your civilization—do you know?"

"We have many different ages—I imagine it is the same for you. Our current age we date as beginning after Turool left us."

"Left?"

"I guess the correct translation for you would be that Turool died. We don't quite have that word in our language."

"OK, keep going."

"The age before that we call the dark age—it was an age of chaos and violence. It lasted about three thousand cycles."

Sam was having a hard time figuring out how herbivores would become a violent species, but they guessed that it was possible.

"Before the dark ages was what we call our 'divine age'—we had developed a peaceful society where everyone was valued and loved."

"What changed, Droat?"

"That, Sam, is the subject of many a... many an academic treatise. Some say that age never existed. Others say that greed and hatred between tribes grew so high that there was violence. I don't have an answer for you."

"Tribes? You have tribes?"

"We had tribes. We no longer do. Turool ended the tribal strife and united us as one people."

"How did you govern yourselves?"

"Turool left us with a... a group of leaders. Twelve in all."

"Twelve? No, really? Twelve?"

"Yes, Sam. Why is that a surprise?"

"Well..."

"What is it, Sam?"

"Never mind, Droat, keep going. So, you all follow these twelve leaders?"

"Yes. When one dies, a new one is elected from among us."

"Elected? They campaign to become a new leader?"

"No, Sam. A slate of candidates comes from a nomination process. And… individuals generally don't want to become a leader."

"They don't?"

"Why should they? It's a hard job. No more mates, you have to be isolated from peers and families, it's not a lot of… fun."

"In our worlds, people actively want the jobs, because it gives them money, power and influence."

"Well, our leaders certainly have power and influence."

"So, who are the twelve now?"

"We don't have twelve anymore, Sam. Seven decided to stay on the planet, five are on this colony ship. There now are only five of us."

"I'm sorry, Droat."

"It is as it is, Sam."

"Wait… you said five of *us*. Are you a leader?"

"I am, Sam. I am the youngest, chosen two cycles before the nova. Do you mind if I ask you a question?"

"Not at all, Droat." Sam wondered what the question was about.

"We sent a probe to your fourth planet."

"I know. I found it."

"You found it? Your ship was in contact with it in that belt of asteroids?"

"Yes, that was me."

"How fortuitous!"

"Fortuitous?"

"Well, Sam, don't you think it is an unlikely event that the first person to make contact with our probe is also the first person to make contact with us?"

"You have a point there, Droat."

"Sam, we don't know why our colony on Mars is gone."

"I have a theory, Droat."

"A theory?"

"The SolGov military will likely have my head for this…"

"Sam! They… decapitate people?"

Sam laughed. "That's a figure of speech, Droat. No, they don't do that anymore, although people used to. They do still kill people as punishment, though. It's not outside the realm of reality that I might be punished in that way..."

"Then don't tell me, Sam."

"You need to know, Droat. When I discovered your probe, and ended up on Mars, I found out that people had found your lost colony. It was abandoned, probably quite some time ago. There are writings on the walls, and they left little shapes behind."

"Shapes?"

"Yes. Um, a colleague of mine called them 'Platonic Solids'."

"'Platonic?' I don't understand that word."

"Plato was the name of a famous old Earth philosopher. Let me remember—they are regular shapes and have congruent sides."

"Ah... you are talking about Holy Shapes. Yes, it makes sense that they left them behind."

"Holy Shapes?"

"Sam, in reviewing all of the language and other information you sent, it seems that some of you, at least, have a concept of some sort of supreme, unifying force or being. I think the word for it in your language is 'God.'"

"Yes, Droat, some people believe in God. I don't really. I mean... I don't really know."

"I understand, Sam. We also believe in a supreme, unifying force. We don't have a name for it, however."

"So, how do you talk about it?"

"We don't talk about it, Sam. We believe that this supreme force is understood best by looking at perfection. One of the ways we look at perfection is in geometry and mathematics."

Sam was a little confused and wanted to finish their story.

"Droat, I'd like to keep telling my story—I need to get it out."

"Of course, Sam. Please continue. I'm sorry for my digression."

"It's OK, Droat. So... when I lived on the Moon, that's Earth's moon, I worked for a mining company. And there was a big brouhaha over a cave that was found on the Moon. I found out later that the writings found in the Mars cave are similar to the writings in that Moon cave. And we also heard about a secret crater that was off-limits to all without the highest security clearance. My friends and I hypothesize that that crater is the site of the colony that moved from Mars."

"Sam! That's wonderful news!"

"No, Droat, it's not. We believe that colony was destroyed some time ago."

Droat was silent for a while, then spoke.

"Is there any chance there are survivors?"

Sam obviously didn't know much about Droat's emotional life and didn't know how the computer would translate the tone of Droat's voice, but the tone had most definitely changed.

"Honestly, Droat, with how they are reacting, I can't imagine it. I'm so sorry, Droat, we humans are pretty problematic."

"Sam, that's not true—all of you aren't this way. You aren't."

"But I'm not in power, Droat. I'm just an asteroid hunter and a scientist."

"I do understand, Sam, why you said that they would 'have your head.' If we were a vengeful species…"

"But you aren't, are you?"

"No, Sam. And we don't even have any weapons, in any case. We are at your mercy."

"Droat, my friends and I will do everything we can to try to make sure they don't destroy you. I just wish I could guarantee that we will prevail."

"I understand, Sam."

Sam realized they were getting very sleepy. It probably made sense for them to get some rest.

"Droat, I'm tired—I need to take a rest."

"Alright, Sam."

"Can you dim the lights?"

"Certainly, Sam. How much time would you like to rest?"

"Just a few hours, Droat. Say, four?"

Tina, April 2107

Tina sat at her desk, transfixed. She had listened to the wideband message perhaps twenty times. Because she loved Sam, she was worried about them, but yet it was clear that Sam was in safe hands—perhaps even safer hands than they would be on the *Corinth* after they got back. Tina figured Sam would be up for treason charges after what they did. Tina was very glad that Sam wasn't badly injured in the process.

The fact that the *Corinth* fired on the alien ship before it was clear that it was a danger, and then continued to fire on the alien ship after they knew Sam was safe, angered Tina greatly. It built upon the anger she was already harboring against SolGov about what they were trying to do to Mars.

She'd had a beer with Kevin last night, and the MIP got a very clear warning from SolGov that if they tried to run any candidates in the next election cycle on Mars, SolGov would arrest known MIP members. SolGov didn't care about Mars democracy—they just wanted to control Mars. Kevin was saying that they were getting ready to break off. Tina thought this situation with the alien ship would be the precipitating event.

Marsies knew the aliens were headed here, but the last poll that Tina had commissioned suggested that over 82% of the people of Mars wanted to give the aliens a home if they proved to be friendly. And this conversation with Sam, the SolGov Captain and the alien made it clear that they indeed were friendly and bore them no ill will. Tina was sure that that number would rise substantially after the transmission with Sam. And she figured that many Marsies would be as angry with SolGov as she was.

She was getting prepared to write the last article for the *Times* she would write. She would pull no punches. She would describe the reaction of Mars officials to the wideband transmission—she'd already booked appointments with the Governor, the head of Mars Air Control, and the Mars Safety Director.

She didn't know what to make of the statement of the alien, Droat, about why they came here. And it was also clear that they had no knowledge of the Moon colony. That was something she would put in the article as well. She composed emails to Holly and Ama, asking for a meeting with the two of them. They should know what was coming. She also sent a message to Jurgen—she'd probably need a job in a few days.

Sam, April 2107

Sam was sad to say goodbye to Droat. They had enjoyed spending most of the last twelve hours with... it. They had a hard time calling Droat "it." That just didn't seem right. Droat was, at the moment, male, but having been female twice before in... "it's" life, calling Droat a "he" didn't seem right, either. Maybe they'd adopt calling Droat ze or they, but Sam somehow doubted it.

Anyway, Sam had learned a lot about Droat and its people. They were finally able to drag out of Droat what had seemed so difficult about their previous encounter with intelligent life. Apparently, sometime before their Revered One, whose name was transliterated as Turool, was born, a ship had landed with about two hundred of the last members of an intelligent alien species from a neighboring star whose planet had become uninhabitable. They tried to make contact out of their desperation. Droat's people had apparently wiped them out.

It apparently was a source of deep shame, and apparently, Turool had helped them out of that shame, find ways to redeem themselves, and told them how to live their lives. And Turool told them to find Sol and that they would need to come here one day.

Apparently, Turool had also told them that the people of this planet would try to wipe them out, too, and might succeed. Droat expressed that its people were rather equanimous about this possible outcome. Sam was sure they were going to do everything in their power to make sure it didn't happen.

Sam had never been much for religion, and their conversations with Droat on that topic had been a little difficult for them. They were agnostic on the issue of whether there was a supreme being or not. Sam figured this supreme being, if it existed, didn't care much about them, so the feeling was mutual. When they had been in the CPS camp, one year they had been visited by a group of born-again Christians, who tried really hard to convert Sam. When they told them about their gender, some of them tried to explain that God could cure their of something they had no interest in changing, and the rest shunned them. Sam had had no patience for religious people after that. They always had some appreciation for some of the religious icons, like Moses, Jesus, and Gandhi. It was clear to Sam that Droat, and Droat's people, were deeply religious. It was hard for them to square that with what they perceived of most religious people. Further, based upon what Droat said about this Turool, it bore a disturbing resemblance to what they knew about the ancient man called Jesus.

"Sam, everything is ready. The corridor between your room and the docking ring is filled with your atmosphere. The ship that is here to take you back is now fully docked, and ready."

"Thank you Droat. I hope we meet again. It has been a pleasure spending this time with you."

"Sam, I have enjoyed this time too. I hope you don't suffer too much for your actions."

"Me too, Droat." They smiled at Droat and waved, then realized Droat probably didn't know much about what a smile or a wave meant. They might have even insulted it. They hoped not.

A door to their room opened, and they walked through the deep red corridor, and could see what looked like an airlock at the end of it. It was open. Sam stepped in and realized they were now at zero gravity. The door shut, and they felt a breeze as the air from the shuttle filled the airlock, replacing the air they had been breathing for a while. They noticed a difference in the smell of the air. This seemed sweeter. Sam wondered about the mix they'd been breathing all this time.

The inner door opened, and they were greeted by two people floating in isolation encounter suits. They guessed it was appropriate, but they had a hard time not being annoyed.

"Mx. Julian, you will need to be in isolation and undergo medical testing before we can release you to the custody of the military police."

"I understand." They didn't like that last part.

"Please go over to that seat and strap in."

There was a seat in the back of the shuttle. They pushed their way back, pulled themselves down to the seat and strapped in. The two in isolation suits moved to the front to pilot the shuttle back to the *Corinth*.

Gareth, April 2107

Gareth and Sharron were sitting around a large conference room table, and the two huge view screens along the long wall of the room had six other conference rooms across the world. The candidate was sitting at the head of the conference table in the Mexico City office. London, Beijing, Johannesburg, Rio, and Melbourne offices were represented.

Gareth had listened to the conversation probably ten times in the past two hours since he heard about it, and the sentence "...It was one of us. We revere It. We follow what It told us to do, everything It told us to do" kept ringing in his ears. He couldn't help it. No one else seemed to care about it, but he cared, deeply for some reason. He wanted to learn more about this one they revere.

The candidate spoke. "Clearly, the Captain was obeying the commands of his Commander-in-Chief, President Volkov. This is perfect fodder for our campaign. We demand that he stop, listen to the needs of the aliens, and not have the blood of a whole intelligent species on our hands."

They spent the next two hours strategizing, and Gareth and Sharron had their marching orders. There were several media appearances already scheduled for him in Washington, including an appearance on Friday at the same time with his brother on a show that had been started to cover the alien story ever since the beginning.

His brother, now the voice of the movement to obliterate the aliens, would be an interesting match for Gareth. He hadn't seen his brother in years, and ever since he not only declined the opportunity to join his brother's institute, but became a vocal opponent, he and his brother were no longer in contact.

Sam, April 2107

Sam slowly awoke, and they were surprised to be in a standard-issue bunk. The last thing they remembered was being given an I.V. once they arrived on the ship, which must have had anesthetic. They looked around the room, and it looked like a standard-issue quarters... except they were the only ones in it. They slowly got up, and got very dizzy, so they lay back down. They could take it slow.

The trip back to the *Corinth* had been uneventful. They had docked with the ship, and they and the crew of the shuttle went through the airlock, into a see-through tent sort of thing. They rolled the tent through a part of the *Corinth*, and they ended up in what looked like a medical facility, and everyone was wearing isolation gear like the shuttle crew. They were put on a gurney and then given the I.V. That was all they remembered.

They had no idea how long it had been since they'd been on the alien ship. Sam had no idea how much closer to Mars they were. They hoped that they hadn't returned to trying to destroy the aliens. They fell asleep, thinking of Droat.

Sam woke again, and nothing in her room had changed. They went to the bathroom and decided that a shower would be a good idea. They looked in the locker next to the bunk, and they were hardly surprised to find their stuff. They pulled out their comfy fleece lounge pants—a luxury of clothing that took up weight and space, but they always thought was worth it.

After the shower, they figured she'd try the door. It was, unsurprisingly, locked. They figured that if they were really, really lucky, they'd just be locked up until they got back to Mars. If they were unlucky... They'd never heard anything good about the prison asteroids, and they honestly weren't sure that they would prefer them to execution.

Sam realized that they'd go crazy without anything to do and just these four walls to stare at. They were just in the middle of figuring out which of the varied theorems they knew by heart and could figure out how to solve in their head when they heard the door click. It opened, and Commander Herman stood in the door. They stood up.

"Mx. Samantha Julian, if you would please follow me."

No one ever called them that. They were in deep shit. They followed the Commander down a corridor, and into a room with two chairs. They assumed that there was a camera, too.

"Please sit." Sam sat.

The Commander looked at her seriously.

"If you were in the military, you would be facing an immediate court-martial, a dishonorable discharge, and life in the brig." It was odd, the way he said it. It was almost as if he was reminding himself.

"How is that relevant to *me?*"

He flinched.

"It's… it's not. You are currently looking at treason charges."

"I see. Then I wish to see an advocate since that is my right. I assume we are under SolGov jurisdiction?"

"Yes, we are under SolGov jurisdiction. There isn't an advocate on the ship."

"OK, I'll wait until we reach Mars." Sam was determined to say nothing more.

He started to look a little desperate. "Look, you have information about the aliens we need."

"I'm sorry, I have the right to not say anything until I have an advocate present."

"You are going to make this difficult for me, aren't you?"

"That is not my intent, sir. My intent is to make it as easy for me as possible." They couldn't help but smile. They figured they'd pay for the smile, too. But when they looked at him, they saw a tiny little upturn of the right side of his mouth.

"I am empowered to make you a deal."

"And that deal is?"

"Nothing you say during this debriefing will be held against you or used in court. We will focus on what happened *after* you got inside the ship, that's all—we won't discuss anything that went before."

Sam considered this. If they lied, it would come out in the trial, and they'd be set free, for sure. They really didn't have anything to lose, and they had something to gain because if they told them what they'd learned, then perhaps they would let Droat and its people alone settle on Mars. But Sam would have to be careful in what they said, and they realized they would have to withhold that they told Droat about the Moon.

"I will agree, but I have one request."

"And that is?"

"That you allow one of the non-military Xenoscientists on board to hear the debrief in person."

Commander Herman rolled his eyes. Sam could imagine him thinking, "Fucking scientists, they always mess things up."

"Alright, Mx. Julian, you will have your wish. Do you have a preference?"

"Yes, I'd like Lodan Greenfellow. I have some biological information that is important for her to hear."

"Very well. I'm sending you back to your room so you can eat dinner and sleep. We'll reconvene tomorrow morning."

"One thing, Commander?"

"Yes."

"What time and day is it?"

"It is 1700 hours on Thursday." Ah, they had only lost two days.

"Thanks."

John, April 2107

The more John heard from Sam about the aliens, the more he was sure that he could not continue in his position. As he left the room behind Lodan, after Sam had been taken back by an MP to the one quarters set aside as the brig on this ship, he walked slowly to Captain McAdam's office. He was planning to resign his commission effective immediately.

He felt as if he was facing a huge void—he hadn't known anything except the military in his whole life—what else could he do? At some level, it didn't really matter—he had no choice but to pull himself out of things.

"Commander Henry!" He looked up to see Dr. Wynn walking briskly down the hall towards him.

"Hello, Dr. Wynn."

"Commander Henry, I have just received word from Captain McAdams that he wants to deploy our weapon. I'm getting everything in place. You'll need to report to the fore weapons array."

"What? On what basis is he deploying?"

"I understand he has received orders from the top."

He couldn't let this happen.

"When?"

"Within twenty minutes. He expects to turn of spin soon."

John tried his hardest to look as if he was going to do exactly what was expected of him.

"Thank you, Dr. Wynn. I will go forward immediately."

"Thank you, Commander."

She continued walking, and John walked to the nearest information screen.

"Location of Lodan Greenfellow."

"Aft lounge."

He ran as fast as he could, doing some quick calculations in his head. He could get back to the lounge, tell Lodan, and get to the fore weapons array within 10 minutes. It would take him about five minutes to arrange the fuel load inside the weapon to vent into space. Yes, that was the way to deal with this.

He saw Lodan in the hallway outside of the lounge, and told her to release the transcripts, and that he had to stop what was happening. He didn't have time to explain, and as he turned to run toward the hub tube, he could see the puzzled look on her face. He knew that she would do as he asked—it was something she wanted to do anyway.

An elevator arrived, and he punched the button that told it to go all the way to the hub. He could feel the gravity decrease the closer he got. He was floating, holding on to a handhold by the time the doors opened to the large hallway in the center of the hub. He found a spare transport cart, strapped in, and set it to go at full speed to the forward section of the ship. During the few minutes as he watched the section signs whizz by, he was struck by how different he felt. How free, even though he realized that his actions might land him in the brig for a very long time.

The cart slowed down, and he unstrapped himself and grabbed the handholds leading to the forward weapons array control panel, which was down one of those totally claustrophobic service lanes. He put his ID plate next to the access control, and the door to the lane came unlocked, and he swung it open, and swung himself headfirst into the lane. He pulled himself hand over hand using the handholds that were on the walls of the lane and came finally to the control panel. He knew the sequence—they had rehearsed this in case of emergency. The fusion fuel was quite volatile, and would endanger the ship in certain circumstances, so a procedure to vent the fuel into space had been necessary. And that was coming in handy right now.

He went through the process—pushing specific sets of icons, and then he finally pulled the large manual lever on the right-hand side of the control panel. He watched the dials as all of the fusion fuel vented into space and stayed there until all indications showed that there was no more fuel. Well, the deed was done, and there was nothing more to do except hand himself in.

He made his way slowly back to the main part of the ship and was not surprised to see Captain McAdams and a couple of MPs greet him as he left the hub tube.

"Captain."

"Do you wish to explain your actions, Commander Herman?"

"Not at this time, Captain. I'll wait for the court-martial."

Lodan, April 2107

Kylee asked, "How is Sam?"

Lodan, Michael, Tai and Kylee were sitting in the lounge. Lodan had just spent most of the day with Sam and Commander Herman in the debrief. What Sam had to say was earth-shattering. Even Commander Herman seemed moved by the description Sam gave of the incident where the aliens wiped out another species, then changed their ways. Lodan couldn't imagine a situation where humans wouldn't let these aliens settle on Mars after hearing that story and hearing the willingness of the aliens to be wiped out as some sort of atonement for their sin.

Lodan answered, "Sam is fine. They are a bit shaken up, and mostly, I think they were bored out of their mind with nothing to do. I got permission to give their some tablets filled with books. They were happy to tell us what had happened, and all they knew about the aliens, who call themselves the Kurool, which, of course, is a rough transliteration from something we can't possibly pronounce."

Tai said, "Have you been given any permission to disseminate this information?"

"No, it's still classified, level seven. Interestingly, before we began, Commander Herman told me in no uncertain terms that I would be prosecuted if any little bit of it got out. But at the end of the debrief, he didn't remind me. Maybe I'm making too much of it, but he seemed different at the end. Anyway, it's going to take political pressure to get this opened up—I'm not ready to disseminate it without authorization."

Michael said, "Well, the good thing is that's happening. Last I heard the opposition candidate Montoya is hammering Volkov's position on the aliens and is now up by 15 points in the latest polling since the wideband transmission. Unfortunately, that seems to be hardening Volkov's position. It's too bad the election won't happen until months after the ship arrives at Mars."

Lodan asked, "How did they think they could stop them from settling on Mars?" Kylee shook her head.

Michael answered, "Well, they could bomb the shit out of them on the ground. Make it impossible to settle in."

"I guess. Silly people. Why is it that we can't live with these aliens peacefully? They certainly seem interesting."

Kylee raised her hand. "Look, people, we have to figure out how we are going to organize the hours of information we got from Sam's debrief."

Michael said, "I suggest we simply divide it by field. I'll take on the anthropological, Lodan, you can take on the biological, and Tai and Kylee can take on the information gathered about the star and planets of Cassiopeia, and the chemical information Sam gained while they was there. We'll collectively write an introduction and conclusion."

Lodan said, "That sounds good. I'm glad that they are interested in talking to us further. I hope we get the chance."

Michael said, "I hope so, too."

They got up to go back to their duty stations. As she was walking down the corridor, Lodan heard someone behind her shout.

"Lodan!"

She turned to see Commander Herman running toward her.

"Tell everyone. Please. I'll take the fall for it—get that whole transcript of Sam's debrief to Mars and Earth! They are about to do something terrible, and I'm going to try to stop it—but I might not succeed."

Lodan was shocked. "But..."

"Please. I have to go now." Lodan watched him run toward the hub tube.

She didn't even have much time for that to sink in when she heard Captain McAdams's voice on the comm.

"Your attention please, your attention please. We will be turning off spin in approximately 10 minutes. If you are on duty, return to your duty station. If not, go back to your bunk and strap in."

Lodan looked around. "Huh? Turning off spin? What can this be about?"

Tai shook his head. "I don't know, but it can't be good."

Lodan looked at Kylee, who was ashen.

"What is it Kylee?"

"It was a conversation I happened to overhear as I walked to breakfast between Dr. Wynn and Captain McAdams. Just a snippet, and, in itself not important, but given what Commander Henry just said..."

"What?"

"Captain McAdams asked Dr. Wynn how their 'baby' was. Dr. Wynn said, 'ready.'"

Lodan said, "I don't get it."

Lodan, Dr. Wynn got her Nobel Prithey for the controlled fusion process that made fusion energy on Earth and other places finally possible."

"And?"

"I read an article written by Dr. Wynn about three years ago detailing how this process could be used to create an extremely powerful directional weapon."

"We'd better go back to our bunks and get strapped in. I certainly hope this weapon can't damage them."

Lodan returned to her bunk, strapped herself in, and prepared the information for release on the Solar net. It would be slow—she had to securely upload it through several proxies and encrypted networks, then send an enigmatic email to a friend, who would then tell the press where to find it. But it would make it happen in the next hour. She worked quickly on her tablet.

Sam, April 2107

Sam heard Captain McAdams and strapped into the bunk. They had no idea what was going on. Lodan had brought some inert tablets with a bunch of books on them, and they appreciated that greatly. It was hard to be disconnected from the world, but Sam was happy at least not to be bored silly. Lodan had filled it with books on advanced physics, geology, astronomy, stellar dynamics, planetology, theoretical Xenoscience, Artificial Intelligence and... a ton of mysteries, most of which they hadn't read yet. They had to smile. These books would likely keep them busy for the entire trip, although they might have to read some of them twice.

Sam got absorbed in reading the latest book by the famous Astronomer Koi Thomas, when spin started back, and they felt her body settle softly into the bunk. In a few minutes, the door opened, and Commander Herman walked in. Someone else closed the door behind him, and he sat on the bunk opposite hers. Sam sat up, and just looked at him.

He looked at them with a crooked smile. Now they were really confused. They waited for him to speak.

Finally, he said, "I'm in the brig, too."

"You are? What did you do?"

"Disobeyed direct orders."

"Oh?" Sam honestly could not figure out what he could have done. "Yeah."

"Are you going to fill me in or just be enigmatic?"

"I stopped the discharge of a weapon."

"What weapon?"

"I can't say. I'm in enough trouble without getting into more."

"Ah, I see. Immediate court-martial and such?"

He laughed. "Indeed."

"I guess you won't tell me why?"

"No, I will. It seemed, well, somehow a crime against everything that is human to allow us to replay what the Kurool did before."

Sam nodded. "It does, doesn't it?"

"I couldn't see it happen. I just couldn't allow it. I didn't think I would ever find anything that would cause me to disobey orders, but I have, now."

"Do you understand me better now?"

He laughed. "Yes, I do. It just took me longer to get there."

"So, what's next?"

"We go back to Mars."

"Can they fire that weapon without you?"

"Not now, they can't. I permanently disabled it and sent the necessary fuel into space."

Sam raised her eyebrows, then stuck their hand out to the Commander. He took it.

"Congratulations, sir."

They laughed together.

"Might as well call me John, Mx. Julian."

"OK, John. And *please* call me Sam."

"You got it."

They both settled down. Sam figured it would be a while. They smiled and turned to John.

"You like mysteries?"

Tina April 2107

An insistent chime woke her. She could see the pulsing yellow light on her desk view screen.

"Accept message."

"Urgent Text Message from Ian Herbert on Earth." She wondered why Ian, of all people, would send her an urgent message.

She got up out of bed and sat at her desk.

"Display, please."

The message was simple—Ian had a friend who was on the *Corinth*. He knew of a drop box to get a large data dump from the *Corinth*—something having to do with a debrief of someone. The message was somewhat cryptic, but it included the password to the drop box. He trusted her to protect his identity. She would, of course.

Ian was a friend of hers in New York City. He was one of her more unusual friends. He was an urban farmer, and urban farming had been in his family since the urban farming heydays of the 2020's and 30's. He took care of about fifty rooftop farms in lower Manhattan, one of which was on top of her building. Tina couldn't imagine what kind of friend Ian had on the *Corinth*... Ah. She remembered Lodan, the agronomist. She bet that was the connection. She'd keep that information to herself.

She logged into the drop box and looked at the information there. One large text file, some audio files, and some other files with date labels from last year. She wondered what those were. She downloaded the whole thing, which took quite a while—the drop box was replicated on Mars servers, but the Mars network had much less bandwidth than the Earth network, so things just took longer.

"Send these files to my tablet once they are downloaded," she told her AI.

"Affirmative."

She picked up her tablet, and went back to her bed, propping up some pillows. She began reading the first large text file, which was the transcript of the debriefing of Sam. She couldn't help but smile. The wideband transmission a few days ago from the ship had been a little bit of a surprise, but somehow, she'd known that Sam would be a central figure in all of this. She kept reading, totally enthralled by the content of what Sam had to say about the aliens. After a long while, she looked at the clock in the lower right-hand corner of her tablet display, and she realized that it was early, rather than late, and she gave up the idea of getting any more sleep tonight.

"Please start the coffee."

"Affirmative."

It would be done in a few minutes. She'd need it. She was already planning how she was going to report on this. And then she remembered that she had a big staff now, and *other* people to do the grunt work. Her article on Sam's wideband transmission, the Mars response to it, and the expose about the Moon cave and possible colony had, indeed, gotten her fired from the *Times*. They threatened a lawsuit if she sent the story anywhere else, but she went and sold it to the *Mars Monitor*, knowing full well that the likelihood that the *Times* would be able to win a suit of that sort was fairly low—it felt like a risk she could take.

This was going to be a total scoop for the *Monitor*. They would, of course, release all of the files when they reported on it, but people were going to hear about this from the *Monitor* first. Jurgen had been happy to have her join the *Monitor*, and she was put in charge of the SolGov department, which seemed humorously ironic to Tina. She had a staff of six reporters, one of whom was Ama, who was happy to stay on Mars and ditch the *Times*. Holly had family connections on Earth, and she went back home. Tina doubted that the *Times* was going to send anyone else to Mars, ever.

Gareth, April 2107

Gareth sat uncomfortably in the chair in the green room, after being made up, and looked at his brother, who was sitting on the couch. They had stiffly greeted each other, but then hadn't said a word. Gareth finally decided to break the silence.

"How's mum?"

Lionel looked at him with steel in his eyes.

"You don't care how she is."

"Excuse me?"

"I said you don't care how she is. How could you, supporting these... these evil beings who will destroy us."

"Lionel, you are going over the top. There is no evidence..."

"No evidence? What evidence is needed? The Bible has no mention of them. So, they must be the work of Satan."

"Lionel, the Bible has no mention of cell phones, television, the net or space travel. And last I looked you weren't Amish."

"They killed your son!"

"They did not kill my son! The damn company that dumped the regolith in the river killed my son!"

"You are being willfully blind."

"Lionel, you are being willfully stupid."

They glared at each other for a while, then stopped. It was clearly going to be of no use. He already knew how his mother was anyway, he'd talked with her just yesterday. His mother was far more reasonable about everything than Lionel was.

The producer stuck her head into the room. "Gentlemen, we are ready."

Gareth got up and followed his brother out of the room. Sometimes, he wondered about the wisdom of his father to name all of his male children after some of the lesser-known knights of the Round Table. He had four brothers and one sister—a very large family by modern standards. He was the second child, oldest son, after his sister Lynette, another character of that tale. Lionel was third, Lucan fourth, Percival fifth, and Tristan had been the youngest. Tristan's life had been tragic and short. He died of an overdose of the designer drug, Thrust, when he was only twenty. Percival had left the family at 18, to move to San Francisco. Gareth was the only member of the family who was still in contact with him. Lucan was Lionel's sidekick, always. Lynette married another high-profile evangelical preacher and moved to Texas to be with him. Gareth had heard that he was considering a run for Texas governor.

He sat catty-corner to his brother, and across from the host, whose name he was currently forgetting, but he was sure he would be reminded of shortly.

"One minute." Everything seemed eerily quiet to Gareth. He knew they used surround imaging, so there wouldn't be one camera to look at.

"And... we're live."

"Welcome, everyone. I'm Henri Rondel, and this is... Alien Talk. Today we have with us two brothers who are staunch opponents. One, Lionel Holbright, is Pastor of Calvary Chapel, in Pittsburgh Pennsylvania, and President of the Institute for the Preservation of Humanity. Gareth Holbright is religious liaison for the Montoya campaign, and just recently returned from a stint as a pastor on Mars Colony 6. Welcome to both of you.

Gareth said, "Thank you, Henri."

His brother answered, "It's a pleasure to be here."

"Now I know that you two feel very strongly about this issue. And I want to give you each time to say your piece. First, let's have a brief statement from both of you, then I'll ask questions."

They both nodded.

"Lionel, will you go first?"

"Certainly, Henri. There is no question that there has never been a more dangerous time for people on Earth. Here we are, on the planet the Father gave us, and we must protect it, and us, from harm from without. I don't know much about these aliens, but they did not warn us of their coming, nor did they stop when asked to. From my perspective, that means that they are hostile, and we have every right to stop them. It's God's miracle that their colony didn't survive—otherwise we would have been destroyed by them hundreds of years ago! Hallelujah!"

Gareth felt the acid in his stomach roil as his brother spoke. He had his speech ready—it was very simple. He bided his time, as his brother continued to spew invective for minutes.

"... We will do everything in our power to destroy this dangerous enemy and protect humankind from harm."

"Gareth..."

"Thank you, Henri. I think the answer is actually quite simple. As evangelicals who are supposed to be following the Prince of Peace, we need to ask ourselves, 'What would Jesus do?' I know it seems simplistic, but it's actually quite profound. I don't need to go further than Matthew 5, which says things like 'Blessed are the meek, for they shall inherit the earth.' and 'Blessed are the merciful, for they shall receive mercy.' and 'Blessed are the peacemakers, for they will be called children of God.' That's all I need to hear. Jesus would have wanted us to still our weapons, listen to the aliens, find out their intentions, and welcome them to our system, if they proved peaceful."

Gareth was done. There was no more to be said. He looked at his brother, who was almost apoplectic. His face was suffused with red, and little drops of spittle had begun to form at the corners of his mouth. Gareth had never seen his brother so angry.

"Lionel, you seem to have something you want to say..."

"My poor, ignorant, naive brother! He sadly has become a tool of Satan, using the words of Jesus to justify his position. How many times, in the Bible, has God commanded His chosen people to go against our enemies and be victorious. These aliens are our enemies."

"Lionel, you don't know that. You have no evidence of that. They have not fired *one* shot, even though we have fired on them repeatedly. They saved the life of one of the *Corinth* crew, when they certainly didn't have to. They could have, I don't know, dissected them or something. What evidence, I mean, *real* evidence do you have that they are dangerous to us?"

Of course, Lionel continued his screed, citing things that were not truly evidence. Henri gave Gareth more airtime than Lionel, and also gave Gareth the last word. He used it wisely.

"We are at a critical time in our history. Do we define ourselves by our violent, xenophobic past, or by our better nature, by the peaceful future we want to build for our children? Until these aliens prove themselves harmful by shooting at us, destroying something, or killing someone, we must be friendly. We must treat them with love and hospitality. We have the power to destroy them if they truly prove dangerous, but let's stay our hand, and show them mercy, where we would like to be shown mercy."

Gareth knew that he would never sway his brother. But he hoped that he could sway others.

Gareth returned to election headquarters, which was pandemonium. Something must have happened, but he didn't know what it was. He went to find Phillip, who always knew exactly what was going on. Phillip was on the phone, and motioned Gareth into the room. Gareth sat down on a chair.

"Yes, yes, I know, Mr. Montoya. We're preparing the précis of this information now for the campaign staff. It's huge, I agree. From what I have read so far, I think we need to highlight their experience with that other species. Yes, exactly. Paid for their sins… right. OK. I'll get on it and send you the talking points by midnight. Thanks, Mr. Montoya, yes, indeed, I think you are right. Good night."

He hung up the phone and looked at Gareth.

"I take it you haven't heard."

"Heard what? I was busy on a debate with my brother."

"Ah, that one. Well, we've got a huge bombshell."

"We do?"

"Yes, an inside job. It was just reported by the *Mars Monitor*, and they released everything. Someone on the *Corinth*, we don't know who yet, leaked the debrief transcript of one Samantha Julian, the crew member who was aboard the alien ship. They got to know one alien, called Droat, pretty well. It's amazing stuff. But the most amazing is this: about two thousand years ago or so, the last of some aliens from a different planet that had become uninhabitable, ended up on this alien's planet. And you know what? They wiped them out."

"You're kidding me."

"No, I'm not. And after that, they had this leader, called Turool, who told them to come here, and find meaning from that shame, or something. Read the transcript. We sent out copies to everyone."

"I'd heard about that one—that's the One they revere, I think."

"Yeah, that's the one—and that's up your alley, ain't it?" Phillip smiled.

"I guess you could say that. I'll get to reading."

He went back to his desk and opened his messages. Before he started reading, he forwarded it to Sharron—he'd want to talk with her about it later. It was long, and he decided to go home, and read in the comfort of his couch, with Sharron, who he was sure had already started to read it. He picked up his jacket, and walked out, and walked the few blocks to the metro station. As he sat on the train to his stop, he realized that he wanted to find a way to talk to these aliens. And that meant going back to Mars. He didn't know what his wife would think of that. But there was plenty of time. They had to win this election, first.

He got out at his stop and walked the few blocks to his apartment. Even though it had been only about a week back on Earth, it surprised him how quickly he had gotten used to breathing regular air, and seeing regular sky, instead of being in caves or under domes. He didn't actually relish returning to that. He walked up to his apartment and walked in the door. Sharron was sitting at the kitchen table with her tablet, crying.

He closed the door quickly and went to her. He knelt down next to her, putting his arms around her waist.

"Gareth, this story is so sad…"

"What part of it? I haven't had much time to read it yet."

"How they destroyed that other species, then almost destroyed themselves with shame and madness when they came to understand what they'd done." She looked up at him, tears streaming down her face, snot oozing out of her nose, eyes shining.

"We can't let that happen to us, Gareth."

"I know, love. We won't."

"Gareth, I want to meet them." He should have known. He couldn't help smiling. He got up and went to get her some tissues.

"I know you don't want to go back to Mars, Gareth, but..." She wiped her face with the tissues Gareth gave her.

"It's OK, dear. I want to meet them, too."

Gareth took off his jacket, poured himself some grape juice, took off his shoes, and sat down on the couch and started to read. He couldn't put it down, and when he finished, he could see some early morning light from the sun peeking in the window. Sharron was gone—she must have gone to bed.

He didn't quite know what to think. Everything he read about this character Turool reminded him of Jesus. He just couldn't help it. Turool taught them to live with nonviolence and compassion. Turool taught them love, and the love of God. Of course, it wasn't phrased that way. The aliens were monotheistic... of a sort. Their approach to understanding God with geometry and mathematics was intriguing, for sure. He was sure theologians would be comparing alien theology with human theology for decades to come. But Turool seemed to serve, for the aliens, the same exact role that Jesus did for humans—except that humans hadn't managed to wipe an alien intelligent species from the universe. Although, Gareth thought, it had managed to wipe out plenty of species from Earth. And humans had managed to make something of Jesus that Jesus had never intended. That wasn't the case for Turool. Gareth laughed. Gareth thought it was almost as if Jesus finally found the right species. Humans certainly hadn't done so well with Him.

He got up and padded into the bedroom, where Sharron was gently snoring. He took off his clothes and sidled into bed next to her. She didn't stir. He figured he could get at least a couple of hours sleep.

Lodan May 2107

Lodan said quietly, "They can't trace it to me."

Kylee looked skeptical. "How do you know?"

174

"Before we left, I thought that I might need something like this. So, with the help of a friend of mine, I set up an anonymous drop box. I'd always accessed it from proxies or in public networks, and there was no link for it back to me. I gave my friend the password and told him to find someone in the press he really trusted, and when I gave him the signal, give the information to them. I sent the material to the drop box by a very convoluted set of encrypted pathways, through many proxy gateways. They won't ever find me by following it."

"But can't they find your friend?"

"Nope. The press will protect their sources, and they are allowed to, so my friend is safe. And there is no way for anyone to know which friend of mine it is. I didn't send the message 'go get the stuff from the drop box!' I used a very generic code sequence. Kinda like 'I'm doing fine, how's your Da?'"

"Ah, I get it."

"More than fifty people on this ship got that transcript, and you can be sure that now that it's public, most people on this ship have it, so mere possession can no longer make one a suspect."

"You're clever clever."

Lodan smiled. "Not nearly as clever clever as my friend."

"Well, the shit has well and truly hit the fan. Volkov is vowing to hang the person who leaked the transcript; I've had fifty meetings with Captain McAdams pressuring me to spy on my team, which, of course, I won't do. And the closer the alien gets to Mars, the hotter things get politically. I'm glad I'm not on Earth right now."

"Remember that guy I told you about? Gareth Holbright?"

"Yeah, the Baptist preacher who lost his son in the regolith fiasco?"

"Yup, that one. He has become an activist *for* the aliens."

"Really?"

"Yeah. He's working for the Montoya campaign, and I've seen him speak. He is incredibly charismatic and convincing. Far better than the videos I've seen of his brother, who is on the other side of the fence."

"It's good to have one such as him on our side, for sure."

"Agreed. Anyway, he sent me an email today."

"Really?"

"He wants to let me know that when a team finally forms to study the aliens, he and his wife want to be the team's theologians."

Kylee laughed. "Is he serious?"

"He is. And he has a point. The whole reason the aliens came *here* was because of their religion, you know."

"Well, you have a point, too." Kylee breathed a sigh. "I'm looking forward to when we can quietly communicate with and study the aliens rather than fight people to help them survive. I want to figure out how herbivores evolved to be so intelligent."

"I thought you were a xenoplanetologist."

"I am, but I have my side interests… T minus five months to home. It's going to be a long one."

"Well, at least we can be entertained by politics on Planet Earth."

Sam May 2107

John and Sam were finishing a game of rummy. Sam was glad that the higher-ups had relented and given them a table and a couple of decks of cards. Reading helped cut the boredom, but Sam's highlight of the day was playing cards with John.

"So, Sam, you still haven't told me about your childhood."

"You haven't told me about yours, either."

"You first. I asked first."

"OK, you did. Well, it was pretty sucky." Sam saw that they had a run of Kings, and they put them down.

"Sucky, how?" John drew from the draw pile and put a King down.

"I spent all of my childhood in Florida, in a CPS camp. My parents gave me up when I was only two. I don't even remember them." They drew a card from the draw pile and discarded a three. When they looked up, they saw his eyes shining.

"I grew up in a CPS camp in Mississippi, from when I was three." They almost heard his drawl come out. "Before that, I had been in a foster home. Apparently, my mother dropped me off in a hospital when I was two months old." He drew a card and discarded it.

Sam drew a card. "Well, John, it appears we have more in common than we thought. Rummy."

"Damn, oh, the things in my hand…"

"At least you got to be in a foster home before the shit completely hit the fan."

"I guess. I don't remember it, really. I was too young."

"I remember talking with some older kids, who were around before the camp system, before there were far too many kids for the number of foster families. They hadn't liked it before, but the camps were apparently way worse. I didn't know any different. And I did hear there were worse camps than Florida. I guess Mississippi might well be one."

"Yeah, it was bad. We sometimes ran out of food, and epidemics would kill off hundreds of kids at a time. It was a miracle to emerge out of it. When I was 18, I realized I had two choices. Join the military, and possibly live a decent life, or join a gang, and die young. I chose the former."

"I thought about the military, and even talked to some people about enlisting, but they all said I was too undisciplined."

John snorted, and Sam laughed. "Well, I guess it's true! Anyway, someone had told me about the recruiting program for the Moon colony, and I wanted to get off that rock called Earth anyway, so I joined up. I graduated from mining grunt to an engineering grunt in about 2 years, and from that, signed on to Strelix to asteroid hunt."

"Did you like that work?"

"I loved it. It was amazing to be out there in space for weeks at a time, looking for the right find. I did very well as a Strelix employee and finally could lease my own ship. And then, well, you know the rest of the story."

"Yes, the last asteroid you found was the alien probe. That must have been quite the rush!"

"No, John, it was far from it. You see, I was screwed. Completely. Let me explain. I hadn't found a good, solid find in way too long, and I had missed four payments on my ship. It was about to be repossessed. Well, it was repossessed. Once I latched on to the probe, the fucker changed direction to move directly through Strelix space on its way to Mars. And I had no choice but to hang on and find a way to Mars. In the end, I lost my ship, and I was broke. Kylee saved my butt."

John laughed. "That's a funny story."

"No, it isn't! It was terrible!"

"C'mon, really. from the perspective of this moment?"

Sam had to laugh. They both laughed and had a hard time stopping.

"Yeah, kinda silly. What do you think will happen to us, John?"

"My theory?"

"Yup."

"We're screwed. Me: I get court-martialed and sent to the brig for life. You: you get charged with treason and spend the rest of your life in a prison asteroid."

"Gee, thanks for that."

"I'll tell you my dream, though."

"And that is?"

"Montoya wins the presidency, and they pardon both of us. Your career will progress, but my military career is over even if I'm pardoned."

"Well, if Montoya wins, then Kylee will get a whole new bunch of money to study the aliens, and you can take my place in the lab while I go hunt asteroids in the Kuiper belt!"

"Sam, you are incorrigible! Don't you want to finish your Ph.D.?"

"Kylee told me I can do it remotely while I'm hunting."

"You're serious, aren't you?"

"Yup. Totally."

Chapter 8:
Mars Revolts

Tina May 2107

Tina was on her way to the central dome of Colony 1. There was a protest being organized by the MIP. Similar protests were happening in each of the 6 colonies. They were designed to let SolGov know how Mars felt about the aliens.

Tina had gotten an email from Kevin making it clear that the MIP was going to use the alien issue as the pivot of their campaign for Mars independence. It was a good choice, Tina thought. The vast majority of people on Mars thought that SolGov's approach to the aliens was wrong. And the last system-wide polls taken suggested that this, in fact, was true everywhere, even on Earth. Volkov's position against the aliens was hardening, and he was certainly going against most of the politicians in SolGov—even those in his own party.

She didn't need to be here—she was an editor, now, not a reporter. But she wanted to see what it was like, firsthand. She knew there were a lot of things happening on the political front—Kevin had hinted at some big things happening for the Mars-wide elections in a couple of months.

As she exited the transit system station, she could already see the dome filled with people. A lot of people. There were signs saying things like "Marsies love Droat" and "Give the aliens a home." She wandered around, although at times it was hard to move around, since the dome was so filled. On one side, she saw a group of SolGov military. They looked quite uncomfortable and were completely outnumbered. There was nothing they would be able to do. She also saw the Mars Militia, who were, unlike the SolGov military, among the crowd, participating in the protest. She could already see how this was going to go down. SolGov, preoccupied with the "alien threat" would be spending their time and effort massing their offense on the aliens. In the meantime, the MIP and others were going to use this preoccupation to slip away.

Tina smiled. She knew that Kevin and the others did actually care about the aliens, but she knew opportunism when she saw it.

"Tina!" She turned to see Patrick, a high MIP official, and a friend of both Kevin and Jurgen, walking toward her.

"Hello, Patrick. You all did a great job here—quite the protest."

He shook his head. "Tina, we barely publicized this, in any of the colonies. We expected maybe a couple of hundred people to show up here, and tens of people at the other colonies. Just enough for the cameras. This has nothing to do with us—this is an outpouring for the aliens."

"Well, it's a good thing, in any event."

"Yes, it is, for sure."

"I hear a rumor that you might run for Governor? Is that true? That might be dangerous, given SolGov's insistence on no MIP candidates this July."

"No danger to me. I am running, indeed, as the Progressive Party candidate."

"Huh? I'm missing something! I know that I hadn't heard of any Progressive candidates saying that they were running yet. But you're MIP."

Patrick smiled enigmatically and nodded slightly.

"I am." He then turned and walked away into the crowd.

Tina didn't know Patrick very well, but she realized he had just dropped a bombshell in her lap—one that he knew she'd have to follow up on. And if it meant what she thought it meant—that the MIP and the Progressives were merging—this would be a big change in the governmental landscape. And a huge blow to SolGov.

On Mars, there were three parties in play. The Mars Freedom Party was the most ironically named. They were currently in the minority and were rigidly loyal to SolGov. They had spent many years in the majority. The Progressive party could generally be counted on to make SolGov give up concessions, but they generally followed SolGov's lead, and let SolGov operate as they would on Mars. The MIP was the small, isolated, marginalized party that had been fighting for Mars independence since the founding of colony 3, thirty years ago.

If the MIP and the Progressive party would merge under a banner of Mars independence, this meant that Mars could pull away from SolGov quite soon—sooner than Tina had thought. It was the only likely conclusion. Patrick was a third-generation Marsie, and a second-generation member of the MIP. Nothing would be more important to Patrick than Mars independence, so the only way he would join the Progressive Party was if they were ready to call for it.

She hurried back to her office. She had a big story to orchestrate. As she walked to the office, she listed the folks who she'd get interviewed, and how she would shape this story. She was very happy she'd left the *Times*. This would be a much more fun assignment to do for the *Monitor*. And she knew for sure it would get printed as they wrote it.

Gareth May 2107

Gareth sat in his hotel room in Chicago, watching Sharron talk at the conference of Concerned Women of America that was being held in Dallas. He was always impressed by her ability to go to exactly where people were at and express her opinions within that context. Basically, he thought, she was a kick-ass prophet. He hadn't gotten to see it much while they were on Mars—but she had been an important part of his ministry when they were here on Earth.

She was talking about concern for children, and their future. She talked about the so-called "Mormon Wars," fifty years ago, which started in the South Pacific, and spread to almost every continent, before it finally ended. She talked about being peacemakers, and how truly making peace was the best way to make sure that our children were safe. And then, surprisingly, she talked about Turool.

Gareth and Sharron had had a surprising conversation after they had both read the transcript. Both of them had been struck by the similarities in what Turool had to say, and what Jesus had to say. It was all the more striking since it was told through someone that Gareth could tell from the transcript was antagonistic toward Christianity.

Gareth shook his head. He still couldn't get used to the fact that the aliens changed gender pretty much at will. Weird system, he thought. He turned off the view screen, and looked at his tablet, with his own notes for tonight's speech in front of a much more friendly audience. He was speaking at the International Conference for the Institute for Noetic Sciences. He could not, in his past, have imagined speaking to such a group—a group that most of his fellow Southern Baptists found heretical and blasphemous. But he had always secretly appreciated their approach, and pretty much agreed with a lot of what they said. That, of course, was something he could never publicly say. And he wouldn't even say it now, exactly.

His speech was basically around the idea that we should embrace what is different and be open to new understandings in the universe. All stuff he knew they would agree with. And he knew already they were going to all vote for Montoya. But, as he was learning, it was often as necessary to talk to what they called 'the base' as it was to talk to more hostile audiences. He hadn't quite finished his sermon for Sunday. He had been given a rare opportunity. An old friend of his, currently pastor of a large megachurch in the Chicago suburbs, had offered him the pulpit this Sunday. He wondered whether his friend thought that he'd fall flat on his face, but perhaps not. He had quite the sermon planned. Discussions from Matthew 15, where Jesus ministers to gentiles, and a few other choice biblical passages—from Isaiah and even Genesis. He and Sharron had spent a lot of time laying out the theological approach to the aliens, and he was going to put it into 30 minutes on Sunday. It felt a little daunting to Gareth, but he had the confidence of his convictions—the arrival of the aliens was God's will, and God's test of humanity.

Lodan, May 2107

Lodan sat in the lounge, looking at the view screen, which at the moment was showing the alien ship. She watched it for a while. Its shape was always mysterious, and although she'd been at the debriefing, and read all of Sam's transcripts, she still knew very little about the interior of the ship.

The *Corinth* was shadowing the ship on its inward journey toward Mars. After the aborted attempt to fire the fusion weapon, Captain McAdams had decided to simply shadow the vessel in-system. It wasn't clear to anyone on the Xenoscience team what his plans were. Everyone on the Corinth was tense. The military were tense, the Xenoscience team was tense—you could cut the atmosphere of the ship with a knife. It was a very unpleasant life onboard the *Corinth*, probably for everyone. Lodan imagined it would be unpleasant for the next five months.

She was in the process of organizing the biological information that Sam had gleaned from Droat. They were an interesting species, for sure. Shifting gender, the different atmosphere, vocal apparatus that was very different than theirs—so different that neither species could shape the words of the other. They were herbivores, evolved to evade some apparently nasty and relentless predators, predators that they eventually exterminated. She had started her long list of questions and investigations she'd want, when she finally got free access to the aliens. She didn't know when that would be—if ever.

"Gah, I had yet another meeting with Captain McAdams."

Lodan looked up from her tablet to see Kylee plop into the chair in front of her.

"I'm getting so tired of telling him that I don't know who released the transcript, and why does it matter anyway, now that everyone has it."

Lodan shook her head. "He has a job to do. I'm sure that he's getting pressure from above."

"This whole thing is completely silly. All of SolGov's best-kept secrets are out. The destroyed Moon colony, the fact that they had a special weapon, it's all out there, now. They can't hide from it, and they know that most people don't want to destroy the aliens."

"At least we stopped firing on Droat's ship."

"Yes. But I'm worried about what happens when we get back to Mars."

"Well, have you been reading about those protests?"

Kylee smiled. "Yes, and Mark has been sending me very interesting dispatches on the political changes going on. I think Mars might actually go independent before we get there."

"Really, that soon?"

"Yes, that soon. And that could change everything. If we arrive at an independent Mars, willing to take the aliens, what can SolGov do?"

"I hate to think about it, Kylee. I hate to think about what they might be willing to try."

Tina, June 2107

"That was quite a coup, my friend."

Tina sat at a table at Filby's, and she could see the soccer match playing on the large screen in the corner. Kevin was sitting across from her, sipping his whiskey. Tina was also drinking whiskey this evening—it seemed to be the right drink for the moment.

"It was in the works for literally years, Tina."

"The merger has left SolGov sputtering."

He laughed. "That was largely the point. They had never really liked the Progressives, but they were useful. They knew that the Mars Freedom Party couldn't possibly win in this election on Mars. So, they compromised, and thought that the Progressives would never call for independence."

"And now that the majority party calls for independence, and the MIP disbands to join the Progressives, what's next?"

"We win landslides in July, and in September, when everyone is sworn in, we declare unilateral independence. SolGov knows this is next."

"What do you think they will do?"

The beginning of his answer was drowned out by the shout of "Gooooooooooaal" and big cheers. Tina looked briefly at the screen. Ah, no wonder, it was US vs. Australia, with Australia just picking up a goal. Australia was, in some ways, Marsies team by proxy. Marsies could never play soccer on Earth, but since Australia had somewhat of a similar history as Mars, Marsies adopted them as their home soccer team.

Kevin started again, and said, "I don't know, Tina. They are so busy with the alien ship approaching Mars, that they don't have very many boots on the ground here on Mars. There isn't a whole lot they can do."

"I also heard that the Mars Militia is planning to protect the alien ship when it arrives?"

"Yes, that's the plan. We don't think that SolGov will be willing to kill people in order to kill aliens."

"I certainly hope you are right about that."

They finished their drinks and said goodnight, and Tina wandered back to her quarters. She missed Sam. Sam had been away for more than eight months now, and the only thing Tina knew was that they was in the brig. She hoped they was being treated fairly, and well, but she hadn't gotten any answers to her emails, suggesting that Sam didn't have net access.

Sam had been clear with Tina when they knew they was leaving they didn't have any commitment to each other, and it would be OK with Sam if Tina found someone new. Tina knew this was not out of Sam's desire to find someone else—Sam could go for years without being involved with someone—their work was more her lover than anyone else. It was out of Sam's desire for Tina to be happy, but it didn't make Tina happy to think about being with anyone else but Sam. It never had, even in the years when she didn't think she'd ever see Sam again. Tina figured it probably was a problem that she felt committed to someone whose only commitment was to space. Sam would never ask Tina to make any sort of commitment to her—in fact, if Sam knew how Tina felt, they'd might even break up with her.

Tina sighed and opened the door to her quarters. She realized that since it had been eight months since Sam had left, it was only four until they'd be back. That made her smile, until she realized that she had no guarantee that she would get to see Sam when they got back. Sam was a prisoner of SolGov and was likely to remain so for a good long time.

John, August 2107

"She walked out of the door, into the pouring rain." Sam put the tablet down ceremoniously.

John said, "That was a great story."

"It was, wasn't it? I love mysteries like that."

"Thanks for reading it."

"It's your turn next. I think you should read *The Mystery of the Saturn Moon.*"

Sam and John had taken up the habit of reading each other mystery novels. It made it more interesting and exciting for them than just reading to themselves.

Over the past few months since their joint incarceration, Sam and John had come to learn how similar they were to each other. They had taken different paths out of the same childhood predicament, but, in fact, they had led similar lives. Neither of them had ever had families or even steady partners. Their work was the most important thing to them, and everything else, including personal relationships, had always had much less priority.

Sam had an independent streak that John didn't have, which John thought explained most of why he had chosen the military and they hadn't. John thought that perhaps he was a little too loyal at times. He certainly felt as if he had been too loyal to Captain McAdams.

Sam said, "I wish we could get net access—at least delayed news, and my email would be nice."

"Sorry, Sam. It's lucky they were even willing to give us inert tablets. These days, in the brig, you get absolutely nothing."

"Nothing?"

"It's a form of punishment in its own right. People break pretty fast."

"I'm sure of that. Before I got the tablets, I was doing theorems in my head."

"You're kidding me, right?"

"Nope. Like the Law of Large Numbers, the Spectral Theorem, Fermat's little theorem, Fermat's last theorem, etc."

John looked at Sam, smiling. "You scare me."

They both laughed.

The door opened, and an MP stood in the door.

"Commander Herman, please come with me."

John looked at Sam and felt trepidation. He didn't know what was in store for him, but he knew it wasn't pretty. He got up and followed the MP, who closed the door. He saw two MPs on each side of the door. He inwardly chuckled. He and Sam hadn't even tried to escape.

He was escorted toward the area where the officer's offices and quarters were. He wondered if he was going to see Captain McAdams. They turned down the corridor that led to sickbay, and the MP stopped at a door that John had never been at before. They opened it, and a vaguely familiar man sat at a desk.

"Please come in, Commander Herman."

He walked in, and the MPs closed the door behind him.

"Please, sit down." The man pointed to the single chair in front of the desk.

"I'd prefer to stand if you don't mind."

"Commander Herman, this is an informal psychological evaluation. It will take quite a while. You will be much more comfortable sitting, I assure you. There is no need for formality."

John considered it for a moment and then sat down.

"I am Dr. Gordon Myers. I am the ship's psychiatrist. Captain McAdams has asked me to do a psychological evaluation on you in preparation for your court martial. I have some questions for you."

"I can't guarantee that I will answer them, sir, given that my counsel is not present."

"These are not questions about the events relating to your court-martial, Commander. They are more general."

"I see. Well, go ahead, then."

He looked down at a tablet and touched it a few times.

"I understand that you had a difficult childhood, Commander."

John didn't respond.

"It seemed the military was pretty much your only option."

John still didn't respond. He kind of got the feeling for where this was going.

"Do you feel as if you have transcended your childhood, Commander?"

"Yes, I do, sir. I feel like I have been able to create a good life for myself, despite what happened to me as a child in Mississippi."

"You don't have children."

That was a statement, not a question, so John remained silent.

"Was that an active choice, Commander?"

"I never really had time for a family, sir."

"Plenty of military officers have families, Commander."

"Yes, they do, sir. And many don't. Do you have a family, sir?"

John thought that Dr. Myers looked a little uncomfortable.

"This is about you, not me, Commander. Do you regret not having a family?"

"No, sir."

"Do you love the military, Commander?"

"I love the structure of the military, yes. And I love working for the good of my people, sir."

"I see. In 2093, there was an entry in your record. You refused a direct order from a superior."

"Yes, sir. It was the end of the Senegalese war, and we had learned that the rebels were about to surrender. My commander at the time, Commander Williams, ordered me to take my platoon to a village that had been home to many of the rebels and destroy it. I refused. I complained to the field Commander, who agreed with my assessment that it would likely prolong the war, and he censured Commander Williams."

"So, you seem to feel that it is right to question your superior officer."

John swore under his breath. He had been totally blindsided. He decided that he would say nothing further. He was furious.

"I will say nothing further."

"Commander, as I said, this is a psychological evaluation..."

"I will say nothing further."

"Alright, Commander, I will ask some very different questions. What is your relationship with Patrick Lohrheim?"

John was taken aback. Patrick had been John's lover over fifteen years ago before he had left for Senegal. Patrick had been the only man John had ever been romantically involved with. It had been a brief but life-changing relationship. John and Patrick had lost touch, mostly because Patrick couldn't quite deal with being involved with someone in the military. John couldn't figure out why this would matter to Dr. Myers, but he didn't want to give anything away.

"I will say nothing further."

"I see. Alright. You are dismissed, Commander."

John went to the door and opened it, and the MP escorted him back to the brig. As he was walking, he was trying to figure out why they wanted to know about Patrick. First, it was a surprise that they even knew that he had known Patrick. At the time, John had been stationed at a base in Austin, Texas. Patrick had been born on Mars and was a student at the university there. Last John knew, Patrick went back to Mars, but John didn't know anything about what he was doing on Mars. Knowing Patrick, though, he was probably deep in the Mars independence movement. He thought they were trying to tie him to the Mars independence movement. John felt scared. They were going to nail him to the wall, throw him in the brig, and throw away the key.

Lodan, August 2107

Michael stirred next to her. They'd both fallen asleep. She shook him.

"Hey, sweetheart, we'd better get up before someone finds us."

He fully woke up, and looked at her, grinning.

"I'm looking forward to when we don't have to commandeer the Xenoscience lab at the wee hours of the morning to make love."

"Me too," Lodan answered.

"I wish I could see the future."

"Why?"

"I'm worried about what might happen when we get to Mars. All we're hearing about how this is stirring up Mars independence feelings, and the insistence of SolGov that the aliens can't settle on Mars. And then there is the thing about that weapon that Commander Herman managed to disable. I'd bet they are already working on fixing it. That's what scares me the most, Lodan."

Lodan held Michael for a while and assured him that things were going to be alright. But in truth, she had no such assurance herself. She was easily as scared as he was.

They put on their clothes and got up from the cushions they had strewn on the floor. Michael started to pick them up and put them back into place on the couches and chairs in the lab. Lodan picked up a few tablets that had gotten somehow misplaced in the process. She looked at Michael as he finished cleaning up, and smiled, feeling her love for him. They had gotten involved only a short time before this trip, and it felt like they'd never had the chance to settle into a "normal" life as lovers. Lodan was looking forward to that time.

They were three months away from Mars, and from who knew what future. She had always liked Mars, although now that she and Michael were getting serious, and thinking about a family, it seemed that her final destination was going to be back on Earth. Michael wanted to settle in Minnesota, on his farm, and Lodan couldn't actually think of a good reason not to go back to Earth. She was proud of the work she'd done on Mars, but it was basically complete, and Minnesota wouldn't be a picnic—just the sort of challenge she would be looking for next.

They embraced, and then parted. Lodan was on her way back to her quarters to get at least a few hours of sleep before she had to report back to the lab at 0930.

As she settled into her bunk, she realized she missed seeing Sam. She had seen their once after the debriefing—they were being generous, or something, and Sam got to visit the Xenoscience lab briefly, with an escort, and see everyone. They looked like they was being treated well, and they'd said that they had the company of John Herman, which they enjoyed.

Lately, there wasn't much that the Xenoscience team could do. They were prevented from communicating with the aliens, so there was no new information they could glean. All remote readings of the alien ship went through the military command first, and none of them trusted what was actually being given to them, so they didn't even bother using it for research. Lodan was one of the few members of the team that thought that SolGov would not succeed in killing the aliens, so the basic atmosphere of the team was very grim.

There just wasn't enough information that they could trust to do any real science on the aliens, so they were limited to analyzing and re-analyzing everything Sam had said in the debrief, which wasn't real science, either, but it was all that they had. Kylee and Tai had lately been diving into early Hubble and Webb telescope images of the Cassiopeia system, to see how much they could learn about the pre-nova conditions of that system. That was promising, but fifty other scientists, and countless amateurs, were doing the same thing. Lodan felt hopeless, and powerless.

Tina, September 2107

"My Fellow Marsies. The time has come. You have made your wishes abundantly clear. Mars will be independent!"

A cheer rose up from the audience.

"There is much work to be done, to truly prove that we can be independent of Earth. But it is welcome work, and I know that we are all up to the task. We are for Mars!"

A deafening cheer greeted the end of the new Governor's speech. Patrick Lohrheim, third-generation Marsie had won a decisive landslide victory over the Freedom Party Candidate. And on his coattails were dozens of Colony managers, senators and legislators, and judges. The politics of Mars had finally begun to represent the true wishes of the people on Mars. It was an exciting moment for Tina.

There as of yet had not been any official response from SolGov, or President Volkov. Tina knew he was staunchly anti-Mars independence, and she could not imagine him letting this go for too long without a response. On the other hand, he was also staunchly anti-alien, and had an alien ship making its way quickly in-system. To Mars. Tina chuckled; glad she was not in his position.

"May I have your attention, please! There is an incoming message from President Volkov. Just a moment."

The background of the stage, which had been showing a picture of billowing Mars independence flags, was replaced by the SolGov seal. A loud "boo" went up from the audience, and when President Volkov's face appeared, it got even louder. Finally, people quieted down.

"Tonight, we have heard that the Progressive Party of Mars, which was violently taken over by the Mars Independence Party..." The rest of what he said was drowned out in a chorus of boos, but Tina could figure out what he basically was saying. The crowd died down again.

"... SolGov will not let this statement of independence stand. The Mars government is part of SolGov, and it cannot unilaterally declare itself independent..." the rest of what he said was lost in the shouts and boos from the crowd. Tina decided to leave the inauguration, and go back to her office, where she could hear the entire recording of the speech. It seemed full of bark, but she didn't know whether or not it would be followed up with bite, and Mars needed to know this.

When she got back to her office, she fired off messages to several old colleagues of hers who were still doing the government beat in Beijing. They all still liked her, and some even envied her new position at the *Monitor*, the new up-and-coming news organization, soon to be system-wide leader. She knew she could get some information from them about any planned retaliation of SolGov. What was interesting for her was that SolGov was insistent on painting the Mars independence movement as fringe, and violent, when neither were true. And Tina didn't think that most people on Earth, or anywhere else, believed that.

Montoya had already read the tea leaves and had come out very much in favor of Mars independence. He was well up in the polls—almost every pundit had said that it would take a miracle for Volkov to recover, even with four months left until the elections in January. But the fact that Montoya had openly pro-Mars sentiments, and that those sentiments matched the popular opinion, hadn't changed Volkov's stand one bit. And that was largely because there were many large Corps, including VirginGalactic, Monsanto, Boyer-Tsiang, Strelix and Chang Galactic, that would suffer greatly with an independent Mars. And Volkov, if anything, was a corporate tool.

She started to set up the assignments for her reporters. And she'd be writing an editorial, once she learned a bit more about the possible sanctions and other nasty surprises SolGov had in store for Mars in retribution for its decision for independence.

Gareth, September 2107

Gareth was in a bar, sitting next to his wife, and they were both drinking ginger ales. Not at all his usual kind of place to go. In fact, Gareth avoided bars like the plague. He had always been a teetotaler. But he was here because of an unusual event. Mars had voted in an independence government, and upon inauguration, the new Governor of Mars declared unilateral independence from SolGov. Everyone in the Montoya campaign was celebrating—they had basically taken over this bar on K Street, and it was overflowing. On the screen were playing varied news coverage of the repercussions of this event. Gareth knew that Montoya was pro-Mars independence, and that

Mars would at worst have maybe six months of problems from the lame duck Volkov, between now and the presidential inauguration in March of 2108.

The campaign for president had gone swimmingly. The latest polls had Montoya up 60% to 25%, with the third-party candidate, who was growing in popularity, at 7%. The good thing about the third-party candidate is that they were also anti-alien, and anti-Mars independence, so that would only take votes away from Volkov. Montoya's numbers had only gotten better in the last few months.

Gareth and Sharron had been across the English-speaking world, and even to China, Russia, and parts of Africa and southeastern Asia. They met with Christian organizations of all types and found almost as much friendliness to their ideas and theology about the aliens as hostility. Gareth's brother was a relentless opponent, writing blog post after blog post in response to Sharron and Gareth's writing. But Gareth could tell that for most Christians, the softer, gentler approach of finding out who the aliens were, and welcoming them if they were friendly, were slowly, but surely winning out. Catholics that followed the Pope were of course a different matter, but Gareth had talked to several Catholic clergy who agreed with him and were agitating for a softer stance from the Pope. Gareth didn't know if that would happen.

And he'd heard that the Mormons had started trying to talk to the aliens by renting time on a strong narrow-band transmitter on the moon. Gareth hadn't heard if they had been successful yet. He laughed out loud at the thought of the first conversation between the Mormons and the aliens, with the Mormons trying to convert them.

"What's so funny, darling? This seems very serious."

Gareth looked at Sharron, who was looking at him with some puzzlement.

"I wasn't thinking about Mars, love. I was imagining the first conversation between the aliens and the Mormons. You heard they'd rented time on a narrow-band transmitter on the Moon, hadn't you?"

"Ah!" She smiled. "Yes, that's funny."

"When do you think we should return to Mars? I'm anxious to get back."

"Darling, the ship won't be there for two months yet. Besides, I think we owe it to Montoya to stay through the election, don't you? Don't be so impatient, Gareth."

Gareth took his hand, and stroked Sharron's arm. "Yes, you are, as always, right. I hope that it will be easy to get passage to Mars once independence is in place."

"I'm sure we can get back. Especially since we will have official status on the Xenoscience team. Somehow, I find that hard to believe. But I do believe it."

"Lodan is a woman of her word. And she seemed… almost intrigued by the idea of having staff theologians. She said that the other members of the team, including Kylee and Michael, were also enthusiastic."

"It will be nice to live in Colony 1—quite a bit more comfortable than our digs in Colony 6, I imagine."

The atmosphere in the bar changed dramatically—a hush fell over the crowd. Gareth looked up to see the SolGov seal on the screen.

"Volkov is giving a statement."

"Tonight, we have heard that the Progressive Party of Mars, which was violently taken over by the Mars Independence Party, has won the governor's election on Mars, and has prevailed in many Colony elections. We have also learned that they have unilaterally declared their independence from SolGov.

"SolGov will not let this statement of independence stand. The Mars government is part of SolGov, and it cannot unilaterally declare itself independent. We will impose an immigration and trade halt to Mars effective immediately. All SolGov personnel have been recalled from Mars, and we have encouraged all Corporations to do the same. We have ceased all talks with the Mars government and will not resume them until they rescind their independence declaration.

"This is a united system! We cannot have colonies go off on their own—we depend on each other and are responsible to each other. We will not let this stand."

The SolGov seal replaced Volkov's face, and a chorus of jeers and boos went out from the crowd.

Gareth said, "Well, my love, it's a good thing you counsel patience—we're not getting back to Mars until Montoya wins."

Sam and John were talking about their childhoods again and sharing stories of the CPS camps.

Sam said, "It sounds like the rules for you were stricter than the rules for us, if that was even possible."

John nodded. "I think that the regimentation of our camp was the only thing keeping us all sane. It was hard losing friends from starvation, medical neglect, or an epidemic every time you turned around."

"Your attention, please!" The loud voice of Commander McAdams rang out. "We are turning off spin again. Please find your places."

"That's odd," John said. "We've just arrived at Mars and have been here only for a day or so. I wonder why..." He turned white.

Sam filled in the blank. "They got more fusion fuel."

"Yes, that must be it. I guess, from their perspective, it makes sense. But it makes me mad, nonetheless."

They got into their bunks, and strapped in, and in a few minutes, Sam could feel the weightlessness. They thought about Lodan, who they hadn't been able to see in months. It was late, and they figured they'd might as well get some sleep. And they thought of Droat, and hoped it was OK.

"I'm going to catch some z's, John. Goodnight."

"Goodnight, Sam."

Sam was awoken by a boom sound, and feeling shoved in one direction, they snapped open their eyes, and saw that the light was dimmed, and a red glow replaced much of the ambient light that had been present in their room. There was a very loud siren blaring. The door was open, and John had gotten out of his harness, and he was hanging onto the open door.

"Sam! We have to get out of here! That siren is the abandon ship siren. Something really bad happened."

"Who unlocked the door?"

"It's automatic—all inside doors unlock and open when we're in abandon ship mode."

Sam got out of her harness and maneuvered herself to the door.

"I need to find Lodan and..."

"Sam, we might not even have enough time to save ourselves. We need to get to the escape pods."

Sam nodded grimly, and they left the room and used handholds in the halls to go forward to the nearest set of escape pods, which John said was four sections toward the forward end of the ship. But they were stopped after traveling two sections—the atmosphere doors between sections were shut.

John said, "We have to go back, and get to the shuttles in the far back! We can't go any further forward."

They turned around and started to go toward the next hub shaft that would take them to the center of the ship. Sam started to smell something acrid and could see that the air wasn't completely clear. Smoke clearly was getting into the air recycling system from somewhere. The siren kept going, deafening them.

As they approached the hub shaft, they saw Lodan and Tai hanging on some handholds, looking lost and scared.

"Lodan, Tai, come with us—we're heading for the shuttles aft."

Sam followed John, and Lodan and Tai followed Sam. They made their way down the hub tube, then down the center hallway to the shuttle bay. They gathered people as they went. At times they felt the ship shake and shudder.

They reached the shuttle bay and saw that both shuttles were still there. Sam and John were the only pilots around.

"Sam, you take shuttle one, I'll take shuttle two. I will get on the com system and tell people that there are shuttles leaving aft, if they can't get to..." The ship shook again, interrupting him. "... the escape pods. We don't have much time, Sam."

Sam nodded and moved into the docking door for shuttle one.

"Lodan, stay just inside the docking door of the shuttle. I'm going to leave it open for as long as I can. Help people in as you can."

Lodan nodded. Sam moved toward the front of the shuttle and strapped into the pilot's seat. They started the launch sequence and then tapped into the *Corinth*'s status feed. The bridge section and fore weapons array... weren't there. There was atmosphere loss in most of the front half of the habitat ring. The front third of the habitat ring was on fire. Sam realized that something had gone badly wrong.

"Sam!" That was John on the comm.

"Yes, Commander Herman." Some sort of habit was kicking in for Sam now.

"We're launching in five minutes. The fire in the habitat ring is spreading. We can't afford to wait. When it reaches the oxygen stores in section fifteen..."

"I got it. I'm synchronizing to your timer."

They noticed Tai hanging out behind her.

"Tai, go back to Lodan, and get her inside, we're leaving in... four minutes, twenty seconds."

Sam saw him propel himself to the back. Zee hoped they were able to rescue some others. They wondered where Michael and Kylee were. Sam brushed that thought away as they did the launch preparations, and white knuckled their way through several more brutal shudders of the ship.

"Sam, everyone is inside and ready."

"Tai, sit down!" Tai strapped himself into the co-pilot's seat but looked like a deer caught in headlights. Sam ignored him.

"Docking doors closed, dock disengaged. Launch in 5... 4... 3... 2... 1..." The shuttle launched, and Sam could feel the acceleration push them back into their chair. As they emerged from the launch tubes, they saw the second shuttle to their left. They looked in the display and saw seven small blips—they must be some escape pods. Four were jumbled up together, and three were scattered around towards Mars. They also saw the very large blip that was the Turool ship, entering into Mars orbit.

"Commander Herman, can you pick up those four shuttles in close proximity to each other. I'll grab the others."

"Affirmative!"

As they pushed towards the escape pods, they put the rear view into the side view screen, and they could see the *Corinth* as it blew itself to pieces. They hoped that most of the crew and passengers had managed to get off of the *Corinth*, but they had no way of knowing. They heard Tai sigh.

"Tai, please go back and help with the docking ring—they will need some manual operation in order to get the passengers of the escape pods on board. I'll get us aligned as closely as possible."

He nodded, and unhooked himself, and drifted out of the piloting cabin. Sam wished they had Jane with them on this shuttle. It's a good thing they always kept several different secure copies of her scattered around. They aimed toward the first escape pod and calculated the trajectory of flight so that the docking ring of the shuttle would nicely nestle against the docking ring of the escape pod. They hoped that Tai and Lodan, and anyone else they could recruit could figure out how to extend the shuttle's docking ring and latch on to the escape pods.

They engaged thrusters, and waited until the proper moment, when they then pushed thrusters again to slow them down and get them next to the escape pod.

After a few minutes, they heard Tai on the comm.

"Sam, docking rings are engaged, we've got four people coming on board."

"Affirmative. Let me know when you've disengaged."

A pause. "Disengaged. We can move on."

Sam repeated this procedure for the next two pods. They were able to rescue fifteen people, total. Sam knew that Kylee and Michael were not among them, because Tai and Lodan would have told her.

Sam connected a call to shuttle two. "Commander Herman, we've got fifteen people."

"Great, Sam. We've got twenty-two more. Next steps?"

"I suggest we land at Mars Colony 1."

"Sounds good."

Sam put in the code to reach Mars Colony 1 landing control.

"Mars colony 1, we have two rescue shuttles from the *Corinth*. We request permission to land."

A stiff, angry voice answered. "I'm sorry, we cannot allow you to land."

"Excuse me?"

"We have broken with SolGov, and the *Corinth* was a SolGov ship. And it also appears the *Corinth* attempted to destroy the aliens."

Sam whistled. What was it that they missed while they were in the brig? Ah, yes, the brig!

"Mars Colony 1 control, this is Sam Julian, and these shuttles are piloted by dissident members of the *Corinth* crew who were in the brig at the time of the accident. We have no allegiance to SolGov, or whatever actions they might have taken. We do have *Corinth* crew among the rescued, and we are willing to turn them over to your custody upon arrival."

There was a brief pause, then a response in a very different tone.

"Affirmative, Sam. Welcome home to Mars! Both shuttles may land."

Sam was relieved. They put a course to Mars orbit. They'd better warn John. They typed in the comm code.

"John, this is Sam."

"Yes, Sam?"

"We have permission to land at Mars Colony 1. But Mars has broken from SolGov. So, any crew of *Corinth* that remains loyal to SolGov will likely be arrested. You should warn your passengers."

"Will do. I guess this means I get a reprieve, eh?"

"We both do, my friend."

They shut off the comm, and looked over at Tai, who had returned to his co-pilot seat.

"Tai, yell if something happens. We're on autopilot to Mars orbit insertion."

"OK. I think I can handle that."

"Thanks, Tai."

Sam unhooked themself and got up, and climbed down to the main part of the shuttle. The acceleration towards Mars was giving them a little gravity to make moving about easier. Once they got on the main level, they walked toward the seats. They saw Lodan talking with one of the *Corinth* crew. They saw that they had rescued only crew. They had some bad news to deliver to those crew members.

"May I have your attention please!"

They all stopped what they were doing and looked at her.

"We are landing at Mars Colony 1. It turns out that Mars has broken from SolGov. If you are a member of the *Corinth* crew, you are likely to be arrested by Mars authorities. I'm sorry about that."

There was a lot of whispering and talking, then one man stood up. They recognized him as one of the MPs that had been guarding her.

"I demand we turn around and find a SolGov rescue ship!"

Sam looked right at him.

"I'm sorry, but I won't do that. Mars is my home, not Earth. If Mars is now independent, I'm with Mars."

"This is a SolGov shuttle!"

"That I am piloting. You might notice I'm the only pilot you have. Wanna try flying this thing yourself?"

He sat back down. Sam figured he had known he wasn't going to win the argument, but he had to put up some sort of protest so that when he returned back to SolGov, he could prove that he hadn't been willing.

They went up to Lodan, who looked determined, but sad and worried.

"How are you?"

"I'm OK. I really wish I knew how Michael was. And Kylee, too."

Sam nodded. "I know. I hope John got them."

Sam heard Tai yell from the pilot's cabin, and they ran to the ladder and climbed back up to the pilot's cabin.

"Sam, SolGov is calling."

Sam took a deep breath, sat down, strapped in, and punched the glowing comm icon.

"This is shuttle one."

"Shuttle one, this is SolGov cruiser *Magellan*. We notice you are on trajectory to Mars orbit."

"We will reach Mars orbital insertion in approximately four minutes."

"We order you to reverse course and head toward our position."

"Negative, *Magellan*. We are landing at Mars Colony 1."

"You are disobeying a direct order and will be subject to court martial. Please state your identity, pilot."

"This is Sam Julian, a citizen of Mars." That wasn't really accurate since Mars didn't have citizenship. But they figured with the break from Sol, they were certainly working on it.

There was dead silence at the other end. They figured they were trying the other shuttle. Sam wished them luck with that.

Sam's telemetry panel lit up with dots as they moved toward Mars.

"What the..." they said under her breath. They pulled up the identifying information. There were probably thirty ships in orbit around Mars. Several of the ships were placed directly in the path between the *Magellan* and some other ship that looked like another SolGov cruiser, and the alien ship. Sam understood. They were *protecting* it.

They reached Mars orbit, and Sam set up the landing sequence. They punched the comm to shuttle two.

"John, did you talk with the *Magellan*?"

"Yes. They offered me amnesty."

"Really?"

"I didn't believe them for a second, even though my actions earlier had clearly saved many lives. We would all have died before rescue got to us out near Saturn's orbit."

Sam smiled. "Indeed. Not only did you save the aliens, you saved all of our lives. OK, we're going down. You all set for landing?"

"It's been a little while since I've landed on a planet, but I think I'm OK."

"Alright—see you on the other side of this, my friend."

"Looking forward to being on the ground, for sure."

For Sam, the landing sequence was generic and predictable. They were a good pilot and had a good feel for this shuttle, even without Jane's help. They thought of Jane and looked forward to grabbing the most recent copy she'd stashed just before the ill-fated first-contact mission.

Once they landed, a rag-tag group of Mars militia—clearly newly minted—met them and took away all of the crew in uniform, except John, who asked for asylum. When Sam explained why he had been detained, they stopped looking at him suspiciously, and he was given provisional asylum pending a hearing.

Neither Michael nor Kylee were among those John had rescued. In fact, there were only 39 rescued from the *Corinth*, all crew except for Sam, Tai and Lodan. The majority of the crew and the rest of the Xenoscience team had clearly perished. The *Corinth* left Mars orbit a year ago with 150 on board. The whole thing was clearly a disaster for SolGov.

Sam found Lodan at a window in the terminal, and they walked up to her.

"I'm sorry, Lodan."

Lodan nodded, and looked at Sam, with tears running down her face.

Lodan said, "I wish I'd gotten to have more time with him. I took his presence for granted, I guess. I never thought anything like this would happen to us."

Sam nodded. "I'll miss him. And I'll miss Kylee, too."

Lodan and Sam embraced, and held each other for a while, both crying quietly. After a while, Sam heard John clear his throat, and speak.

"Sam, there apparently is a huge crowd outside of this terminal waiting to see us."

Sam and Lodan broke their hug, and Sam looked at John, feeling a little puzzled.

"Why?"

"Apparently the story has gone out that we saved the aliens. And, of course, *you* are the only one that has actually seen them."

"Well..."

John shrugged. "What can I say?"

"OK, let's go meet our public." Sam wiped her face on her sleeve, and they looked at Lodan, who still looked devastated.

"Lodan..."

"I'll be OK, Sam." She had a cloth in her pocket, and she wiped her eyes and nose with it.

They walked toward the terminal exit, which had two militia people at the entrance, Sam guessed ostensibly to keep people out. As they walked through the door, they could see a large crowd gathered, with news imagers in the front, and other people that must be press gathered on one side. Sam saw Tina among them, in the front of the pack, smiling broadly. Sam resisted the desire to run to Tina and give her a big hug, and Sam expected Tina was resisting the same desire.

There was a podium, and Sam, Lodan, Tai, and John stood behind the podium. Sam didn't have anything in particular to say—they had more questions than statements.

A voice said, "Will you take questions?"

They nodded.

"Do you know the reason the *Corinth* was destroyed?"

Sam turned to John, indicating he should answer.

"We don't know for a fact, but it is my surmise that the fusion fuel they were using for a new type of weapon somehow misfired and caused the destruction. That's the only logical explanation."

Tina spoke next.

"Commander Herman, we understand you have requested asylum on Mars. Why is this?"

"I was in the brig for preventing the firing of this fusion weapon near Saturn's orbit. I would be subject to court martial and possible execution for that act."

"Why did you act in that way?" Tina was good at using what might seem too obvious as a vehicle for letting people express a lot of what is behind their intentions.

"After hearing what Sam said about the Kurool, and about what they had done, and what had happened to them, I couldn't stomach the possibility that we would repeat their history, wiping them out. They are peaceful, and don't deserve our violence."

Another man that Sam didn't recognize spoke next.

"So, you don't think they are a threat to us?"

"They have clearly proven themselves not to be a threat. They have no weapons on board, they saved Sam's life, and all they want is a place to settle peacefully."

He seemed insistent for some reason. Sam wondered where he was from.

"SolGov insists they have information that proves their threat that you don't have privy to."

Sam said, "There is no such information! Look, I spent time with them—they are no threat."

The questions continued for a few more minutes, and Sam got worn out.

They said, "Folks, we have just had a harrowing experience, and we need rest. There will be ample opportunities in the near future to hear more from us, I promise." They got down from the podium, and the crowd dispersed somewhat.

Sam saw Kylee's husband, Mark, standing toward the front, and Sam walked toward him. They didn't know him very well, but they could tell he looked lost.

"Mark..."

"Kylee didn't make it, did she?"

"I'm sorry, no. She wasn't in any of the escape pods, and Lodan last saw her in the Xenoscience workspace, which was in the far forward part of the habitat ring on the ship. We expect that part of the ship was destroyed during the initial blast. I'm sorry, Mark."

He nodded. They put her hand on his shoulder and could feel him shuddering slightly. Sam didn't know what else to say, so they said, "Call me anytime, Mark. Let me know how I can help."

He looked up at them, nodded again, turned, and walked away. Sam watched him silently and sadly.

Some of the militia members stood beside them, and they all started walking toward the terminal transit station. They realized belatedly that John didn't have a place to stay.

"John, we'll go to my apartment—you can stay there."

"Where are you going to stay?"

Just at that moment, Tina was walking toward them, and one of the militia went to block her, and Sam indicated that it was OK.

"I'll be with Tina." Sam smiled at Tina, and they embraced.

Tina whispered in her ear, "I was afraid I'd lost you."

Sam pulled back a bit and looked at her, grinning. "You should have known I'd get out of it."

Tina smiled, and they continued walking to the transit station.

"John, this is Tina, Tina, meet John, my former commander, and then brig companion."

"Wait... Tina Fiorici? Do you remember me?"

Tina looked at him for a moment, and Sam wasn't sure what was going on.

"John! Vito's friend! I can't believe it!"

"When Sam told me about you, they never used your last name. I had no idea you were on Mars!"

They chatted amiably during the transit to dome complex 3, and the walk to the section 9, where Sam, Tai, and Lodan's quarters were. They stopped in front of Sam's apartment, which was the first line.

"Hey, we'll meet up at the Xenoscience lab tomorrow morning? We should make plans."

Everyone nodded, and Sam could feel the weight of grief. The Xenoscience lab without Kylee and Michael would never be the same.

"John, give me your ident card." He handed it to them, and they swiped theirs on the door, then used the guest mechanism, and swiped his.

"OK, you should have no problem getting in again. Make yourself at home. Lodan, and Tai, I'll see you tomorrow."

Everyone went their own way, and Sam and Tina got on another transport train to complex four. They traveled silently, Sam deep in thought about their next steps. They were now SolGov *persona non grata*. This meant that, at least for the time being, they weren't going anywhere else except Mars. They looked at Tina, who seemed off in her own world.

Sam asked, "Are you going to get to stay now that Mars is independent from SolGov?"

Tina turned to Sam. "I was fired from the *Times* six months ago, Sam."

"Fired? From the *Times*? Tina..."

"Yes, fired. I wrote one too many articles insinuating that SolGov wasn't giving Mars enough autonomy. And actually, the article that clinched it was reporting about your wideband transmission, and I did an expose on the Moon, too. They fired me and refused to print the article. So, I sold the article to the *Mars Monitor.*"

Sam shook her head. "Tina, your career..."

"Is completely intact—better than intact, actually. I expect that no Earth news organization will ever hire me. But right after I was fired, I was hired as an editor by the *Mars Monitor.* They had a standing offer for me for months. They want to beat the *New York Times*, Sam, and I'll do what I can to make that happen for them. I'm making almost twice what I made at the *Times*, with more autonomy and authority." She grinned. "Besides, living on Mars is so much easier."

"I could never understand how you stood living on Earth."

"Sheer strength of will. I've since learned the price I paid for six years there."

"Well, your body will certainly thank you. And, frankly, I'm glad you're staying around, since I can't see how I'm going to get off this rock anytime soon given the political climate."

"So, that's what it's going to take for me to keep you here, eh? Government action?"

Sam laughed. "Speaking of the Government, fill me in on what happened!"

Chapter 9:
Resolution

Sam, November 2107

Sam had been to their share of funerals and memorial services, but these last two had been wrenching. Yesterday was Kylee's service. Kylee had more friends than Sam had known, and the relatively small hall that Mark had arranged to hold the service was overflowing. There had been many flowers, and people speaking about how well they knew Kylee, and how much she would be missed on Mars. She'd seen Curtis, who they hadn't seen since they'd left. He had declined to come on the *Corinth* with them, for reasons of his own. They suspected that he did not regret his decision.

Today's service for Michael was a much quieter affair. Members from his team and his friends on Colony 6 had arrived last night, and they were joined by the remaining members of the Xenoscience team, Tina, and Mark. John and Curtis were also there. Lodan had been quiet for most of the service. It was her turn to speak. Sam watched her get up from her chair in the front and stand in front of the podium that had a picture of Michael surrounded by flowers.

"I met Michael on the ship that first brought us both to Mars. We were wet behind the ears, and knew nothing about Mars, but we came to solve a puzzle. Working with Michael had become a pleasure, and even though our fields were different, he always seemed to find the similarities and congruencies in the situations we faced, or the problems we were trying to solve. I think I really fell in love with him when he helped me solve the problem of the nanoparticles, and he told me once he'd fallen in love with me when he learned I'd braved the frozen wastes of Massachusetts."

There was light laughter in the audience. Lodan continued.

"We had been planning our futures, oblivious to the danger that faced both of us. There is the deep sadness that I won't get to spend more time with Michael, but there is the great joy that I had while he was with us. It is that joy I will remember."

The service ended soon thereafter, and a small group of them, Lodan, Sam, Curtis, Tai, John, Tina and Mark, went to Lodan's quarters to spend time together.

Sam said, "I don't even know how we're going to do this without Kylee and Michael. I don't quite know what to do without them."

Lodan said, "They'd both want us to figure it out. I, for one, want to do work that would have made them proud."

Sam knew that Tai had been offered Kylee's position by the Terra University administration. Tai was still considering it. Sam didn't know whether Tai wanted the position—he was a great scientist, but they didn't think he liked management at all, even though they imagined he might be good at it anyway.

Sam said, "We can do it. I know that. We have the support of Terra U, and all of Mars."

Gareth, January 2108

Their things were strewn around the apartment—it was a disorganized mess. Gareth couldn't imagine how they had managed to accumulate so much stuff in the nine months that they had been on Earth. Gareth was trying to figure out what he needed and wanted, and what he could throw away. They had a baggage allowance of only one hundred pounds each for their passage to Mars, and they needed to slim down.

It had been impossible to get from Earth to Mars, or back, since the declaration of independence four months earlier. SolGov had put a complete blockade in place, so that no ships could travel to or from Mars. Now that Volkov had lost the election, and a whole host of pro-Martian candidates had won in the SolGov legislature, the first thing that the transition teams had negotiated was an end to the blockade. Now that it was over, the backlog of people who wanted to travel to Mars was enormous. Gareth and Sharron had gotten passage because of their new official role, but they were cramming in as many people as possible into the transports, thus the unusually small luggage allowance.

Gareth was glad that they had been involved in the momentous election process. Montoya had won a stunning landslide victory, as everyone expected. The unintended result of the Montoya victory, as well as Mars independence, was a running battle for the control of the asteroid belt.

The Mars government had declared that all space from Mars orbit outward was new Mars Gov territory. Some of the companies that ran asteroid mining in the asteroid belt had always been aligned with Earth-based corps, and others were strictly independent. Neither group liked the idea of Mars sovereignty over the asteroid belt. Montoya and others were trying to negotiate, but it didn't look good. It looked possible that there would be all-out war for the asteroid belt.

But that wasn't Gareth's concern. Gareth and Sharron were heading back to Mars, to Colony 1 this time, to help study the Kurool. Sharron had already begun a book on Kuroolian theology, and Gareth had been in touch with many religious leaders on Earth about the kinds of things they wanted to know about the Kuroolian people, and Turool in particular. Both he and Sharron would be busy studying and talking with the Kurool and writing and communicating with the world about what they were finding.

Gareth had been surprised by the overwhelming support for the aliens, especially after the transcript was released. Even his brother had to admit that perhaps they weren't the threat he thought they had been. He, and most of his fundamentalist colleagues, were not ready to admit that the Kuroolians were God's creation. In fact, there was a new sect that had arisen out of this crisis that insisted that the Kuroolians were products not of God, but of Satan, and would only be a temptation to humans to stray from God's path. They were going so far down the path that they even suggested that the nonviolence of the Kuroolians was Satanic. Gareth could hardly even figure that one out.

Sam January 2108

Droat's people had been in radio silence for months. Sam had been worried at first, but they'd been monitoring satellite imagery of the colony site, and they could see that they had been busy. The five sections of their ship had separated in orbit and come down to the surface individually. They were set in a perfect pentagon, with one edge on the rock face that contained the caves where they had originally found the artifacts and carvings, and there were domes and corridors going up inside the pentagon, and outside of the other sides of it.

Unlike the domes that humans could manage to make on Mars, the Kuroolian domes were massive in size. One of the smaller domes was easily twenty times the size of the largest central dome of Colony 1. Clearly, they had technology that humans didn't, and Sam wondered whether or not they would be inclined to share.

Sam looked forward to seeing Droat again, and spending time with it. At the same time, Sam was itching to get out to the Kuiper Belt, for one last go at being an asteroid hunter.

Lodan, April 2108

They landed the shuttle where they had been told to and waited as a long docking tube grew out of one of the domes that was toward the edge of one side of the pentagon. It was one of the smaller domes, and Droat had said that it had been specially designed to allow humans and Kuroolians to live and work in the same space.

Lodan, Sam, Tai, Curtis, John, Gareth and Sharron were to be the first team to spend a month with the Kuroolians in their colony. In addition, they had along two journalists from the *Mars Monitor*, who would spend only a week with them. Lodan had been especially excited about seeing this new dome. Last month, one of the Kurool, Jorat, had requested a rather large shipment of Earth plants of a wide variety of types, and Lodan was intrigued to find out what they had done with them.

The Kuroolians had been in radio silence until February, when they had requested an exchange of information. They had provided the Xenoscience team with a frankly astonishing amount of data on their planet, people, history and technology. It had taken weeks to transmit over relatively high-bandwidth connections the exabytes of data. It would take generations to analyze it. In return, the Xenoscience team had given the Kuroolians the entire Library of Congress, which now included a worldwide collection of books, a collection of all scientific articles from all journals published in the past two centuries, several public domain net encyclopedias, as well as the collected content of several commercial online content libraries that were donated by their owners.

Lodan heard a series of clunks, and Sam announced that the docking tube was engaged, and it was time to disembark. They picked up their things and started to roll the cart containing all of the food that they needed for the month, as well as supplies and personal belongings, through the tunnel. As they approached the end of the tunnel, they saw a cabinet that had what looked like simple facemasks. Lodan opened the cabinet and put one on. It was mostly white but had a bright green stripe. Lodan looked back at the cabinet, and saw next to it a bin, that had a yellow stripe. She assumed this meant that when the stripe on the mask turned yellow, it was time to discard it.

Lodan had learned that the Kuroolians used oxygen as well, but they also used ammonia for metabolism, and their home atmosphere had high concentrations of ammonia and carbon monoxide, as well as higher concentrations of methane and nitrous oxide than humans could handle. But Lodan figured that since they didn't need carbon monoxide, methane or N2O, if they got rid of those, the only thing that humans couldn't deal with would be the ammonia. And a filter could certainly take care of that.

This way, they could live together, and not have to have separate atmospheres. Wearing the mask would take getting used to, but being in direct contact with the Kuroolians would be worth it.

They all donned masks, and then walked through the airlock. They were greeted by several Kuroolians. They all looked quite similar, and Lodan wondered whether one was Droat. One of them started to speak, and with a short delay, an electronic sounding voice spoke.

"Welcome to our colony. We are very happy that you have come to spend time with us. I am Jorat, and Droat, Froat, Kloft and Horat are here to greet you. This is an area that has been specially designed to be habitable to both species, although each of us needs to make adjustments. The air pressure is quite a bit higher than our native pressure, so we have had to adapt to it. And, as you see, you have to wear the masks. We have set aside an area for you, through those doors at your left, which has only your atmosphere. We also will be forced to leave here once a day. But we expect to be able to accomplish much."

Lodan was touched by the effort that the Kuroolians had put into making it hospitable for them, and she could hardly imagine human beings doing the same thing for aliens. True, the Kuroolians clearly had superior technology, but their thoughtfulness seemed above and beyond the call of duty.

Sam, June 2108

Sam settled into the pilot's chair and looked at the small frame with Tina's face sitting on the top of the control panel. They smiled. They knew Tina was far from happy that Sam was leaving now, but they also knew it was in Sam's nature. And Sam knew that their nature was changing.

Sam was a celebrity in the new, free Mars, which now included a colony of aliens. Everyone on Mars was getting along swimmingly, and Sam didn't like being in the limelight. They hoped that by the time they got back, people would have forgotten them. The rest of the system, however, was frankly in chaos. The Moon was agitating for independence, and there were some all-out battles happening in the asteroid belt for control of that very precious resource. Weird things were happening in the outer system as well. Sam had mapped the path through the belt to avoid the most dangerous areas.

Between the pay that they'd been saving up, which had thankfully accumulated even while they were in the brig, and a small loan they got from Tina, they were able to buy a ship outright. This one was used, but it was better and faster than the ship they'd leased. They and their ship were on their way to the Kuiper belt.

She'd always wanted to hunt asteroids in the Kuiper belt. Most bodies in the belt were ice, or mostly ice. But about 2% of the asteroids in the belt were prime. Really, really prime. And it was easy to see from a distance which were prime, and which were a waste of time. Kuiper Exploratory had a monopoly out there—and all asteroid hunters sold their asteroids to Kuiper Exploratory. Sam didn't mind—what they'd heard of KE was a lot better than they knew of Strelix. And there seemed always a lack of good asteroid hunters out there. It was too far to go for most people.

Sam's plan, surprisingly to them, was to go out to the belt, find a few asteroids, and then go home to Mars. They'd work on her Ph.D. in Xenoplanetology remotely. They felt her age more these days and realized that this was, in a sense, their last hurrah. They would be ready to settle down on Mars when this was done.

"Jane, time to the inner Kuiper Belt?"

"105 days, 13 hours."

"Thank you, Jane. Jane, do you have *Mystery of the Saturn Moon* on file?"

"Affirmative, Sam."

"Read it to me, please?"

The Saturn Moon

Prologue

Somewhere near Saturn, September 2095

Henry sat looking at the gas meter on his wrist. It was fully in the red zone now. He tapped on it, hoping that perhaps that might magically make a difference, but it did not. He was going to die.

He'd spent the last week drifting in space, near Dione, all of his plans coming to dust. A year ago, he had proposed a grand plan of finding needed rare earth elements on Saturn's moons. No one had been able to find them before, but he had been sure he knew things no one else knew. And he was good at convincing people. He had been able to borrow a ship, borrow money for fuel and equipment, and set out for Saturn from Earth. Finally, he'd escaped the stifling life he had in Pennsylvania.

Yet, ultimately, he'd been unsuccessful. First, he ran out of fuel; then, slowly, the systems of his aging ship began to come to a halt. Three days ago, the life support system had gone, and now he was forced to live in his suit full-time. Distress signals had resulted in several answers from people who were too far away to help him in time. When he was almost out of oxygen, he decided it was time to pray.

"Father God, I know I've been a wayward son, not praying, or tithing, or going to church. I have failed to give you glory, Father. I ask your forgiveness in Jesus' name. Please, God, save me, somehow. I know that you have plans for me, Father. I know it."

His prayer was interrupted by a proximity alert, but he was too groggy to do anything about it. His mind drifted, and he tried to bring it back to his prayer.

"God, I promise that I will bring you glory if you save me. I will fulfill the destiny that I know you have set out for me..."

His mind drifted again, and he saw images of his favorite zoetrope, the one with the dancers he'd built when he was ten. He went back to praying.

"Father God, please help me in my hour of greatest need..."

He was interrupted again by clanging noises, and he turned his head toward the motion he saw out of the corner of his eyes. He blinked. As he blacked out, he saw cats moving around his ship, and he could swear he heard a meow or two before he lost consciousness.

When Henry woke up, he realized that his helmet was off of his head, and he was breathing fine. His suit was off, and he was sitting in his skivvies on the floor of his control room. He looked around and saw several... creatures working at the controls. He shook his head and imagined he must be dreaming. Or maybe he was dead already.

One of the creatures, a small, short but lithe biped, covered in fur, with a long tail and ears that looked a little bit like a cat's, turned toward him. Now that he could see the creature's face, the fur, tail and ears were the only thing that in the least resembled a cat. The creature didn't have a nose, and its mouth was crowded with two rows of equally sized, and equally sharp, teeth. It had two tongues, which flicked constantly in and out of its mouth. Its eyes were small and beady, without whites or iris.

He felt, rather than heard, a voice.

You are awake.

That was the best he could interpret what he felt. It wasn't really words; it was more like a combination of feelings and images.

He nodded, even though he knew that it was not a question.

You are alive. Again, this was the best he could interpret this feeling. He nodded again.

I am Koth.

"I am Henry."

We saved life.

He nodded again. "Thank you."

We bring this ship to our home. You come with us.

And then he thought, *I will come with them. I will help them.*

Chapter 1:
Artifacts

Sky threw the thing to Mikhail, who almost missed catching it.

"George sent it."

"And?" Sky could see Mikhail feel the thing a little bit, then put it in a cubby in Nilesh's workstation.

"And he says there are a lot more where that came from. Prime mysterious alien artifacts."

Mikhail sighed. "Sky, we've talked about this how many times?"

"I know, you're tired of this trade."

"It gets on my nerves."

"Mik, it's saved our asses at times, and our asses need saving right now. We haven't done this kind of trade in almost a year, man. We need it now. We'll be dead in the water with no fuel or food in about... what, three months if we're lucky? I don't really want to go back to working for Strelix, thank you very much."

Sky was trying hard not to think of their empty contract pipeline, or the fact that they had no leads to new cargo or service work whatsoever. The economic slowdown that had happened system-wide after Mars independence still hadn't let up, and all of the economic pundits telling them that things were going to get better didn't make their situation any less dire.

"Alright, so how many of these can he make?"

"He claims these are real."

"Yeah, right. And pigs can fly."

"He was very adamant, although frankly, he wasn't willing to say over the comm why he thought so."

"That's our George, alright."

"So?"

"I won't block it, if Lesh and Cait agree."

"I floated it by them when you were stationside."

"Of course. They seem to like fraud."

Sky laughed. "Mik, for someone who robbed a bank, you have an odd sense of morality."

"Eh, whatever. Look I have some things to take care of..."

"What the heck is going on, Mikhail? You've spent more time stationside this time than ever."

"No worries - nothing to do with you guys or the *Callista*. Old family shit."

"Ugh, sorry."

"My Yemeni uncle is on station, and he's demanding that I go back with him to Yemen and get married. Unfortunately, my mother agrees with him."

"Well, you could just stop talking to them." Sky calculated that she had not talked with her own family in over a decade.

"I know that was your answer, Sky, but it's not mine. I'm working to convince him I'd be a terrible husband. The problem is that for my family, my faithfulness doesn't really matter much."

"Ah, so explaining how many lovers you've had isn't helping?"

"Not in the least. So, I have to take another tack."

"You could claim to be in love with Lesh."

Sky heard a bit of bitterness in Mikhail's laugh. She wondered what that was about.

"I don't think they'd believe me, since I've already told them I've slept with hundreds of women."

"Good point, there. Well, good luck."

Mikhail turned, grabbed a handhold at the entrance to the workroom, and propelled himself out of the room. Sky turned toward Lesh's workstation. She wasn't really in the mood to examine the thing. She knew it wasn't real, and in general, George was pretty good at making top-notch fake artifacts. She'd look at it later.

With Mik agreeing, it was time to signal to George that they'd meet him. She left the workroom and moved hand-over-hand around the central hallway to a hub tube, then climbed through the hub tube to the hub, then up to the main control room. Nilesh and Caitlyn were doing a standard maintenance routine.

"Mik agreed."

Nilesh looked up from his board with a grin on his face.

"Alright. Let's make contact with George. I'm looking forward to seeing him."

Caitlyn snickered.

"What?"

"You have a crush on him."

"So what?"

"I can't quite get my mind around that."

"Cait..."

"You two, can we do this business thing now, and you can discuss your love lives later?"

Caitlyn screwed up her face and said caustically, "Yessir!"

Sky sighed and floated over to the comm system. She brought up George's system net address and left him an encrypted voice message.

"George, we're all in, but we'd have to go consignment. We don't have much in the way of spare cash. Send us the coordinates, and we'll be there as soon as we can. We're at Moon Station Delta and can leave within 24 hours."

Nilesh said, "Good thing George likes consignment."

Sky looked up from the console. "George likes us. We can always get rid of his fake artifacts."

They went together through some pre-launch items and then Sky heard the ping of an incoming text message. It was George, who only gave his coordinates. Sky brought up the system map and swore.

"What in blazes is he doing in the fucking asteroid belt?"

Caitlyn looked up. "The asteroid belt?"

"That's what the coordinates say."

"Is it in one of the war zones? We can't risk that."

"No, it's very safe within Strelix space."

"It will take us weeks to get out there!"

Sky asked the ship AI for an accurate estimate. The toneless voice responded, "It will take an estimated thirty-five days, seven hours, at normal thrust."

Nilesh said, "What are we going to do?"

Sky answered, "What else can we do? We can sell some of this stuff at Strelix station, to begin with—so that's a good thing. We can probably at least pay for the fuel it took to get out there."

Caitlyn screwed up her face. "I don't like this, Sky. Something is weird here."

"I know, but George is reliable. We're his main customers, and he wouldn't steer us wrong. We'll be fine. Maybe he decided to settle out there. I'll signal to Mik to get on board. We're leaving in 24 hours."

Asteroid Belt, May 2112

Sky woke up and looked at the clock on the wall next to her bunk. It was 0600 hours: time to get up. She switched on the light over her bunk and swung her legs over. She'd never quite gotten used to how small her quarters were, even though she'd been on the *Callista* for almost three years now. Somehow that was hard to fathom, though she'd mostly enjoyed her time here.

Once she'd decided, twelve years ago, to leave Earth and spend her life in space, she'd had pretty good luck. She felt happy to live a relatively normal life. Being the daughter of the richest man in Latin America and one of the most well-known actresses in the world had not been something Sky had taken to very well. It wasn't something she'd taken to at all. As soon as she could, she left Ecuador and headed into space, wrangling a job in Strelix by pulling some hidden strings in her father's company.

When her parents found out, they threatened to disinherit her, which she responded to with a brief text message, "Please do." She had had brief email exchanges with her mother for a while, but they'd petered out to nothing ten years ago. She knew they were both fine—anything that happened with her parents on Earth was system-wide news. And because her parents had taken pains to shield their children from the press, her disappearance was not noted.

As she finished her morning rituals, she couldn't help but feel happy. They were about to meet George, who would give them a ton of artifacts to sell. Nilesh had already made contacts at Strelix station, and they expected to sell a good chunk of them to one of their regulars, who did a lot of trade with Mars and Io. They would be in good shape again. Things were looking up.

She walked out of her quarters and down the hall to the mess room.

"Morning, sunshine." Sky looked up to see Caitlyn grinning at her. She looked to be in an especially good mood.

"Morning, Cait." Sky went over to the freezer cabinet, got out a breakfast sandwich packet, and threw it into the microwave.

"Mik says he's going to turn off spin in about 30 minutes. He spotted George's asteroid a while ago."

"It's funny that we haven't heard from him in a couple of weeks. He's usually a chatty sort."

"Maybe he's worried about someone overhearing our conversation."

"Maybe. Anyway, we'll know soon enough."

They chatted amiably while Sky ate her breakfast sandwich, then headed together back to the hub and up to the control room. Sky liked *Callista*. It was a ship large enough to have a habitat ring with spin, and good cargo space, but small enough to be pretty nimble. The control room could feel a little crowded sometimes with the four of them, though.

Mikhail said, "Turning off spin. Deceleration is just about complete. Making final adjustments in attitude. The asteroid is a large one. We'll be orbiting it, and two of us will go down in the shuttle. I volunteer Sky and Nilesh."

Sky said, "Alright, Mik. We make the most sense, anyway. We know George the best."

"And he likes you both. He doesn't like me."

"He doesn't like Russians."

"I'm only half Russian. I don't like Russians, either."

Nilesh spoke loudly. "Guys, there's something wrong."

"What?"

"I can't find George's beacon."

"What do you mean, can't find it?"

"I can't find it. It's not there. Yesterday, I thought it was odd that I hadn't picked it up, but I chalked that up to a weak signal. But now... we absolutely should have found it."

Caitlyn said, "Is it possible he's not here?"

"We got a message from him a couple of weeks ago..."

Mikhail said, "That was a couple of weeks ago, Sky."

Sky said, "Alright, look, we're here, there's no point in turning around. We'll take the shuttle down, and look around, OK?"

Mikhail sighed. "I knew there was something about this I didn't like. Actually, there was a lot about this I didn't like."

Sky was exasperated. "Mik, you agreed to it. Look, let's just look and see what's going on, OK?"

They did the final approach to the asteroid and got into orbit. Sky and Nilesh went to the shuttle bay, and they launched the shuttle toward the asteroid. They did a slow orbit, looking for the place where George might have been, but saw nothing. Then Sky saw what she thought was the entrance to a cave.

"Nilesh, look over there—see that large opening. It looks like a cave. Could that have blocked the beacon?"

"Possibly, depending on how deep it is. Let's go investigate." He touched his panel. "Guys, we're going into a cavern. We might lose contact."

Mikhail answered, "Alright. Be careful."

Sky steered the shuttle into the cavern entrance and turned on the strong exploration lights at the front. They couldn't see much except the walls of the cavern. As they kept going slowly into the cavern, it widened. It was clearly a large internal cavern. But they still couldn't get his beacon. Then Sky saw what looked like the pieces of a wrecked ship.

"Whoa!"

"What is it?"

"Look there."

"Oh, my. That's George's ship—see that part of the insignia on a panel on the ground?"

"Fuck. What happened?"

"We need to find out."

They landed the shuttle, got into their suits, and went out to explore. George's ship, or rather, varied pieces of it, lay scattered about in the cavern. Sky discovered a spacesuit leg with a leg still in it. The suit and end of the leg were badly burned, and there were flakes of frozen blood.

"Nilesh."

She heard his tinny voice over the comm. "What?"

"Come over here, please."

She watched him bounce carefully over, holding a large piece of bulkhead.

"I think this is part of George."

Nilesh looked at the suit leg. "Ugh. Did you find any other parts?"

"No, this is the only one."

"I can't imagine he survived this."

"No, he didn't, Lesh."

"So, Sky, look at this bulkhead."

She looked at the edges. They were blackened, with tinges of blue and green. In some places, the layers were completely melted together.

"That's really strange-looking."

"I'm going to take it back with us, along with a few other strange things I found. The damage done here doesn't look like any weapon I've ever seen."

"I feel sorry for George. I wonder what he got himself into."

"You mean, what have we gotten ourselves into? Believe me, Sky, whoever was willing to do this to George is going to be willing to do this to us. We'd better get the hell out of here."

They hurriedly picked up a few more assorted pieces of ship, including the one with the partial insignia. When they arrived back in the shuttle, as Nilesh was stowing what they had, Sky called Mikhail on the comm.

"Mik, get prepared for the quickest exit you can make. The instant we are in the bay, start maximum thrust for Strelix station."

"What's going on, Sky?"

"I don't have time to explain now, Mik, just do it. And keep the AI's ears open for any sorts of incoming signals. We need to avoid anything coming this way."

"Alright. See you back soon."

They were all in the control room; they hadn't turned spin back on because they were proceeding to Strelix station at Maximum thrust. Sky regretted this, as they would use up a lot of their available fuel. They would be basically stranded at Strelix station until they could find a cargo or service contract, and Sky didn't think that was especially likely at Strelix station. But it was better that, then get caught by whoever or whatever had destroyed George's ship, and George with it.

Mikhail said, "Gods, we're screwed."

Sky exhaled. "This is strange. George was always reliable in the past."

Nilesh spoke up. "We don't know that it was him who was being unreliable, Sky. Maybe he discovered something that other people didn't want him to discover."

Caitlyn said, "Look, we're three days away from Strelix station. Let's just get there and figure out what to do, OK?"

Sky looked at Nilesh, who was pensive. He finally said, "I need to take the samples down to the workroom and examine them. If we can figure something out before we get to the station, that would be good. We have to report this."

Sky said, "I know. We need to come up with a story as to why we were meeting with him. George is SolGov and MarsGov *persona non grata*. I'd rather not have that attached to us."

Mikhail laughed. "You really think that they think of us any differently?"

"No, but at least we don't have any warrants out for our arrest at the moment. Last I heard, he had several, and we could get slapped with aiding and abetting."

Nilesh unstrapped himself and left the control room. Sky, along with the rest, were lost in their thoughts.

"Guys!" It was Nilesh on the intercom.

Sky tapped the intercom button on the side of the wall near the entrance to the control room.

"What?"

"That artifact that George gave us?"

"What about it?"

"When I got down here, it was glowing. I took some pictures. It stopped, though."

Caitlyn asked, "Glowing?"

"Yeah, glowing. I've never seen anything like it. I thought you should know. I'm going to do some analyses of the bulkhead damage, and then I'll tackle the artifact. I have a theory, but I don't want to share it until I have more evidence."

Mikhail grunted. "I don't like Nilesh's theories."

Sky asked, "Why?"

"The dude is always right."

After no evidence of any sort of pursuit for 48 hours, they slowed down and turned on spin. Sky was waking from a well-deserved sleep in her bunk. They'd arrive at Strelix station in about two hours. Sky hadn't heard a peep from Nilesh, so she decided to head down to the workroom.

When she arrived, the workroom was in a state of chaos. Pieces of the ship lay about, and more instruments than she knew that they had on Callista were strewn almost randomly around the workroom. Nilesh looked like he hadn't slept.

"Nilesh, how is the analysis going?"

"I don't quite know how to tell you this, but we need to make contact with someone who is in contact with the Kurool."

"Huh? They don't have any weapons!"

"I know. But they might know who these people are. This damage was definitively not done by any weapon humans have ever made."

"How do you know that?"

"Just trust me. I know it. I can explain it to someone who knows chemistry and physics..."

"Try me. If this is what you say it is, we'll have to explain it to a lot of people."

"Alright. So... I've taken a look at the damage patterns and found the relative temperature that these bulkheads must have endured, as well as the chemical residue left on them. George's ship was attacked with a directional weapon—it wasn't an explosive weapon."

"OK..."

"And our directional weapons have real limitations."

"Unless they managed to perfect the fusion weapon that destroyed the *Corinth*."

"No, no, that would have a different signature, and leave radiation. There was none of that. And in any event, this one was more powerful than that would be."

"Really?"

"Yeah, much smaller beam, and much, much more powerful. Basically, from what I can recreate, George and his ship were probably destroyed in one short strike."

"Oh, my. Powerful, and alien."

"Yup."

Sky thought that the one person she could trust with this information was Sam.

"Just a sec." Sky walked to the intercom.

"Mik, do we have enough fuel to make it to Mars?"

"Mars? Nilesh wants to go home?"

"No, Mik. We have a mess on our hands, and the one person I trust to deal with it is on Mars."

There was a pause.

"We'll need to refuel, Sky. But we have the funds to buy enough fuel to make it to Mars. We'll be totally broke and empty when we get there, though."

"We'll be OK, Mik, I promise."

Sky had met Sam back when they both worked for Strelix. Sam was one of the asteroid hunters, while Sky worked for Strelix as a pilot, mostly shuttling people from the station to one of the large asteroid mines. They didn't see each other often, but when they did... Sky smiled. Sam was one of her most favorite exes. They had kept in touch, mostly, and when Sam became famous during the Kurool incident, Sky couldn't help but be proud of what Sam had done. Sky trusted Sam implicitly, and Sam had all of the right connections to help them out. This was going to be delicate. Time to call Sam. She headed up to the control room.

She left the video message short, sweet, and a little bit mysterious. Sam loved mysteries. Well, truthfully, it *was* mysterious. She then called up Strelix Fuel.

"Hallo, Strelix Fuel." A balding, light-skinned man with an unfamiliar accent answered.

"Hi, this is the *Callista*. We need a brief refuel, six hundred units. We won't be stopping at the station, just a flyby."

"Six hundre' units? That all?"

"That's all we need."

"Al'light, whateva." He looked down. "You cleared for bay six."

"Thanks." Sky turned to Mikhail. "Hear that?"

"Roger. On my way to fuel bay six."

Getting refueled and getting to Mars was uneventful, even boring. Sam had called back, welcomed them to Mars, and even arranged housing for the four of them at Colony 1. They hadn't asked too many questions, which was a little unnerving for Sky, but she didn't worry about it too much. She figured that Sam trusted her about as much as she trusted Sam.

Mars Colony One, May 2112

Sam and Tina were sitting in their living room. Sam was reading a draft of an article that Tai had recently written detailing the new information about the Cassiopeia supernova. Tai had become good friends with Kloft, a Kurool scientist who studied stars. The Kurool were much further along in their understanding of how stars worked.

Sam looked over at Tina, who they could tell was subvocalizing. Tina was pretty busy these days as the SolGov editor for the *Mars Monitor*. After Mars independence, SolGov had been in some disarray for years. And, of course, there was the little problem of the war in the asteroid belt.

"Sam, message from Sky Alvarez." Jane's dulcet voice spoke softly. Tina looked up, her head cocked to one side. Tina knew that Sky was Sam's ex. Sam could not imagine what would prompt a video message from Sky. They hoped she was OK.

"Play, please, Jane."

"Sam, I hope you are doing well. I need your help. A friend of ours was killed in the asteroid belt when his ship was destroyed, and Nilesh has a theory that I really need to speak with you about. We're on our way to Mars. We should arrive in about six days. Thanks in advance for anything you can do to help."

Tina said, "Well, wasn't that enigmatic."

"I suspect there is something she doesn't want to say over an open channel."

"You think it's about the war?"

"I don't know that she'd contact me about something like that—I think this must be different."

"So, what are you going to do?"

"Respond, then arrange for some housing for them, and wait and see. I haven't seen Sky in a long time—it will be nice to see her."

Tina responded to that with a look.

"Tina, love..." Sam got up from her seat on the couch and walked over to Tina, who was reclined in the settee.

"I love you. Sky is my ex, and she's just a friend. There's nothing to worry about." They kissed.

"I know, Sam. I guess, somehow, I haven't gotten used to the fact that you've decided to settle down. I keep worrying about the next thing that'll take you away."

"Tina, if you'd experienced what I experienced in the Kuiper Belt, you'd want to stay home from now on, too."

"I know. Sorry."

"It's OK, love, I understand."

The next day, after making reservations at the Colony One hostel for the *Callista* crew, Sam visited the Xenobiology lab. Although they'd resigned from their official position, they still had a desk there. They hardly ever used it; they were much more comfortable working at home, and as long as they had Jane, Sam didn't need much. The lab had meetings once a month, and they were always present for those, but hardly ever darkened the door otherwise.

"Howdy, stranger!" It was Curtis.

"Hey Curtis. How was your trip to the Kurool colony?"

"Great, as always. I love spending time there."

"Yes, you and everyone else."

"Why don't you go more?"

"I don't know, Curtis, I'm kinda busy with my own research."

"Alright. Well, Droat says it misses you."

Sam chuckled. They should really go visit Droat. It had been months. They always found it surprising that time seemed to move much more quickly when they were on Mars than when they'd been asteroid hunting.

Sam had been planet-bound for two years now, after a very successful but almost catastrophic trip to the Kuiper Belt. Sam had found two very prime asteroids during that trip, prime enough to allow Sam and Tina to retire in comfort on Mars, then later on the moon when Mars became too much for Tina's body. Of course, Tina had no interest in retiring, nor did Sam, but it was nice to never have to scramble again, and to get to do the research they wanted to do.

But during that trip, Sam had come closer to losing their life than they ever had in 15 years of asteroid hunting. After they'd claimed and sold the second asteroid of the trip, they'd been on their way back to Kuiper Exploratory to take a break before doing one last run when their ship ran into a cluster of small asteroids. They were so small they hadn't shown up on any telemetry, and Sam hadn't had time to change course to avoid them. One asteroid turned the engine to pulp, while another made hash of the life support system. They sent out a distress call, dropped into the survival pod, and drifted in space for a long time.

It turned out they'd drifted for five months. The new type of escape pods, which they were lucky to have on their ship, were designed to put you in a sort of stasis, reducing your need for oxygen, water, and nutrition to a bare minimum. But five months was still, they later heard, a record for survival in a new pod. Eventually, they'd been picked up by a cargo ship on its way to Mars. Somehow, that seemed appropriate. All they wanted to do after waking up was to go home.

Sam had come in to see Tai and give him their in-person critique on the article he'd written, but since he wasn't in his office, they decided they would just go home and record it. They said goodbye to Curtis and were on the way out when they ran into Sharron walking in.

"Sam! How are you? Haven't seen much of you. Coming to the meeting next Monday? I have some big news."

"Sure, but if the news is theological..."

"Really, it's interesting. I promise."

"Alright. I was going to show up anyway. How's Gareth?"

"He's alright. He had to go back to Earth for his mother's funeral."

"Oh, I'm sorry. I hadn't heard."

"It's a bit of a sticky situation. His brother still blames him for the horrible Earth economy after Mars independence."

"Uh, what?"

"I know, Sam, it's completely silly. But his brother feels that if Gareth hadn't been working for Montoya, he wouldn't have won."

"And Earth would be dealing with a Mars revolution. I'm sure that would have been great for the economy."

"And Gareth can hardly be to blame for his brother's church dying because people actually *like* the Kurool."

"Well, I wish him the best. When will he be back?"

"He leaves Earth in a few days, so he'll be back in a few weeks."

"OK, I'll see you next Monday."

Sharron nodded, and Sam continued to walk out of the lab and back home. For some reason, they suspected that next Monday's meeting was going to be more interesting than any of them knew.

Pittsburgh, Pennsylvania, May 2112

Gareth sat in one corner, munching on the fried chicken leg. The last few days had been some of the most trying of his life. His mother's death seemed to be bringing out the worst in his family, and he was barely welcome there. He'd mostly successfully avoided his brother Lionel, except for the moment when Percival showed up at the funeral. Lionel had had the temerity to ask him to leave the church, but Gareth had stepped in, taken Percival to the back of the church to sit, and stayed with him.

He had not, however, been able to avoid Evelyn, Lionel's wife, who blamed him for everything—from the fact that Lionel's church was now largely empty of people and couldn't pay his salary anymore, to the death of their mother. It was all completely silly. He'd also had a run-in with Lynette, his sister. Her husband, the new governor of Texas, had pulled him aside to give him a talking-to about his theology.

Gareth had simply come back to Pennsylvania to pay his respects to the mother he loved, who'd died of MLS at the young age of 70. He'd been in contact with her throughout her illness; she loved him and cared about what happened to him and had largely ignored his siblings' opinions of him.

"Gareth." He looked up to see his brother Lionel looking at him.

"Hello, Lionel."

"Unfortunately, we must all be present at the reading of mother's will tomorrow. I've sent the address to you. It will be at 10:00 am."

"Alright. I'll be there."

His brother didn't move. "Is there something else, Lionel?"

"Yes, there is something else. I heard a rumor about you."

"What kind of rumor?"

"That you're starting a new cult."

"That's absurd, Lionel."

"Well, you left the Southern Baptist Convention three years ago."

"Yes, I did. And you know why. That doesn't mean I'm starting a cult."

"I hear that you're writing a paper which suggested that Jesus visited those evil aliens."

"Lionel, look, we'll never see eye to eye on this. I've written several papers now comparing the teachings of Turool, the leader that changed Kurool society, to the teachings of Jesus. That's all. Can we stop talking about this?"

"I pray for your eternal soul, brother, every day."

"And I pray for yours."

Lionel glared at him, spun on his heels, and walked away. Gareth shook his head. He did wonder where Lionel was getting his information. It was true that Gareth had come to believe that Turool was indeed the Son of God, incarnate as a Kurool. He hadn't quite been able to get himself to finish the paper which laid out the theological argument for that stance, but in his heart, he knew it was the truth.

The next morning, he picked up Percival at his hotel—he didn't want him to have to arrive alone.

"So how is Seattle and the family, Percival?" Percival had moved to Seattle about a year before with his long-time lover Roger, and their two children.

"I love Seattle. I liked San Francisco a lot, but Seattle really is becoming home. Roger is fine; it's his turn to be the stay-at-home dad. Joellyn and Gareth are a handful, but wonderful. Gareth wants to be a space pilot, at least for now. Last week he wanted to be a fireman."

Gareth smiled. It had been such an honor to hear that Percival and Roger had named their son after him.

"How's work?"

"It's a bit slow but picking up because we got a big contract with a company on Mars that does similar work. They want some of our code."

"I'm glad to hear that."

"Speaking of, how's Mars? And how's Sharron?"

"Mars is great. Being part of the new, independent Mars has been an amazing experience. And getting to study the Kurool up close and personal has been more rewarding than I'd ever imagined. And Sharron is fine. We'd love you to visit. I know I could wrangle a visit to a real space pilot for Gareth."

Gareth saw Percival's eyes tear up.

"I'd love that too. It's been so hard to be separated from the family."

"I know. I hate that some of our clan are still living in the twentieth century. But we're not, so please, come visit. Sharron would love to see you—it's been too long."

They had arrived at the building where the attorney's office was, an old building that looked like it had been built in the nineteenth or early twentieth century. It did look like it had some modern overhauls, with new windows with displays, and a green roof. They made their way up to the fifth floor, where the door to the conference room was open. When they walked in together, they garnered stares from Lionel, Lucan and Lynette.

Gareth and Percival sat next to each other at one corner of the large glass conference table. The lawyer cleared his throat.

"Hello. We are all here to hear the Last Will and Testament of Marielle Holbright, of Pittsburgh, Pennsylvania. She chose a more traditional text-only will.

"I hereby leave one million Yuan to the Designer Drug Rehabilitation Center of Walnut Creek, California, in honor of our dear Tristan." Gareth heard Lionel groan.

"I also leave one million Yuan each to The Center for Alien Understanding, and the Cetacean Rescue Center." Gareth smiled, and thought, *Well, well, mother is certainly putting her money where her mouth had been. The triumvirate across the table must be writhing in pain.*

"I leave one point five million Yuan to each of my living children, and a trust of approximately one million each to my seven grandchildren, to be used for their education, and given to them when they turn twenty-one."

Gareth was stunned. First, he'd had no idea his mother had so much money. Second, Lionel had two children, Lucan one, and Lynette two, which meant that mother had included Percival's children in her will, too!

Lionel said loudly, "Wait, excuse me! There are only five *true* grandchildren. There must be a mistake."

The attorney said patiently, "Mr. Holbright, there is no mistake. There are seven legal grandchildren in your family, and your mother provided for each."

Percival said, "Lionel, get over it. My husband Roger and our children are legally part of this family, whether you want to admit it or not."

"How dare you..."

Gareth got up. "Look, we're here to honor our dear mother in her death, which means honoring her wishes. Let's move on, shall we?"

He could see Lionel's anger, and he was very interested in avoiding being around it for much longer.

The attorney said, "That is all, that's the full will. I will be in contact with each of you regarding the status of your inheritance and the trusts for your children. Thank you for being here today."

Lionel, Lucan and Lynette filed out first, and Gareth waited until they got an elevator before he got up. Percival followed.

"I'm sorry he's such a dickhead, Percival."

Percival laughed. "I don't hear that kind of language from you very often, Gareth."

"It's the only language that is appropriate for that brother of ours.

Mars Colony One, May 2112
Sam stood near the entrance to the shuttle port, waiting for Sky and the other *Callista* crew to arrive. Sam was a little nervous. They hadn't seen Sky in more than seven years when Sam was taking a break from

asteroid hunting at Strelix station. And they hadn't seen Caitlyn in a lot longer. So much had happened to all of them in that time. They'd been in touch, although Sky was always pretty circumspect about how the *Callista* and its crew stayed employed. Out of respect, Sam didn't ask questions. Sky had always been running this or that racket at Strelix, always staying barely on this side of the law. Sam wouldn't be surprised if the *Callista* did some illegal trade now and again.

Sam saw Sky first—tall, with dark eyes, and very close-cropped dark hair. She was wearing frayed coveralls and miner's boots. She was flanked on one side by a tall, thin woman with long red hair—that was Caitlyn, from the moon. She was an old friend of Tina's. On the other side of Sky was a tall man with olive skin and curly hair. He reminded her suddenly of Lodan. Following them was a slight man with tousled blond hair. They all looked tired, and, if Sam was reading them right, nervous.

"Sam!" Sam and Sky hugged, and then Caitlyn hugged Sam.

"Sky! God, it's so good to see you. And great to see you too, Cait! It's been like forever."

Caitlyn asked, "How's my Tina?"

"Tina's great. She's sorry she couldn't be here to meet you all—but we're cooking dinner for you at our place tonight."

"She's a busy gal, I hear."

"Indeed, she is."

Sky said, "So, Sam, I want you to meet Mikhail, and Nilesh."

"Nice to meet you both. Look, I'm sure you're beat from your journey. I've got you quarters at the hostel, pretty decent digs, and we'll meet up later..."

Sky interrupted. "Sam, we need to talk now."

"Now?"

"Yes. It's really important."

"OK, why don't I just take you back to our place then, and we can talk."

They took the transport to dome complex 4 and made their way to Sam and Tina's place—the same apartment where Tina had lived since she arrived on Mars. They walked into the apartment, and Sam heard some "oohs" and "aahs" at the view. They'd looked out on construction for a long time, but now that the construction was over, it was quite nice.

"Please, make yourself at home. What can I get you? I've got some beer, juice, coffee..."

Sky said, "I think we all could use some beer."

"Alright, beer it is."

Sam got out a six-pack of Cassiopeia 2081 and passed containers around.

When they were settled in place, Sam said, "Alright, Sky, what's going on?"

"We had a friend, this guy George. He used to give us stuff to sell. But this time, when we went to meet him in the asteroid belt, we found him and his ship in pieces. And he was nowhere near any of the war zones—he was safe in Strelix space."

Sam chuckled. "*Safe* in Strelix space?"

Sky said, "Sam, there's more."

Nilesh said, "I examined the pattern of destruction and the damage to pieces of his ship. It wasn't done with any weapon known to humans."

"Are you sure?"

"Absolutely."

"What was he selling you?"

Sam saw Nilesh reach into his bag. He said, "These." He handed her the artifact.

Sam looked at it. It was cylindrical and made of a kind of dark substance that she'd never seen before. It seemed to have several openings that were covered in a smooth, glossy material, sort of like glass, but not quite. It looked old, pitted in many places.

"What is this?"

"George claimed it was a genuine alien artifact. We assumed it was fake."

"Why would you go meet George to get fake alien artifacts... oh, I get it."

Sky said, "Trade in counterfeit alien artifacts made up some of our revenue."

"Sky!"

"Sam, don't judge me, please."

"Alright. So Nilesh, what exactly made you think it was a weapon we don't have?"

"First, it was clearly a beam weapon, not an explosive. The pattern of damage made that clear. The beam sliced through the ship, and George, and some of the ship's components exploded because of the heat of the beam. But it wasn't a bomb. Second, the beam was narrow, but more powerful than anything we have. Even more powerful that that fusion weapon, if anyone ever got it to work."

"You know this because?"

"The pattern of damage on the remaining pieces of ship. A part of George that was left. I think that his ship was destroyed by a single, short pulse of an extremely powerful beam weapon."

"I'll want to see your detailed analysis. And we need to look further at this." She held up the artifact.

Nilesh said, "Of course, Sam."

Now Sam understood why Sky had come to her.

Sam said, "So, you think George found these alien artifacts, and then the aliens found him, and eliminated him. Do you think they know you have one of these?"

Nilesh said, "We have no idea. I noticed this glowing when we were near the asteroid."

"OK, send me everything you've got, and I'll get the Xenoscience team on it tomorrow."

Sam watched as everyone relaxed. Well, everyone except them. How did they get themself into the center of these things?

Mars Colony One, May 2112

Sam sat watching the team filter into the all-too-familiar conference room. They still missed Kylee and Michael, even though they had been dead for more than four years. And Lodan had left two years ago to go and farm Michael's land in Minnesota. She'd planned to go back to Earth with Michael at some point, but Sam had been surprised that she'd chosen to go back without him.

Tai led the lab now, and Curtis had been promoted. There were several other scientists who had joined the lab, and then there were

Gareth and Sharron, the resident theologians. The new scientists included Ted, Xiang, Rosalind, and Abdi. Getting a position in the Xenoscience lab at Terra University was about as high as you could get in Xenoscience these days, and these four had already been at the top of their field when they arrived. It was one of the reasons Sam had resigned their position. They didn't need it and didn't quite feel like they deserved it.

Sharron sat down next to Sam.

"Sam, I just wanted you to know that I didn't feel bad that my announcement got postponed. It really wasn't nearly as big as this seems to be."

"Thanks, Sharron. I was looking forward to hearing what you had to say, though."

"You'll hear about it soon enough. This is fascinating."

"Indeed, it is."

Once everyone was seated, Tai motioned to Sam to start.

"Hi everyone." Sam told them the story, holding nothing back. They showed slides of the detailed analysis of the weapon residue and effects, as well as the new analysis of the alien artifact, which showed definitively that it was not human-made. It was largely carbon and silicon, and based on the carbon dating, it was very, very old, or from very far away, or both.

Tai asked, "So, are we dealing with one new alien species, or two?"

Sam answered, "That is a very good question, one we can't answer at the moment."

Sharron said, "We need to ask the Kurool if they know who it might be. They know of other species in the galaxy."

Xiang, who had come directly from China several months ago and had become an expert in Kurool culture, said, "They have been reticent to talk about those species, however."

Sam said, "But I know they'll talk if they hear this story."

Tai said, "They will certainly talk with you, Sam."

There was some murmuring in the room. It was no secret that the Kurool liked Sam and told Sam more than they told the other scientists. It was a point of some contention, and they and Xiang, who was supposed to be the lab's culture expert, sometimes argued about it.

Tai spoke up, "OK, crew, we need a plan. Sam, you go with Sharron and Xiang to the Kurool colony, tell them this story, and get whatever information you can. I need to tell someone official about this, and I think it's going to be John. He'll know what to do. In the meantime, Ted, Rosalind and Abdi, work with Nilesh on further analysis of the pieces of ship left, and the artifact. We need more data. Let's get to it."

They got up and filtered out of the room. Sam, Xiang, and Sharron met outside the conference room.

Sam said, "I'll schedule a shuttle to the Kurool colony and let you know when we're leaving."

They split up, and Sam headed toward the shuttle port.

Chapter 2:
Mysteries

John walked briskly from General Tsang's office, shaking his head. The process of moving the Mars Militia—the rag-tag assembly of Marsies with no SolGov military experience and no discipline—to an actual military structure, was a moving train wreck. The war in the Asteroid belt was serving as an object lesson in how not to run a military. John was now a Major General, which really meant nothing except that he was training the General of the Mars Army how to build a military.

He sighed. He really didn't have anything to complain about. After almost losing everything, including his life, he had a new life as a respected man on Mars, and he was busy with work that he largely enjoyed and that did not place him in harm's way. Further, reconnecting with his old love Patrick had come as a complete surprise. And what was also a surprise was that he was doing rather well at holding himself together in the relationship. That was something he hadn't expected. Of course, Sam giving him advice over beer had been a real help.

He loved Mars. He loved the people, loved their spirits, and the new energy that came from independence. He was happy being a part of building a defensive military force that could take care of those people no matter what SolGov decided to throw at them. Luckily, SolGov seemed intent on leaving Mars itself alone, even though they wanted to fight over the resources of the asteroid belt. It was mostly the Corps that demanded that SolGov protect them from nationalization from Mars, but the truth was, Mars had no interest in owning the asteroid belt—they just wanted some modicum of legal jurisdiction over the system from the Mars orbit outside. John, and most Marsies, couldn't understand why the corps didn't understand this.

The current state of the conflict was a standoff. Unfortunately, Montoya, who would have been a reasonable partner to negotiate with, had died in office two years earlier, and his vice-president was very uninterested in Mars' jurisdiction of anything besides Mars. In fact, before Mars independence Prak had been a loose ally of President Volkov. There was a cease-fire in place, and in a few days, Patrick, Prak, and several CEOs, like Jeevan Fredlund, the CEO of Strelix, were going to meet on Mars Station One, to hammer out terms. Patrick was hopeful of a settlement, because he'd gotten signals that the corps were finally figuring out what Mars wanted.

He got back to his office and started in on the several progress reports his colonels were working on. They had decided on having three services: Ground, Sky, and Star. The third was a bit of a fantasy, but it was designed to begin the process of putting together a structure that could provide leadership for space exploration outside of the solar system. Since Mars was the most populous planet outside of Earth, and it was the home to the only interstellar-traveling species humans knew about, it seemed to the right place to be the new center of that effort. John was arranging things so that once the three services were up and running, he would get placed as the head of the Mars Star Service.

He heard the quiet chime of his AI signaling that he had a message marked urgent. It was Tai Xien, the head of the Xenoscience lab at Terra U, and a friend he'd gained after the fiasco of the *Corinth*. The message was short and cryptic, but John could tell it was important. Tai suggested a meeting at the lab tomorrow morning, and John sent his confirmation. He was curious, but he had a lot of work to get done this afternoon before he got his last night with Patrick for a while. Patrick was heading up to the station for diplomacy, and he was heading out to the new Mars Military academy being built off of Colony 4.

Mars Colony One, May 2112
"Wow, Tai, that was a lot to dump into my lap. Thanks, *friend*." John made it sound ironic, but he knew Tai would take it well.

"I know, man, I'm sorry, but I needed to find someone official to report all this to, and the only person that came to mind was you."

"So right now, the only people who know about this are the Xenoscientists, and the four criminals?"

"John..."

"I don't have much tolerance for that stuff. I know they are friends of Sam, but I'm going to have to give Sam a talking to."

Tai chuckled, and John could hear a "good luck with that" undertone to the laugh. Tai was right, of course. Sam would never do that sort of thing themself, but they did have a tolerance for other people's law-breaking that John didn't quite understand.

"I'm trying to figure out how I am going to push this up the chain without those folks getting themselves arrested for intent to sell counterfeit artifacts. There are hefty fines and even time at the prison asteroids for that stuff these days. Mars is taking a hard zero-tolerance approach."

"John, I'm leaving that up to you. They knew there was some likelihood that they would get into hot water reporting this, but they *did* report it. That should get them some leniency."

"Agreed. Alright, Tai, thanks. I think the next step is for me to have a meeting with General Tsang and Governor Lohrheim. Unfortunately, Patrick is busy meeting with the SolGov president and Corps at the Mars station, so it will be a few days before I can get that meeting arranged. And it would be good to have any information the Kurool have on this new species before we have that meeting, anyway."

"I'll send you the report the minute I get it from Sam, Xiang and Sharron. I'm hoping there will be some good news in it."

"Good news? Like?"

"I don't know—something that will make me feel less like we're about to get ground to dust."

"Well, there isn't much hurry, anyway. If they are in our system right now, and inclined to hurt us, there is nothing we can do about it, based on the information you've shared with me. I don't think any level of preparation will help us when they have weapons like they used on poor George. He deserved to be knocked upside the head into next week, but not blown to bits by one alien shot."

Mars Colony One, May 2112
"Sam, hello. I've missed you."

Sam sat in a chair across from Droat, who they hadn't seen in way too long. They were in the area where they could stay together, and Sam was wearing a mask, which they didn't really like, but they were at least glad they got to be in Droat's presence.

"I'm sorry, Droat. I've been a terrible friend, haven't I? I'll try to do better. I really do enjoy spending time with you."

"I have the feeling that you have some news for us, however."

Sam was always surprised by how well the Kurool could read human emotion. None of the humans had managed to master understanding the Kurool emotions, but perhaps that was because they didn't really have them in the same way as humans did.

"Yes, Droat, I do. Some weeks ago, a friend of mine and her ship crew were given an alien artifact by a colleague of theirs and asked to meet the person at an asteroid to see more of them. When they arrived at the asteroid, their colleague's ship was completely destroyed, and their colleague was dead. We are certain that the artifact is indeed alien, although it doesn't look like anything of yours. In addition, the damage to the ship was also clearly done by an alien weapon. We thought perhaps you might know who these people are."

Droat seemed frozen in place, and Sam thought something might be wrong. After a pause, Droat said, "Show me the artifact, please, Sam."

The mechanism by which the Kurool talked with humans was still something of a mystery, but it definitely included some artificial intelligence and voice generation. Sam very rarely heard any variations in the tone or timbre of Droat's voice, although each Kurool did sound different from each other. Now, though, Sam was sure they were hearing a different tone; they just couldn't quite put their finger on how it was different. As they reached into the bag with the artifact, they looked over at Xiang, who was ashen. He clearly had heard a difference, too.

Sam held out the artifact, expecting Droat to reach to pick it up, but they did not. Droat cocked their head, and looked at Froat, who also had their head cocked. There was silence for far, far too long. Finally, Froat, who rarely said anything, spoke.

"I am sorry. I am sorry for you, and sorry for your people. I am also sorry for us. Clearly, our sin followed us here, and you will pay with us for it." There was more silence, for almost two minutes, and then Sam lost her patience.

"What? Is that all you are going to say? You have to explain!"

Droat spoke. "Sam, forgive us. We will explain it all. Remember the story I told you about the people we wiped out?"

"Yes, of course."

"Well, I left out part of the story."

"Oh?"

"We didn't actually end up killing all of them. The reason we were scared, and tried to wipe them out, was that we knew about them. They were, at the time, a species always at war with each other, and when they could, they drew other species into their wars. They slowly but surely were killing each other off. When what we thought was the last of them arrived at our planet, having made their planet uninhabitable because of their conflicts, we originally gave them refuge. But after a few years, their conflicts became our conflicts, and a period of wars started because of them. We couldn't tolerate it, so we tried to exterminate them.

"We thought we'd killed them all, but we learned some years later that a small group had survived, found refuge with another species, and vowed to do to us what we tried to do to them. It has been several thousand of your years, Sam. They have had time to grow, multiply, and develop the weapons they need. They found us here."

"Are you absolutely sure this is them? You haven't even really looked at this. And besides, we've found out that it is really old." Sam held up the artifact.

"Yes, it dates from the time that they were on our planet. It is a homing device. I've seen images of it."

"But why would they use an ancient homing device now?"

A series of clicks and grunts emanated from Droat and Froat—Sam had never heard their native language before, but they were sure that was what was going on.

Froat said, "Perhaps we were wrong. Perhaps they don't know we are here—perhaps they got here before we did and destroyed your ship to prevent being discovered."

Xiang said, "Honestly, I like that explanation much better, don't you, Sam?"

"Indeed, I do."

Sharron said, "Just when we were getting used to these aliens, we have some new ones to learn about."

Sam turned to Sharron. "You almost sound like you are enjoying yourself! Did you hear what they said about those guys?"

"Yes, I did. I'm not worried. God will provide."

Sam shook her head. Although they and Sharron got along fine, sometimes they thought Sharron and Gareth were simply crazy.

Sam turned back to Droat. "Droat, can you send everything, I mean *everything*, you have on these aliens? We won't judge you, no matter what you send. We just need every single piece of information you have."

"We will send what we can." That sounded strange to Sam, but they didn't really have the inclination to press them.

"We have to go, Droat. It seems we have our work cut out for us. Do you have any suggestions?"

"Pretend you don't know they exist."

"Is that for our protection, or yours?"

"Both, Sam. If they are here, and don't know about us, once they know you know about them, they will draw you into their conflicts. If they learn about us, they will destroy you along with us because you gave us refuge."

Sam had only one thing to say. "Oh, fabulous."

Pandora, May 2112

Lindsey Ali was exhausted. She had finally managed to plug the slow leak in her habitat by spending the last twenty hours circling around the habitat with a hand-held spectrometer, trying to get a whiff of air. It was a challenge, as the sublimating water from the surface of Pandora had a habit of masking the signals of air coming out of the habitat.

Finally, though, she'd found the offending leak, and patched it, and now it was time for a long sleep. Sometimes she thought she'd been on Pandora too long, but every time she went onto the surface and got a look at the majesty that was Saturn, she was sure she was in the right place. She didn't have any plans to leave... yet.

As she stripped out of her suit, checked the seals and hung it up in the locker, she heard the insistent beep of her AI telling her she had an inbound message. These days, it was one of two things: her lawyer, or the supply depot on Rhea. Since she had just gotten a shipment from the supply depot, it wasn't them. That meant it was her lawyer. Oh, joy.

She looked at the comm screen, and saw that the message wasn't marked urgent, and it *was* from her lawyer, so she decided to get some food and sleep, and deal with it when she woke up. She quickly heated up a cheeseburger from a box full of pre-packaged food, and headed to her quarters, where she wolfed down the burger sitting on her bunk, then lay down and promptly fell asleep.

After she woke, she did her standard routine, which included a mist shower and a half-hour run on the treadmill inside the centrifuge. She sat down to breakfast and decided to listen to whatever message her lawyer had for her.

"Lindsay, hey. Some good news, and some bad news. First, the bad news. Arcadia died in a horrible accident when she was traveling in India. I know that you did love her, although the two of you certainly hadn't gotten along lately." Lindsay snorted, and said under her breath, "That evil stepmother? Not hardly. Good riddance!"

The message went on. "The good news is that her estate is withdrawing all of the suits against you, so you are free and clear. I guess that means you don't need me anymore. I don't know if I'll ever see you again in person, but if you do make it back to Earth at some point, please make some time to let me take you out to lunch."

Lindsay breathed out heavily as the message ended. She was finally free of her stepmother's conniving to get money from the estate left for Lindsay by her father. That was a good chunk of the reason she'd moved out here to the middle of fucking nowhere. The job given to her by Kuiper Exploratory was to hang out on this tiny little piece of ice a hair's breadth from Saturn and check out the bodies moving around Saturn for hints of precious metals. It had been her excuse to get off of Earth, where Arcadia had made it her personal mission to make Lindsay's life completely miserable. Arcadia had been insulted, incensed and angry that Lindsay's father hadn't left her any money when he died, even though their marriage had ended badly. Between the lawsuits, private investigators, and surprise visits by Arcadia at very inopportune times, Lindsay realized that Arcadia was fighting a battle of attrition, and unless Lindsay got herself as far away as possible, she would cave and give Arcadia a lot of money.

But what had happened just a few days after moving here was that she fell in love with Pandora, and in love with Saturn, and was happier than she'd been in her entire life. And that was three years ago. She had been alone here all that time and had enjoyed pretty much every minute. She couldn't imagine going back to Earth, but she could imagine going to Mars, where she'd spent a few months before she got this position. She liked Mars and had gotten caught up in the exuberance that had been created by independence. She'd made some good friends there.

She heard a beep she realized was the proximity alert. That was strange—she'd just gotten the supply drop a few days ago, and wasn't expecting anything, or anyone. She turned on the external monitors and whistled. A ship was coming in between her and Saturn. It was small—but it was a design she'd never seen before. It made her very curious. She wondered what it was. She turned her comm system on.

"Hello there! This is Lindsay of Kuiper Exploratory on Pandora. Who are you? That's quite a fancy ship you've got there."

She heard nothing as it continued to move away from her. She took lots of images of it as it moved away from her, toward the G ring. She had a feeling she'd see it again sometime.

About three years ago, she'd thought it would be a good idea to buy a shuttle, but somehow, she'd put it on the back burner. Now, she thought it was time, for many reasons. She had a survival pod, which was fine in emergencies, but having a shuttle would mean that she could more easily go about the system without having to hire ships, which was inconvenient and expensive. Now that she knew there would be no claims on her money, she decided to go ahead and order one. She brought up the latest catalog, and saw that there was a nice, small shuttle, used, that wouldn't take too much of a bite out of her account. It would take several weeks to get here from Kuiper's ship depot in orbit around Titan, but she was patient.

Sky was pacing. She felt like a rat in a cage. They were stranded on Mars, with no money and no fuel. They were waiting on some high muckety-muck to get back from negotiations with some other high muckety-muck. And, to make things worse, Sam was unreachable, because she was busy talking with the Kurool at their colony. She had nothing to do. Nilesh was happy to be home visiting family, and he was spending a lot of time working at the Xenoscience lab doing further investigations on the artifact and wreckage of George's ship. Mikhail was busy finding women to fuck, and Caitlyn was off doing who knows what. Sky was bored, and antsy, and worried.

Sam had been doing her best, but Sky had the feeling that once this got out of Sam's hands, there was no telling what kind of trouble the four of them would get into because there was clear evidence that they had been intending to sell what they thought were counterfeit artifacts. Nevermind they didn't turn out to be! And it turned out that there was an outstanding SolGov warrant for Mikhail's arrest— one Mik hadn't bothered to share with them. Sky wasn't sure why only Mik had a warrant, but the only good news was that on Mars, a SolGov warrant wasn't worth the bytes it took to store it. Sky didn't know how long that would be true. So, she kept pacing, not sure what to do with herself.

It was nice to have her own space at the Colony One hostel. It was larger quarters than she'd had in a long while. That didn't seem to make much of a difference, though.

"Incoming message from Sam Julian." Her AIs voice spoke, startling her.

"Play, please."

"Hey, Sky, it's Sam. I just got back from the Kurool Colony. We have big news to share. We are all in some very deep shit, I need to tell you that up front. Anyway, we're convening a big meeting at the Xenoscience lab tomorrow morning at 0900. Be there or be square."

Mars Colony One, May 2112

Sam grabbed the towel and dried themself off after they left the mist shower. Sam remembered fondly the first time they took a mist shower on Mars—they'd just arrived and had been somewhat astonished by the lavishness of the digs they had. Now, all of this was old hat. Sam heard Tina moving about in the living room, so they threw on their bathrobe, and walked into the living room, to find Tina looking at the viewscreen. The image that flashed on the viewscreen at that moment made Sam's blood run cold.

"Sam, love, hey."

Sam eyes were still glued to the screen.

"Sam?"

Sam turned to Tina, and asked quietly, "What's that?"

"Some very weird shit happening on Io. Why do I get the impression that this is something you already know about?"

"Well, not really... what do you know?"

"You know that self-described 'warlord' Zoetrope on Ganymede?"

"Yes, he's a nut. I can't believe he's managed to get as far as he has."

"Well, last week, he managed to arrange a silent coup of the Ganymede colony government."

"What?"

"Yes, and this week, he threatened both Io and Callisto. One of his ships destroyed the old abandoned SolGov military station on Io in a few shots—that's what this picture is. No one knows where he got that weapon—it looks like something straight out of the SolGov labs."

"No, it's not. I know exactly where he got that weapon."

"You know where he got that weapon? Sam, does this have to do with what happened to Sky's friend?"

Sam was torn with indecision. Tina was her partner, and as such, they had never kept secrets from each other. But it was possible that the future of the human race depended on keeping this secret. Sam would just have to trust Tina with it.

"Love, let's sit down."

Sam told her the whole story—what they knew about how George's ship had been destroyed and what the Kurool had told them about this other species, as yet unnamed. Tina was quiet through all of it.

"Sam, something doesn't make sense."

"What do you mean?"

"If these aliens were here in force, why would they get involved in what is a very petty local conflict? I hear you that their M.O. seems to be to get themselves inserted into local conflicts, but they could have just as easily destroyed everything on Io, not just an abandoned base. There were five ships that attacked Io. Two of them didn't fire a shot, two of them had conventional weapons, and only one of them had this super beam thing."

Sam thought a moment. The Kurool had assumed that this species had taken a couple of thousand years to grow and search them out—but that struck Sam as unlikely, given the information they shared. It seemed more probable that the aliens had scattered—and then wherever they landed and began to grow, they would get themselves into conflicts and trouble, and decimate themselves again. Tina was right—if there were more of them, there would have been evidence of that on Io.

"Thanks, Tina, I think you're right—I think perhaps there are fewer of these aliens than we think—perhaps not even enough to be a substantial threat. But I don't want to make that assumption yet. You know I need to ask you to keep a lid on what you know. I promise, promise that you'll get the scoop when we're ready."

Tina smiled. "You'd better, sailor."

"Is the *Monitor* writing a story about Zoetrope and the thing on Io?"

"Yup. It will be up tonight."

"Great! We'll need it at our meeting tomorrow!"

"Are there any more momentous pieces of news significant to the history of humankind you want to tell me tonight?" Tina was smiling *that* smile.

"Besides the fact that the SolGov/Corps/MarsGov talks collapsed today?"

"Of course, I knew that already."

"Well, then, I think we're done with momentous news for the moment."

"I'm glad to hear it." Tina began to widen the opening of Sam's robe, and Sam forgot about everything else.

Mars Colony One, 2112

Sky walked into the meeting room with Caitlyn and Mikhail. She could see that Nilesh was already there, talking with a man she hadn't yet met. She looked around the room and saw Sam at the head of the conference table, along with a lot of people she didn't know. It was chaotic, and everyone seemed to be talking at once. They made their way around the table and found empty seats.

Sky heard a man say loudly, "OK, everyone, please take your seats—we have a lot to talk about today."

People settled down and took their seats.

"Hello and welcome. For those of you who don't know me, I am Tai Xien, the head of the Xenoscience lab. I think since we have some new faces here today, we should go around, and have everyone introduce themselves."

Sky paid attention as everyone said who they were, and what they did. The person who had been speaking to Nilesh was some Major General of the Mars military. That made Sky very nervous. The rest were just scientists.

When her turn came around, she just said, "Sky Alvarez, crew on the *Callista*." She knew everyone knew what that meant, anyway.

Sam had sent her a private message letting her know that Sam was doing their best on the side to make sure that they didn't get into any trouble around the trade they were involved in, but they'd also made it clear that once the Mars police found out about all of this, they didn't know whether they could stop them from trying to prosecute. Luckily, since Mars and SolGov were still officially at war, the warrant for Mikhail wouldn't be honored.

Tai said, "Thank you everyone. So, Sam, first, I think we need to hear both of your reports—the details of the conversation with the Kurool, and what you know about what happened on Io yesterday."

As Sam spoke, Sky realized that she was happy that they had reported this, even if they got into trouble for it. This was way too important to have kept to themselves. She hoped the rest of the *Callista* crew felt the same.

After Sam wrapped up, Tai said, "Thank you, Sam. First, is there any discussion of the potential conclusion that there may only be a few of them here?"

The Major General, John Herman, said, "I agree that it is likely that there aren't very many of them, but I do not want to depend on that as a fact. We don't have all of the facts. We need to plan for the possibility that there is more than just one ship with this weapon."

There were murmurs of agreement around the room, and Sky certainly agreed with him.

The woman named Sharron spoke next. "I know how we can find out."

Everyone stopped talking and looked at her. From the look on people's faces, it was clear they were surprised she'd spoken.

Tai said, "Sharron?"

"Zoetrope's real name is Henry Gardinia. He was born and raised in Pennsylvania and was a regular member of Gareth's father's church. He was a childhood friend of mine."

Sky looked around and saw quite a number of open jaws.

Sam said, "You're kidding me."

"No, Sam, you know me. I don't kid."

"How did you find out?"

"Well, when I saw a video of him a few years ago when he first went public as Zoetrope, he looked very familiar. When he was a kid, he would say these really quirky things, things that mystified everyone. Well, Zoetrope says those same quirky things. It's him, I'm sure of it. Besides, when he was a kid, one of his hobbies was building zoetropes." Sky had no idea what a zoetrope was.

Sam looked at Sky with a calculating look on her face. Sky wondered what Sam had in mind. She was sure she'd find out.

Sam said, "Tai, I'd like to meet with Sharron, John, and the *Callista* crew. I have an idea on how to infiltrate them and get some answers."

Tai said, "Alright. Let's split up into two teams. John, Sam, Sharron and the crew of the *Callista* are on task to figure out how many aliens we're talking about, and how much of a threat they might be. The rest of us need to get busy analyzing that huge boatload of data the Kurool sent us on these folks. We have a lot to learn, people. Let's get busy.

Sam, you have the room." Sky watched as the scientists filtered out of the room.

Sam said, "OK, folks, I have a hair-brained idea, but it needs work. I'm depending on all of you to make it work."

Sky chuckled. She looked forward to hearing it.

The Major General said, "Outline it for us, Sam."

"We all know that the negotiations between Mars, SolGov and the corps were a dismal failure. We just found out that SolGov totally refuses to cede jurisdiction to any territory in the system outside of the orbit of Mars. That's useful for us, because it makes Zoetrope a natural ally, certainly from his perspective. He needs us, and, given that he's a narcissistic sociopath, he'll think we need him. Ganymede and Io aren't food sustainable yet and might never be. We'll offer him help, but we'll pretend it's on the down-low: we don't want SolGov to know that we're helping him—which of course is mostly true. If he's done any research on the *Callista*, he'll know it's a bit... shady, so he'll believe us. We send the *Callista*, and you offer to join up with him. He'll agree, I'm sure."

Sky was liking this plan. It would get them back on their ship and doing something useful. She might even be able to wrangle some payment for it.

Sam continued, "The quiet approach is where Sharron fits in. Sharron, if it's OK with you, I want you to go with the *Callista* to Ganymede, and act as part of the crew."

Sharron let out a yelp. "Sam!"

"You can do it, Sharron. I know you can."

"What would my role be?"

"We need someone who he knew—it's a sort of implicit threat. Kind of like 'we know who you really are.' Carrot and stick, as it were."

Sky didn't know Sharron, but she could tell the woman looked petrified.

"OK, Sam, I'll do it, but I hope you aren't sorry later."

"Sharron, really, I know you have it in you. So, Sky, Mikhail, you guys on board?"

Mik put his arm on Sky's, and said, "Under certain conditions."

Sky could see the Major General bristle. Sky thought this might get ugly, but she'd be good cop to Mik's bad cop.

Sam said, "What conditions?"

"First, we get a complete pardon of all pending charges. Second, we get enough fuel to get us there and wherever we want to go after we're done. And third, we get paid for this. A million Yuan seems an appropriate fee."

The Major General's face got really red. He spat, "You are lucky that you're not in the brig right now. We will *not* be blackmailed!"

Sam said in a quiet but steely voice, "Mikhail, there are no pending charges on Mars against you. But believe me, there will be if you don't go on this mission. And there's nothing stopping us from handing your ass to SolGov on a platter right this minute."

Sky jumped in, removing Mikhail's hand from her arm. "Mik, be quiet. Sam, we want to be reasonable, and we want to be useful." She turned to Mikhail. "Right, Mik?" He looked away from her. She knew she'd pay for this later.

"We're on board for this, really we are. But we do have needs, Sam. Obviously we need fuel to at least get us there and back. And we're completely broke."

Sam sighed. Sky knew Sam would do for them what they could and hold the dogs at bay for as long as they could.

"Sky, Mikhail, we'll fill up your tanks. I'll talk with Tai and see what a reasonable fee for a service contract like this should be. I have no power whatsoever, nor does John, over what the Mars police might choose to do with you. I can imagine if you help us out in this important task, they will be more likely to forget anything untoward ever happened. And of course, after this is done, you don't need to come back to Mars anyway. This is the best we can do."

Sky said, "Thanks, Sam, that's all we ask." She looked at Mikhail, who she could tell was very angry. Caitlyn was impassive, and Nilesh thoughtful. He, at least, would have her back when she needed to face Mikhail later. Cait would likely take Mik's side. Sky thought that the next few hours were going to be far from fun.

Sam said, "OK, we all have our work cut out for us. I'll go talk with Tai, and get numbers for you, Sky. Sharron, find out whatever you can via your family about what they know about Zoetrope. John, walk with me. We need to plan the *Callista's* trip out to Ganymede."

The walk back to the hostel was frosty and silent. The four of them had done very well over the last few years together. There had been a couple of big fights over contracts or decisions, but largely they all got along. Nominally, Sky was the leader, because she'd fronted most of the down payment on the ship, so she owned more of it than the other three. But in practice they worked by consensus. Sky hoped she wouldn't have to pull rank on Mikhail to make this all work. He might never forgive her for that. But she couldn't see any other way out of this. If they didn't agree to do this, they'd still be completely broke and stranded on Mars, and likely to get slapped with intent to sell counterfeit goods. At least if they took the mission, the likelihood of getting into legal trouble was greatly decreased, and they might even get a legitimate service contract out of this—not to mention credit for helping save the human race, or something.

They filtered into the living room of the suite they had at the hostel, and Sky saw Mikhail go to the refrigerator box and get a beer.

Caitlyn said, "Sky, that wasn't a nice thing to do to Mik."

"I see. What should I have said, then?"

"You should have stood up for him."

"And get us all into deeper trouble?"

Mik said, "They would have never turned us in. They need us!"

Sky turned to Mik and said, "Mik, Cait, you both are being stupid. All they need is a somewhat shady ship to go to Ganymede and be an agent for them. They don't need *our* ship, just *a* ship."

Mik was silent, and Sky could tell it was sinking in.

"Everyone, we need them far more than they need us. If they actually pay us for this, that will be more than we should expect. There are twenty other ships, just as marginal and shady as we are, that would be happy to do this duty. Let's count ourselves lucky."

Sky could tell they understood, but she could also tell they weren't happy about it. Not that she was, either. She never liked the *Callista* to be in this sort of situation. But there wasn't much any of them could do about it at the moment.

Mik said, "So we just bend over, then?"

"Mik, look, this is our only way out of this predicament. And we get to do something useful in the process. If you can think of a better way out..."

Sky thought she saw something in his eyes, but he only said, "No, you are right. Let's just do this."

After they'd talked practicalities for a while, Nilesh went off to spend time with family, and Caitlyn and Mikhail left to go out to a bar. Sky was left with her thoughts. She realized that she didn't trust Mik and Caitlyn anymore, and perhaps they didn't trust her, either. And that wasn't a good thing - she wasn't going to be able to keep working with people she didn't trust. She was trying to identify when this had happened. Was it that Mik hadn't told any of them about the SolGov warrant for his arrest? Or was it his earlier lying to her about the Venus contract? Or maybe it had happened even before that, when she'd discovered he'd taken a kickback from one of their sales from an old client. As she thought about all these things, she realized that this was going to be her last trip with the *Callista*. She'd sell, or maybe even give away her share, and go find some other way to live her life. She was done with Mik.

Chapter 3:
The Mission

Mars Colony One, May 2112

John had been trying to avoid this meeting for as long as humanly possible but given that the *Callista* would be leaving orbit in less than three days, he knew he'd better get this meeting over with. Patrick was back from the disastrous attempted negotiation with SolGov and the corps, and was in a foul mood, but John figured that he would appreciate something else to talk about. John had already told Patrick the outlines of what was happening, so this wouldn't be as much of a surprise as it would be for General Tsang.

As he arrived and was ushered into the office by Patrick's aide, he saw that the General had already arrived. Patrick was speaking.

"Lei, I don't really know what to do. SolGov and the corps ambushed us in the talks. Clearly, they had been in discussions, and planned to force our hand... John, come in, have a seat. I was just filling Lei in on the dismal details of the talks."

John simply nodded, expecting Patrick to continue.

"It's just untenable, and I don't want to commit any more forces to the effort, especially given the state of our military at the moment. But we can claim jurisdiction over the space we've taken and refuse to allow any SolGov ships to refuel at the Mars Station fuel depot. That'll make it a lot more difficult for SolGov to hold sway over the belt."

The General said, "But of course, SolGov already has several fuel depots just inside Mars orbit, and I don't think we should think about attacking those."

"No, originally, we asked for jurisdiction over the system from the Mars orbit and beyond. I'm sticking to that. I don't want them to think we're reaching. John, do you have any comments?"

"Of course, sir, I think we do as you say, and wait. SolGov's ability to keep control over space outside Mars orbit is already pretty bad. With the current problems that SolGov has got insystem, plus that nutcase Zoetrope making Jupiter a problem for them, we'll be in shape to have defacto jurisdiction in just a few years."

Patrick nodded, as did General Tsang.

"Alright, John, you convened this meeting, and I know a little about the situation, but why don't you start from the beginning."

John laid out the facts and plans, clearly, and without editing.

"You think this will work—we can get the information we need about these aliens from Zoetrope?"

"I think so, yes. I think Sam can make it work, even if the *Callista* crew can't."

General Tsang said, "I think we need to notify SolGov military about all this. I don't know what they'll say..."

"Yes, Lei. The sooner we explain what's going on, the better. I don't want them accusing us of really allying with Zoetrope. They would believe that."

"Indeed, they would. I'll leave it to you, how and when you want to tell SolGov."

Patrick sighed. "Yes, I guess that would be my job, wouldn't it? And I would have bet a week ago that Prak would be OK with all of this and trust us with yet another set of aliens... but now, I don't know that I think that will happen."

John looked at Patrick and tried to smile a comforting smile. Sometimes it was hard for him to meet with Patrick in his official capacity because he wanted to make him feel better or comfort him... but that would have to wait until later.

A knock at the door startled John, and he turned to see Patrick's aide in the doorway.

"Governor Lohrheim, Mr. Jason Snow is here to see you about the new station contract."

"Thank you, Marianne. General, Major General, thank you for all of your hard work on this. I'll keep you posted on SolGov's response, and please keep me apprised of any progress from your efforts, and that of the Xenoscience lab."

Patrick nodded and walked out of the office with General Tsang.

General Tsang said, "I don't envy him one bit."

John nodded. "He has a really tough job."

General Tsang smiled, and patted John on the back. "I'm glad he has such a good companion to help him through this."

John smiled back, nodding. His relationship with Patrick was public knowledge, although few people referred to it. His dual role could sometimes be a little bit dicey, but the informal culture of Mars made it possible to pull off.

They parted ways, and John made his way back to his office to order something he needed to give to Sam before they left for the mission.

Mars Colony One, May 2112

Sam and John were sitting in Tai's office. Sam could tell John was angry, but he was doing fairly well at keeping it to himself. Sam knew that if John had his druthers, he'd march the four *Callista* crew over to the Mars police and get them charged with a dozen things. Sam could tell that the idea that the crew might get paid for this mission rankled him.

Tai said, "Well, it's probably a six-month mission, between getting to Ganymede, and joining up long enough to get the info we need. Service contracts like that tend to be from ten to fifteen Mars units a month."

John said, "Give them ten."

Sam said, "Why don't we offer 75K Mars Units for the contract, half to be paid up front, half to be paid on completion."

Tai said, "That sounds reasonable. With the current deflation of the Mars currency in the system, that would end up being about 200K Yuan."

Sam said, "I'm sure they'll accept that."

John shook his head. "They'd better. Or else I'm calling Zhen."

Sam knew that Zhen was the head of the Mars police force. Sam hoped they could keep Zhen in the dark about all of this for as long as humanly possible.

"OK, I'll go talk with Sky. The *Callista* should launch ASAP. I'm not sure what I think about the fact that you want me to go with them."

John said, "Sam, how else are we going to make sure that they go through with their mission? You are a credible backchannel for

MarsGov, given your connections. You're no longer a member of the Xenoscience lab, and only a few of us know that you are still in close touch with the Kurool."

Sam sighed. "I know, John, I know. I just don't really want to have to tell Tina."

"She'll understand, Sam."

Sam nodded. It was logical that they should accompany the *Callista* to Ganymede. But even apart from telling Tina, Sam really wasn't all that interested in being in space again. But perhaps this would be good for them—a way for Sam to finally face their fears of space.

They walked out of Tai's office, and Sam made their way back home. Sam picked up a tablet.

"Jane, find Sky Alvarez. Ask her to meet me at my house as soon as possible."

There was a brief pause, then, "Done, Sam."

"Thanks, Jane."

Sam wondered whether or not the *Callista* had a matrix capable of handling Jane.

"Jane, what are the current matrix capacities of the *Callista*? Can you find out?"

"They got an upgrade to 5 THz with .5 K cores two years ago."

"That's all?" Sam was surprised. That was about what the old small asteroid hunter had.

"Yes, Sam. Not enough for me."

"OK, can you talk with Ched at the shipyards? Order an upgrade for the *Callista* that gets it up to spec to add you to the matrix. Tell him it's on the lab."

"Will do, Sam."

Sam could hardly imagine Sky would mind.

Sam got home and had just poured some juice and made a sandwich when they heard the door chime.

"Come in."

Sky walked in, looking worried.

"Hey, Sky. Have a seat. Hungry?"

"No, thanks, I'm fine."

"I hope you don't mind me eating my sandwich while we talk."

"No, not at all. Go for it."

They sat at the dining room table, Sky across from Sam.

"A few things, Sky. First, I got you 75K Mars units as a contract fee, half paid up front, half on completion. And as we said, we'll fill up your tanks here and at Ganymede at the end of the mission."

"Alright. Mikhail won't like it, but I'll make sure everyone agrees."

"This probably won't help, but John threatened to call Zhen, the head of the Mars police if you don't agree to these terms."

"I understand."

"Second, I checked into your matrix. We're ordering a big upgrade for you, and it's on our tab."

"Why?"

"Because I'm coming with you, as is Jane, my AI."

"Sam! No, no way. No one will agree to that."

"You don't have a choice. That's part of the terms of the deal."

"You don't trust us?"

"Honestly, Sky, what do you think? We're handing you 37.5K Mars credits and a tank full of fuel. One of you is a fugitive from SolGov, and you're known to take part in illegal trade. What would you do in our shoes?"

"Well, we wouldn't abandon Sharron. But the truth is, I wouldn't trust us either. Alright. Sam, you're making this hard."

"Sky, I'm trying to make the best of this situation. Most everyone else wants to throw you in jail and hire a trustworthy crew for this mission..."

"I know you are trying your best. I trust you, Sam."

"Sky, if it were only you, I'd trust you, too. But it isn't only you. I don't trust Mikhail."

"I don't trust him either, honestly."

Sam was taken aback for a moment, but they saw in Sky that she was telling the truth—and perhaps it was a new truth for her.

Sam said, "The matrix upgrade can be done in a day. We can launch in 48 hours. I want to get in the shuttle up to *Callista* in about 40 or so."

"Alright. Let me gather everyone and twist arms."

Sky got up and walked out, and Sam couldn't help but see how much seemed to be weighing Sky down. And then, there was what was weighing Sam down—the talk with Tina. She'd be home in a few hours, so Sam had time to get some work done in preparation for the trip. Oh, and to cook Tina a very nice dinner.

"Mmmm, Sam, this dinner was amazing, and a bountiful feast. You haven't cooked a meal like this since... Saaaammm?"

Sam looked up, busted. The last time they'd cooked a meal like this was when they'd chosen to take an assignment at Colony 7 for three months, helping them get off the ground.

"Tell me you're not going to Ganymede, Sam."

"I'm going to Ganymede."

Tina sighed, then smiled. "I can imagine that it's harder for you to think about going back into space than it is to tell me you'll be away for... how many months?"

"Probably around six. And no, I'm not looking forward to going back into space."

"There isn't anyone else they can send?"

"No, Tina, I'm one of the most credible backchannel people they can send. And that's one less person they have to let in on the secret."

"I'll miss you, Sam. Promise me you'll be home for Christmas?"

"I promise, Tina."

"I'll be worried about you. And don't tell me you'll be fine."

"This really isn't a dangerous mission."

Tina laughed. "Really, now?"

Sam grinned. "Well, alright. There is significant risk. And I'll be scared as hell for most of it."

"I bet you'll get right back in the saddle, sailor."

Sam hoped Tina was right.

The evening before they were going to leave, John came by. He looked concerned.

"Hi, Sam. I just wanted to have a last unofficial conversation before you left."

"Well, I think we're in good shape. Our initial contact with Zoetrope seemed successful. He seems completely ready to believe that Mars wants to ally with him. And for some reason, he seems to especially look forward to meeting me."

"I bet I know what it is."

"What?"

"If he had first contact with the Zeloso, then he thinks he and you are two of a kind."

"Ah, that makes a kind of sense. I imagine he wants to brag." Zeloso was the name that they had given the new aliens. The materials that the Kurool had given them used a name that was not translatable, but transliterated to something vaguely approaching Zeloso, so they'd taken it on.

"Yes, I imagine so. Anyway, a couple of things..."

John took out something wrapped in cloth.

"Here, you might need this. It's a multi-mode beam weapon. Mode 1 is dome stun, mode 2 is dome lethal, mode 3 is outside stun, and mode 4 is outside lethal."

"John, I..."

"Sam, you need some protection. I don't trust Zoetrope, and I don't trust Mikhail."

"John, I don't even know how to shoot."

"There's a laser sight. You don't need to know how to shoot."

"OK. Thanks, John."

"Keep it hidden. Don't even tell Sky you have it. Keep it on hand."

"Alright."

"Second, the Kurool are busy."

"Busy?"

"Yes, some satellite imaging of their colony suggests that something is happening, but it's not clear what. Two of the five shapes that made up the ship have separated from the main pentagon."

"That's strange. Have you thought about asking Droat?"

"We did. They just said something enigmatic."

"What did they say?"

"'We have debts to repay.'"

"John, that's not enigmatic, that's clear."

"It is?"

"Yes, they are headed for Ganymede. They hope to talk with the Zeloso. I suspected as much when I talked with Droat. They seemed to be suggesting that they would want to make amends in some way with the Zeloso, if it were possible. I'm sure that they gathered from my last set of questions that there likely aren't a lot of the Zeloso around."

"Well, that might make things a little more complicated, won't it?"

"Let's hope that they are circumspect about it, at least until we get our intel."

"Well, Sam, I sort of wish I was going with you, and I'm also glad I'm not. Good luck, my friend."

"Thanks, John. And thanks for the piece." Sam picked up the wrapped weapon.

They hugged, and John left Sam, who finished some last-minute preparations and work before Tina got home for their last evening together.

Potemkin, May 2112

Gareth was relieved to finally be leaving Earth. It had been an unpleasant two weeks. The only thing he had enjoyed was getting to spend time with his brother Percival, who had grown into a mature, graceful man. Before Percival had left to go back to Seattle, he and Gareth had had a long leisurely dinner and spoke honestly about the family. Percival had confirmed what Gareth had long suspected— Tristan had been transgender, but hadn't been able to deal with it, or tell anyone in the family except for Percival, and had become addicted because of it.

Gareth was settling into his small stateroom on the Mars leisure transport, the *Potemkin*. Usually, he traveled by more utilitarian means, on cargo or colony transports. This was his first time on a leisure transport. It was quite a different experience. But he figured since he and Sharron were about to be one and a half million Yuan richer, a 5,000 Yuan luxury transport back home wasn't a big deal.

He heard his AI's message alert—he had a message from Sharron. That surprised him. She'd just sent him a message yesterday about the whole new alien presence. It was fascinating. Perhaps there was more news.

He said to his AI, "Display on viewscreen, please."

When he looked at Sharron, he saw a look on her face that he'd never seen before. It was a combination of pride, fear, and excitement. He wondered what was going on.

"Hi Gareth. I have been asked by Sam and the Xenoscience team to accompany the *Callista* to Ganymede."

Gareth was stunned. Sharron, go to Ganymede? Then he smiled. He knew now that she really *wanted* to go. She explained the rationale, which made sense to him. She was asking his permission. Ah, that one. It was more than time to let that one go.

He said to his AI, "Record a message, please."

"Sharron, I am excited for you! That sounds like an amazing adventure. I am almost even jealous, but it's also not my kind of thing.

"Dear heart, it is time for us to stop this game we've been playing for the last couple of years. I know that both of us were raised and lived with this notion that you should follow me and obey me, but we both know that we now believe differently—it's time for us to act like it. If you wish to go to Ganymede, you should go to Ganymede. You don't need to ask my permission.

"I will miss you. I know this means that you'll be gone by the time I get home. Be safe. I know that Sam will look after you. Send me a message once you get underway. I love you."

Gareth had a feeling that perhaps this trip would be a very good thing for Sharron. It was time for her to finally get out of his shadow.

Mars Colony 1, May 2112

"Fuck no!"

"Mik..."

"Sky, did you hear what I said? I said, FUCK NO! Having that Sharron person is bad enough, but I will not accept Sam on this mission!"

Nilesh said, "Mik, Sam is trustworthy, and we'll want to have Sam on this mission. I'm not worried about it, and I don't see why what's-his-face-trope would want to talk to us without someone like Sam along."

Mikhail was fuming, angrier than Sky had seen him in a very long time.

He said, "Great, that's two babysitters we have now. I don't want Sam on this mission!"

Sky said reasonably, "Mik, if we don't agree with these terms, they call Mars police, we go to jail, and some other ship takes the mission. This is our only chance off this planet with our skins intact. 75K isn't a lot of money, but it's better than nothing, and not all that much less than we would have originally made selling George's artifacts."

Caitlyn muttered, "This sucks. I don't like it. I know they are your ex, but I don't like Sam."

Sky was exasperated. "Alright, Mik, Cait, do you have an alternative plan? Let's hear it."

Both Mikhail and Caitlyn were silent. Sky knew they didn't have an alternative plan because there wasn't one. Sky had spent hours making contacts all over the system, but there was no work, no cargo, and nothing that would get them out of this bind... except this mission.

"OK, I'm taking silence as assent. We're meeting Sam at the shuttle bay at 0800 hours the day after tomorrow."

Sky felt bruised and battered by this whole thing. And tired. Tired to the bone. She left the suite and went to drown her sorrows for an evening.

As she sat drinking her vodka tonic at the closest watering hole, she couldn't help but regret the last few years of her life. There had been some excitement and some good times, but as she did an inventory, she realized that it had been a harder time than she'd been willing to admit to herself. She'd been far more broke than she'd ever been when she worked for Strelix, and the stress level she dealt with on a daily basis was far worse. She sighed. Why did she have to make her own life so hard?

She heard, "One whisky sour, please."

She looked to her side to see Nilesh sitting down. He nodded to her. "Lesh..."

"Don't say it, Sky. Don't apologize. This isn't your fault."

"I'm glad you don't blame me. I know Mik does."

"Fuck Mik. I'm tired of him, tired of his attitude. I walked out of the hostel while he was in the middle of delivering a screed against you for taking the original offer from George, and me for feeling the need to report it. The truth is, we got in a bit of bad luck with George, and this mission is the only way out of it."

"Lesh, I can't work with Mik anymore. I'm going to need out after this mission."

Nilesh chuckled. "I'm done too, Sky. I talked with Patrick—he's going to give me a job when I get back."

"That's great, Nilesh!"

"Yeah, it's more than time for me to stay home for a while."

"I don't know what I'll do, but I'll figure it out."

"You could always go home, Sky."

"No, not even now. I can't stand the thought of going back to Earth."

"Well, Cait and Mik can buy us out with their shares of the contract money, if they want. Or we'll just sell *Callista*—we should get a decent price for her."

"You've kept her in good shape."

"I have, that. We'll be OK, Sky."

Sky somehow didn't really believe that, but she was trying hard.

Mars Colony 1, May 2112

Sam and Sharron sat in the shuttle port waiting for the *Callista* crew, who were fifteen minutes late. Sam was already annoyed. Just as Sam was about to ask Jane to track them down, they saw them saunter into the port area towards them. Well, only two of them were sauntering, really. Mikhail and Caitlyn. Sky and Nilesh walked behind them, looking relatively depressed. Sam shook their head. This was not going to be a pleasant month.

Sam stood up, and Sky approached, and said quietly. "Sorry, Sam, we had a little argument before we left the hostel."

"Don't worry about it, Sky. Let's just go."

They all walked out toward shuttle aisle 17, where the *Callista* shuttle was sitting. Sam knew that although Sky would have let their pilot, none of the other crew would agree. Well, they didn't know about Nilesh, but certainly neither Mikhail nor Caitlyn would agree. Caitlyn had spent a little time with Tina, and Tina had said that she felt she no longer knew her. Sam didn't think they knew her anymore, either.

On the other hand, they'd enjoyed getting to know Nilesh a little bit. John said that Patrick really trusted him, and even though his sense of legality was sometimes a bit askew, his sense of morality never was.

Sam was happy not to pilot—they didn't know whether they trusted themselves. Sam wasn't looking forward to being in space, and they'd spent the last night sleepless, scared out of their mind. Sam couldn't imagine how the night would have gone if Tina hadn't been there.

The matrix upgrade had gone fine, and a copy of Jane was happily ensconced in the *Callista* matrix. She would remain accessible but sort of to the side of the standard AI routines. Jane had said they were extremely "primitive." Sam couldn't help but chuckle. Sometimes Sam was sure Jane had an ego.

"Alright, please stow your stuff and strap in everyone. We're launching in five."

Sam found a cubby to put her bag in and helped Sharron strap into one of the extra seats in the back. She sat next to Sharron, and strapped in, too.

She looked at Sharron, who looked nervous.

Sam said, "You OK?"

"I'll be fine. I'm sorry, I hope I'm not a bother."

"No worries, it will be great."

Sam subvocalized, "Jane, status?"

She heard in her ear, sort of, "No further communication from Zoetrope. The Kurool haven't launched."

"Thanks. Make sure to alert me of any changes in either situation."

"Of course, Sam."

Sam had resisted communication implants for years because they didn't like the idea of having silicon and metal in their head, but on this mission, they needed a silent interface with Jane, so they'd gotten a subvocal electrode, a cochlear implant, and a transmitter all well-hidden. This meant Sam could communicate with Jane and others without anyone knowing. Sam hadn't even told Sky. That felt sneaky and bad to Sam, but they realized they didn't really have a choice.

Sam felt the side pocket of their pants, where the weapon was. It was strange carrying it—they'd never carried a weapon before.

They hoped they didn't need it. Sam was as ready as they were ever going to be.

They launched, and it was a fairly uneventful ride for Sam. Nothing unusual happened, and Sam relaxed into the familiar feelings of a shuttle launch and dock. As they disembarked from the shuttle, Mikhail took Sam aside, pulling her bodily away from the others.

"Sam, you'll be staying in your quarters, with Sharron. There is a matrix terminal that should be adequate for your needs, and your quarters are close to the mess. I don't want either of you up in the control room, or, really, anywhere in the hub, nor in the workroom. This is *our* ship, and you are just passengers, hear me?"

"Alright, Mikhail, that's fine with me. You don't have anything to worry about. We will stay well out of your hair."

Although Mikhail knew that Jane had been installed, he probably didn't know that there was a failsafe, and Jane could take complete control of the *Callista* if need be. Sam didn't need to be in the control room to change the course of the *Callista* if it came to that. And they wouldn't get bored. One of the things Sam intended to do while on this trip was to comb through with Jane several thousand exabytes worth of space surveillance data.

SolGov had started to place surveillance satellites all around the Solar system more than twenty years ago, and most of that data was simply stored. It was only in the unusual case when something needed investigating that this data was looked at. Sam wasn't sure exactly what she was looking for—it was likely needles in a haystack, but Sam had the time, and Jane had the processing power, so they were going to go through it, year by year. Jane would look for events that were unusual, things that didn't fit the usual patterns: these might indicate the presence of alien ships in the system.

They followed Mikhail. He gave them a brief tour of the mess, and of the few other spaces, like the toilet and shower and sickbay, that they would need for the trip. He floated next to a door and opened it.

"Here are your quarters. There are straps in the bunk. We should be turning on spin in about an hour."

"Thanks, Mikhail."

"Don't thank me. I don't want you either of you here, and I've taken it on myself to make sure you in particular don't get into any trouble." He was pointing right at Sam.

She nodded. They went into their quarters and closed the door behind them. As Sharron took the bottom bunk, Sam took out her tablet, and stowed their bag in a small cubby above the top bunk. They pulled themselves up into the bunk, and strapped in.

"Need any help with the straps, Sharron?"

"No, Sam, I'm all set. Thanks."

"Alright. I'm going to get some work done."

"Sounds like a good idea. Me too."

Potemkin, June 2112

Gareth was sitting in the lounge area of the transport taking him back to Mars. He'd arrive in about a week. He'd been glad to finally leave the horrible drama of his family behind. Percival had promised to come with his family to visit soon, and Gareth knew that Sharron would enjoy that.

He'd gotten a message from Sharron yesterday from the *Callista*, sharing what it had been like to be on board. It sounded like it was tense, but Sharron seemed to be having a good time, nonetheless. She'd been working on their most recent treatise.

Gareth and Sharron were finally finishing the paper for the International Journal of Christian Theology that laid out their arguments that the Son of God had incarnated as a Kurool in the man of Turool, the One they revered. The truth was, Gareth had known it more than four years ago, when he'd first read the account of the visit to the Kurool ship by Sam Julian, while he and Sharron were on Earth to work for the Montoya campaign.

Then, it was his heart telling him that this was so. He and Sharron had spent the last four years working to find the right theological and biblical arguments that other Christians might agree were plausible. It scared him to go public with this; he had no idea what the repercussions might be. They had sent a brief letter in response to another theologian's earlier paper discussing the similarities between

Turool and Jesus, and the journal had requested a full article from them. Gareth wasn't sure that they would really print it once they saw what it said.

It was the linguists working on the Kurool language that had made all the difference. They initially hadn't been so keen on it, but Gareth had asked them to translate what he had been told by the Kurool was a particularly important teaching of Turool. And what emerged was stunning, both to him and to the linguists. The teaching was absolutely the Beatitudes—there wasn't any other explanation.

The dominant Kurool language, the one that Turool spoke, was conceptually different from any human language. That was not a surprise. But the linguists had been working hard with the Kurool to come up with a kind of key—the best human concept that corresponded with a Kurool one. For instance, the part of the Beatitudes that said "Blessed be the meek..." The Kurool had no concept of "meekness" or "humility" but they did have a concept that translated as "lying horizontally and folding." It meant the same thing to Kurool that "meekness" or "humility" meant to humans, even though it was really conceptually completely different.

Using that key, what emerged from that central teaching of Turool was the same as the Beatitudes of Jesus. It was striking, so striking that even the linguists were beginning to agree with Gareth's point of view and had continued to do similar translations of other Turool teachings.

Of course, the interesting thing was that Turool arrived after the Kurool had significant technology, so all of Their teachings were actually recorded. Jesus was on Earth before any kind of technology, and all of his teachings were handed down verbally, then written and translated and re-translated. Gareth had gone back to an old mainline Christian biblical scholarship group from the twentieth century called "The Jesus Seminar". Earlier in his life, he had dismissed this as heretical, but he realized that ultimately, it made a lot of sense. It found the parts of what was in the Gospels that was likely truly authentic, and he and Sharron compared those to the recorded and conceptually translated teachings of Turool. The result had been uncanny, and, he was told, extremely unlikely to be accidental. Many of the sayings of Jesus considered by the Jesus Seminar to be authentic, or likely authentic had a corresponding saying by Turool. There were many, many other sayings of Turool that seemed meant just for the Kurool, which was no surprise to Gareth. He expected that the sayings of Jesus that were missing from the Kurool teachings were meant for humans specifically.

And, of course, there was the whole thing about Earth. First, it had become clear that Turool was born on the Kurool planet at least one hundred years after Jesus' time on Earth. In translating the teachings of Turool about Earth, there was absolutely no mistake about what planet Turool was talking about. He specifically talked about Sol, specifically mentioned the third planet, and even had things to say about the beings on the third planet, things that were true.

The Kurool technology at the time of Turool was like human technology in the last half of the twentieth century. There was no way to get much information about planets around distant stars at that time. The Kurool hadn't launched a telescope into orbit by then. There is no way that any Kurool could say much of anything about the third planet in the Sol system. There was no way for Turool to know much of anything about Earth.

This all added up to one thing in Gareth's mind. Turool had been on Earth. And Turool had been Jesus. He gulped. And they were about to tell the world about it.

Pandora, June 2112

Lindsay had set her AI to sweep the space one thousand kilometers out from Pandora and warn her loudly when something approached. She wanted more time to have a look at what was out there. It had been a while since she saw that ship, but in doing a bunch of research, she had come up with nothing. There was no ship she could find with similar design. She was stumped.

She'd gotten some new data from the remotes she'd sent out all over the F-ring—Kuiper Exploratory wanted to know how much money were in the rings. It didn't look good. This was the fifth set of remotes she'd sent, and none of them so far had come back with anything promising. It wasn't going to be too much longer before

Kuiper decided that this wasn't a good investment after all and pulled the plug on funding Lindsay. Lindsay could fund herself for a while, but she realized that it wouldn't be the best use of her inheritance, now that it was totally free from the danger of being lost to her evil stepmother.

It wasn't all that surprising, the lack of metal in any body she looked at. Saturn's moons had first been explored in the forties, and consistently, they were relatively worthless in the metals department. She'd read several theoretical papers suggesting why. It involved something having to do with the formation of gas giants. Jupiter's moons were pretty metal-poor as well. But someone at Kuiper wanted to make sure, and Lindsay was here to do that.

She decided to delay sending this data for a week or so. They mostly forgot her existence, which was a blessing. But some bureaucrat got antsy if she didn't send in a report at least once every month or so with more data.

Now that it was looking like her time on Pandora would come to an end sooner rather than later, she started to think about what was going to be next. Settling on Mars sounded like the best plan—Jupiter was crazy, with that Zoetrope dude. She was going to stay as far away from that as possible. Nothing further out-system felt attractive, and she was never going back to Earth again, so Mars sounded like the best bet. Besides, she'd gained some friends on Mars, and she liked the society that independent Mars was growing into.

She went back to look at those images she was able to take of that ship. She wondered whether she should tell anyone about it or ask anyone whether or not they'd ever seen anything like it. She decided she wouldn't for now—she wanted to learn more first, if possible, if it came this way again.

Chapter 4:
Zoetrope

Ganymede, June 2112

Zoetrope looked at the text message sent by the governor of Io and laughed. His attack on the old SolGov military installation on Io had clearly scared the Io governor, which, of course was the point. Zoetrope smiled. Soon, very soon, all of Jupiter would be his. And after that... who knew how far he could go.

He had been quite satisfied by the communication with the new Mars government. Yes, they would be his allies, and they would need him in their fight with SolGov. He had been especially satisfied to learn that Sam, with whom he shared the honor of being a human who had made first contact with an alien species, would be coming to visit. It was unfortunate that he could not tell Sam anything about Koth. He had promised them to not expose their presence in the system. But he was sure that Sam would be awed by him anyway.

He was, of course, awesome. He had gone from being someone just about ready to die in a borrowed ship during a failed mission, to a wealthy man who now owned Ganymede, and was about to own Jupiter. He might say it was God who had answered his prayers— and answered them quite dramatically, at that. God had proven that Zoetrope was worthy.

He heard a knock at his door.

"Enter."

The small man who had been Ganymede's governor and was now acting as its manager walked in, looking at the floor.

"General Zoetrope..."

He turned, bored already.

"Yes, Manager Holcomp?"

"Sir, the owner of the fuel depot refuses to acknowledge that you have become governor of Ganymede. They will not pay their taxes."

"I see. You are dismissed."

"Is there...?"

"That is all, Mr. Holcomp."

The small man nodded and fled the room. Zoetrope shook his head. How did he get surrounded by such imbeciles?

He spoke to his AI. "Who is the owner of the Ganymede fuel depot?"

"Millicent Woeller."

"Please tell Commander Kaleen Creal that Millicent Woeller has refused to pay her taxes."

"Done."

Zoetrope smiled. No, he was not surrounded by imbeciles. Kaleen would convince Ms. Woeller to pay her taxes... or else Ms. Woeller would be found unfortunately floating in space without any oxygen. Zoetrope knew that Kaleen would be quite amenable to this task.

He didn't really want to run Jupiter, he just wanted to control it, and benefit from its riches. He didn't have any interest in running it - that he would leave to the plebes like Holcomp. He had better things to do, like plan the zoetrope that would awe the system.

Callista, June 2112

At least Sam wasn't getting bored in their small, cramped quarters. It had been three weeks, and the only *Callista* crew member they'd seen much of was Mikhail, who seemed to be keeping everyone else away from them. He didn't seem to care much what Sharron did, which was useful. Sharron had been relaying to Sam all sorts of stuff about the goings on of the *Callista* crew, and Sam had been working hard with Jane, combing the massive amounts of data from the surveillance monitors scattered all over the system.

Sam had garnered a lot of very interesting data. They had first looked at all of the data from two months before George's destroyed ship was discovered. It turned out there was a surveillance system in an asteroid only ten thousand kilometers from the asteroid George was found. It showed one ship, presumably George's ship, arriving, then another ship arriving and leaving, and then, about two weeks later, the *Callista*. Jane was now going back as far as there was data to see if there were any other significant arrivals or departures.

Jane had also been looking for anomalous events, such as distress calls and evidence of ships without identity beacons. So far, she had only gone back a year or so—there was so much data to comb through.

Sam stood up from the bunk and stretched, and decided it was time for dinner. Mikhail hadn't come to get them for dinner yet, as he usually did, but Sam was hungry, and tired of being polite to Mikhail by following his lead. Sam walked out of the room and down the hall to the mess room, where Sky, Sharron, and Nilesh were eating. They looked up as Sam entered.

Sky said, "Hey, haven't seen much of you."

"Mikhail has been doing his job keeping me away from you, from what I can tell."

Sky laughed. "I don't know what his problem is, really. You are so completely harmless."

Sam grabbed a meal from the freezer cabinet and put it into the microwave. As they were waiting for it to heat up, they were having an animated discussion about the data they'd found so far.

Nilesh asked, "Could you tell anything about the ship that destroyed George's ship?"

"Not really. The surveillance monitor was too far to get visual data. It registered the heat and exhaust profile and a series of strange signals coming from it. I sent it to the Kurool—perhaps they can understand it. It didn't have a standard identity beacon, of course.

"There are also about twenty anomalous readings so far from this year—ships where there are clear exhaust or heat signatures and strange signals, but no identity beacons. Jane is doing further analysis of those to determine whether about how many ships she thinks that represents. I'm hoping that by the time we get to Ganymede…"

"What? That you can get all of us on your side?" They all turned to see Mikhail in the doorway with an angry look on his face.

Sam turned back to Sky and finished her sentence. "… I can estimate how many alien ships are likely flying about the system at the present time."

Sky said, "Mik, Sam was explaining to us that there is some interesting data from the surveillance systems."

"I don't care what Sam is explaining. They should be in their quarters."

"I was hungry. I came to eat. My food seems to be done now. I will eat, and then I will leave, alright?"

"No. You will take your meal and eat it in your bunk."

Sam sighed. They were tired of Mikhail's attitude.

"No, Mik. Sam is eating here. Sit down, be civil, and have something to eat, alright?"

Sam could tell that Mikhail was fuming as he prepared a meal for himself. Sam had mostly lost their appetite, but they went ahead and finished dinner. Everyone ate in silence. They and Sharron left the mess and got into their quarters.

Sam said, "Gah, I'm tired of that man."

"You and me both. And by the way, so are Sky and Nilesh. Basically, they don't much talk to one another."

"I'm not surprised. I know this is the last mission they will be doing together."

"Yup, indeed."

Sam got up on the bunk. As they picked up the tablet, they saw a few lines in the analysis results highlighted in red.

Sam subvocalized, "Jane, explain items five and six."

"Item five occurred September 23, 2095."

"You went back that far already?"

"I had sent several subroutines to start at the beginning, Sam. They flagged several thousand events for me to analyze, and I did so while you were at dinner."

Yes, Sam thought, this proves it. Jane has an ego.

"Explain this item."

"A ship near Dione sent out a distress call suggesting a lack of fuel and complete life support failure. This would be a minor anomaly, except that no ship was ever found, but that same ship was sold on Ganymede one year later. That ship was owned by a man from the Moon named John Garfield. More investigation determined that it had been lent to Henry Gardinia."

"In other words, he somehow survived."

"Yes. And that's where we get to item six, which occurred also near Dione, six months earlier. An unknown ship was in visual view by the Dione surveillance monitors. Here's the picture."

An image came up on the screen. It was fuzzy, but it clearly was a ship of a design Sam had never seen.

"Any idea how large it was?"

"I estimate it was 75 meters long or less, and about ten meters wide."

"That's a pretty small ship! Either the crew were very small, or there weren't many of them."

"I am now looking for any images that are similar to this, as well as exhaust profiles or signals that match."

"Looks like we have our answer about how Zoetrope survived, and first contact. I wonder if it was random, or if the aliens knew he was in trouble."

"I can't say, Sam."

Sam said to Sharron, "Well, it looks like Jane figured out a big piece of the life of Henry/Zoetrope."

"Yes?"

"Yup. There was a distress signal sent from a ship that had lost all fuel and life support. When help got there, no ship was found, but that same ship was sold at Ganymede a year later. It had been owned by John Garfield."

"Oh, I knew John."

"You did?"

"Another old friend from school. He moved to the Moon pretty much the minute he graduated from high school."

"So that's the connection. There is data that Henry borrowed his ship. There isn't any information about Henry being on Ganymede, but the first entry about a 'Zoetrope' happens on Ganymede about the same time as the ship was sold. So, Henry became Zoetrope during the time of contact with the Zeloso. Jane also found evidence of a Zeloso ship in the area around the same time as Henry's ship was there."

"So, you think that the Zeloso rescued Henry?"

"That's what the data seems to suggest."

"I wonder why."

"That is a key question, Sharron."

John lay down with Patrick on the couch, Patrick's head on his chest. There were several minutes of silence. John could already tell that Patrick had had a horrible day. It sometimes took him a while to finally tell John the details of how it went. It was almost as if Patrick was afraid that telling John would somehow make it all real, but John knew that Patrick always felt better after he'd talked about it.

"So, I told Prak about the whole thing."

"And..."

"The shit hit the fan."

"Really?"

"I am so out of my depth, John."

John put his hand on Patrick's shoulder. "No, you aren't! Stop saying that."

"Silly me, I thought Prak would be happy to have us deal with this. And I stupidly assumed he knew that I only tell the truth. He was sure I was lying when I said that we were going to pretend to ally with Zoetrope to get info about the aliens. I tried to explain over and over that we thought he was a nutcase, and by no means wanted him to be running things on Ganymede. He thinks that we want to ally with Zoetrope, contact the Zeloso ourselves, and capture the weapon. I should have known he'd think that."

"But then why would we tell him?"

"I asked him that, and he said that he didn't have a good answer, but it must be some subterfuge. I gave up."

"So, what's going to happen?"

There was more silence. John was worried.

"They are sending two *Corinth*-class ships to Ganymede immediately. They are sending three more to the shipping lanes to enforce a blockade of traffic between Mars and insystem. He said that if Zoetrope does anything more to take over Io, SolGov will blame us. I got calls from the Mercury, Venus and Lunar governors begging that I do not ally with Zoetrope and pledging their support for the actions of SolGov. They have been more friendly than not since our independence and were working behind the scenes to help get us jurisdiction in the asteroid belt, and this is a bad turn. We are well and truly screwed."

"Well, the good thing is that Sam and the *Callista* will beat the SolGov ships to Ganymede. I'll let Sam know what's up, and that we need to speed up the timetable of getting our intel. Hopefully, Sam and the *Callista* will get their intel, and get out of there before SolGov destroys Zoetrope."

"I don't like this, John. I can manage Mars no problem, but this stuff?"

"This is why you have a military, sweetheart."

Patrick sighed. "I know, I know. This just isn't my strong suit."

"You'll do fine. Listen to Lei, take his advice, and it will be fine. I promise. This will all work out."

"Why are you so confident?"

John smiled. "I'm not so sure. But I do know we have the Kurool on our side. That's got to count for something. And besides, Zoetrope is a narcissistic sociopath—they don't last long."

"I know, John, but they can take millions of people with them."

Callista, June 2112

Sam was in the middle of looking at five more possible images of unidentified ships, and they could tell that at least three of them were truly alien. Unfortunately, they were also different than each other and the one other identified alien ship. That meant that there were sightings of at least four alien ships in the system in the last twenty years.

Jane had estimated that for each image they got of an alien ship, there were likely five to ten or more that existed. This meant that, at a minimum, there had been twenty alien ships in the system. They were all small, which was a relief to Sam, but the number was not. They had no idea whether all of the ships had this beam weapon, and the more ships there were, the more likely it seemed that there were many beam weapons. And the more beam weapons there were, the worse things were for humankind.

"Sam, priority encrypted message from John."

"Play the message, Jane."

Sam could see John's face on the tablet. He looked haggard, as if he hadn't slept in a while. "Sam, sorry to give you bad news, but SolGov went bananas after hearing our plan. They are sending two *Corinth-class* ships to Ganymede. They believe we actually *want* to ally with Zoetrope. You need to get as much intel as you can, as fast as you can, and get the hell out of there."

Sam sighed. They should have predicted this. The death of President Montoya had been a huge blow to Mars. Montoya had been outright friendly to Mars, and quite amenable to the idea that Mars have legal jurisdiction over all of the solar system from its orbit outward. Earth couldn't manage it in any event, and a Mars friendly to Earth governing the outer system was in Earth's best interest. But, sadly, his vice-president, picked as a concession to the right wing, had been an ally of the old President Volkov, a hawk, and uninterested in ceding any jurisdiction to Mars for anything except Mars. He even wanted jurisdiction over Phobos, which was ridiculous, given that it was mostly an industrial outpost for Mars. Rumor had it that he was even planning to try to take Mars back.

Sam also could tell that John hadn't shared the whole story, suggesting that there were other consequences. Sam figured they included another blockade. The funny thing about that was that it was, for Marsies, largely an inconvenience, but it was a disaster for the Earth economy. Sam chuckled. Some politicians didn't much care about that sort of thing, as long as they could make their point, and, more importantly, protect the interests of the corps. None of the corps liked Mars independence—Mars had always been somewhat of a renegade planet when it came to corporate relationships. The corps always thought of Marsies as people who bit the hand that fed them—once Mars got a toehold, it put in place all sorts of worker protection rules that the corps had to obey. They didn't much like that, and the idea that Mars would control the outer system was anathema to them. Sam thought about whether to tell Sky this news or not. She decided that they would wait and see how things played out at the beginning of the mission.

A week later, when they were only a couple of days from Ganymede, Jane had completed the analysis of all of the anomalous images, as well as the other data regarding evidence of alien ships. Jane estimated that there were from twenty-five to forty alien ships in the system, all sharing the frequency and pattern of signaling and of about five different types. All of the ships were small, the largest was only two hundred meters long by fifty meters wide. Jane suggested that only the largest of the ships they had seen had the capacity to hold enough energy to create a blast like they'd seen at Io, and like the one that had destroyed George's ship. Sam theorized that the weapons would need significant recharge time, and the images taken during the Io attack seemed to support that theory. All in all, the data suggested that there were likely few ships with this capacity, and those ships had significant weaknesses.

Sam hoped that they could at least confirm some of this information when they arrived at Ganymede, but they had no idea how close to his chest Zoetrope would keep his cards. They would just have to find out. Mikhail had been making noises about being the primary contact with Zoetrope, and Sam had nixed that, but they didn't know what Mikhail would do once they arrived at Ganymede.

"Sam, message from Tai, marked urgent."

"Play, please."

"Sam, I hope your trip has gone well. We've analyzed a lot of the data that the Kurool gave us about the Zeloso, and we can't say a lot. It's a bit of a confused hodge-podge. One thing we can say is that they found that the Zeloso are empathic and perhaps telepathic. The Kurool seemed to have spent some time theorizing the mechanism of this capacity—but they pointedly left their theorizing out of the materials they gave us.

"Anyway, what is clear is that this is how the Zeloso insert themselves into conflicts. They read the emotions of others around them, and also project emotions and thoughts that they think will manipulate others. Apparently, not all individuals are subject to this, but most of the Kurool seem to be, and they say that from what they have heard, most individuals of most species are subject to it. My suggestion is that if you are offered a chance to meet one of the Zeloso, do not take it! I hope this information will be helpful to you. I'm attaching the packet of some of the analysis we've been able to make so far. Good luck, Sam!"

Good luck. Well, that was certainly what they needed, given this information. If Zoetrope is under the spell of these Zeloso, who knows what to expect. Sam sighed and started to read the packet of info that came along with the message. Sam was deeply engaged with reading when they heard a knock on her door. They got up and opened it and saw Sky and Mikhail standing outside the door. Sky looked nervous, and Mikhail looked angry. Sam was not looking forward to hearing what this was about.

Sam said, "What's up?"

Mikhail glared at Sky, who said, "We need to talk. Let's go to the mess."

"Alright." Sam followed them into the mess, where Sharron, Caitlyn and Nilesh were already sitting. She sat down, and Mikhail and Sky sat as well.

Sky started. "Sam, Mikhail wanted to talk with you about how we will communicate with Zoetrope."

Sam looked at Mikhail and wondered what was going on.

"Well, I'm the official representative of MarsGov, and MarsGov is making the overtures to Zoetrope for an ostensible alliance with him. As an independent crew, the idea was that you would also join him for a time, long enough for all of us to get the intelligence we need on the presence and strength of the Zeloso. You are empowered to tell him whatever you want in order to help us accomplish this mission. Sharron's role is a little more delicate—it's hard to know how he will react to her presence."

"I don't trust either of you." Sam turned toward Mikhail, who had spoken those words in a very nasty tone.

"I understand that. Frankly, I don't trust you, either. So, we're even. What is it that you are worried about, Mikhail?"

"That you will betray us."

"Why would I do that? We have only one goal: to find out how much of a threat the Zeloso are to Mars, and to the system in general. I don't care about anything else. I can't imagine how we could possibly betray you in the accomplishment of that mission, unless you betray Mars somehow."

"I don't want you to be able to judge what betrayal is."

Sharron said, "Mikhail, I understand how this is difficult for you, but really, we are not working at cross purposes. You can watch what we do."

Sky said, "Mik, come on, Sam and Sharron are reasonable people."

Mikhail looked at Sky, and Sam could tell by the way they looked at each other that they weren't getting along anymore. Sharron had observed that the *Callista* crew were now in two factions, and Sam could see it in everyone's demeanor.

Sam decided to play most of the cards they had in their deck. Sam said, "Look Mikhail, I really did my best to try to make sure that the four of you didn't end up in jail, and to provide you with pay for this mission. I know you don't like me, and I honestly don't much like you. As long as you do what we've asked, which, frankly, isn't much, we're good. We were clear that if something didn't feel right in working with Zoetrope even for a minute, you had the right to pull out and go wherever you wanted. But know this, Mikhail, if you screw us, everyone in MarsGov, including me, will happily produce you in particular to SolGov on a silver platter, and make sure that the rest of the *Callista* crew spends the rest of their days in an asteroid mine. Are we clear?"

Mikhail looked at Sam with more hatred than they had ever seen on another person's face. It made them physically draw back.

"Yes, Sam, you have made it clear."

Sam realized that there was nothing they were going to be able to do to make him change his mind about them or about this mission. Sam knew that they certainly could not risk even telling Sky about the *Corinth*-class ships coming their way—it would absolutely be seen by Mik, if he were to find out, as betrayal. They needed to set Jane on the task of finding them alternative transportation home. With a crew this fractured, even though they trusted Sky, they could not be sure that Sky was going to prevail. And the time they had to get this mission done was much shorter than they'd anticipated. They were not hopeful.

When Sam and Sharron got back to their quarters, they discussed the situation.

Sam said, "Sharron, I'm going to give Jane the task of finding us alternate transport back to Mars. This mission is going to be short, and I'm not all that sure how much we are going to accomplish in the short time we have before SolGov is knocking on Ganymede's door."

"I know. The *Callista* crew is a disaster. And that Mikhail, he's up to no good."

"I agree. Well, I'll keep you posted on what Jane finds."

"Thanks, Sam."

Sam heard Jane say, "Sam, urgent encrypted message from Lindsay Ali on Pandora."

Sam subvocalized, "Urgent? What's in the message?"

"A bunch of image files, both still and moving, some transmission recordings, and a short voice message."

"Play the voice message."

"Sam, it's Lindsay. The weirdest shit ever just happened to me, and I sure hope you have a clue as to what it all means. Let me know what you think."

Sam said to Jane, "Alright, then, Jane, let's go through what she sent, shall we?"

Pandora, July, 2112

Lindsay swam awake, hearing her AI's proximity alert. She got up quickly and went to her workstation to see how far away the ship was. It was still almost 700 kilometers away.

She said to her AI, "Start constant imaging, and include remote spectroscopy. What direction is it going?"

"It is headed directly here."

"Here?"

"Yes. And it is sending some high-frequency signals this way."

"Any standard identity beacon?"

"Negative."

"Play the signals, please."

A relatively deep voice with the strangest accent Lindsay had ever heard said, "Hello, hello, I would like to meet you."

She said to her AI, "Use the same frequency."

"Transmission starting."

"Hello, I am Lindsay Ali, Kuiper Exploratory, stationed here on Pandora. Who are you?"

"I am Koth."

Well, that was enigmatic.

"Why are you using this frequency?"

"It is what I use."

"Who are you working for?"

"I am Koth."

She wasn't getting anywhere.

She asked, "Where are you from?"

"The seventh planet."

Well, that was useless. No one was from Saturn.

"You live on Saturn?"

"I am from the seventh planet."

Lindsay shook her head. This guy was crazy. But he was flying one of the most interesting ships she'd ever seen. She couldn't imagine it would harm her to meet him. She could handle herself. She remembered the bar brawl on the moon. She'd sent three guys to the hospital that night.

"Alright, do you want to dock?"

"Yes, I would like to meet Lindsay-Ali-Kuiper-Exploratory." It was said as if it were all one word. Oh, my, she thought. This was going to be interesting.

She watched as the ship got closer, and very deftly landed in close proximity to her docking ring. She'd never seen any flying quite like it. The ship's dock looked quite different than any she'd seen - it didn't seem as though it would fit, but a tube extended from his ship that ended up matching perfectly. She checked the airlock, and it was completely solid. She started cycling the air in the airlock, when her AI started beeping.

"High levels of Carbon Monoxide and Ammonia are present in the air of their ship."

"What?"

"Levels dangerous for humans."

"How is that possible?"

"The ship cannot have any human beings on it."

"But... wait, possible explanations?"

"The ship could be of alien origin."

"The Kurool?"

"The Kurool are not known to have ships of this type."

"Can you prevent the CO and Ammonia from entering the habitat's atmosphere?"

"Yes."

"Do that. Start internal imaging—I want this whole thing recorded. Open the door on my mark."

Lindsay sat for a moment, getting ready for who knew what. Then, from out of nowhere, a thought came to her mind.

I need to open the door.

She knew she hadn't thought that - it was foreign. It felt foreign.

I need to open the door. What I want is through that door. My curiosity will be satisfied.

This was weird, very, very weird. She didn't like it one bit. It had the feeling of someone trying to manipulate her somehow. She was tempted not to go through with this—to tell them that she didn't want to meet them after all, but somehow, she knew she needed to know more. She opened the door.

A smallish animal that looked to be the love child of a cat and a kangaroo, but without a nose, and with nasty, nasty looking teeth, walked through the door. Alien, indeed. What in God's name did it want with her?

She heard a thought in her head. Different than the first. She could tell it was from the creature in front of her.

I am Koth.

She said, "Alright, then, Koth. You've met me." She was thinking furiously—what was she going to do?

You explore here.

It was not a question.

"Yes. I'm here trying to find precious metals for my company."

Metals. There are metals on Rhea.

Then came the same sort of compelling thought as the earlier thought: *I need to go to Rhea. I need to leave here and get to Rhea.*

No, she didn't! She had no intention of going to Rhea. There was nothing she needed there. What was going on?

Before she knew it, the creature had turned and run through the dock, and closed their side of the door. She had only a few seconds to tell her AI to shut her side, when the ship took off. She was stunned. She collected her wits.

She said to her AI, "Please send everything, the first set of images, the second set, all internal recording, all recordings of the messages, everything, and send it to Sam Julian on Mars, encrypted and marked urgent. Add the following note: 'Sam, it's Lindsay. The weirdest shit ever just happened to me, and I sure hope you have a clue as to what it all means. Let me know what you think.'"

"Collecting... Sending... Done."

She'd wait and see what Sam had to say. She didn't know what else to do.

Mars Colony One, July 2112

Gareth was on his way to a Xenoscience meeting. The team had been unusually busy analyzing the data that Sam was generating about the presence of the Zeloso in the system, as well as the abundance of information from the Kurool. It wasn't really up Gareth's alley, but he was enjoying being a spectator.

Today, they had asked him to give his short presentation about the Turool/Jesus comparison that Sharron had planned to present to the team before the whole thing with the new aliens erupted. He wasn't really looking forward to it. Sharron was better at talking with atheists and agnostics about theological topics than he was, surprisingly. He was good at listening, and being respectful of other ideas, but Sharron really excelled at explaining theological concepts to people who would rather not hear them. But he would do his best.

He walked in and took his standard seat at the table. Curtis and Xiang were in animated discussion about something, and Rosalind and Abdi were busy at their tablets. Tai and Ted hadn't shown up yet. Gareth took out his tablet and started to review what he would be presenting.

Tai and Ted walked in together.

Tai said, "Alright, let's get started, shall we? We have a packed agenda. First, we have some new data from Sam, apparently sent to her from Lindsay Ali, stationed on Pandora. Lindsay apparently has been in contact with the Zeloso. We need to add this new data to the analysis of the Kurool material we've gotten on the Zeloso. And, Gareth, we have the long-awaited presentation about your theological work on Turool."

Ted said, "Tai, can we postpone that? This is all much more important than theology." Ted always belittled the work of Gareth and Sharron.

Tai said, "No, Ted. I would like to hear it, and I head this lab. Gareth will give his presentation."

Gareth heard Ted sigh heavily. He decided, impromptu, to focus his presentation not on the analysis of the teachings, but on the analysis of what Turool said about Earth. That was pretty incontrovertible stuff. He chuckled internally. Sharron had originally had that as the focus of her presentation, and Gareth, in his arrogance, had changed it, since he thought that the comparisons of teachings were more important.

He listened with some interest as the team reviewed the new information from Lindsay. Gareth vaguely remembered meeting her at a party that Sam and Tina had given at one point a few years ago, just before Sam left for the Kuiper Belt. Then they gave each other sets of assignments, and surprisingly, Tai gave Gareth one.

"Gareth, can you dig through the teachings of Turool for any discussions of the Zeloso, and figure out whether there is any information there useful to us?"

Gareth nodded. "I'd be happy to. I haven't studied those yet."

Ted said under his breath, "Yeah, too busy making Turool like your silly Jesus."

Tai glared at Ted, and he went silent.

They discussed the new data Sam had sent about the number of possible Zeloso ships in the system, and a few other topics, and then it was time for Gareth's presentation.

"Thank you, Tai, for this opportunity. Given how short the time is, I'm going to focus the presentation almost entirely on what Turool said about Sol and Earth. You can read our full analysis in the report I've sent all of you. Most of that has made it into the article that will be published in a few weeks.

"So, as you know, most of the teachings of Turool were recorded by audio and video recording devices—they had that technology at the time. Therefore, we have very complete information about what It said. And you also know that the reason they sent the initial colony here, and they came after the nova, was that they were following Turool's commandment to come here. So here is an outline of what It said.

"First, since they had a well-developed astronomical system by then, better developed than we had at a comparable time in our technology development, there is no question that Turool identified Sol as the star It commanded them to visit. Sol is a relatively bright star in their sky, and an important star of one of their major constellations. It's as if someone here told us to visit Betelguese.

"Second, It said very specifically that the third planet had intelligent life, and that it was bipedal, instead of quadrapedal, as they were. Life that, It said, was violent, and in need of what they could teach them. It also said that they would not be able to live on the third planet, but the fourth might provide what they needed. It explained that at some point, those beings would be in the position to possibly destroy them and would attempt to do so.

"Remember, although they did have a well-developed astronomical system, they had not yet launched an orbital telescope, and I have been told their atmosphere would have been less hospitable to astronomical observation. There is no evidence that they were any further along in studying planets of distant stars that we were in the mid-20th century. In fact, although Turool's new religion eventually swept the entire society, They did have his detractors at the time. One of the biggest points that these detractors made was that there was no way It could know what the planets of this star were like."

Ted said, "OK, so it happened to have guessed correctly. What's the big deal?"

Gareth answered, "Ted, you have a statistical background, correct?"

"Yeah, so what?"

"What is the probability that you would be correct if you picked a random star, and guessed that oh, say, there was intelligent, insectoid life on the second planet of that star, and that it had an atmosphere poisonous to you?"

Ted was silent and brooded. Gareth figured he'd hit the nail on the head.

"I was talking with one of the linguists about this, and he described to me what is called 'Occam's Razor.' He seemed to think that Occam's Razor would suggest that Turool had either been here, somehow, or somehow actually had information about Earth. There just isn't a possibility that It could randomly guess that much that right.

"Sharron and I have a detailed analysis of the teachings of Turool compared to that of Jesus, but you can read them at your leisure. Suffice it to say that the comparisons are as impossible to happen by chance as this, and the combination of the two is simply unbelievable, but it's all true."

Tai said, "So your conclusion is?"

"Our basic conclusion is that Turool, who was born chronologically after Jesus died, was somehow connected to Jesus. He either was the same being or was somehow in communication with him. There isn't any other explanation. Our theological conclusion is that Turool was the Son of God, incarnated as a Kurool."

Gareth looked around the room. He knew that Tai had grown up as a Christian, as had Curtis, but neither were observant. Ted was the lone atheist, and Rosalind was agnostic, and an active Buddhist, as was Xiang. He knew that Abdi was an observant Muslim. They all looked very thoughtful, even Ted.

Xiang said, "Gareth, have you run this theory by the Kurool? They have more scientific knowledge than we do, and they might be able to come up with an alternate theory than your theological one."

"I haven't. That's a good idea—I'd love to hear what they think of our theories."

Tai said, "OK, everyone, we're done here, and we all have our work cut out for us."

Mars Colony One, July 2112

John was looking at his AI's projection of when the *Callista* would get to Ganymede, and when the two *Corinth*-class ships would also arrive. It was much tighter than he'd wanted. Sam and the *Callista* crew would have about a week before the ships arrived to get intel. And John made a bet that Zoetrope would likely find out about the ships before they arrived. He'd gotten the message from Sam that things on the *Callista* were falling apart, and they had not shared with them knowledge about the SolGov ships. John agreed with their cautiousness but hoped that it would not get Sam into trouble.

It had been a harrowing month since the ship left. SolGov had cut off all communication and was basically back on a war footing with Mars. Marsies were up in arms about the inconvenience of the blockade, and Patrick had decided not to make the reasons public yet. SolGov wasn't spilling the beans, either. John and the rest of the Mars military had all of their development plans laid aside while they dealt with the SolGov threat. SolGov was saying basically that Mars had declared war on the asteroid belt, which was, of course, nonsense, and everyone on Mars knew it.

There wasn't really anything John could do at the moment—this all had to play itself out. Once Sam had gotten as much intel as they felt they were going to get, they were going to decide when and how to make this all public. John was especially glad at this moment that they had a very sympathetic press contact in Tina, whose news outfit, *The Mars Monitor*, would get the scoop.

He heard a knock at his door, and he looked up to see his second in command, Colonel Joan Brosco, looking into his office.

"Colonel, what can I do for you?"

"Sir, you asked me for those reports on ship strength in the alpha sector of the belt?"

"Ah, yes, so I did. You could have just sent it to me."

Colonel Brosco smiled. "But then you would not have gotten to see my face when I told you the good news."

"Ah, good news! Come in, please, Colonel."

"Thank you, sir." She sat down.

"So…"

"Remember that we'd put in that order for five new *Zoar*-class cruisers, and the company said they couldn't get the parts, etc.?"

"Sadly, I do remember."

"I managed to wrangle what they needed from Kuiper Exploratory's ship factory on Tethys."

John could see the self-congratulatory smile on Joan's face. She deserved to congratulate herself—it would make their lives so much easier.

"And so that means we can expect those ships..."

"Within the year, sir."

"And how much did this cost us?"

"Only 15% over what we would have needed to pay Strelix, Virgin, or Tata for the parts."

"Well, you deserve some congratulations, Colonel. Thank you."

"You are welcome, sir. And Kuiper Exploratory is happy to continue to get our parts business."

"Are they now?"

"Yes sir."

"That's very good to know. Have you told...?"

"Yes sir, he knows. He's on it."

John chuckled. At this rate, she'd have his job in a year or two.

"Thank you, Colonel. Anything else?"

"No sir. The full report is already in your inbox."

"Why am I not surprised?" John smiled and rose.

"Dismissed, Colonel."

She rose, saluted, and left his office. Well, John thought, that was good news, for once. It might be considered to be too little, too late, but John had the sense that this conflict with SolGov wasn't going to be short-lived. Five *Zoar*-class cruisers, only one step down from *Corinth*-class, weren't anything SolGov could completely ignore. Further, the economics kept being in Mars' favor. The blockade made things much more expensive on Earth, and suppressed the economy, but for Mars, the blockade only made luxury items from Earth more expensive— everything else was made cheaper because of the lack of the in-system market. The economy kept doing better, and since Mars did govern about 1/3 of the belt, between the good economy, and taxes from that part of the belt, MarsGov was swimming in money. Now that they had a reliable parts supplier, more money meant more ships.

John really hadn't wanted to spend his time thinking about the long game of war with SolGov. He'd been more interested in building an interstellar exploration service. That would have to wait, but hopefully not for too long.

Ganymede Colony One, August 2112

They left the shuttle, Sam leading the group into the main spaceport area of Ganymede Colony One, Zoetrope's home base. Sam was reminded of the moon as they carefully bounced down the tunnel from the shuttle dock. Sam turned to see Caitlyn take up the habitual long gait of someone born on the Moon. Sam was never quite able to master it. As they exited the tunnel, Sam saw several people gathered in a small knot on one side of the large room in dusty gray uniforms. They moved toward the group of the *Callista* crew. One of them, a tall woman with ebony skin and very short-cropped hair loped forward and reached out her hand. Sam took it and shook.

"You must be Sam Julian. I'm Commander Kaleen Creel. Zoetrope asked me to meet you and show you to your quarters. He would like to meet with you all in one hour."

"Hello, Commander Creel. Thank you for the welcome."

"It is an honor to meet someone of your stature." Sam was embarrassed.

"Well…"

"Don't deny it, Mx. Julian. Zoetrope is very much looking forward to meeting you."

Sam could feel, more than see Mikhail fuming behind her. This was not what they needed now.

"Thanks. Anyway, can you show us to our quarters? We'd like to get a break before we meet General Zoetrope."

Kaleen nodded and seemed disappointed somehow. "Of course. This way."

As they walked, Sam was taking in the surroundings. The halls were gunmetal gray, with lots of doors, and the ceilings were only about six and a half feet high. It was all very spartan and utilitarian and looked to be well-kept up. They arrived at a door, and Commander Creel waved her ident card, and the door opened to a hallway. She pointed to their individual rooms. They were all quite small. There was what looked to be a tiny bathroom at one end of the hall.

"I'll meet you out here in an hour and take you to see Zoetrope."

Sam nodded. "Thank you, Commander Kreel."

"Please call me Kaleen."

"Alright. Thanks, Kaleen. See you in an hour."

Sam went through the door to her quarters, which was only slightly larger than the room they'd just shared with Sharron over the last month. They stowed her belongings. It was time to talk with Jane.

Sam subvocalized, "Jane, status, please."

"The *Callista* is in safe orbit, and there are no ships anywhere near it. SolGov's ships are about six days from Ganymede. The Kurool are about twelve days away."

"Any more results from your analysis?"

"No, Sam. I've not received any more flagged data from the subroutines. I think we've probably found everything we're going to find."

"Jane, please wake me in fifty minutes."

"Acknowledged."

Sam felt like a nap was in order.

As they walked in, Sam looked around at the large room with the domed roof. This room was a stark contrast to most of the colony that they'd seen so far. The view of Jupiter above was quite spectacular. On the far side of the room was a large desk, reminiscent of the desk that their old boss at Strelix had had in his office except that this one looked to be even older, if that were possible. Sitting behind it was a man who was a lot smaller than Sam had imagined. He had a large head, and thinning, straight jet-black hair.

"Well, if it isn't Sam Julian from Mars! Welcome to Ganymede!"

"Thank you, General Zoetrope."

"I am so glad that you have come. I am honored that Mars considers me an ally."

"Well, as you know, we need allies in the fight against SolGov, and I know that they are our common enemy. It seems that you have some resources that might come in handy."

"Indeed, I do. I do. Please, all of you, sit. Joseph, bring out the new vintage, would you?"

Sam saw a man nod briefly and walk out of a door on one side of the huge room. She noticed that Zoetrope had not yet recognized Sharron.

"We grow grapes here on Ganymede. I have perfected the art of hydroponic grapes."

Sky said, "Remarkable." Sam inwardly smiled. Sky understood what was needed.

"Yes, it is, actually. There is much remarkable about what I've done here."

Sam said, "So tell us more."

"Well, we are beginning to build Colony Four, and I have a waiting list of emigrants from Earth and the Moon itching to start it. If there is one thing the outer system needs is manufacturing capacity, which is my focus right now."

Sam nodded, playing the game. "Yes, the outer system really does need that capacity. Mars has been looking for reliable manufacturing partners."

"Yes, yes, well, we'll be able to be a partner like that soon enough."

The man who had left returned with seven glasses and a wine bottle. Sam could see the label on the bottle. A zoetrope, of course.

Sam took the glass with the dark purple wine and sipped. It was pretty good—as good as any wine Sam had had before, which wasn't actually saying much.

Sky said, "General, this is a very nice wine."

"Thank you. I take that as a great compliment from someone from Earth."

"Well, my parents were great wine connoisseurs—Ecuador has some wonderful wineries."

Sam looked at Mikhail, who by now was glaring at Sky.

Zoetrope said, "So, my friends, you came all the way to Ganymede to talk with me. How can I be of assistance besides just promising to be a good manufacturing partner to Mars?"

Mikhail began to speak, but Sam interrupted.

"First, we wanted to let you know that the *Callista* and its crew are at your disposal, General Zoetrope. And, as you know, Mars is in the fight of its life with SolGov. We couldn't help but notice that you have a very powerful new weapon in your arsenal. We'd like to hear about it and find out how to obtain one."

Zoetrope looked surprised, then smiled thinly. "That weapon is not for sale."

"We would like to hear more about it—how did you develop it?"

Sam could tell that this subject was touchy for Zoetrope. They didn't expect him to explain anything outright, but this question upset him for some reason. They decided to let it go.

"Actually, General, it's fine. You say it's not for sale, and I take you at your word. We'd just like to join you and be of use in any way we can be."

Sam could see him relax. "Well, thank you. We could definitely use the *Callista* for some scouting—we lack good scouting ships. We need some intelligence about what is happening on Io and Callisto. We think that SolGov is gathering forces in an effort to dislodge me. You could go in the *Callista* without arousing suspicion and find out."

Sam filed this away for investigation later. The fact that Zoetrope needed the *Callista* for pretty simple reconnaissance was interesting. It indicated something, but Sam wasn't quite sure yet what that was.

Mikhail said, "General, I'll be happy to do that scouting for you."

"And you are?"

"Mihkail Odeh, General."

"Interesting name you have there."

"I am half Russian, and half Yemeni."

"Ah, I see. Yemeni on your father's side?"

"Yes, sir. Very conservative family."

They chatted amiably about family and such for another few minutes. Sam observed that Zoetrope gave up absolutely no information about his own origins, but that wasn't necessary. They already knew just about everything there was to know about Henry and his family. It was time for Sharron. Sam looked at Sharron and nodded.

Sharron said, "Do you remember me, Henry?"

Zoetrope looked at Sharron sharply.

"My name is not Henry."

"I am Sharron Holbright. I was Sharron Snyder. Remember now?"

His face lost several shades of color. He said, quietly, "I am no longer Henry. Please call me Zoetrope."

"Alright, I will."

"What are you doing here?"

"I'm just a member of the crew. It took me a while to figure out who you were."

Zoetrope looked uncomfortable. Sam thought it had worked perfectly.

They left soon after and went to the dining hall to get some dinner. As they sat around the table, no one spoke much, but finally Sky broke the silence.

"OK, so we'll go scout Callisto, and come back in a couple of days. Sam and Sharron, do you want to come along, or stay here?"

Sam said, "I'll stay here. There's plenty to check out."

Sharron nodded. "Yes, I want to check out the place and hear what they are saying about Henry."

Sky said, "Alright. Crew, we leave at 0800 tomorrow morning." There were nods all around.

Sam kept herself busy while the *Callista* crew was gone. They found all of the watering holes and watched and listened. They overheard one very interesting conversation one evening, close to bar closing time. Both individuals were wearing the uniform of Zoetrope's army. One was a brawny Asian man, and the other was a thin light-skinned blond woman.

"I wish I didn't have to deal with them," the blond said.

The burly man said, "I hate the way they get into my head. But you seem not to hear them."

"I don't hear them at all. It's a little weird, since everyone else seems to."

"I've noticed Martin hears them but doesn't seem to care what they say. I can't stop myself. I hate it."

Sam realized that they were talking about the same phenomenon that Lindsay had experienced. Lindsay seemed to be like that Martin guy they were talking about.

"Well, it doesn't matter. They are going to help us take over the system."

The burly man laughed. "No, they aren't."

"What do you mean?"

"I heard that something happened, and suddenly, a bunch of ships left orbit to go back to Epimetheus. There are still some left, but not enough for us."

"You're kidding! If that's so we're..."

"Screwed. We can't beat SolGov without them."

"I don't..."

"You need to find yourself an escape route. This Colony will be toast in a matter of weeks. I've booked passage back to Mars."

They began to look as if they were leaving, so Sam made herself busy looking at her beer, and subvocalizing.

"Jane, are there any surveillance monitors near Epimetheus?"

"Negative. It's not a body of interest. It's deserted."

"Perfect place for an alien base, I think."

"Yes, Sam, it is."

"What's the closest surveillance monitor?"

"There are several in orbit around Mimas."

"How close is Mimas to Epithemius now?"

"Opposite sides of Saturn."

"Find the times when they were close. Look at the data from those surveillance monitors during those times."

"Will do. I should have information for you within an hour."

By the time Sam finished the beer, and got back to their room, Jane had the analysis done.

"Sam, there is definite evidence of alien traffic to and from Epimetheus starting about ten years ago. The last time Epimetheus and Mimas were close was about one month ago, there were several ships coming and going from Epimetheus, almost all towards Jupiter. One ship was headed towards Pandora."

"Ah, the ship that came in contact with Lindsay."

"I expect so."

Well, Sam definitely owed Lindsay some information. They'd responded to Lindsay with basically a "hold on, more coming later" message, but they'd been procrastinating, and then they decided to hand the decision over to Tai and John. Both had said that given that Lindsay had been in contact with the Zeloso, it made sense to just give her all of the information they had. When Sam got back to quarters, they composed a video message to Lindsay.

"Hey, Lindsay, sorry it's taken me so long to finally fully get back to you. I had to kick the decision about whether or not to tell you everything up the chain of command, as it were. Just so you know, this is still classified, so I'd appreciate it if you kept mum for now—even to Kuiper Exploratory. I'm sending you a summary report of what we know that we prepared for some brass a few weeks ago, as well as some more recent information. It turns out that you're a lucky one. Most people are compelled by the Zeloso. A few can't hear them, and fewer still can hear them, but don't need to obey. If you hadn't been so special, you would have been on the next available ship to Rhea. I imagine they were going to destroy your habitat on Pandora while you were gone—it's the closest to their base on Epimetheus. Anyway, have a look at the data—it's pretty darned interesting. And we have quite a challenge on our hands, my friend. I hope you are still enjoying being on Pandora. Later."

Ganymede One, August 2112
He heard/felt him. *I am in danger. Koth can no longer help.*
"Danger? What could be danger to you?"
My enemies of old draw near. Come here.
"They come here?"
Yes. Will be here soon.
"But I need you. You can't stop helping us!"
I must retreat to the sixth planet.
Zoetrope was furious, and desperate. How could Koth stop helping him at this critical juncture? Without Koth, he knew he couldn't even hold Ganymede, let alone push forward his plans of taking over Jupiter. He had to do something.
"If you stop aiding me, I will expose your presence here, and tell them where you are."

He heard/felt a rush of thought that he did not understand. It was so strong that he was literally pushed back a few steps from Koth. He watched as Koth left through the small door hidden in a corner of his large office. He'd had that corridor made especially for Koth, and Koth had come and gone as he pleased. Well, some Koth. Zoetrope knew that he'd been visited by numerous individuals, but they all talked of themselves as Koth.

He assumed that Koth would relent and keep on helping him. They always did. He sat back down at his desk and began to work on the plans for the next phase. Io was in his sights. Yes, here was a plan to take over Io, and controlling Ganymede and Io would probably give him enough leverage to then take over all of Jupiter.

He heard the sounds of footsteps approaching, and saw his assistant approach his desk.

"Yes?"

"General, Mikhail Odeh from the *Callista* would like to speak with you."

"Is he alone?"

"Yes, sir."

"Send him in."

Zoetrope watched as the tall man with dark eyes walked toward him with deliberate steps. Zoetrope could see that he had a lot on his mind.

"Welcome, Mr. Odeh. I want to thank you for that scouting mission—very helpful information."

"You are welcome, General."

"How can I help you?"

"I have some critical information for you."

Zoetrope looked at the man and could see the plotting in his eyes. "I take it your colleagues don't want you to share this information with me."

"No. Sam would have me thrown to the SolGov wolves if they found out I was talking with you."

"I see. And what would you like in return?"

"I will work for you, and so will Caitlyn. I mean *really* work for you, not fake work for you like we are supposed to. You give us a salary, and a bit of a bonus, and we're yours."

"I see. Alright, that's a reasonable trade. So, part of your information is that you are not really working for me. I take it this means that Mars doesn't really want to be my ally."

"Yes. We were sent here to find out more about the aliens. Oh, and Sharron? She's part of the Xenoscience team—she's never been *Callista* crew, although it is sort of random that she happened to know you. She's here to provide the implicit threat to you."

Zoetrope was taken aback.

"How did they know?"

"The *Callista* was contacted by an old friend who said he had some alien artifacts to sell. We assumed they were fake, because they always were. We tried to meet him at the rendezvous point, but his ship had been destroyed with a weapon we determined wasn't of human origin. When Sam saw videos of the attack on Io, she recognized the weapon as being the one that destroyed our friend's ship."

"And Sam told the Kurool?"

"Yes."

"I see."

Zoetrope thought a moment. First, he needed to get rid of Sam and Sharron. Second, he needed to test this Mikhail, to see how loyal he was. He was forming a plan in his head.

"There is an old SolGov installation on the other side of the Nicholson Regio, right at the Khumbam crater. It has some sophisticated communications equipment I need. I want you to go out there with the whole crew and, while you are out there, kill Sam and Sharron."

"I can take care of that."

"Good. I'll send you the specifications for the mission and get you any gear you need."

"Send the specs to Sam, please. I don't want them to suspect..."

"Of course, Mr. Odeh. I know how to be discreet."

Mikhail nodded and turned and left his office.

Zoetrope returned to working out the details of the next phase. Yes, he was confident he could do it, as long as Koth cooperated.

Chapter 5:
Betrayal

Ganymede Surface, August 2112

Sam was sitting in a scrunched position inside the rover, with their helmet off. They were glad they'd been given a rover with atmosphere. It was small, but at least they weren't going to be breathing their own recycled air for the five-hour trip. Sam chuckled internally. No, just breathing the recycled air of the six of them!

They'd gotten this assignment from Zoetrope, and Sam had noticed how Mikhail and Caitlyn seemed especially interested in what seemed to Sam to be a routine mission that Zoetrope could have sent some teenager on. The mission frankly stank to Sam, but Sky seemed willing to go ahead with it, assuming it was some sort of test. Sam had asked Jane about the installation, which had been abandoned by SolGov five years before, because of cost-cutting. Several of the items that Zoetrope claimed to want were models that Jane said were manufactured *after* the installation had been abandoned.

Sam relented, given that no one else seemed to smell the problem. It was nice to get out of the Ganymede colony and see a bit of the surface. She'd never been on one of Jupiter's moons before. The surface bore some vague similarity to Mars, but only vague. The surface of this part of the Nicholson Regio was pretty smooth, with a few hillocks and such they needed to climb over.

"Sam."

"Yes, Jane," Sam subvocalized.

"I have today's update on the position of the SolGov fleet, as well as the Kurool."

"Continue."

"The SolGov fleet is decelerating and should be entering Ganymede orbit in about 40 hours. The Kurool are about 72 hours out of Ganymede orbit."

"Thank you, Jane."

Sam had no idea what was going to happen when SolGov showed up. Zoetrope would learn soon that they were coming, and so far, they hadn't been able to learn a thing about the aliens. Sam was beginning to realize that there just wasn't going to be enough time. And further, they were here out in the middle of nowhere on a dubious mission. Sam was frustrated.

The rover suddenly slowed down and came to a halt.

Mikhail said, "Something's not working properly. Sam, can you come with me outside? You can probably help me best with this."

Sam's attention perked up. This did not sound right. Nilesh was the best of them, technically and mechanically.

Sky said, "Hey, it's a good time for a stretch, anyway. I'm going to come outside too."

Sharron said, "I'm happy to stay inside."

Mikhail said, "Thank you, Sharron. I'd appreciate it if everyone else stayed inside, too." Mikhail's voice sounded strained.

Sky said, "I'm coming outside, Mik. What's the issue?"

Everyone had to put on their helmets anyway, because the rover didn't have an airlock. Mikhail pushed the cover release locks, and Sam heard the air sucked back into the recycling system before the cover was fully opened. They unfolded from their position and stood up, and climbed out of the rover. Sky and Caitlyn followed.

Sam heard in the suit comm, "Come over here, Sam."

"Sure." Sam bounced over to where Mikhail was and followed him around the other side of the rover. Sam noticed Sky wasn't following and looked back to see Caitlyn physically holding Sky back.

Sam heard in the suit comm, "Cait, what the..."

Sam was on instant alert and put their hand inside her leg pocket where the weapon was. When Sam got around the rover, they were unsurprised to see Mikhail pointing a weapon at them.

"I'm sorry, Sam. Zoetrope knows everything, and he wants you dead."

"Mikhail, really, how is this going to help you? I didn't tell you that SolGov is on its way here. Once they deal with Zoetrope, you'll be on the first shuttle to a prison asteroid if they find you."

"Sam, be quiet. Let me just get this over with."

Just as he raised his weapon to shoot, they saw a blur behind him, and someone else in a suit tackled him. Sam saw his weapon fly out of his hand, falling about two feet towards them. They belatedly pulled out her weapon, pointing towards him. Saw saw the blur of someone else rushing toward them with a weapon drawn, and they turned and fired. The front of their suit erupted in flying plastic and blood, and they crumpled to the ground. Sam turned and saw Mikhail bounding quickly away, back toward Ganymede One. When they looked around and didn't see anyone else, they walked back to the other side of the rover and saw someone bending over someone else on the ground.

Sam said into her suit comm, "Sky, Nilesh, Sharron?"

Sam heard Nilesh in her suit. "Caitlyn shot Sky, Sam. She's dead."

Sam turned to see the person who'd saved her life walk towards her and realized it must have been Sharron.

Sam said into the suit comm, "Sharron, that was brave. You saved my life."

"When I saw what was happening between Sky and Caitlyn, I realized you were in danger, so I jumped out and ran around the rover."

The adrenaline rush faded suddenly, and all that was left was a feeling of sadness. It was all so unnecessary. Sky was dead, Caitlyn was dead, Mikhail probably wouldn't have enough air to get back to Ganymede One. And then Sam realized that they couldn't go back to Ganymede One. Zoetrope wanted them dead. They were in a pickle, for sure.

"Lesh, Sharron, I think the best thing we can do is to keep going to the installation. It will have enough air, water, and food for us for a while, and we can strategize what to do from there."

Nilesh said, "What should we do with Sky and Cait?"

"Let's bury them here."

Nilesh, Sharron, and Sam worked for a couple of hours using the rover's digging attachments to dig graves for Caitlyn and Sky. The ground was very brittle, and it took a long time to get deep enough to cover the bodies. They did a brief ceremony, which Sharron led, and Sam had Jane record the exact spot of the burials. Someday, Sam would come back to lay a memorial stone or plate for Sky. Sam cried for a while and was still crying as they climbed back into the rover and went to the installation.

It was easy to get in—Jane had figured out a way around the security lockouts, and they all gratefully took off their suits after a few minutes, when the atmosphere had fully become breathable.

Nilesh said, "Fuck, what a nightmare."

They all hugged for a minute.

Sharron said, "I'm sorry about your crew, Nilesh."

"We were bound to break up after this mission, but I couldn't have imagined Mik defecting like that. And trying to kill Sam? And Cait..."

Sam said, "It's hard to fathom. But Zoetrope got to them, somehow."

"So, what are we going to do?"

Sam said, "I'd like to take the *Callista* back to Mars, if we can, so we need to find someone willing to pick us up here. Jane has put out some feelers, and I'm waiting to hear back from her."

Nilesh said, "OK, I guess I can be patient. I'd like to take the *Callista* back myself. I'm glad you know how to pilot—the *Callista* requires a crew of at least three. Sharron, you're going to get to learn some cool things—we'll need every hand."

Sharron looked a little nervous. "I'll do my best."

Sam heard Jane say, "Sam, Ganymede One is under attack."

"What? SolGov arrived already?"

"No, Sam. Ganymede One is under attack by the Zeloso. Ganymede One has been destroyed."

Ganymede One, August 2112

Zoetrope took his time dressing before the big strategy meeting. He liked to keep his lieutenants waiting a little—keep them on their toes, so to speak. As he buttoned the last button and made sure his shoes were free of scuffs, he thought again about how far he had come. Indeed, God had big plans for him. First, Jupiter, then... the universe was the limit.

He thought for a moment back to his old friend Sharron. He had indeed been nervous that she would expose that he was just Henry Gardinia, a nobody and failure from Pennsylvania. He hoped that Mikhail would take care of things.

He left his spacious quarters and walked to the conference room, flanked by two guards. As usual, he stopped a few meters from the door, and listened via his cochlear implant to the conversation in the conference room.

"Koth's ships are gathering in some sort of weird formation in orbit—not their usual holding patterns."

"I wouldn't worry about it too much. Koth is unpredictable."

"I'm not happy with our relationship with them."

"They are why we are in charge on Ganymede, how can you not be happy?"

Zoetrope decided it was time to interrupt. He knew who liked Koth, and who did not. He soon would rid himself of those who didn't. As he walked in, there was complete silence in the room. He sat down. Zoetrope smiled, in control. He looked around the table at his lieutenants and imagined that Mikhail Odeh was among them. Yes, if Mikhail managed to kill those Martian agents, Sam and Sharron, that would be a nice reward and surprise. Mikhail would be loyal to Zoetrope from then on.

Zoetrope said, "We are in position. Koth is on their way, and you should launch in five hours for Io. Targeting the two SolGov military stations first, destroy the communications satellites, then go in for the kill. Once you take over Io One and Two, we'll be well on our way to victory over Jupiter."

He looked around at the lieutenants, all of whom were nodding their heads. The Koth gave him confidence that they could win. He was just beginning to think about what owning Jupiter meant. It meant that Mars and SolGov would have to deal with him as an equal, finally.

"General Zoetrope!" One of his lieutenants looked up from his tablet.

"What?"

"Koth..."

At that moment, Zoetrope heard a deafening noise and felt a deep shudder. The glasses and mugs on the table rattled and shook, and alarm bells went off. He heard another deafening sound, this time much closer. He got up, as did all of the lieutenants.

"To your posts, SolGov must be..."

"No, General, it is Koth attacking!"

"That cannot be! They wouldn't..."

Zoetrope's last sight was of a beam of light, slicing into the conference room, destroying everything it touched. His last thought was regret that he'd never get to build the zoetrope of his dreams.

Ganymede Surface, August 2112

Sam subvocalized to Jane, "Send a priority encrypted message to John on Mars. Tell him that Nilesh, Sharron, and I were not in Ganymede One when it was destroyed and that we are safe, Sky and Caitlyn are dead, and Mikhail is missing, presumed dead. Tell him that we're stranded without a shuttle back to the *Callista*. Send him all the logs and ask him to tell SolGov the story. Maybe they'll pick us up here if we're lucky."

Sam said aloud, "I just told Jane to send John a message. He needs to hear from us that we're alive when he hears that Ganymede One got destroyed by the Zeloso. I don't want to think about what he, Tina, and Gareth will think when they find out that Ganymede One is toast."

Nilesh said, "You know, Zoetrope and Mikhail's plot to assassinate you is what saved our lives. Ironic, huh?"

Sam replied, "I don't quite know what to think of that."

They spent several hours wandering around the installation, figuring out what was there, and what would be useful. Sharron was following Nilesh's lead on what to look for, and Sam was busy sorting through the surveillance files for the last several years, looking for any anomalies, mostly just out of curiosity, when Nilesh came running towards her.

"Sam, there's a shuttle!"

"A shuttle?"

"Out there is a tiny shuttle bay and a small shuttle in it. Barely big enough for three. I've been running tests. It may well be spaceworthy."

"Fuel?"

"There is some fuel in storage here, and some in the shuttle. I think there are enough units to get us to the *Callista*."

"You *think?*"

"I'll do the calculations and make sure, of course."

"Thank you. I'd rather not die an ignominious death of running out of fuel after having managed to escape an assassination attempt and a destroyed colony."

Nilesh smiled. "I can understand that my friend. Oh, and Sharron has been really useful, and is quite enjoying herself. She's fun to work with."

Sam nodded. "There's more inside that gal than she thinks."

As Nilesh walked away, the full weight of the loss of Ganymede One became clear to her. They didn't have friends there, but there had been twenty-five thousand people living in Ganymede One. They assumed most of them didn't survive. Why would the Zeloso destroy it after they had become allied to Zoetrope? Sam wondered if they'd ever know the answer to that question.

Later, as they were eating dinner, Nilesh said, "So, we're all set. There is more than enough fuel to get us to the *Callista*. We've got about three more hours of testing and repairs to do, and then we can get the hell out of here."

Sam said, "That will be just in time. The SolGov ships are due to arrive in 20 hours. I'd love to be out of here before they arrive."

"Yes, I'd rather be on my way back to Mars about then."

"How much room is there in the shuttle for cargo?"

"Not much, since we've got three people. No more than a hundred kilos, to be safe."

"OK, I'll start gathering up the stuff that might be useful."

Sharron said, "Can I help, Sam? The shuttle testing stuff is out of my league."

"Sure thing."

When the shuttle was ready and packed, they all got in. It was small—smaller than her old asteroid-hunting ship. There were two main seats, a jumper seat, and instrumentation where there wasn't seat. She looked out and could see the little shuttle bay doors.

"Nilesh, do you know how to..."

"Took care of that." He pushed a button on one of the panels, and the doors opened to the sky.

"Let's get out of here." Sam set the take-off thrusters to maximum and put in the coordinates for the *Callista*. The take-off was gentle;

Ganymede's gravity was a bit less than that of the moon, so it was easy to get out of orbit. Sam watched the viewscreen as the surface of Ganymede below them retreated, and the installation they had left got smaller and smaller.

Once in orbit, their path to the *Callista* would take them over Ganymede One, so Sam swung the shuttle 180 degrees so that the moon was above them. As Ganymede One floated above them, they could see how utterly destroyed it was. There were a few outlying domes that seemed to have been spared, although those in them wouldn't last long without the resources of the main dome. The main dome was completely open to space, and there was debris spread everywhere. Sam could see whole neighborhoods open to the sky, and others completely turned to ash.

Sharron said, "Oh my God. That's terrible."

Nilesh agreed. "They were serious."

Sam asked, "I don't get it. Why would they do this?"

Nilesh answered, "I bet the Zeloso got a wind of the Kurool coming, said something to Zoetrope, and he pissed them off—maybe threatened them?"

"Ah, that's a reasonable bet. He's the sort that would do something that stupid. The bad news is that they have enough firepower to destroy a decent-sized colony. I don't like that."

"I bet that's the best they have, though."

Sam said, "May well be, but it still isn't going to make anyone happy. We have to find a way to communicate with them."

"Well, it sounds kind of unlikely that we could communicate with them."

"Why? Zoetrope certainly did. I'm thinking that maybe we should head to Saturn instead of Mars. Jane has identified the most likely location of the Zeloso base—it's on Epimetheus."

"Epimetheus? That's a tiny little rock, barely more than an asteroid, with nothing of value in it! Nobody cares... ah, right, of course. Is this a good idea, Sam?"

"It's the only one I've got, Nilesh. We need to talk to the Zeloso before they do any more damage to the system."

"They might kill us in the process."

"I know, it's a risk we'll need to take. That is, if you're game."

Nilesh said, "I'm game, I'm game. I've already managed to escape death twice in one week. What's one more? Sharron?"

She said, "Yes, count me in! This has been a disturbing combination of harrowing and fun."

They laughed, and then Sam saw the *Callista* growing in size in the window and smiled. They'd never thought that the *Callista* would be a welcome sight.

Sam jutted her chin toward the ship. "You going to keep her, Nilesh?"

"Nah. Once we get to Mars, I'll sell her. I'm looking forward to settling down, maybe finding a boyfriend. Haven't had one of those in far too long."

Sam smiled. They were way overdue in sending a message to Tina. That was going to be their first task once again on the Callista.

Mars Colony One, August 2112

John sat in his office, looking over the latest personnel reports. The nice thing about the Mars military was that there was no shortage of recruits. They had many more recruits than they did ships to place them in, so there was a rather long waiting list of applicants, some of whom would likely get too old before they could be allowed to enter the service. SolGov had always been lacking in recruits.

His AI signaled an urgent message, and he indicated to accept it.

"Major General, this is Lieutenant Sanders from Communications. I wanted to let you know that we have received information that Ganymede One has been destroyed."

"Destroyed? By whom?"

"That is unclear, sir. The SolGov ships are too far away. I'll have visual images soon."

"Thank you, Lieutenant."

"Certainly, sir."

John didn't quite know what to do. If Ganymede One was destroyed, that certainly took care of the Zoetrope problem, but that meant they'd lost Sam and Sharron in the process—and any hope of figuring out what was going on with the Zeloso. He looked to see another urgent message, this time from Jane, Sam's AI. It was in text. Sam was fine and hadn't been at Ganymede One. John breathed a sigh of relief. He sobered when he read further. Sky and Caitlyn were dead, and Sam, Nilesh, and Sharron were stranded at an old SolGov installation.

There wasn't much he could do for them from here. The closest Mars Military ship was weeks away from Ganymede. He was sure they would figure something out before then, but he sent a message to Colonel Harold in logistics to get a small ship going toward Jupiter anyway, just in case. He also fired off a quick message to Tina, who was sure to hear about Ganymede One faster than just about anyone else, and Gareth as well, so that he'd know his wife was safe.

He wasn't sure what the right next steps were. The last report from Sam about the analysis of the surveillance data over the years had suggested activity around the moons of Saturn. Luckily, Mars was still friendly with the Governors of the Titan and Rhea colonies. He composed a message to Patrick, outlining a plan. He'd run it by Sam, of course, since they were central to the idea and had to agree to it. The more he thought about it, the more it seemed like it might work.

Later, he sat with Tina in the apartment she shared with Sam, having dinner.

"I'm glad Sam's safe, John. Thanks for sending me that message. It came a scant minute before the news of Ganymede One hit."

"I figured you'd hear about it quickly."

"We got some very interesting images—looks like the same exact weapon that attacked the base on Io. Our editors are writing up a story, but it's hard for me since I know exactly what's going on, and the public doesn't."

"I know; I'm sorry, Tina. I'm hoping we can make this public soon."

"SolGov is blaming Mars for it."

"They know it wasn't us. First, they accuse us of partnering with Zoetrope to take over the outer system, and then they blame us for the destruction of Ganymede One? Not very logical. But they are afraid of people hearing about the new aliens, and they know we won't say anything until we know more. No one believes them, anyway."

"So, you're going to make this public after you and Sam contact the Zeloso, aren't you?"

"Tina!"

"I know you, and I know Sam. Whose idea, was it? Sam's, right?"

"Well, actually, we both came up with it. Before I could send them my idea, they sent me their idea—basically the same."

"You two..."

"Look, Sam seems to be a lucky one—they managed to escape death on Ganymede not once, but twice. And I'll be their backup. We're an unbeatable team, Tina."

"But this... I know they are the best choice. Sam is out there anyway, and they are experienced, and smart, blah blah. But I want Sam home, here, now, not out there chasing deadly aliens."

"I understand, I do, Tina. But this is important—more important than anything since the Kurool."

"I know." Tina sighed. "Anyway, I'm pretty busy dealing with the stories around the embargo. We'd hoped it might end soon, but with this, who knows how long they will want to maintain it."

"Luckily it hasn't hurt our economy much."

"Yes, but it is making life difficult for a lot of people who depend on traveling back and forth."

They talked about life on Mars for a while, then John took his leave to go back home. Patrick was sitting on the couch, watching the news.

"Ach, what a mess," he said as John sat down next to him on the couch.

"Yes, a mess it is indeed. But I think we will get something out of this."

"I hope you are right. President Prak has been sending conciliatory messages to me lately."

"At the same time as SolGov is publicly blaming Mars for the destruction of Ganymede One?"

"He knows no one believes it—it's politics, John. He's just happy the Zoetrope problem was handled."

"Along with twenty-five thousand deaths? What an asshole."

"John, relax. I think he mourns, really, I do. I think he's just making the best of the situation. That's what politicians do, you know."

"Ugh. I'm glad you're not the typical politician."

"Well, I'm not so glad you're going off to Saturn."

"It will be fine. Sam and I are old hands, right? You'll be too busy governing, anyway."

Patrick smiled, and John relaxed. He didn't want to talk anymore, so just as Patrick was about to speak again, he turned to sit straddling Patrick, put his hands on both sides of his head, and gave him a long, passionate kiss. John felt Patrick relax underneath him. It was going to be a nice evening before he left for a while, John thought.

Callista, August 2112

"Jane, plot a course to Epimetheus. How long will it take us to get there?"

"One hundred and twenty-two days, Sam, Saturn and Jupiter are very far from each other right now. Also, I would suggest that we aim for Janus, not Epimetheus."

"Why?"

"Janus and Epimetheus are co-orbital. They are currently approaching each other. If we go to Janus, we may be able to observe the Zeloso without being detected for a while."

"That sounds reasonable. Explain the co-orbital behavior of those two moons, please?"

Jane talked about how the moons were discovered in the 20th century, which was thought to be only one moon for a while, and how they behaved according to the "circular restricted three-body problem" of classical physics. Sam remembered that one well.

"Ready for a long trip, Nilesh? It looks like this mission might end up being almost a year long."

"Yeah, let's get this party started."

"Jane, engage. Let's get out of here."

"Leaving Ganymede orbit. We'll start thrust for Janus in ten minutes."

"Acknowledged."

They had gotten fuel at the Ganymede fuel depot, then stopped briefly at the Ganymede station, which was serving as a refugee point for the several thousand who had managed to survive the destruction of Ganymede One. It had been chaotic, and getting supplies had been a challenge, but a message from Patrick to the manager of the station had helped. They were now fueled up and had enough supplies for quite a long time.

Sam had never been to Saturn. On both of her trips out to the Kuiper Belt, Saturn hadn't been nearby. Like the Kuiper Belt, Saturn was part of the wild west of the solar system. There were very few established colonies, and those were small, and generally rough and tumble. Titan and Rhea had the only really viable colonies in the Saturn system, even though Saturn had a ton of moons. There was an outpost of Kuiper Exploratory on Iapetus, and some fly-by-night exploratory outposts on some of the smaller, outer moons, but the inner moons were largely untouched. They remembered Lindsay, who they'd gotten to know a few years before. Lindsay had been stationed on Pandora, a tiny little ball of ice in the F-ring. Sam was excited to get to see Saturn, and hopeful, but scared about the mission.

Based on Jane's research, and the data from the Kurool, they knew which frequencies the Zeloso used. When they were ready for contact, they would start sending out messages of peace and communication in English and Chinese, on those frequencies. They figured the Zeloso must know some human language by now, even if it was rudimentary.

And they had their ace in the hole, Sam hoped. They'd sent a message to Lindsay, asking if they'd meet them on Janus, and be part of the contact team. Since Lindsay was the one they knew for sure couldn't be compelled by the Zeloso, Sam thought she was a necessity for the team.

Things at home seemed to be calming down. There had been no more attacks on any colonies on Ganymede, and it seemed from surveillance monitors that a large group of Zeloso ships were headed back to Saturn ahead of the *Callista*. Sam bet it was the last of the ships they had in the Jupiter system. Jane said that those ships would arrive at Epimetheus in about forty days—three times as fast as the *Callista* could travel. Sam had to wonder what kind of fuel and propulsion system could get them going that quickly. It certainly wasn't fusion.

Tina had been very unhappy that Sam was off to Saturn, rather than returning home. Sam could understand—they'd almost gotten themselves killed, after all. But here they were, alive and well. And now that Sam thought of it, enjoying being in space. It came as a little bit of a surprise to them—they liked it, after all.

They got into a rhythm on board. Sam did most of the piloting, except when they were asleep—Jane took over then. Nilesh kept the *Callista* in good shape, with Sharron's help. In their spare time, they played cards, and talked about news of home. Nilesh had the unfortunate job of telling Sky and Caitlyn's next of kin what had happened to them. He also couldn't help but obsess about what happened to Mikhail. They were discussing it one day over a game of gin rummy.

Sam said, "Lesh, face it, he's got to be dead. He couldn't have had more than fifteen hours of oxygen in his tank—that was the limit. The closest structure with air was the installation we were at, and we were there for more than fifteen hours, so even if he followed us and waited for us to leave, it's impossible that he didn't run out of air before we left. The next closest structure was Ganymede One, and it was destroyed. Further, I don't think he could have walked there in less than fifteen hours, even at .14g."

"But then why did he run?"

"Because he realized that it was that, or be captured or killed by us?"

"I don't know—it doesn't seem like Mik. Mik would have a plan B."

Sharron asked, "Did plotting to kill me and Sam seem like Mik?"

Nilesh answered, "It's true, the whole thing didn't seem like Mik. He could be problematic, for sure, and I knew he was getting to the end of his rope with Sky. But still..."

"I don't think we'll ever know." Sam lay down her cards. "Gin."

Sharron groaned. "Damn, I just needed one card."

A few days later, Sam was listening to a message from Tai back on Mars. It was in response to the full report about the surveillance monitors that Sam and Jane had analyzed, the number and types of ships, and every other bit of information collected on this mission so far.

"Sam, you've given us a lot to chew on. I think we'll be analyzing that ship data for a long time. I'm glad it's you going out there. You know John is coming out with an *Acheron*-class ship, and I'm sending Xiang and Rosalind with him. John agrees that you should not meet with the Zeloso until that ship arrives at Janus. You'll need the support.

Because of the more favorable position of Mars, it should reach you only a few days after you get to Janus."

Sam felt mixed about the new people on the mission. On one hand, he was right—they needed the support, and they were quite glad that John was coming as well. The idea of just the four of them pulling this off, even with Lindsay, was sort of crazy, and Sam was glad someone recognized that. On the other hand, they didn't get along with Xiang so well, and wasn't looking forward to working with him. Sam started to record their response.

"Thanks, Tai. Glad to hear we're getting support. We'll hold off on any action until the two crews are together and in sync. I'm looking forward to hearing what you think of Jane's analysis of the ships from the surveillance data."

Mars Colony One, August 2112

Gareth watched the message from his wife with some bemusement. God was good. She had avoided death, once at the hands of that Mikhail character, and also because she hadn't been at Ganymede One when it was destroyed.

She seemed to be a new woman. Not only had she saved Sam's life, but she had been enjoying herself learning new things about traveling in space. Apparently Nilesh had taken her on as something of an apprentice, and she was learning a lot.

He was happy for her—happy that perhaps she'd really found what gave her joy. It wasn't his thing at all, but that didn't matter. He was glad that she was in her element. He should have seen it coming. She was always the technical one of the house, the fix-it person, and on Mars, she had gotten herself involved in all sorts of things he didn't understand. He just wished that she hadn't been in so much danger.

Gareth started to record his reply.

"Dear heart, I am so glad to find out that you are safe and sound, and that you are on the *Callista*. I know that you'll be away for much longer than you expected, now that you are going all the way to Saturn. I'll miss you, but I can tell that you are happy, which makes me happy.

"I am on my way to meet with the Kurool. I am glad that the journal accepted our paper, but I feel that it would be irresponsible for us to publish it without some sort of official commentary from the Kurool. I have already spoken at length with Kloft about my theory, and it is willing to compose some sort of companion piece. We're going to speak about it in detail today. I look forward to hearing its thoughts on our theories.

"I love you, and miss you, and I am praying for your safety every day. Be well."

He left their apartment and walked to the transport tubes to take a train to the shuttle depot. He was being joined this trip out by Ted and Xiang. He met them at the shuttle depot, and the three of them got into the shuttle to the Kurool Colony.

He liked meeting with the Kurool—they were such good hosts, and they were truly interested in everything he had to say. They went out of their way to find answers to questions that he asked. Gareth could hardly believe that humans would have done better in the same situation.

The shuttle docked with the Kurool colony, and he, Ted, and Xiang got out.

Xiang said to the pilot, "We'll be leaving in about three hours."

The pilot nodded, "I've got a run from Colony Three to one of the outposts. I'll be back for sure by then."

They walked into the tube leading to the area that both humans and Kurool could work in together. He grabbed a mask, and donned it, and indicated to Xiang that he was ready. They opened the door into the large, shared dome.

Three Kurool were there to greet them: Droat, Kloft and Jorat. Although Gareth had spoken a lot to Droat, Kloft was really the theologian among them.

Droat said, in the familiar treated voice, "Welcome. We are happy that you have come again. I know you have some very specific questions."

The three of them sat in chairs, Ted and Xiang took recordings and made notes. The Kurool took their usual relaxed position: their bodies sat on top of their folded legs.

Gareth started. "I take it you've had time to read the paper?"

Kloft said, "We have. We have a few... clarification questions for you."

Gareth said, "Go ahead."

"We don't understand who the 'Son of God' is to you. For us, what we would call 'God' isn't of a nature to have children. Anything that can have children is by definition imperfect, and perfection is what we understand."

"To most Christians, the 'Son of God' was basically the incarnation of God on Earth, in the form of the historical man, Jesus. When he died, and was resurrected..."

"Resurrected? I don't understand that word."

Gareth heard Ted snicker. He ignored it.

"It means to come alive after death. For us, we believe that Jesus was killed, then became alive again."

"How is this possible? Does this happen often on Earth?"

Ted laughed. Gareth glared at him.

"No, only Jesus was resurrected. He was special, because, basically, He was God. He had the power to resurrect others, and He resurrected one person in His life that we know of."

"Ah. I see. Keep going, please."

"He eventually went back into heaven..."

"Heaven?"

"It's a place that many Christians believe exists, that we go to when we die. A different place than Earth. An idyllic place. The place where God lives."

"I see."

"Jesus forms one third of what we call the 'Triune God.'"

Droat said, "This is all very strange, I hope you don't mind all of the questions."

Gareth said, "No, no, not at all. In fact, my colleague Ted here would probably agree with you about how strange it is."

Kloft said, "So if I am to understand what you are proposing correctly, you are saying that this Jesus, who died, came alive again, and then became God again, became our Turool."

"Well, in outline, yes. The theological particulars would be stated a little differently."

Kloft paused. "Your cosmology is much more... limited than we thought."

Xiang said, "Kloft, Gareth's cosmology is only one of many. For instance, my tradition, Buddhism, has a completely different cosmology, and the Buddha, who is the one we follow, was completely human. We think that people are reincarnated into different beings. From my cosmology, Jesus perhaps was reincarnated as Turool."

"Ah. I see. So they are not consistent?"

Ted said, "Basically, all of the religious cosmologies are mutually exclusive."

Gareth said, "Ted, that is not true—in fact, there are many similarities. You deride all of them without knowing any of them."

Kloft asked, "Ted, what is your cosmology?"

Ted answered, "I'm an atheist. Life arose on Earth, and other planets, relatively randomly, and evolved through complex, but completely natural, impersonal means. When people die, their molecules are scattered, and nothing of their personality remains. Any attempt to suggest otherwise is not supported by science."

Kloft said, "Ah, well, that's quite limited as well. And by supported by science, I'm assuming you are talking about human science?"

Gareth laughed, and Ted glowered.

Kloft spoke again. "Gareth, given your limited concept of what you call 'God' and the theological concept of Jesus as part of God, I would say that it would be quite reasonable for you to come to that conclusion. Xiang, your conclusion would be consistent as well. We have not yet had a chance to digest all of your analysis, but we agree that the only possible conclusion to draw is that Turool either knew this Jesus of yours and was in communication with him or was this Jesus. There isn't any other alternative that we think works with the data."

Gareth was largely satisfied by that answer, but he couldn't shake the feeling that he was being thought of as a child.

"Is there anything more you can add?"

"I'm sorry, Gareth, we can't. It will take us years to fully theorize how these two beings were connected. And you are well over a thousand of your years behind us in math, physics, and biology, so none of you yet would be able to understand whatever theory we came up with. Imagine if someone from an era a thousand years ago asked you a question that you could only answer with your quantum physics of today. That's what we face."

Ted whistled. "Back then, they still thought the Earth was flat."

Gareth asked, "You have said that you wish to be careful, that you don't want us to get ahead too fast. I can certainly understand that. I hate to think what humankind would do with the knowledge you hold. But there has got to be a way for us to slowly learn this. I want us to finally be able to understand the universe as you do."

Droat said, "We've been thinking about this a great deal, Gareth. We have a suggestion."

Gareth said, "Please, go ahead."

"We think that a colony close by, and eventually connected, should be built, where human children and Kurool children could learn side by side. We would have to choose both the parents and the children quite carefully and collaboratively, but we think that those children might have a chance to learn a small part of what we know.

"But we also need to make sure that those children are brought up with the teachings of Turool. Otherwise, we would not be willing to trust this knowledge with your species."

Ted said, "That's a tall order, Droat."

"Yes, it is. But I think it can be done. And in a few hundred years, we will finally be at the same level."

Xiang said, "That long?"

Gareth knew several things at once. First, he was going to spearhead this effort. Second, he got the definite sense that the Kurool were evangelists for Turool. This didn't really surprise him or bother him, given that he'd concluded Turool was really Jesus. Third, his brother might be more prescient than he'd given him credit for because Gareth, indeed, was going to start a new religion.

Pandora, October 2112

Lindsay sipped her tea while she debated her options. Kuiper Exploratory had just sent her a message telling her they were firing her, but not because she hadn't done her job well. In fact, she had done her job too well. She had tried the hardest she knew how to find value in the rings and came up empty. KE didn't want to spend any more money on her, or this effort, and she could understand. They'd given her a nice little going away bonus. They said that she was welcome to stay on Pandora as long as she could afford it, and she was tempted to stick around a while.

But she'd also gotten that bolus of data and information from Sam about the creatures they were calling the Zeloso, and she was greatly intrigued. She'd just gotten delivery of her shuttle, so she could meet Sam on Janus, and help with contact with the Zeloso. Lindsay thought it would be a fun way to end her time on Saturn.

She realized there was no way she would have imagined a few years ago in searching for a way to escape her ex-stepmother that she'd end up where she was and doing what she was about to do. And she realized that she was having a whole lot of fun. The weirdness of the contact with the Zeloso had worn off some, and she was intrigued about what might happen next.

Well, she had some work to do. She had to mothball the habitat, pack all of her stuff, and make it to Janus. Sam would arrive at Janus in about 40 days, enough time for her to take care of everything here. She'd miss Pandora, and perhaps sometime she'd be able to return for a little vacation, or something.

She had done a lot of work on the habitat, and she had to consider what equipment she wanted to take with her to Mars, and what equipment could stay. She had already scoped out several isolated habitats on Mars—she liked living alone, and she liked the idea of braving Mars on her own—it was a lot cushier than being on Pandora, that was for sure. She had already put an offer in on one of the best she'd found, a small cave and dome complex, about 1000 square meters, and the beginnings of a small agriculture operation. It was located near Aesacus Dorsum and had a spectacular view of Hecates Tholus. The only drawback was that it was pretty far off the beaten path. She'd have to buy a long-distance Mars rover—the trip to the nearest colony, which was Colony Three, would take thirty hours over land. But that wasn't so bad, and the complex had real potential. She hoped she'd be the winning bidder.

Atreyu, October 2112

Xiang sat in the seat next to John. He'd been largely useless as a co-pilot, but it didn't matter. The *Atreyu*, the Acheron-class transport that they were taking from Mars out to Janus, basically flew itself. It had the most sophisticated AI that John had ever encountered, save for Sam's "Jane." And John knew that "Jane" hadn't been quite so sophisticated before Sam got their hands on it.

Xiang commented, "I have to say, I've never really enjoyed space travel."

"Really?" John asked. "Why did you choose Xenoscience?"

"I was a *theoretical* Xenoscientist, until the Kurool showed up and made the theoretical not so theoretical anymore."

John chuckled.

"What's so funny?"

"Well, it seems to be a case of 'be careful what you wish for.'"

Xiang laughed out loud. "Yes, yes, you are quite right about that, aren't you?"

John hadn't really warmed to Xiang yet. He was overly formal, but not in the familiar military way—in some different way that John couldn't really quite get his head around. And it didn't help things that Sam, who was basically John's best friend, didn't get along well with Xiang. While Sam was busy supporting John in his relationship with Patrick, John had to listen to Sam complain about how hard it was to work with Xiang. John could see why.

But they had at least been pleasant and civil, and Xiang had been willing to follow John's lead. They were about ten days out from Janus, where they would meet Sam and their friend Lindsay, and plan their contact procedure. He wasn't quite sure what was going to happen or how they were going to pull this off, but everyone realized the necessity of making contact with the Zeloso and letting them know that they'd been found out. They needed to find out what the Zeloso wanted and try to make sure they didn't do any more damage to the system.

The decision to hold off on telling SolGov what was happening was Patrick's. Of course, it was impossible to argue very well over an asynchronous connection, and since Patrick was officially John's boss, John couldn't really argue anyway, but he thought it was an unwise move. He understood it—Patrick felt completely burned by what SolGov was doing and didn't trust them. But John thought that it might make things more difficult later.

The AI, who had a thin, metallic voice, said, "Incoming message from Sam Julian."

"Play, please."

Sam's face appeared on the small comm viewscreen.

"Hey, John. Jane just filled me in on something. We'd lost track of the Kurool, who left Jupiter soon after the destruction of Ganymede One. She'd been monitoring all of the surveillance systems from the Kuiper Belt to Mars, and found them, finally. They are heading on a beeline to... you guessed it, Epimetheus. We'd suspected this but needed to be sure. They won't be there for another thirty days or so. I sent a message letting them know the outlines of our plan, but I haven't heard back yet. Just thought you'd want to know who all the guests at our party are going to be. Looking forward to seeing your face in realtime, my friend."

Xiang made a sound, and John turned to look at him. Xiang was making a sour face but remained silent. John didn't bother to ask. Instead, he commented with mock cheerfulness, "Well, that's going to make our lives quite a bit more interesting, ain't it?"

Xiang's face had become impassive. He said nothing.

Chapter 6:
Contact

Approaching Janus, December 2112

Lindsay's AI had scoped out the best possible approach to Janus, allowing her to avoid being seen from Epimetheus. Janus was still tens of thousands of kilometers away from Epimetheus but was approaching quickly. They would be closest in about five days. Sam's team would arrive in several hours.

Lindsay could see Janus growing ahead of her and found a shallow cavern on the side of Janus facing away from Epimetheus to drop into. There was just enough gravity to keep her shuttle settled in the cavern for the wait.

She had heard just before she left for Janus that her offer on the wonderful cave/dome complex on Mars had been accepted. She'd already transferred the funds to Mars for the purchase, and filled out all of the varied paperwork, including detailed immigration papers. Mars was being very picky about immigrants but having Sam as a reference made all the difference in the world; Lindsay's application had been approved almost immediately, which, from what she knew, was unheard of.

She decided that she might as well take a nap, since it would be several hours before Sam arrived. She dreamed of her father, and as she awoke, she felt tears in her eyes. It seemed that she'd never really had time to mourn him; right after his death she'd had to enter the battle of her life, trying to honor his wishes and have his second wife inherit nothing. If it had been up to Lindsay, she'd have just given the woman some money and let it go, but her father had been quite clear that Arcadia was to get none of it, so Lindsay fought in his name.

She was, for a moment, sad for Arcadia. The woman had only lived with Lindsay and her father for about a year; her father had gotten involved with Arcadia just a few months after her mother was killed in an accident. Lindsay and Arcadia had never gotten along; Arcadia was always jealous of the time her father spent with Lindsay, time that was precious to her. Arcadia knew she wasn't her husband's first priority and did rather horrific things to get back at him for it. Finally, her father had had enough.

Lindsay's father had been an explorer before he settled back down on Earth relatively late in his life to marry her mother and raise a family. He'd been out as far as Uranus and had pioneered some specific methods for identifying promising asteroids that KE, Strelix, and other companies still use today. Lindsay had never expected to go out into space; her father hadn't wanted her to follow in his footsteps. He'd wanted a more safe, stable life for her.

But here she was, in the outer solar system, about to make contact again with a troublesome alien species. How did she get into this again? Ah, right, they were the ones who'd initiated this. And somehow, she'd managed to be special. She did appreciate that—she would have been sad and angry to have been manipulated to leave Pandora, only to return to see it destroyed.

She checked on the status of Sam's ship, the *Callista*. She could already hear the ident beacon. They were about fifteen minutes from Janus, approaching carefully to avoid being seen by anything on Epimetheus.

She opened a comm channel. "*Callista*, this is Lindsay. I'm hiding in a little cavern on Janus. Shall I come to meet you—have room for a shuttle?"

Lindsay heard a voice she didn't recognize. "Affirmative, Lindsay, we've got an open shuttle spot. Come on board."

She woke up her systems and quietly launched from the cavern. As she approached the *Callista*, Sam came on the comm.

"Lindsay, hey, it's Sam. The shuttle bay door is now open. The bay is about two-thirds of the way down the hub. The signal beacons are active."

Lindsay instructed her AI to find the beacons and navigate into the bay. She didn't quite trust her own piloting yet for that delicate maneuver. She settled into the bay, and saw the doors close overhead. Her AI signaled that she could disembark from the shuttle.

As she left, she saw Sam floating at a door close to the shuttle.

"Lindsay, it's great to see you!"

"Glad to see you too, Sam." They did a zero-g hug.

"Let's get you out to the habitat ring. You can meet Nilesh and Sharron, the other crew members. The *Atreyu* will be here in a few days, so we have some leisure time before we start all this in earnest."

Lindsay grabbed her bag, and followed Sam.

Atreyu, December 2112

Sam looked around the table at John, Xiang, Sharron, Rosalind, Lindsay and Nilesh. They were the group that would figure out how to contact the Zeloso. It seemed daunting to her. Sam didn't get along with Xiang and had never really gotten to know Rosalind. She seemed like a nice person, but John had mentioned that she and Xiang seemed to be striking up a bit of a romance. Sam figured this meant that Rosalind would be on Xiang's side when there was a conflict.

The good thing, Sam thought, was that they trusted Sharron, John and Nilesh with their life, and had always thought Lindsay a reasonable person with whom they could get along well. If things got dicey, Sam knew that they had folks who had their back.

Sam and John shared leadership of this mission, which worked well for them. It was time to get started.

Sam said, "OK, folks, let's start. The current plan is to contact the Zeloso via their high-frequency transmission wavelength and suggest that they meet with us. Xiang, Lindsay and I will take the *Callista* to Epimetheus, and meet with them. Since Lindsay can't be compelled by them, she will be the commander of that mission."

Xiang cleared his throat.

"Xiang?"

"I think I would be of better use analyzing the data feed from the meeting than actually being there."

Sam tilted their head toward him. "Are you sure? Xiang, you are supposed to be the culture expert."

"Yes, and I'd rather study their culture at a distance."

Sam inwardly smiled. They'd always thought he was a coward. Now they really knew.

"Alright. Well, we need three folks on that mission. John needs to stay with the *Atreyu*. Any takers? Rosalind?"

Sharron said immediately, "I'll go."

"You sure?"

"Yes. I'm up for it, and I'm intrigued by the aliens. Nilesh has taught me enough that I can take care of the *Callista*."

"So, it's Sharron, Lindsay and I. We'll be sending back constant feeds."

John said, "To be safe, we'll be moving the *Atreyu* back out to Rhea."

Sam said, "Makes sense to me. We'll be fine, I'm sure. We've been watching Epimetheus for a while now, and we've seen about four ships come and go since we arrived. We're assuming that most of the ships are in deep caverns inside Epimetheus, since there are no surface buildings of any sort except for an old habitat that was built in the sixties, long abandoned."

John said, "Have you been able to get an idea of how many ships might be there?"

"No, there's no way to know. There could be four ships, or there could be a hundred. Jane estimated twenty-five, but that's a rough guess. If fifty ships had just been sitting inside Epimetheus all these years, we'd never know it."

The next day, Sam was sitting with Sharron and Lindsay in the control room of the *Callista*, heading for Epimetheus. They'd been sending a message on the high frequency bandwidth that the Zeloso had used before but had yet to hear back from them. They were going to orbit around Epimetheus until the Zeloso answered, or until they were forced to leave. Sam hoped the latter wasn't going to happen.

Jane said, "Sam, incoming message from the Zeloso."

"Open the channel, Jane."

A strangely accented voice said, "Hello, hello, go away."

Lindsay said, "That's the same voice I heard before—that's Koth."

Sam said, "Hello, Koth. We would like to talk with you."

"No talk. Go away."

"Koth, everyone knows you are here. We human beings are at home in this system, and you are visiting. We need to talk with you."

There was silence on the end of the line. Finally, after a few minutes, they heard, "Come down to the surface. We talk."

Sam let out a sigh of relief.

"Agreed. We will launch momentarily."

Sam still didn't know what was in store for them. They decided to take Lindsay's shuttle—it was better equipped than the one they had, and more comfortable for three, and room in its systems for a copy of Jane. As they launched toward the surface, they saw a ship emerge from the mouth of a cavern.

Sam said to Lindsay, "They are close enough that it is time for this. Lindsay Ali, I give you full authority as the leader of this mission."

Sam could tell Lindsay was nervous. Sam said, "Don't worry—it will be fine. It's not a big deal. You know the plan."

She nodded.

Sam said, "Jane, send John a message. 'We've made contact with the Zeloso and are meeting them on the surface. Lindsay is in charge.'"

"Affirmative, Sam."

"And you're sending him everything?"

"Yes, Sam."

They approached the surface and assumed that whatever ship had emerged from the cavern was going to meet with them on the surface. But the ship kept going outward.

Sam said, "Jane, where is the Zeloso ship headed?"

"Toward the *Callista*."

"Toward the *Callista*? Show it on screen."

The viewscreen showed the *Callista*, which was in a slow orbit around Epimetheus. The Zeloso ship entered into view, and Sam gasped as she saw the beam weapon slice into *Callista*, sending pieces of it flying in all directions.

Sam heard Lindsay exclaim, "Fuck!"

Sam said, "I thought there was an outside chance they would do that, but I'm still a little surprised."

Lindsay said, "These are bad creatures, Sam."

"I'm getting that impression."

Jane said, "Sam, incoming message from John."

"Put him through."

"Sam, you all right? What happened?"

"We're fine, John. Don't come close to Epimetheus. They destroyed the *Callista* without a howdy-do."

"You need to get out of there!"

"No, we need to see this through, John. They knew that we were in a shuttle headed toward Epimetheus. If they wanted to kill us, they would have already."

"Well, that's true. Nilesh is livid."

"Yeah, I'm not surprised he's mad. Tell him that I'm sorry. I'm assuming they think that they can compel us to do something, and that's why they spared us. We'll see how it goes."

John said, "Be careful, my friend."

"I will, that. Talk to you later."

Jane said, "Sam, I suggest you land at the abandoned habitat. You might be able to get it going again, and that would give you some shelter, and a relatively safe place to meet the Zeloso."

"Agreed. Let's head for it."

Mars Colony One, December 2112

Gareth looked at Sharron's face. It was shining.

"So, Gareth, I'm about to head into a new adventure. I volunteered to go with Sam and Lindsay to contact the Zeloso. It seems like such a wonderful opportunity. I don't think there will be much danger, but we can't be sure. Pray for me, and the success of this mission.

"I hope you are doing well. Have you gotten that final statement from the Kurool to append to our article? I look forward to reading what they have to say. I have been increasingly confident of our conclusions, Gareth, and I would find it unlikely that many reasonable people would disagree. And we already know what the unreasonable people will say.

"Be well. I pray for you every day. I miss you dearly and look forward to seeing you soon. Love you."

Yes, Gareth knew what the unreasonable people would say when they read the article. The Kurool had just delivered to him their very short statement.

It read: "Based on the data that we gave you about the teachings of Turool, as well as what we have seen of the teachings of Jesus, it is clear that they are somehow truly connected. We cannot, at this time, theorize how, but the explanation given in this article would certainly make this data consistent with the theology and cosmology of the religion you call 'Christianity.'"

It wasn't what he'd hoped for, but it was enough. He wasn't sure what he'd hoped for. Perhaps the old evangelical in him had hoped that this article would convert the Kurool to Christianity. But the truth was, the article was more likely to convert Christians to worship Turool. He supposed people might even think he'd converted himself, though it didn't really feel that way to him. It felt more like he'd found the true Christianity, after all. It surprised him deeply that it was alien.

Epimetheus, December 2112

Sam found the habitat and docked their shuttle. It turned out to be in impeccable shape—it had clearly been mothballed with the idea of someone coming back to it.

Sharron and Lindsay stayed there, working to get the atmosphere started, and inventory what was there. Meanwhile, Sam kept up with the status of the Kurool, who were about five days out from Epimetheus, as well as tracking the coming and going of ships into the cavern. Jane was doing some calculations based on the size of Epimetheus, estimating how big the internal caverns might be, based on caverns known in other Saturn moons.

Sam was glad they got to shirk engineering duty and stay in the shuttle, without having to work in a suit. Sharron and Lindsay were quite good at it anyway, and Sam would have just gotten in the way.

"Jane, any results on your search for the history of this place?"

"Yes, Sam. In 2061, the founder of Strelix and Kuiper Exploratory, Brodric Tata, came out here with theories of finding rare earth elements and precious metals. He didn't find anything, but he put a claim on all of the inner moons of Saturn, which no one has challenged. When he died in 2080, ownership of the moons fell to KE."

Sam—along with everyone else interested in the solar system—knew the history of KE well. Brodric Tata was a scion of the very powerful Tata family, owners of one of the largest Corps on Earth. He broke with them over space exploration—they wanted to stick to working on Earth, and he wanted to roam the solar system and find precious metals. He first founded Strelix, then sold it, came to the outer system, and founded KE before he was killed in a ship accident in the belt in 2080.

Of course, he'd been right about the precious metals, most especially in the asteroid belt. Although their delay in getting into space had cost Tata a precious decade or two, they were now trying hard to play catch up to Virgin Galactic, who had been one of the first corps in space. There were at least a dozen other corps vying for power in the solar system.

"Thanks, Jane." Sam took in the information that they were trespassing on KE space—but then, so were the Zeloso.

"Jane, send a quick message to John with the details of what you just gave me. He needs to know that KE owns this space, and they should be the first to hear what's going on here."

"Affirmative, Sam."

Sam knew that Mars had a very good relationship with KE, as did they. They doubted that they would take issue with what was happening here. KE was one of the rare corps that played nice, realized their dependence on others, and returned favors. Sam wished that Strelix had kept the culture Tata seemed to have nurtured at KE.

Sam heard Sharron on the comm. "Sam, come on in. We're out of our suits. The heat is on, the air is sweet, and there are some decent quarters. I even just had a nice shower."

"Thanks! Be there in a flash."

Sam got out of the seat, lightly pushed to the back of the shuttle to grab their bag of essentials, and then bounded out of the shuttle into the habitat. Epimetheus' gravity was tiny—but it was enough to know up from down, keep things pretty much where you left them, and kind of walk. Sam saw Lindsay squatting in front of an open panel, working on something inside.

Sam said, "Hey, thanks for getting this going. Very nice space here. Won't be the most horrible place to spend Christmas."

"Yeah, it's not bad. It's bigger and nicer than my habitat on Pandora. I'll see if I can find a tree."

Sam smiled. "Well, in case you are interested, the habitat was built by Broderic Tata."

"Ah, that doesn't surprise me. He built the one on Pandora as well."

"I didn't know that KE owned all this space."

"Yup. But they've finally realized that there's no money here. That's why they fired me. I was the last person out here they had."

"Do you think they'll care about what we're doing here in their space?"

"I don't think so. I heard a rumor they were going to try and sell the space to a tourism company."

"Oh, well, that won't work at all, will it, with the Zeloso here?"

"Not so much, Sam. I guess we'd better tell them, eh?"

"I'm leaving that decision up to John, but yes, they'll be the first to know what's happening out here."

Sharron came up to Sam, and asked, "Any word yet from the Zeloso?"

"Not a peep. I don't quite know what they are waiting for."

"Perhaps planning what they want to try to compel us to do?"

"Yup."

Sharron looked at Lindsay. "I'm so glad you're here, Lindsay."

Lindsay smiled.

Sam said, "I'm hungry. Any eats? Or do we have to make do with MREs from the shuttle?"

Sharron said, "I haven't checked the galley yet. Let's go look."

Sam realized that the food would be almost fifty years old. She didn't know whether or not one could eat fifty-year-old food.

Sharron opened one of the cabinets. "Oh, my. Fifty-year-old freeze-dried food. I think we need to go back to the shuttle for the MREs."

"Lemme look."

Sam took out a package, which said "Roasted Chicken with Rosemary, mashed potatoes, and peas." Nice Christmas dinner, and it sounded delish, but the expiration on the package said May, 2063. So much for that.

"OK, I'll get them. You keep working."

"Alright, thanks."

They sat around the table in the galley eating MREs from the shuttle. They had about a ten-day supply; Sam wondered if it would be enough. She said, "I don't like the fact that the Zeloso haven't said a peep since they destroyed the *Callista*. I guess we should wait here until we're out of food, then head back to Rhea."

Lindsay said, "I have a feeling they'll contact us soon."

"I certainly hope so."

Life in the habitat for the next few days settled into a routine. All of the systems in the habitat were working well. John had decided to let KE in on what was happening at Epimetheus, and they'd appreciated the heads-up, as they'd been about to close a deal with VirginGalactic's tourism subsidiary for the inner moons of Saturn. They chose to withdraw from the deal for the time being, and John said that VG was upset. KE wasn't explaining yet, which made VG even madder, apparently. Ah, Sam thought, life in the solar system.

Chapter 7:
The Kurool and The Zeloso

Epimetheus, January 2113

Lindsay was doing a check on one of the atmosphere monitors—it had become a bit flaky the day before. She had been pleasantly surprised at how well the habitat had stood up all this time being empty. Her habitat had been empty for many years, but not nearly as long as this one.

She heard Sam shout, "Sharron, Lindsay, come to the control area!"

Lindsay dropped what she was doing and headed toward where Sam was.

"Jane said that the Kurool are now in visual range of Epimetheus, and there is a small Zeloso ship headed here. Should land in a few minutes."

Lindsay said, "So *that* was what they were waiting for."

"Funny, I thought it might be their way of celebrating the New Year. Anyway, Lindsay, you're on."

Lindsay nodded. She didn't feel ready for this, but she knew she might be the only one who could resist the Zeloso. She had her medical injector handy, in case she had to subdue Sam and Sharron. They both knew this was a possibility. She also had a small weapon that she could use against the Zeloso if necessary, but she hoped it wouldn't come to that.

Their ship docked on the other side from the shuttle and sent out that familiar tube to connect with the habitat. The doors opened, and then the familiar little cat/kangaroo with no nose stood looking at her.

Destroy. Destroy.

"Destroy what?"

Destroy big ship coming.

"You're kidding, right?"

It is dangerous to us. You must destroy. Then, in that familiar compelling-but-not thought: *We must do our best to destroy the Kurool. They are a danger to everyone.*

Lindsay looked at Sam, whose eyes were glassy.

Sam said, "Jane, calculate what we would need to destroy the Kurool ship. Does the *Atreyu* have the capacity?"

Lindsay was surprised. This was no simple kind of compelling.

Sharron looked at Sam, then at Lindsay, then at the Zeloso. "What is happening?"

"Jane, this is Lindsay. Do not obey anything Sam commands as of now."

"Affirmative."

Sam looked at Lindsay, confused. "Why did you do that?"

Sharron said, "Sam, you aren't yourself."

Lindsay said, "Sam, listen to me."

"I will not listen to you. We have a mission here, and we must carry it through. The Kurool are dangerous, and we need to eliminate them."

Lindsay sighed and turned to the Zeloso.

"You don't have any power over me, and I am in command here—my colleagues here can do nothing. We need to talk."

No talk. No talk. Destroy.

"What are you so afraid of?"

Enemy. Enemy. No talk. Destroy.

Koth ran back out of the habitat into its ship and took off quickly. Lindsay shook her head.

Sam put their head in their hands and said, "Oh my god. Oh my god. Shoot me now. I can't get this idea that I should destroy the Kurool ship out of my head!"

Lindsay said, "Sam, it's OK. We knew this would likely happen."

Sharron said, "I'm special too, I guess. I didn't hear or think a thing from them."

Lindsay said, "That is quite useful. I'm glad of that. What do we do now? They seem hell-bent on trying to destroy the Kurool."

Lindsay heard Jane say, "Lindsay, a much larger ship has exited the caverns. It is a ship that has the same design and size as the ship with the beam weapon that destroyed Ganymede One."

"Is it heading here?"

"Negative. It is going toward the Kurool ship."

Sam said, "The Kurool have no weapons, and... they should be destroyed... what am I saying?" Sam looked rather distressed.

Sharron said, "I sure hope that the Kurool ship is immune to whatever the Zeloso throw at it. Maybe then they'll talk."

Lindsay said, "Sam, listen to me. If you feel that you cannot be trusted, let me know. We have contingency plans for that."

Lindsay could see that Sam was struggling. Struggling was good, as far as Lindsay was concerned.

"Lindsay, ask Jane to monitor me, and to tell you whether she feels I'm a danger. I'll trust her judgment."

"Jane, did you hear that?"

"Affirmative, Lindsay. I will monitor Sam."

"Jane, status of the Zeloso ship?"

"Closing on the Kurool."

"Display."

On the viewscreen was the image of the Kurool ship. Jane zoomed out so that the picture included the approaching Zeloso ship. They all watched, transfixed, as the ship got closer. It stopped. Lindsay could see what looked like bands of light moving down the ship. She was worried.

Lindsay said, "Jane, analysis?"

"It appears that the Zeloso ship is about to fire its weapon."

"Oh no!"

As they watched, the bright, thick beam of the Zeloso weapon flew out of the front of their ship. It seemed to simply be absorbed by the Kurool ship—there was no evident damage.

"Jane? How is the Kurool ship?"

"It appears undamaged."

Nothing happened for several minutes, then Jane said, "The two ships are communicating on a high-frequency bandwidth."

Sharron said, "Well, that's a relief. I guess now that the Zeloso know they can't harm the Kurool, they'll talk."

They waited, while the two ships were close to each other. Then, finally, the larger Zeloso ship with the beam weapon left, and the smaller ship came back to the habitat. Again, the cat/kangaroo was at the door.

We could not destroy them. And they offer us help. We do not trust them.

Then, in that compelling-but-not thought: *I must make them go away. I will convince the Kurool to leave Saturn.*

Lindsay turned to look at Sam who was staring at the Zeloso.

Sam said, "Lindsay, can we make the Kurool go away?"

Lindsay said, "We will do no such thing." She turned to the Zeloso. "Stop trying to compel us. Stop it now! It won't work, and it's just making things more complicated—and believe me, they will be more difficult for you if you continue this way."

Sam said loudly, "Oh, man, you are little creepy bastard. Stay the fuck out of my head."

Lindsay nodded. Well, that seemed to have worked.

"Thank you."

Maybe we trust you?

Lindsay was taken aback. "What is your name?"

I am Koth.

She looked more carefully at the creature, which looked different than the one she'd seen before. Same name?

"I am Lindsay Ali. This is Sam, and over there is Sharron. By the way, she can't hear you at all."

I know. I must go now. I will see Lindsay-Ali again.

It turned around and left. The ship took off and entered the caverns.

Lindsay shook her head. What was that all about?

Jane said, "Lindsay, the Kurool are on the comm."

"Connect please."

The familiar almost-mechanical voice of the Kurool started. "Hello, this is Huroat. We haven't met yet. I was chosen for this mission because I have characteristics that make it unlikely that I can be compelled by the..." and a word that Lindsay couldn't possibly pronounce but sounded vaguely like "Zeloso."

"Hello Huroat. We call them 'Zeloso'—it seems the best transliteration of the word you have. We're glad their weapon didn't harm you."

"Our ships are very tough—we knew they could not harm us. I will use 'Zeloso' from now on. We have been in communication with the Zeloso, and they will cease contact with you. We have offered them assistance and assurance that we won't harm them again, but they don't really trust us. I can understand that."

Sam asked, "Why have they been busy inserting themselves into our affairs, Huroat?"

"That's what they do. That's what they know. We hope to prevent that from happening in the future."

Lindsay wondered how successful they would be. She said, "What should we do, Huroat?"

"It would be best to make sure no one enters this space. This ship will stay here and help them as much as we can. It is all we can do since this predicament is our fault."

Lindsay wasn't quite so sure of that—these creatures seemed to be able to make enough trouble all by themselves. If they'd never rescued Zoetrope... well, anyway, it seemed that this was over. Perhaps it was time to go home.

"Thank you, Huroat. Is there anything we can do to assist?"

"No, not at this time. Goodbye."

Lindsay was relieved. "Sam, you're back in charge. Let's get the hell out of here."

Atreyu, February 2113

Sam said, "I'm so embarrassed by the whole thing. I mean, me, want to destroy the Kurool? I couldn't help myself."

Sam, Lindsay and Sharron were sitting around the conference table on the *Atreyu*, relaying to John, Xiang, Nilesh and Rosalind what had happened on the Epimetheus habitat.

John said, "Sam, no need to be embarrassed! We knew this was likely. They clearly have a very strong mechanism of telepathy. I wish that the Xenoscience team was further along in understanding it."

Xiang said, "That's years and years away, John. There are some theoretical physics that apparently, we have to get to understand before we'll even get close. And even then, we'll only have theories—nothing certain."

Rosalind said, "I'd love to work on the evolutionary mechanisms of such a talent."

John said, "So anyway, we have our work cut out for us, guys. First, we have to tell SolGov that Epimetheus, and about five million cubic kilometers is off-limits to anyone except the Kurool and the Zeloso. Then, we have to make this all public."

Sam said, "Tina will handle that part, John. We just need to feed her the info."

John nodded. "I need to contact Kuiper Exploratory and explain the full situation before this hits the press, Sam."

"Understood."

"They are likely going to want to let VirginGalactic on it before that as well."

"Just give me the go-ahead when it's time. I'll work with Lindsay on crafting the material."

Xiang said, "I'd like to contribute to that."

Sam nodded, although they were internally bristling. The guy chickened out, and now he is going to want his name on the report? Sheesh.

John said, "We're forty-five days from Mars. I'm sure we can work this all out by then."

They left the conference room, and Sam went back to their quarters. They'd gotten a message from Tina several days before, which they still hadn't watched and, frankly, were scared to watch. Sam suspected that Tina was about to break up with them.

Sam didn't blame her one bit. If Sam had been Tina, they'd never have gotten re-involved with Sam in the first place. Sam thought that missing Christmas last year was probably the final straw.

Sam had promised to make it home for Christmas, and they knew how important it was for Tina—not because Tina was religious, but because she had some amazing memories of family Christmases on Mars and wanted a little piece of that. Sam well remembered a couple of those—they could understand.

Sam sat down on the bunk. "Jane, play message from Tina."

Sam looked into the screen with Tina's face. It looked sad. Yup, here it comes.

"Hi Sam. Thanks for your message letting me know that you were safe and sound. It was a really hard Christmas without you. I have come to realize that I can't do this anymore. I keep almost losing you, and it has finally penetrated my thick skull that you *like* doing this sort of thing. I know, you have told me more times than I can count, but somehow, when you came back from that... that *disaster* in the Kuiper Belt, I thought that had all been worked out of you. I now realize it hasn't.

"I will always love you, Sam, and I do hope we can be friends. I want to be able to support and cheer you on from a safe distance.

"I'm taking a long-delayed trip to the Moon to visit family, so I'll be gone when you get back. I'll look forward to seeing you again once I get return."

Sam knew Tina. That was code for "Please feel free to remove your stuff from my place before I get back." Sam would oblige. They were going to have to find some quarters of their own.

Sam was sad. It would take some time to get used to not being Tina's partner anymore. Tina had always been the closest person to Sam's heart, but Tina was right: nothing could match space, work, and the adventure that was the combination of the two.

Sam didn't know what was going to be next. It would take a bit of figuring out.

Atreyu, February 2113

John looked at Patrick's haggard face. This was all taking a huge toll on Patrick. He'd never bargained for this kind of trouble.

"So, John, SolGov is sending three, count them, three new *Corinth*-class ships to Epimetheus. They are livid that we didn't tell them what was going on, and livid that these little creatures managed to wreak havoc in the system.

"And possibly worse, VirginGalactic is suing both Kuiper Exploratory and Mars because this nixes the deal that KE had made with VG to sell the inner moons of Saturn to VG once KE determined that they were of no value to them. Apparently, VG had already spent billions of Yuan on research and planning, and they're going to extract that from someone's hide. And they've unilaterally canceled all contracts with Mars entities, which is making a lot of people here really mad.

340

"What makes it even more complex is that VG has a case in front of the SolGov supreme court, which could decide that SolGov has the right to jurisdiction in the system—the whole system."

John thought, *Unless Mars caves in, war is coming.*

"And, to make matters worse, public opinion of the Kurool is dropping like a stone, because of the perceived Kurool responsibility for this mess, and the deaths of twenty-five thousand on Ganymede. SolGov is making major hay out of it, and Prak is almost certain to win re-election, possibly by a landslide. Mars independence is at risk, John."

John sighed. This was going from bad to worse. He needed to tell the Kurool what was going on and figure out how in God's name they were going to get out of this mess. It was a complete disaster for Mars.

He recorded a message to Patrick on his personal account—he wanted to let him know that he loved him, no matter what happened, and that they would both get through this. Things would be chaotic when he returned, and he realized that if Mars lost independence, John was possibly going to be captured and thrown in the brig. He needed to make arrangements so that didn't happen. Perhaps one of those remote Mars outposts? That would be his safety valve. He made a note to mention it to Lindsay.

The trip back to Mars was filled with messages from Patrick and General Lei Tsang about Mars' military readiness for war with SolGov. It was all very sobering. Even given the horrible economy that Earth had been suffering since Mars independence, and particularly since the more recent blockade of Mars, there was no way that Mars could match the military power of SolGov. They would lose a full-out war with SolGov and lose it badly. Patrick was trying his best to mend fences and build bridges and make as many concessions as he dared make without jeopardizing independence. He'd ceded jurisdiction to everything except Mars, Phobos and Diemos to SolGov, and so far, that had been enough to keep the dogs at bay. But John had no idea what would happen if or when Prak won re-election. All bets were off.

Mars Colony One, May 2113

Lindsay was on her way to the new Mars Colonial Authority. No one seemed to know exactly what the Authority did, though there were some rumors about creating small colonies. She'd gotten a cryptic message when she returned to Mars, suggesting that she talk with one of the agents of the Authority regarding the compound she had just purchased. They said there were a lot of things they could offer to help her. Lindsay thought she could use some help.

She had spent most of her inheritance on the compound—it was large and could easily house twenty people. She didn't quite know why she'd jumped at it, but it felt right to her, like a good next step and a good way to spend her father's money. But she didn't have a lot left to spend on improvements, and she hadn't quite figured out how she'd make a living out in the hinterland of Mars.

She walked into the office with the small label on the side of the door and saw a receptionist and a few chairs.

"Hi, I'm Lindsay Ali."

The man sitting behind the desk had sandy hair and a nice smile.

"Hello, Lindsay. Have a seat for a moment. Jason will be with you in a little bit."

She found a seat and started to take out her tablet to check for messages, when she heard, "Hello, Lindsay. Please come into my office."

She looked up to see a large man with a balding head standing in the doorway to an inner office. She got up and followed him inside.

"Please, have a seat. I'm Jason Welles, and I'm the coordinator of the Mars Colonial Authority. I imagine you're wondering why I sent you that message?"

"Yes, indeed I am."

"Well, MarsGov has realized that there is no way that we have the capital to build another large colony, like Colony 1 or even 6, so we're going a different route. We're looking for people who own property on Mars that has potential—potential to grow into full-fledged colonies."

"I see."

"We have a very specific offer, one that is quite lucrative, I think you'll agree."

"Go ahead and tell me."

"We give you one million Yuan to do upgrades and changes that allow for a colony of thirty, within one year. Once you've reached what we're calling Colony Stage One status, we will start assessing income tax on all members of the colony, except you, of course. You will get 75% of that income tax, at least two-thirds of which you are required to invest back in the colony. When the colony has grown to Colony Stage Two, or one hundred colonists, we take 50% of the taxes, and you keep 50%, again at least two-thirds of which must be re-invested in growth of the colony. At Stage Three, or 500 colonists, you keep 25%. At Stage Four, or 1000 colonists, you keep 10%. At Stage Five, it is 5%, and finally Full Colony status, with 10,000 colonists and up, you keep 2%, with no expectation of further investment on your part. That will continue until you die, but that percentage is not inheritable by any offspring. You will never be assessed income tax on colony-related income."

Lindsay did some quick math in her head. She stood to make tens, perhaps hundreds of millions of Yuan! She would be one of the wealthiest people on Mars if the colony made it to Full Status. She guessed that was the incentive. But...

"What's the catch? There must be a catch."

"Well, you must sign over ownership of your compound to MarsGov. MarsGov does reserve the right to revoke Colony status during stage One or Two, but ownership of the compound would revert to you in that case. After Stage Two, no matter what happens, MarsGov retains ownership. There are mileposts you must make in terms of growth and GDP of the colony, but those aren't too onerous. The governance of the colony is up to you until Stage Four, when you will need to adopt standard MarsGov colony governance. Not making the targets reduces the percentage of taxes you can keep, and MarsGov reserves the right to invest more in the colony than you have chosen to."

Well, that seemed obvious—no government was going to make a deal like that without demanding ownership, and without providing targets to reach. Lindsay wondered whether she really wanted to do this. She had liked living alone for all of those years on Pandora, and she'd expected to live alone on Mars as well. But she knew that she'd run out of money before long, and this looked like a way to make serious money—enough to buy her a small dome nearby to live in alone, if she wanted to. It seemed a very sweet deal.

"I need to think over this for a while. When do you need to know?"

"No hurry. Decide whenever you want. The offer will remain open as long as you own the property, and don't make changes to it that preclude the sort of colony building we have in mind."

She added internally, *as long as Mars stays independent.* "Alright, thanks!"

She left the office and asked her AI to send Sam a message to meet her.

Mars Colony One, August 2113

Gareth was poring over the three proposals he had gotten from contractors for building the new compound close to the Kurool Colony. MarsGov had given Gareth and a small group a large lot of property a few kilometers from the Kurool, outside of the toxic regolith area. In return, Gareth and Sharron would spend a big chunk of his inheritance building a compound which would grow into a colony according to the new ideas that MarsGov had.

So far, their group included Sharron, Xiang and Rosalind, and, surprisingly, Ted. Sharron had returned from her adventure a completely different person. Gareth loved the person that she'd become, even though he felt he hardly recognized her. He'd always known she had this confidence and ability within her, but she'd chosen to limit herself for a long time. Clearly, that was over.

She was currently wading into the storm they'd created when the article about Turool and Jesus was finally published. He hadn't the stomach for it. The Pope had dedicated an entire encyclical to the "horrific and damaging theology" that Sharron and Gareth were proposing. Scientists were up in arms because the Kurool refused to teach them their science and suggested that they were simply trying to convert everyone to worship Turool. That last part, Gareth knew, was probably true.

The good news was that somehow this new idea that Turool and Jesus were connected had helped bolster what had been sagging approval for the Kurool. Mars needed that, in the face of an increasingly hostile SolGov.

Sharron busy giving interviews and talks. Between their article, her adventures with the Zeloso, and the fact that she had saved Sam's life, she was the celebrity of the moment. He was happy for her—she deserved the limelight.

It was his turn to do domestic things and begin to build their new colony—the colony that would educate human children with Kurool children, and, importantly, the colony that would follow Turool. He had already gotten thousands of inquiries from people all over the system.

Ali Compound, September 2113

Lindsay brushed the dust off of her coveralls as she walked into the dome, where Sam was on some scaffolding working to make sure all of the dome panels were properly coated.

"Sam, looking good!"

"Yeah, I figured I'd clean them off while I was at it, so we could see the sun sometimes."

"You sure you're ready for this, Sam?"

Sam climbed down the scaffolding to join Lindsay.

"I need a new adventure, Lindsay, it's in my blood. Tina finally realized I was hopeless, and she found herself someone who would always be around. I rather like Angeline, and I don't blame Tina. We'll be friends for life."

"Starting a new colony isn't going to be easy, my friend."

"I know, but it's just the kind of problem for me to be sinking my teeth into right now. I like the new Mars approach of organically growing colonies from small compounds. We should be ready for seven or eight emigrants in a few months, and if we keep going, we could be a full-fledged colony in less than ten years."

Lindsay laughed. "Sam, you won't be here ten years from now. I don't quite know where you'll be, but it ain't here."

Sam had to admit that Lindsay was right. As they looked over their life, they never had been in one place, save perhaps a ship, for more than a few years. It just wasn't in Sam to stay in one place for very long. They didn't know what adventure was next, but this adventure was fine for now.

"Hey Linds, it's time for lunch. Let's break out the new cuisine shipment we got yesterday. Oh, and the wine!"

"Did I hear correctly that you found a cache of Zoetrope's Ganymede wine, and bought all of it?"

"Yeah. It was dirt cheap. The person selling it had no idea of its significance. I figure in a year or two it'll sell for a hundred times what I bought it for."

"But we'll drink some first."

"That we will."

About the Author

Max has been a science fiction fan since he could read. He has written and published poetry, creative nonfiction, and technical writing. Max lives and works in Cazadero, CA and Seattle, WA.

Connect with him online:

https://author.maxwellpearl.com